'Clements truly lets rip with the pollaxes, billhooks and glaives, sparing no detail as he recreates the blood and thunder of the battlefield . . . But mere retro-bloodfest this is not – amid the butchery emerges a tender, heroic love story.' *Sun*

'I loved this from the first page, and if you ask me, this is what it's all about. There's an immediacy, an accessibility to Clements' writing that makes the story leap from the page in all its vivid, vibrant glory. In fact this story reads like a film script, which shows that here is a writer who knows his business. Atmosphere, drama, great characters and a brilliantly imagined medieval world – *Kingmaker: Winter Pilgrims* took me on a journey. I'm already looking forward to the next one. Storytelling doesn't get much better than this.' **Giles Kristian**

'The first of what promises to be one of the best historical adventure series to hit the shelves this year . . . an author born to be a storyteller . . . *Kingmaker* proves to be a thrilling, stomach-churning odyssey into the grime, gore and guts of the brutal medieval world. There is an addictive, raw excitement to Clements' writing . . . Prepare to be shocked, amazed . . . and thoroughly entertained.' *Lancashire Evening Post*

'The narrative, quick-paced, direct and written in the vivid present . . . the repression, anger and bloodshed of the Wars of the Roses was itself frequently beyond belief. Clements' pages are aflutter with that conflict's every emotion.' *Spectator*

'Toby Clements has provided ripping action we can be absorbed by and relate to; a talent that many more experienced authors have yet to grasp.' *The Bookbag*

'Toby Clements has a rich knowledge of the history of the times and this is evident in his writing. His depictions of the way people lived their lives during this turbulent time in our history is so vivid you feel a definite sense of being there . . . the most enjoyable historical novel I have read for some time.' *Culture Fly*

Also by Toby Clements

Kingmaker: Winter Pilgrims

Kingmaker
Broken Faith

TOBY CLEMENTS

CENTURY

1 3 5 7 9 10 8 6 4 2

Century
20 Vauxhall Bridge Road
London SW1V 2SA

Century is part of the Penguin Random House group
of companies whose addresses can be found
at global.penguinrandomhouse.com.

Penguin
Random House
UK

First published by Century in 2015

www.randomhouse.co.uk

A CIP catalogue record for this book
is available from the British Library.

ISBN 9781780891705

Penguin Random House is committed to a sustainable future
for our business, our readers and our planet. This book is
made from Forest Stewardship Council® certified paper.

MIX
Paper from
responsible sources
FSC® C018179

Typeset in Fournier MT by Palimpsest Book Production Limited,
Falkirk, Stirlingshire
Printed and bound by Clays Ltd, St Ives plc

For Alex, Isabel, Justin and Matt (1967 and 1968–1989),
still with us every day, in heart and mind.

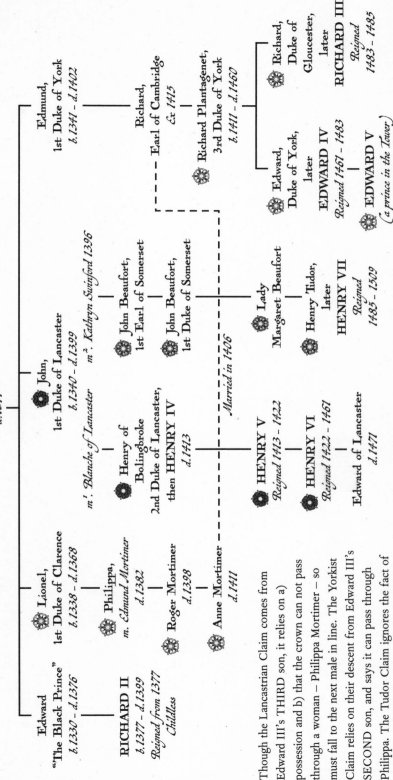

Key: York   Lancaster   Tudor

Though the Lancastrian Claim comes from Edward III's THIRD son, it relies on a) possession and b) that the crown can not pass through a woman – Philippa Mortimer – so must fall to the next male in line. The Yorkist Claim relies on their descent from Edward III's SECOND son, and says it can pass through Philippa. The Tudor Claim ignores the fact of passing through a woman – Lady Margaret Beaufort – or that John, Earl of Somerset, was born illegimate.

Factions in the Wars of the Roses,
November 1463.

HOUSE OF YORK

King Edward IV:
   victor of the battle of Towton, crowned king in 1461.

Richard Neville, Earl of Warwick:
   architect of the Yorkist victory, later known as the Kingmaker.

John Neville, Lord Montagu:
   younger brother of the Earl of Warwick, warden of the East March,
   commander of Yorkist forces in the north. Tough, resourceful,
   pitiless.

Henry Beaufort, 3rd Duke of Somerset
   defeated leader of the Lancastrian faction at the battle of
   Towton, attainted but then received into King Edward's grace in
   1463 and made Gentleman of the King's Bedchamber, to
   everyone's disgust.

HOUSE OF LANCASTER

King Henry VI
   Deposed king, in exile in Scotland, returned to England in 1463. His
   strong labour'd wife Margaret of Anjou is in exile in France.

Ralph Percy
   Brother of the Earl of Northumberland, commander of Bamburgh
   Castle

Lords Roos and Hungerford
  Northern lords, with unreliable retinues
Sir Ralph Grey
  Castellan of Alnwick Castle. There is no evidence of him being a drunk.

Kingmaker
Broken Faith

Prologue

The Battle of Towton, fought in driving snow on Palm Sunday 1461, saw twenty thousand Englishmen killed, more in one day than ever before or ever since. Although Edward of York carried the day, and was afterwards crowned Edward IV, his victory was only by the narrowest of margins, and it did not mark the end of the Wars.

The old King, Henry VI, of Lancaster, and his indomitable French Queen Margaret, escaped and fled north, to Scotland, where they tried to lure the Scots and the French into attacking newly-crowned King Edward's much-weakened England. But despite promises of help, neither the Scots nor the French were to be drawn in, and after two years all that was left to the dethroned Henry's cause were a few castles in Northumberland, mere toeholds in his vanished kingdom.

These castles – Dunstanburgh, Bamburgh, Alnwick – became beacons of hope, attracting the dispossessed, the attainted, and those whose loyalty to the old Lancastrian King could not be bought off with the promise of titles and positions from the new Yorkist one. Among such men were the Dukes of Somerset and Exeter and the Lords Hungerford and Roos, and from these castles they kept the last flames of Lancastrian hope guttering.

But life in these mighty castles on their bleak North Sea shores was far from comfortable. And now the Earl of Warwick, King Edward's mighty ally, is marching north with ordnance enough to batter down the thickest walls, and with an army at his back bigger than was ever gathered at Towton. So while some pray the castles' *fall will mark the end of a sorrowful chapter in the nation's story, others pray that some miracle will avert disaster, and that the old King will survive and thrive and return to right the wrongs of the last few years . . .*

PART ONE

Cornford Castle, Cornford, County of Lincoln, England, After Michaelmas 1462

1

It is the hour before noon on the second day after St Luke's, late in the month of October, and in the grey light slanting through the castle's kitchen doorway, Katherine inspects the small, skinned body of an animal lying on the scrubbed oak table. The animal is gutted, headless and footless.

'Rabbit, my lady,' Eelby's wife tells her. 'Husband caught it this morning. Out near the Cold Half-Hundred drain.'

Katherine knows the Cold Half-Hundred drain, and she knows Eelby, who sits with his broad back turned on her, eating his bread so that she can hear him chewing. He says nothing, doesn't even grunt, but his brawny shoulders are up and she can see he is waiting for something, so she prises open the narrow trap of the animal's ribs and counts. She makes it thirteen pairs.

'Not a rabbit,' she says. 'A cat.'

Eelby stops his chewing. His wife holds Katherine's stare for a moment, then drops her gaze to the rushes and rubs her swollen belly. She must be nearly ready now, Katherine thinks, and she must be frightened of what is to come. Her husband swallows his bread.

'It's a rabbit,' he says without turning his head. There are creases of pale skin in the dirty fat of his neck. 'As wife told you. Killed it meself.'

Katherine knows she still seems odd to them – an interloper in a good dress, small, thin, with her hat pulled down to hide her ear and her already sharp features honed by sorrow and privation – but it has been like this ever since she arrived at Cornford Castle more

5

than a year before, since the first time she led Richard Fakenham on his horse over the two bridges and in through the gatehouse to take possession of her late supposed father's property.

The curtain walls had seemed taller then, rough grey stone, stained with damp even in the summer months, weeds growing from every crevice and all sorts of filth underfoot. Eelby's wife stood on an unswept step of the kitchen, washing beetle in hand, while unfed dogs snarled on chains and the air was sour with the smell of their waste.

'What is it?' Richard had asked, wrinkling his nose. Eelby's wife had stared at his bandaged eyes and then looked away, quickly crossing herself and whispering some prayer.

'A welcome,' Katherine had told him. 'Of sorts.'

'Where is everyone?' he'd asked.

'Dead,' someone had answered. This had been Eelby, the castle's reeve, emerging from the lower door of the gatehouse from where he'd been watching them cross the fen. She'd disliked him from the moment she saw him – broad and squat, with fleshy ears and small, mean eyes – and neither did he like her.

'Dead?' she'd asked.

'Aye,' Eelby had said. 'Every man save meself went north with Sir Giles Riven and we've given up on 'em coming home now.'

Eelby had said this as if it were somehow her fault, as if she, Katherine, had been responsible for their deaths, but she had ignored him and had taken a moment to look around at the castle, to note the accretion of filth, the dilapidation of the stone, the rot in the wood. There were jackdaws in the roof, and a bush of some sort springing from between the stones up by the crenellations. Apart from the new stone badge of Riven's crows that had been put in place of the old Cornford arms, she supposed, the castle looked to have been falling to pieces for some time. It was strange to see how little it had been valued by Riven while Sir John Fakenham and his son Richard had spent so much time, energy and blood to acquire it.

She had not thought it would be like this. Nor had Richard.

They had come up from London with some of William Hastings's men, ten of them, keeping guard over them and a wagon loaded with wedding gifts which they'd received, mostly from the newly ennobled Lord Hastings: two feather pillows, a bolster, a standing coffer, two small chests of oak, a hundred carpet hooks, three pounds of wire, and a hemp sack of shoe nails. There had been two gowns of Kendal green, one of damask, a bolt of russet and a pair of stockings. For Richard there was a velvet jacket and a doublet, a horse's harness and a short-bladed sword. Not much, Hastings had admitted, but what else do you give a blind man?

They had come along the same road they had travelled with Sir John and the others the summer of the year before, and to console themselves for their losses and for the absence of men they loved, they had tried to imagine what they would find when they got to Cornford: something sound and well-founded, with slate roofs, stout walls and three glazed windows in the solar. They'd pictured a reeve out collecting dues. They'd imagined beehives, orchards full of geese and chickens, fat pigeons in the dovecotes, a watermill chuntering away, a saw pit perhaps, and a priest at the door of his church. There would be breweries, a baker, a smithy and an inn. There would be men to keep the oxen straight and to shear the sheep. There would be boys to fetch in wood from the forest and girls to mind the goats. There would be women in woollen dresses with babies on their hips and barrels of ale fermenting in the cellar's cool.

But it was not like that. Instead there were only widows and orphans. The mill wheel was broken, the priest unpaid and gone, and such crops as had been planted before the men had left for the north now lay rotting in the sodden fields. Katherine had thought at the time that perhaps Richard was lucky not to be able to see it.

And now, a year later, here she is, standing in the kitchen with the body of a cat in her hand and a mere twine of smoke from the twigs that make up the fire in the hearth. She looks down at the little body and thinks of asking to see its head, to see its fur and feet, but she has too often demeaned herself with Eelby in the past, sinking to his level and later finding herself begging him to accept her apology so that there is food on the table for Richard to eat. She has promised herself she will not do it again and so she won't now, and besides, what is so bad about eating a cat?

She places the body back on the table and leaves Eelby and his wife there, closing the door behind her. Outside it is cold, the first hint of the winter to come perhaps, and her ear begins to throb as she hurries across to the keep and ascends the stairs to the solar where Richard is sitting just as she left him, on a bench by the piled ashes of a cooling fire. He seldom leaves this spot. He is too anxious to venture out these days, too scared of the unfamiliar, but in place of his absent sight, his other senses have sharpened.

'Is he trying some fresh fraud?' he asks.

'How did you guess?'

'Your gait. You walk as if you are angry.'

She laughs quietly and crosses the threshes to touch his shoulder. He turns his face to her, smiles blankly, puts out a hand.

'Margaret,' he says.

Katherine knows she must take his hand. She does so, looking down on her husband. She wants to change his dressing; the linen is grubby and there are sooty finger marks where he has adjusted it after fiddling with the fire. He pulls her to him, puts his arm around her waist. It is always like this. He cannot just – be. He has to clutch at her, paw at her. Even now his palm drifts from her waist to her hip and she cannot help but stiffen, and he feels it, and his already absent smile slips and he lets his hand drop. He is like a whipped dog.

He has declined sharply over the past year, lost the muscle he'd acquired from all that fighting practice he used to do, all that riding with the hounds and going out with the hawks. It turned to fat in those first few months, but now the fat is gone too, and his skin hangs from his bones. There is no one to shave him, no one to comb his hair, so Katherine has learned how.

'Shall we go for a walk?' she asks.

He sighs.

'Yes,' he says. 'Take me somewhere high from where I may slip and fall to my death.'

'Come on,' she says. She takes his arms and he needs hauling to his feet.

She indulges him and leads him out of the solar and stumbling up the circling stone steps to the top of the tower. On the way up there is an unglazed window through which she can see the castle's one remaining touch of ornament: a gargoyle in the shape of a lion's face, dripping water into the courtyard below. Everything else of value is gone, stripped and sold, and she supposes that the gargoyle remains only because it is too difficult to reach. It is not clear whether it was Riven's men who carried everything else away before they left for the north, or if it is Eelby and his wife who have been slowly stripping the place and selling it bit by bit.

When they emerge on to the walkway at the top of the tower she guides Richard across the treacherous flagstones to stand facing into the brisk east wind in which she imagines she can taste salt from the sea that lies just beyond the horizon. It is cold enough to bring tears to her eyes, but not his. He stands and grips the edge of the stone merlon and rocks himself backward and forward, backward and forward. He is like a simpleton in his misery.

She looks away and watches the land beyond the castle, seeing all the things that require attention: the silted moats and flooded furlongs, the sagging fences, the fruit trees in need of pruning, the hazels in need of coppicing, the willows in need of pollarding. Nearby, across the first bridge, the roofs of the cattle shed and the hayloft are sunk in and green, and beyond them the wheel of the mill remains jammed while water flares through the broken dyke below. There are a few houses by the causeway, some of them occupied, their roof lines softened by a haze of pale woodsmoke, but there are others there too, abandoned, and their rooflines are softened by their neighbours having pilfered their beams for firewood.

'Soon be winter,' Richard says.

She wonders what in God's name they will do then.

'How does it look?' he asks.

'Sad,' she says.

He tries to encourage her.

'We've no men to work the place,' he says. 'And Eelby – if I had eyes in my head I would kill him now.'

'Then we'd have one fewer,' she sighs, 'and be in an even worse state.'

She remembers again his high hopes as they'd ridden here. Richard had asked her what they might find, since she was supposed to have passed her youth in the castle, but she told him she could remember almost nothing of it.

'It is a castle,' she'd said.

'Yes, yes, but Windsor is a castle. The Tower is a castle. What is it like? My father said it was well set up, though cold, and there are two moats?'

'There are moats,' she'd agreed. 'Yes. Yes. That is right. Moats.'

Although she'd thought, why have more than one?

'And who will be there?' he'd pressed. 'The steward and the reeve, of course, but do you remember them? Or I suppose it is too long ago?'

She'd agreed again.

'And anything might have happened to the place,' she'd cautioned. 'Or to them.'

In truth she'd had no idea what sort of welcome to expect. For the first few days after their arrival she had looked in the village for anyone so old they might have been able to recall Margaret Cornford as a girl, but there was no one above ground to do so. The longer she remained, the more confident she became.

And so now she takes Richard's arm and leads him to face north-ward. They say nothing for a while. She watches the river, a snaking grey ribbon among the reeds. It is motionless and looks broken too.

'Do you miss Marton Hall?' she asks.

He cocks his ear, his way of glancing at her.

'Marton Hall?' he says. 'No. Or not exactly. I miss – I miss the people. I miss my father, of course. And Geoffrey Popham, the steward, and his wife. They were – well. There was Thomas, of course. You met him. And the others. Do you remember Walter? He was a brute, wasn't he? But by great God above, he was – anyway . . . and Kit, of course. I think about him sometimes. I don't remember where he came from. I think we found him on a ship, can you believe it? But do you know he cured my father's fistula? He was no more than a boy, but he cut him, like a surgeon, and we all stood by and we knew it was the right thing to do. By all the saints, when I think of it now. That summer. Everything rang with life.'

She thinks back to Marton Hall and remembers the long summer she spent there pretending to be a boy, answering to the name of Kit. No one – not Richard, not Sir John, nor any of the others – had suspected she was anyone other than who she claimed to be, as why should they? And so later, when she needed to, she was able to return in another borrowed guise, that of Lady Margaret Cornford. The summer is a happy memory, dominated in the main by Thomas, of course, but it is inevitably spoiled by the thought of the winter that followed. Since then she has learned not to sniff when the tears come, and so she can weep silently.

'But,' Richard continues quickly, just as if he knows, 'they're all gone now. And anyway, why have a hall when you can have a castle?'

He is half in jest. He gestures, little knowing he is opening his arms to a vista of burdensome and ruined countryside, peopled by worrying responsibilities and petty shames. She twists the ring on her forefinger and together they pace along the tower's walkway to where she stops and forces herself to stare westwards, across the fens to the huddle of grey stone buildings scarcely visible in the distance.

It is the Priory of St Mary at Haverhurst. In the year she has been in Cornford she has never been along the causeway that leads to its gates, never even left the castle in that direction. All she can manage is to make herself look at it at least once a day and every time she does so she still feels a hot flare of panic. Looking at it now, she can see there is almost nothing to the place – a church, a few low buildings encircled by that wall – and it seems absurd that for the larger part of her life it encompassed her entire world. She wonders what they are doing there now, and knows instinctively it is the hour of None and the sisters will be gathering in observance.

She is relieved when there is a flurry of barking from below and she can look away. Eelby's wife is down there, feeding the dogs God knows what. The head of the cat perhaps.

'It is Eelby's wife,' she tells Richard. He grunts. Katherine wonders again how many days she can have left. She has asked Eelby about her lying in, but Eelby laughed in her face and told her that women such as his wife did not lie in. He told her that it was not her concern anyway, and he told her that he had delivered cows of their calves and ewes of their lambs and that there was nothing very special about delivering a woman of her baby.

Katherine had then tried to talk to Eelby's wife, to avoid the forestaller as it were, but the woman had been fearful and backed away, shaking her head as if she did not want to hear what was being said, and Katherine could not tell if it was the prospect of the birth that frightened her most, or the prospect of her husband. Katherine asked if there was a woman in the village who attended births.

'There was,' Eelby's wife said, 'but she is in the churchyard since St Agnes's last year and her daughter alongside her, so now there is no one.'

From her vantage point at the top of the tower Katherine watches Eelby's wife and wonders how she can work on like that. She must be due any day. She may even be overdue. She imagines her fear. What must it be like to know what is coming? She has seen men's faces as they troop to battle, the grim set of their mouths, their distant gazes, their skin the colour of goose fat and trembling hands that can only be stilled by wine or ale. But what about women as they prepare for childbirth? Their chance of death is the greater, and terrible pain a certainty.

'We must do something for Eelby's wife,' she tells Richard. 'And soon.'

Richard grunts again.

'Perhaps we should send for the infirmarian at the priory?' she asks.

Even as she says the words she feels that familiar flutter in her chest; her breath comes a little faster and she feels unsteady.

But Richard is dismissive.

'St Mary's is a Gilbertine priory, remember?' he tells her. 'An enclosed order. The women are only supposed to see the outside world through an aperture that must be no thicker than a thumb, no taller than a finger. Did you know? It is supposed to be brass-bound, too. To prevent the sisters enlarging it over time. So their infirmarian could not come out even if it were worth her while because, after all, what experience can she have in childbirth? Among those women who have not seen a man in – ever?'

Richard knows little of the sisters in the priory, she thinks, but he is not really thinking about them: he is thinking of himself and her, and once again the subject of their own lack of offspring is between them, dark and heavy. It is not as if she has not tried. They were married in the first month after King Edward's coronation, when she had given Thomas Everingham up for dead, and since then they have lain together as man and wife on occasion. She does not care to recall those first encounters, but since then they have reached not so much an understanding as a way of doing things.

Yet still there is no child, and she feels there is none on the way

13

either, and so she wonders if their way of doing things is the right way after all, or if such a union, forged in hidden sorrow, will ever be blessed.

Eelby's wife has now fed the dogs and is retreating slowly towards the kitchen.

'I could find some woman myself?' Katherine suggests. 'Have her here when the baby comes.'

'Is there someone in the village?' Richard asks.

'No,' she admits. 'But at one of the other villages? Or I might go as far as Boston? I need to sell such russet as we have left. You could come with me?'

Richard nods but they both know he will not come.

The next morning it is Eelby who waits alone for her across the first bridge with two horses in the falling rain. He makes her walk through the courtyard, past the dogs, quietened now with a bone apiece, and the kitchen door where his wife leans against the wall. When Katherine sees her she is brought up short. The woman's skin is taut and her eyes bulge almost grotesquely. She is breathing noisily, too, almost panting, and when she raises her hand Katherine can see it is horribly swollen.

'Good day to you, Goodwife Eelby,' Katherine calls. 'We will be back as soon as we can. Rest until we return. Do nothing, do you hear?'

Eelby's wife does not speak, but nods stiffly, as if she cannot move her head for the swelling in her neck. She looks terrified, Katherine thinks, and she hurries out through the gatehouse and across the first bridge to where Eelby looks unhappy in his wet straw hat.

'Your wife—' Katherine starts.

'Will be all right,' he interrupts.

She makes up her mind. She will find someone in Boston. She pulls herself up into the saddle and settles herself. Then they ride out across the second bridge to the causeway.

'Needs mending,' she says.

There is a pause.

'Hard to mend a bridge when you've no wood,' he says. 'Or nails. Or a hammer. Or anyone to use it to drive them in.'

'Is there really no one?'

He lifts his hands off his reins and gestures at the houses along the road ahead. There are five or six of them, low and dark, with rotting, green slicked daub, and further on is a boy, the oldest in the hamlet yet still beardless, wrestling a pig into a pen while his sisters look on. The detritus of rush weaving is in a pile all around their ankles, and baskets and mattresses are heaped and hooked on the fences. The boy is smacking the pig with a stout stick now, and if the pig turns on him, they will have one fewer hand.

'Help him, Eelby,' Katherine says.

Eelby slouches from his saddle and joins the boy. Together they kick and hit the pig until it retreats into its pen.

'Thank you, lady,' the boy says. He is breathless. Then he adds a thank-you for Eelby but there is some side there, and Katherine notes it.

Eelby mounts up and she says goodbye to the children and they kick their horses on. Further along the causeway a skinny-looking mother — their mother? — with a bald-headed newborn sits in her open doorway and stares at them as they pass. Katherine smiles but receives nothing in return. She wonders who delivered the child.

'My wife did it,' Eelby tells her when they are out of earshot.

Eelby rides with his head down, hunched under his hat, letting the horse lead the way. She imagines he is probably thinking of all the men who used to live in the hamlet, the men who did all the work and kept the place alive. She supposes they must have been at the shambles on the fields of Towton, and she shies away from recalling the day, from her memories of it, but even here they come back, almost crushing her.

She cannot stop herself remembering going up to the plateau with Richard and the surgeon's assistant whose name she cannot recall, just after she'd heard news of Thomas, and she remembers how in the light of the looters' torches she'd seen the valley so choked with corpses that the river was dammed with them and water frothed through the bodies. She remembers the piles of dead men all around, four, five, six bodies high. She remembers that the ground under her feet was glutinous with blood and melted snow and God knew what else. She remembers the smell and the sound of the wounded still crying, trapped under the weight of the dead above them, and even then, as if there had not been enough killed, there were still more men being put to death, even in the night. Their bellows and shouts were cut off with clumsy flurries of hammer blows and everybody was terrified, even the men with the hammers. It was the evening of the day on which God and his saints had slept.

She remembers when she thought she'd found him, Thomas, only for it to be some other man, a Welshman who also answered to the name of Thomas and thought it was his wife calling for him. That was when the tears really began, that was when the misery of it settled in her guts with the weight of a stone, and even now, months later, she feels herself skinless against the pain of it, and she thanks the rain for hiding her tears and giving her reason to hunch and shudder on the back of her horse.

She supposes that any hope that the men of the villages would return slowly withered over the summer, as hers did for Thomas. She had cleaved to William Hastings all those months, hoping that Thomas would know to find her in his household, but her position there was uncertain, and there was gossip, even though she had given them no evidence to assume she was Hastings's mistress. She did not know how to enforce her own claims for Cornford Castle either, nor, really, what she should do with herself during that febrile time when new masters were sweeping into new properties and new positions all over the country, and the old King's men were being attainted and exiled and all that had been theirs was suddenly there for any well-placed man to take.

She had been utterly stilled with grief during those months, and as the days passed the complex mutual responsibilities between her and Richard Fakenham hardened into dependence. As the days turned to weeks, and Thomas did not appear, the more obvious it became that she would have to marry Richard, and go with him and such household as they had to Cornford.

The rain is persistent now, sharp and fine from a dingy wind-blown sky wherein pigeons and gulls are bundled in the gusts, and a little later they meet a friar sheltering under a tree by a crossroads. When she sees him, Katherine can't seem to find the right words in greeting, so Eelby says something and the friar has a soft, wet cough that she does not like the sound of and he tells them he is on his way to Lincoln, intending to stay the night at St Mary's Priory at Haverhurst if they will have him.

They wish him a safe journey and ride on.

'Bad luck to meet a friar on the road,' Eelby says after an interval. She tells him that is superstitious nonsense and on they go.

She has been this far east of the castle since, to the town of Boston, but every time she travels the road, she remembers the first time she was ever in the town, two years previously, and she looks again for the wood in which she and Thomas spent their first night as apostates, sleeping in the mud with the pardoner. There are some trees clumped on the horizon that may do, but elsewhere there is nothing to guide her, only the road on its dyke among the wet sedge of the fenland. She imagines that the river down which they floated might be a little way to the north. Further on a heron is hunched over a pool and she knows that Richard might once have tried to hit it with an arrow, or set a hawk at it, but Eelby is not like that, and so the bird sits and hardly bothers to watch them as they pass.

17

Soon they come to a stretch of dry land, tilled and divvied into neat furlongs and beyond is Boston under its halo of coal smoke and pale winged gulls. She sees the tree wherein the thief's dead body hung, now empty, and ahead is the bridge where the pardoner was made to pay extra pontage for his mule.

She tries to imagine herself as she was then. How things have changed and yet how they have also remained the same. She was in rags the last time she was here, a barefoot apostate in terror of everything around her, and now here she is again, in a cloak trimmed with fox's fur and a dress of Kendal green given to her by the greatest lord in the land, riding a horse with a servant trailing behind. Yet she feels almost exactly the same gnawing anxiety, still the same dread that someone will recognise her for who she really is and call her out on it, and then where will she be?

She steels herself and rides on to the bridge. At the end is a guard, waiting in his hut to collect pontage, and it could be the same man. They always look the same anyway. She digs out the coin and pays him without getting down from her saddle and he nods and lets her pass with no more than the speculative appraisal she has come to expect from any man, and she leads Eelby off the bridge and on into the marketplace.

It is perhaps her imagination, but every time she visits, the town seems less busy than last time, or perhaps having seen more of the world she is less impressed by it. The familiars are all there, including the hunched fripperer, though the sad-faced bear has gone. They have made progress with the church tower, she notes, and the scaffold looms ever more perilously over the river's bank.

She wonders how to set about finding a midwife. The church, she knows, regulates their practice fiercely. This is because the priests are frightened of anyone with knowledge of matters to which they themselves are not privy. And naturally if it is something within a woman's realm, if it is something a man cannot control, then it is

18

stigmatised and she has heard men mutter darkly that the better the witch, the better the midwife.

She decides to give Eelby one more chance.

'While we are here,' she says, 'I shall ask the friars if they know of anyone who might assist at your wife's lying-in.'

He glowers at her. His cheeks are wind-mottled, purple-veined, his eyes small and watery blue.

'She doesn't need any help,' he says. 'Least none from some old witch.'

'But the swelling. You saw her hands? Her face?'

'It's natural,' he says. Then: 'By Christ, I should have seen the Cunning Woman when she came. She has a tincture, you know, that she can give a woman? Raspberry leaves and a root of something? It smothers the baby before it grows, like a stillborn lamb.'

Katherine does not even want to think about what Eelby has just said.

She realises she needs a different tactic.

'Very well,' she says. 'I will sell the cloth now.'

He nods and now that she looks to have backed down, he is scornful, as if this sign of weakness is his permission to dismiss her concerns. She is weary of him, but says nothing further and only turns and he follows her with the bolt of cloth folded over his shoulder to where she stops before the window of a tailor's shop and begins the bargaining process. The tailor has a lively eye, and from his hatch, he enjoys the process as much as she, and she remembers with pleasure all the lessons in bartering that she learned from Geoffrey during their time in Calais. The cloth is good and the price is fair. Eelby looks on.

When she puts the coins in her purse and straps it closed, she asks if he knows any people here. He shakes his head. He has been to Boston before, twice he thinks, though it is hardly any distance from Cornford. It is then that she sees the woman coming from the market. She is a merchant's wife, Katherine supposes, in a good coat and stout wooden pattens, and though she is conventional in that she is hardly broadcasting the fact that she is pregnant, it is clear that she is pleased with her state, and happy to let the world know it.

'I will ask her,' Katherine says.

Eelby draws in his breath. Behind the woman trails a servant, carrying a heavy basket of beetroot. The servant is anxious when Katherine addresses his mistress but then stands glumly by while she tells Katherine the details of the impending lying-in, and that a widow named Beaufoy is to attend her birthing.

'She is licensed by the Bishop in Lincoln,' the woman says, 'and can read letters and knows all the words needed to baptise an infant. Should that prove necessary.'

There is a trace of wariness in her face as she says this, and Katherine thanks her and wishes her well and together she and Eelby follow her directions to the widow's house, around two corners and along a narrow street. When they find her house they knock and a girl answers and shows them into a hall where she leaves them to fetch her mistress. Katherine is reminded of visiting the pardoner's widow in Lincoln, but this time she is with Eelby.

'Why are you so concerned about my wife and child?' Eelby asks her.

Katherine does not answer for a moment. She thinks it ought to be natural for one human being to care for another, but perhaps there is more to it than that? She supposes that with the arrival of a baby, something at Cornford will change, that there will be a rebirth, she hopes, and their fortunes will pick up again. She wonders if she is being fanciful, whether she should tell Eelby of the burden she is placing on his unborn child, but he continues.

'Is it because you have none of your own?' he asks. 'Because you are barren?'

She says nothing. They wait. It is a fine room, she thinks, not unlike the pardoner's in Lincoln, with panelled wooden walls and an aperture through which the fire's smoke can rise to warm the rooms above. When Widow Beaufoy comes she is wearing a dress that is almost identical to Katherine's, as if she might also have been given it by Lord Hastings, and a softly folded headdress in deepest red. She is a handsome woman, perhaps thirty-five or thereabouts, taller than Katherine by a handspan, with sharp cheekbones and quick, assessing eyes.

'You are Lady Margaret?' she asks. 'You are the daughter of the late Lord Cornford, of Cornford?'

Katherine agrees she is and steels herself to endure Widow Beaufoy's further scrutiny. It endures for a long moment. What will she see? Once she has seen beyond Katherine's physical appearance – too sharp-featured and thin to be beautiful, she knows – will she divine anything else? That Katherine is not who she says she is? That she is an impersonator? That she is an apostate? That she is a murderer? As she stands before Widow Beaufoy, Katherine cannot stop herself touching her half ear, hidden beneath her own headdress.

'Perhaps we have come to the wrong place,' she says, stepping back, but Widow Beaufoy collects herself, and waves aside Katherine's protest.

'No,' she says. 'No. You are here now. Though your lying-in is not soon?'

Katherine explains the case but to answer some of the widow's questions she must defer to Eelby, who stands askance and will not look at either of them, as if the business offends him. Katherine wonders if he isn't just as frightened as his wife at the thought of the birth. Widow Beaufoy asks when his wife last flowered, and he does not know, and she seems to think this typical of men, but when Katherine describes Eelby's wife as being swollen, Widow Beaufoy becomes alarmed.

'Around the face?' she asks. 'And the hands?'

Eelby nods.

'We must go quickly,' Widow Beaufoy says. She instructs the girl to summon the ostler and someone called Harrington, who turns out to be a servant.

'Bring the bag,' she tells the girl, 'and make sure it is ready, particularly with hawthorn and garlic.'

They hurry to their horses and, with Widow Beaufoy riding side-saddle like Katherine, the girl on the back of the servant's horse, they ride out through the marketplace and back across the bridge. When they are in the road, Widow Beaufoy urges her horse on.

'We must be quick,' she says. 'Or we are more likely to have need of a priest and a man good with a spade.'

2

When they arrive at the castle, the gates are still open and the hungry dogs are barking.

'Woman!' Eelby calls. Only the dogs answer. He is off his horse first, running for the kitchen where the door stands open. The fire has gone out and it is dark within.

'Woman!'

They find her behind the table, lying in a pool of her own making, her face fixed in a terrible grimace. Widow Beaufoy calls for a candle and orders the girl to bring her bag.

'Can we move her?'

Eelby and the servant lift Eelby's wife on to the table. Her body is swollen, hot and rigid.

'Put the jars there,' Widow Beaufoy tells the girl, 'then open that shutter and find more candles.'

She turns to her servant and Eelby. 'You, get the fire going. You, fetch some water. Then feed those dogs. Shut them up, at any rate.'

Harrington fixes the fire while Eelby hurries away with the cauldron. Widow Beaufoy begins concocting a mixture, of herbs and some wine, in a small bowl of dark stone.

'How can I help?' Katherine asks.

'Pray for her,' Widow Beaufoy says.

'I have worked in a hospital,' Katherine tells her, 'after two battles, and have sewn men together.'

Widow Beaufoy looks up.

'We may have need of your skills then, if they are both to survive. In the meantime, mix this, make it fine.'

She passes Katherine the bowl. The smell is strong, earthy and rich, like a country lane in high summer. Widow Beaufoy turns and stands by Eelby's wife. She feels her face, her limbs. Smells her. Even tastes whatever it is that has made the pool under her.

Eelby returns with the pot and hangs it over the blossoming fire and Widow Beaufoy dismisses him and Harrington both before she raises Eelby's wife's dress and shift, both heavy with what must be her broken waters. Eelby's wife is breathing fast, her face still clenched, the muscles around her mouth twitching peculiarly, and though her eyes are open she seems to see nothing.

Widow Beaufoy uses a knife to cut away her braies and together she and the girl raise the dress over Eelby's wife's belly, as big as a moon, with an upright belly button. Widow Beaufoy peers at her nethers.

'Rue, wormwood, marsh mallow. Rub her hands with laurel oil. Quick, girl.'

The girl makes a mixture from two bottles and passes it to Widow Beaufoy who stands by Eelby's wife's head.

'Lift her,' she says.

Katherine puts aside her bowl, slides her hands under Eelby's wife's heavy shoulders and hauls her up. Widow Beaufoy tips her head back, pinches the point of Eelby's wife's nose and pours the contents of the bowl into her mouth so that she must drink or drown. The fire is cracking behind them, throwing shadows.

'More light,' Widow Beaufoy says, and, 'that needs to be ground finer still. And add oil.'

The girl lights another of the goat-fat candles before unstopping a clay jar and adding oil to Katherine's mix. Katherine keeps stirring, creating a thick paste, wondering what it is.

'Now warm the wine.'

There is a small jug, half-empty, in the buttery. Katherine pours it into a scrubbed pot and places this on the stone among the ashes.

Now Eelby's wife goes into spasm. Her body is stiff for a long moment, her back arched. Her mighty legs are shaking, and her hose slips from her calves to bunch around her ankles. She is grimacing. Widow Beaufoy is bent over her now, embracing her, holding her gently, soothing her with words Katherine does not understand. Eelby's wife starts shuddering and a tendril of foam slips from her mouth. Then blood. And then – dear God! Eelby's wife is – changing colour? Katherine brings one of the smoking candles closer. She is not sure now, but for a moment it seemed Eelby's wife's skin darkened, turned almost blue.

After a moment, Eelby's wife relaxes. Widow Beaufoy stands. Then Eelby's wife falls asleep, but it is not a good sleep. The girl has a cloth to mop her face, to wipe away the spit and the blood.

'She has bitten her tongue,' she says.

Widow Beaufoy nods.

'She will wake soon,' she says, 'but she will not be with us long before the fit comes again.'

'Why? What is it?' Katherine asks.

'It is something to do with the womb. It is misplaced, perhaps.'

'Misplaced? How?'

'It is what the books say. I have never seen it myself, but I was taught that the womb may rise into the body. It can choke the heart. I think this is what we have here.'

Katherine looks at Eelby's wife. Her womb looks very fixed, very low with the child within, but is it possible, she wonders, that the heart might be pressed by the size of the baby?

'What can we do?' she asks.

'The books suggest we write some formulation of words in any cheese or butter you may have? Then apply it to the surface of the womb.'

How would that help? Katherine wonders. It sounds like witch-craft.

'The books also suggest the womb must be fixed in place by burning the bones of a salted fish, or the hooves of a horse, even the dung of a cat, and letting the smoke rise up and fumigate her from below . . .'

'But?'

'But none of this works.'

'What then?'

'I have given her something. I have seen it work, but I have also seen it fail. Hawthorn. Garlic. Poppy, too, to calm her.'

The girl puts more wood on the fire.

The three stand and watch Eelby's wife. Her hands are huge, lying in loose fists by her sprawling thighs. Blood and the other liquid cover the table and have pooled on the slates underfoot. Only now does either of them take off their riding cloak. Widow Beaufoy's is held with a fine gold brooch and pin. They drape them over a coffer by the door.

They wait. The girl lights another candle. Widow Beaufoy prepares some other unguent with the warmed wine. Then Eelby's wife stirs. Widow Beaufoy is quickly by her side. Eelby's wife is confused and touches her face, looks around as if dazed, wonders what they are all doing there. She settles back down on the table and stares up at the low, sooted rafters, the bunches of brown herbs that hang from them. It looks as if she is going to say something but, before she can, she gives a long cry and her mouth starts twitching again and the fit is on her.

Widow Beaufoy holds her down again, and whispers more words, but already she is spitting froth again and this time Katherine is certain her hands, bigger than ever now, are turning blue.

But it passes. Eelby's wife relaxes and, when it is over and she is asleep again, Widow Beaufoy stands up.

'Tell Harrington to fetch a priest.'

26

The girl looks to Katherine.

'The priest has gone,' she tells her. 'He will have to ride to the priory. Eelby can show him.'

'You have no priest here?'

Katherine shakes her head. They cannot afford a priest. They can scarcely afford a greyhound. Widow Beaufoy nods, as if she understands.

'Tell Harrington to be quick,' she tells the girl, who nods and is gone. A long moment slides by. The fire catches brightly. Eelby's wife makes a noise in her throat. She starts to snore. Widow Beaufoy places a palm on Eelby's wife's belly.

'Come,' she says. 'Feel.'

Katherine extends a hand to the hot drum of the belly.

'There,' Widow Beaufoy says. She takes Katherine's fingers and presses them down on something harder still within.

'A knee,' she says. 'Or an elbow.'

She thinks for a long moment. Then the girl returns.

'He has gone for the priest,' she tells them.

'Help us,' Widow Beaufoy says and together they turn Eelby's wife on the table so that her legs swing down one side. Widow Beaufoy is surprisingly strong, and, standing behind Eelby's wife, she grips her under the arms and sits her up, and for a moment she sits slumped over her belly like an old drunk.

'Hold her,' Widow Beaufoy tells Katherine, and to the girl: 'Rose oil. All over. Vigorously now.'

Katherine stands behind Eelby's wife and takes the weight. Eelby's wife is solid, her chest and shoulders broad and deep, her large muscles well covered with fat. Widow Beaufoy fiddles with some concoction while the girl starts massaging oil into Eelby's wife's nethers and her marbled thighs.

The mixture Widow Beaufoy is making is penetrating, sharp and sweet. Widow Beaufoy pushes the girl aside and once again takes Eelby's wife's nose, tips back her head and pours in the contents of the bowl. Eelby's wife starts. Katherine struggles to hold her. The girl helps, her hands fragrant with oil. Then Widow Beaufoy places a pinch of something from a china pot in each of Eelby's wife's nostrils. There is a moment, then Eelby's wife stretches backward. Katherine staggers, has to use her shoulder to keep the body upright – then the woman sneezes.

'Good,' Widow Beaufoy murmurs. 'And again.'

Eelby's wife sneezes three more times.

Widow Beaufoy keeps a hand on her belly. She is frowning beadily. After a moment she shakes her head. Nothing is happening.

'I will have to help her myself,' she says. Widow Beaufoy takes the oil jar and washes her hand in it. Then she stands before Eelby's wife, spreads the younger woman's solid knees, pushes her backward against Katherine and then crouches down. Widow Beaufoy narrows her eyes, pushes her hands forward and twists her wrist. It seems to Katherine that she must have her hand inside Eelby's wife.

'I can't – I can't get it.'

She stands.

'The baby is the wrong way around. Like this, you see? Not that.'

The girl is watching, learning. So is Katherine.

There is a voice at the door.

'The priest is here.'

'Don't let him in. I will try again. Hold her.'

She does so, but with the same result. After the third attempt she gives up.

'Let her sleep undisturbed,' she says.

They let her down and turn her around so that she is lying along the table again.

'Will we need a surgeon?' the girl asks.

Widow Beaufoy shakes her head.

'It is too late for that,' she says, and the girl pulls a face and nods. Katherine realises what has happened. Although Eelby's wife is not yet dead, Widow Beaufoy has given her up as such. She has passed from one state to another, hardly noticed. The girl starts to pack away the bottles and the pestle and mortar. Then she brings out another earthenware bottle and a crucifix made of folded rushes, long-faded brown. Widow Beaufoy anoints her hands with more oil.

'We must baptise the baby,' she says.

Katherine feels a great weight of sadness, a crushing disappointment. She has placed more hope on this child than she expected.

'It will die?' she asks.

Widow Beaufoy nods.

'But if I can pull a limb out,' she says, 'then at least we may absolve it of sin, and ensure it does not pass eternity in Purgatory.'

She inserts her hand into Eelby's wife again. This time she is less gentle. She no longer cares whether she hurts the baby, or Eelby's wife, since she has already given up on them both. The girl looks on, clutching the bottle to her chest.

After a moment Widow Beaufoy shakes her head sadly and withdraws her hand.

'It is stuck fast,' she says.

There is a long silence. Katherine can feel tears gathering weight in her eyelashes. This cannot be, she thinks.

'What would a surgeon have done?' she asks.

Widow Beaufoy shrugs again, and says: 'He might have cut her, perhaps, across here.'

She runs a finger over Eelby's wife's belly.

'But that would kill her, surely?'

'Of course. It is only done to save the baby, only *in extremis*. And usually after the death has occurred.'

'But now?'

Widow Beaufoy looks at her and shakes her head.

'It has been too long,' she says.

'The poor soul,' the girl adds.

Eelby's wife is slack now. The fire has gone out in the hearth, too. It seems very dark in the kitchen.

'So that is it?' Katherine asks.

Widow Beaufoy nods. The girl is returning the jar and cross to the leather bag.

'But the baby?' Katherine asks. 'It might yet be alive?'

She cannot help but glance at the expanse of belly. There is another life buried in there hoping to escape, but . . .

'But we must try, surely. What have we to lose? You say she is almost dead, but the baby?'

Widow Beaufoy stops and looks at her.

'Is probably already dead.'

'But we can't be sure?'

Widow Beaufoy looks at Katherine for what seems like a long moment.

'The mother is still alive,' she says, indicating Eelby's wife. 'To cut her in the manner in which you suggest would be to kill her, and it will be for nothing if the baby is already dead.'

Katherine feels panicky. She feels they are losing more than just the life of an unborn child.

'We must do something.'

Widow Beaufoy shakes her head.

'I must wash,' she says, 'and then I will find the priest.'

And she leaves Katherine and the girl alone in the kitchen with the great mound of Eelby's dying wife. The girl hurries to close the door behind her and then comes to stand close to Katherine. She looks confiding.

'She would not cut her,' she says in a low voice, 'even if she knew the baby were alive.'

'Why not?'

'It is murder.'

'But surely? In the eyes of the Lord—'

'Oh, she is not worried about the Lord. She is worried about the

30

law. About the bailiff and the coroner, about the deodand, and all the fines she would have to pay.'

Katherine has no idea what she is talking about, and so ignores it.

'What if I do it?' Katherine asks.

The girl shrugs.

'She would help, I dare say.'

When Widow Beaufoy returns Katherine has the midwife's roll of knives out on the table. Widow Beaufoy stares at her and the girl, who buries her head in her tasks, and the knives.

'What are you doing?' she asks.

'I will cut her,' Katherine says.

Widow Beaufoy nods.

'Very well,' she says, 'but do not use any of those knives. Use one of your own.'

Katherine looks at the kitchen knives on the far table. Both are fat-bladed, clumsily wrought, probably blunt.

'I have none other that is suitable. Come on, we must hurry.'

Widow Beaufoy is anxious. She fiddles in the roll and passes a small blade to Katherine.

'This will never do,' Katherine says. 'Pass me that one.'

Widow Beaufoy is reluctant.

'That knife is the dearer,' the girl suggests.

'I will pay you for it,' Katherine says. Widow Beaufoy nods and suggests a price to which Katherine agrees, but only because time is fleeting. The knife is very fine: eight inches long, perhaps, with a short, ornamented blade so sharp she can almost already see it parting the layers of taut skin that cover Eelby's wife's belly. This thought frightens her, but she remembers how she cut Sir John's fistula, and how she could see herself doing that before she actually did it. In the moments after the operation, when she knew Sir John would live, she had wondered to herself if her hand had not been guided by God. And now here she is, having those same feelings again.

31

'Will you help?'

'I will call the priest first, yes, then I will be there to keep the blood from your eyes.'

'Would you show me where to cut?'

'It hardly matters where you cut since you will kill her wherever you do it.'

Katherine looks at Eelby's wife. Her breathing is quick, her skin waxy and she is sweating heavily. The soporific must be strong.

'But she will die anyway?'

Widow Beaufoy nods.

'She is almost there now.'

'Then fetch the priest,' Katherine says, and she steps back, into the shadowy pantry where the dry goods are kept. She does not want to be seen, even though she knows the priest will not recognise her. Widow Beaufoy draws Eelby's wife's dress down, pushes her knees and ankles together and then calls the priest.

When he comes in he is not the snow-haired old man of whom Thomas used to speak, whose voice she had so often heard floating over the wall at Mass through her youth, but a much younger man, her own age perhaps. He is wearing a pale cloak over his cassock and when he removes his worsted cap, his fringe of hair is nondescript brown.

Harrington calls him Father Barnaby.

Katherine stares at the priest from the shadows. Can this be the same Barnaby whom Thomas mentioned as his friend in the priory? It must be. Distractedly she wants to reach out and touch him, to retrieve some notion of Thomas.

But he is mumbling to Widow Beaufoy, who gives him the correct responses to his questions, before he turns and retrieves a phial of liquid from his purse; he moves to stand over Eelby's wife, at her head, and he begins chanting some words. He shakes the phial, speckling her with water, before anointing her with some chrism and making the sign of the cross over her body. When the ceremony

32

is over, with Eelby's wife all the time unconscious, Widow Beaufoy hurries the priest from the kitchen and calls for the girl.

'Get as many cloths as you can,' she says. 'Take them from anywhere, from the table, from the cupboard in the solar. And Harrington, we need more water, plenty of it.'

She returns and throws more wood on the fire, and something else, some herb or other, that fills the room with an acrid smell. As Katherine steps out of the pantry, Widow Beaufoy is scattering wands of the herb into the puddles on the floor and on the table around Eelby's dying wife.

'It helps keep the miasma away,' she says.

Katherine's hands are trembling. She feels jittery, as if she has not eaten for a day. She tries to calm herself, to remember the hospital in Towton. The surgeon's assistant's name was Matthew Mayhew. She remembers Sir John and his soporific.

'Will she feel anything?' she asks Widow Beaufoy.

'No,' Widow Beaufoy tells her. 'She is still alive, but I have given her a sedative to put her beyond the realm of suffering.'

Dear God, she thinks. Dear God.

But she takes the knife and places its point just below the belly button.

'Lower, I think,' Widow Beaufoy says.

The line on Eelby's wife's belly is the line that Katherine will follow. She presses in the tip and produces a bead of blood that slips down the oiled skin. She edges the blade down, from the belly button towards the pubis, hardly scratching the surface, but the skin parts under its tension. Blood runs, following the point of the knife, but there is nothing like the amount Widow Beaufoy predicted.

'You have only parted the skin,' Widow Beaufoy tells her. 'Now you must part the flesh.'

The flesh is harder to cut. It is tense and sprung, and as Katherine cuts through it so the blood begins to pour from the wound. It seethes out, and covers her hands and arms, and is all over her dress,

33

the one that Hastings gave her, and the knife is slippery with it. Blood washes across the table. It gurgles in the wound from where it runs to the stone floor. It keeps coming. It is like a bowl that fills from below, like a spring, a rising head of a conduit, filling up. They could spoon it out of her.

'Dear God.'

'Keep going,' Widow Beaufoy says. 'Another pass.'

Katherine slices again. There is so much blood she can see nothing of the wound, almost nothing at all. The texture, though, is softer, as if she is into a different layer. Something like thickened water, as warm as a bath, spreads from the heel of the wound, across the table. She can feel it on her knees, filling her boots. Eelby's wife seems to have deflated. Her skin is wrinkling, and the belly that a moment ago had been ripe has now gone over.

'There,' Widow Beaufoy says and she points at something within the lips of the cut. Katherine drops the knife on the table. Widow Beaufoy shoulders her aside. She slides her hand into the wound. She is frowning. But then her eyes go wide. They are very white against the blood on her cheeks. She looks at Katherine, then at the girl, and she nods at her. The girl breaks into a smile and scrabbles in the bag once more.

Now Widow Beaufoy is gentle.

'Here we are,' she says. 'Here we are. Great God above. It has caught my finger!'

She is beaming. Her hands are in the wound, now up to her wrists. Blood is everywhere, her clothing drenched. Widow Beaufoy stretches, then pulls, just as if she were harvesting something from the garden. After a brief tug of resistance, she has it out, feet first, through the lips of the cut and out into the blood-scented air.

'A boy!'

It is disgusting, repellently ugly, blue almost, coated with blood and a thick layer of bloodied fat. A grey tube connects it to the wound.

'Take it,' Widow Beaufoy says. She passes the baby to Katherine, who is half-laughing, half-crying. She holds a life, small, but miraculously there, scorching and stinking, in her bloody palms. And now Widow Beaufoy is quick and deft. She ties something around the cord three or four times, finishing it with a quick knot and then, collecting Katherine's new knife from the table, she slices it through. The cord falls loose, looping from the wound, tied off at its end.

Katherine cannot stop staring at the baby. It is moving gently in her cupped hands, hot and restless, terrifying. Then the girl steps over, quickly taking it from her. She wraps him in a piece of cloth and takes him away to rub him with wine and butter. Katherine is left empty-handed, with nothing now to do. She is wet with blood, every inch of her skin beaded with it, her dress heavy with it. She can taste slate in her mouth.

She looks around the kitchen. Widow Beaufoy stands at the far end of the table, and she closes Eelby's wife's eyes with a bloody palm.

Then it breaks on Katherine what she has done.

She has killed another woman.

Lying on the table is Eelby's wife, gutted and splayed, just as the cat had been the day before. She is a puddle of deflated flesh, an empty bucket. Her dress is pulled up around her ribcage and her legs apart either side of the table, and there is nowhere that is not blood-soaked, even the rough beams of the roof. The kitchen reeks. It steams.

Katherine takes a step back, the hem of her dress in the blood on the floor.

It is dark outside now.

'We had better get the husband in,' Widow Beaufoy says, and the dogs that have been quiet all this time, start howling again.

35

3

Thomas Everingham sleeps in the hall with his brother, his brother's wife, their two boys, three dogs and a cat that shits in the corner where the rushes are oldest. Of them all Thomas is held in the least regard. His brother's wife, Elizabeth, calls him a simpleton and shouts at him.

'Do this, simpleton!' she says, or 'Do that, simpleton!'

And her husband John watches with tired eyes as his younger brother stiffens, then shuffles to do what she has ordered in that slow, tripping manner of his. Thomas has been on the farm since he turned up last spring, when the weather had just turned, some time after Eastertide, and though he has made himself useful in the year that has passed, Elizabeth wants him gone.

'We did not expect the idiot to appear,' she tells John, 'so we will not miss him when he has gone.'

'He is my brother,' John tells Elizabeth, and they look over the fire at Thomas and he looks back, but his eyes are as blank as a mule's. They have learned he understands almost nothing they say, or at least reacts to none of it, unless it is one of the Elizabeth's orders.

'Strange,' John says, watching him. 'Strange that he only knows the things he knew as a boy here.'

Elizabeth mutters something under her breath. John ignores her.

'Though I suppose anyone'd forget a thing or two if they'd been walloped like that,' he concludes.

When Thomas arrived at the farm the year before it had been

the time for lambing and his hair had been matted with blood and there was a wound on the side of his head into which Elizabeth thought she might be able to slide her finger to touch his brain. She did not, though, and as the summer passed the wound had healed itself; now, a year later, the hair over the scar has grown back in a silver streak.

'Let's make up the bed,' John says, for it is nearly dark.

'Idiot!' Elizabeth calls. 'Idiot!'

John tuts but Thomas looks up.

'Fetch the mattress.'

Thomas gets to his feet and shuffles to where the mattress is stored rolled on long pegs hammered in under the eaves. He brings it to the firelight, stepping over the boys and a dog where they lie, and he unrolls it for John and Elizabeth. He himself sleeps further from the fire, beyond the dogs, in a dip in the hard earth floor that he has worn with all the twitches and jerks that wrack his body when he sleeps.

In the mornings he is always awake first and he leaves the rest of the family bundled together by the fire's covered ashes while he goes out into the yard and through the stock fence to relieve himself in the privy. Every time he does this he pauses a moment. He stops and looks around him with narrowed eyes, as if remembering some long-forgotten time, but after a moment he looks up at the pale sky and seems to forget what it was that he's remembered, and he presses on, scattering the pigeons that peck at the straw by the cow's byre. He feeds the sheep hay from the rick and then collects a crooked armful of the logs he chopped in the autumn, takes them in, lays the fire and then returns to milk the cow.

His days continue like this; small tasks punctuated by bread and ale first and last thing, and at dinner some meat in a sauce with root vegetables. When it is very cold the red wheals on his hip and across his shoulder ache, and he limps, but otherwise he seems mostly content to do what is he is told, and to do it until he is told to stop.

And at least he is warmly dressed. They have given him a woollen coat and a sheepskin hat, and his boots do not let in, though the soles are without a heel, so that he sometimes slips, and when he does, and falls in the shit, John's boys laugh out just as if they have engineered the accident themselves.

He does not speak and so he cannot tell them if he remembers arriving at the farm, or how he found his way there from wherever he came, though Elizabeth will tell anyone who will listen that when he first appeared he was more like an animal than a Christian, and that his clothes were stiff with blood and worse, and that if John had not recognised him, she would have set the dogs on him and got the boys to drive him away with shots from their practice bows.

They would not let him in the house for those first months and all summer he slept with the sheep on the hills above the farm. After a while he began to bring water in unasked and John remembered that this had been Thomas's task when he was a boy, before their father went off to the wars in France, before their mother died. Day by day they got him to do more. Soon he was looking after the cow and then helping the shearers when they came to do the sheep. He helped John take the wool to the market and the grain to the windmill. He dug over the vegetable plot, guided the oxen across the rye field and broadcast the seeds.

When Thomas had first arrived, people – especially those who knew him as a boy – were interested in him. After Mass they would look at him as he stood waiting outside the church and they would ask him questions, but he would never say anything, just gaze back at them, sometimes smiling, sometimes more fearful, and soon it was known he was an idiot, and it was only the boys from the other farms who followed him around and threw things at him, though that stopped after the elder of John's two boys – Adam – fought one of them almost to the death, and would have gone beyond had not Thomas been there to pull them apart. He'd held each boy up in the air, at arm's length, their toes straining to touch the ground like men being hanged, and when he dropped them they scrabbled away in silence, their eyes fixed on his pale face.

Adam's brother William is the gentler soul, with red hair and the palest blue eyes that come down from his mother, and he can happily sit in the yard helping her spin yarn on the wheel while Adam roams restless about the woods looking for things to kill. William is generous to Thomas, and gives him things Elizabeth would not want him to have: a pair of fulled socks, a salve for his hands made from honey and sage leaves, a shepherd's cow-horn crook he has made himself.

John let him sleep in the hall when the weather turned at the end of autumn, at about the time they cut and butchered the pigs and the air was filled with the smell of burning hair, and that was when they discovered that he had terrible nightmares, and that he could speak after all, for he would call out in the dark, crying out to the Lord and to someone else whose name they can never agree on.

'Who was it last night?' they'd ask in the morning.

'Dick,' Adam would say.

'Azrin,' William would say.

'That's not a word,' Adam would counter.

'Doesn't need to be,' William would say and Elizabeth would agree with John and Adam would be sent to see if the geese had laid any eggs, or if the malt in the malthouse was likely to sprout that day. After a month or so the family came to accept Thomas sleeping in the house. They came to understand that when he shouted out in the dark and when he screamed and when he was rigid with what John said was terror, it would soon pass. They covered their ears and waited until he slipped back into burbling slumber, only occasionally interrupted by twitches and writhings. John said this was even a comforting sound, better at least than the sound of the mice or the cat chasing them, better than the sound of Adam farting.

As autumn gave way to winter, the soldiers started coming through the valley. They came up from the west and the south, small companies making their ways to join the road that led northwards to the castles in the East March, castles such as Dunstanburgh and Bamburgh, those that were still holding out for the old King. Sometimes they were organised and led by well-dressed men on good horses, with gloves and rings on their fingers, and baggage mules; others were in worse straits, down to their last loaf, horses in need of shoeing. Both sorts and all those between were fugitives, though, always careful about where they went, what they said, and to whom they said it. Some did stop and talk though, in return for bread and ale and hay for their horses.

'Put off my land,' one of them told John. 'His grace's been attainted and some new man's arrived, some connection of the Earl of Warwick. Met me with the offer of serving him, or shifting for myself. So.'

The soldier shrugged his big, archer's shoulders and adjusted his straw hat over his ruddy face. He eyed Thomas, recognising something in him perhaps, and nodded slowly, his hand resting on the hilt of a big knife stuck in his belt.

'But why don't you serve this new man?' John asked.

'Thought of that,' the soldier said. 'But what happens when his grace gets back? He'll have something to say then, won't he? That's for sure.'

'Will he get back?'

'Course he will. Can't keep someone like the Duke of Somerset down.'

'The Duke of Somerset? You served him?'

'Aye,' the man said proudly. 'And his father before.'

John nodded.

'So where is he now? The Duke?'

'Alnwick?' the man says. 'Or Bamburgh? Or the other one. There are three of them up there. Three or four. Dirty great big castles, each held against this new King and the Earl of fucking Warwick.'

The man spat but John was surprised.

40

'Are there many of the old King's men left?'

'Not so many as there were,' the soldier admitted. 'Not after Towton Field. But there are some and they're all making their ways to the castles up there to wait until the Queen comes with her men, from France, you know, or maybe Scotland, and old Tudor comes with his Welshmen, and then we'll see a clean pair of heels from the Earl of Warwick and this new King of his making.'

'You mean there'll be more fighting?' John asked.

The man barked a laugh.

'Course there'll be more fighting,' he said. 'There's *always* more fighting, isn't there? It won't stop until everybody gets what they want, and that isn't going to happen before heaven opens her gates.'

John shook his head at the thought of it. The man took a loaf and filled his flask with ale and left them to follow the causeway that led up over Stanage Edge towards Sheffield and beyond.

When he'd gone, John turned to Thomas and stopped.

'You all right, you daft bastard? You've gone all pale.'

More men came by in the next few weeks, bands of them in riding cloaks, bows and poles slung over their packs, moving furtively through the countryside on hungry horses. Things started to go missing from the farm – a couple of geese, one of the sheep – and Thomas helped bring the animals inside the hazel fence that surrounded the farmhouse and then every night the dogs woke and barked and John would grope for his bow.

That winter they did not go up into the hills to mine for lead as they usually did, and though at night they could see the fires on the hilltops all around where other men were smelting the grey metal, and they thought of the money they were missing out on, they stayed close to the farm, and waited.

Nothing happened all through Advent. Christmastide passed, then Epiphany, and then Candlemas and then Ash Wednesday came and went and still nothing happened. So now it is the season of Lent, when the statues in the church are masked, but the land without is opening up and life is returning to the valley, and it is now that eight men on horses turn off the road and come up the track to the farm, halting their horses before the stockade gates. John watches them come, shading his eyes from the low spring sun. The man who seems to be their leader gets off his horse well before the stockade's gate and John tells Elizabeth to stay within the house with William and he asks Adam to find Thomas.

'Quickly now.'

The man who has climbed off his horse is weary, and from his walk it is obvious he has been riding a good while. He relieves himself in the sheep-cropped grass, then turns to John. He has a bitter-set face and is wearing a buff jack with no sign of a badge to show his allegiance. He greets John cordially, but he does not smile.

'Good country, this,' he says. He has a thick, soft accent.

John nods.

'Hard in winter, I'd imagine?'

Again, John agrees.

'But all right in summer?'

'Yes.'

'Hunting?'

'A little, in the valleys.'

'Not on the hills?'

'Not so much.'

'Still though, eh?'

There is a long silence. It is as if the man doesn't quite know how to start whatever it is he wants to start. His men are lined up behind him, still mounted. One of them is chewing something – a twig, or a piece of straw. He takes it and throws it down.

'We are in need of a few things,' the first man says, as if reminded to get on with it. 'Something to eat. And ale, of course. But horses too, if you have them.'

'I have a horse,' John says. 'But not for sale.'

'I was not thinking of buying.'

'Then?'

Adam comes back.

'I cannot find him,' he tells John.

'Find who?' the man asks.

'No one,' John says, then to the boy: 'All right, Adam, go in now.'

Adam is uncertain. John gives him a push.

The man smiles, watching him go.

'Fine boy,' he says.

There is another moment of silence, then: 'May I see the horse?'

'Why?' John asks.

'See if I want it,' the man says.

'Makes no difference if you want it. You can't have it.'

'But I am willing to trade something for it.'

'Such as what?'

The man smiles and gestures at the hall, the fields, the hills above them.

'All this,' he says. 'You. Him. Her, probably.'

'They are not yours to trade,' John says.

The man frowns.

'Well,' he says. 'No. Not for the moment, but there are more of us than you.'

The man pulls half his sword from his sheath. His eyes are unnaturally bright. He stares at John. John stares back. John does not know what to say now. He opens his mouth to say something, when an arrow flits past him and catches the man in the chest with a thump. The blow knocks the wind from him. He staggers back four or five paces, reaching out for John, then he falls on his heels and his backside.

John is as surprised as the man with the arrow in his chest. He stands stock-still for a moment, his mouth open, his arms by his sides. Then he looks up at the other men on their horses who are likewise paused in mid-gesture. Then at once they move, throwing themselves off their horses, and John turns and runs, back to the stockade.

Thomas is there. He has another arrow nocked and he draws and looses without seeming to aim. His arrow hits one of the men, bundles him with a cry from his saddle. Then Thomas nocks, draws and looses again and he hits another who is running with his back turned. A man shouts.

'Kill him!'

Then there's another arrow. Another cry. Adam has loosed and caught one of the men. He nocks and looses his practice bow just as he has been taught. The arrow carries less weight, but from this distance it may still turf a man from his horse, may still kill him.

John runs through the gateway and slams the hazel stock gate behind him. It is to keep animals in, or out, and not much good for anything else. Thomas sends another arrow through a gap in the fence but sees it wicker into the distance. Already there is another arrow nocked.

And now the remaining men beyond the fence have scattered. They are circling the farmhouse. Thomas has lost sight of them. Then there is a sudden thunder of hoof beats behind and a man looms over the fence and crashes his horse into it and through it. Thomas turns and looses. The arrow catches the horse below the jaw and the horse rears and the man is thrown back and falls from the saddle and the horse stamps forward into the yard and then thunders past, whinnying and screaming, and out through the other side. Geese scatter everywhere.

John emerges from the house with a billhook just in time to stop the fallen rider getting to his feet. He crashes the billhook down on his head, knocking his helmet off, and as his fear is replaced by anger, he crashes it down on him again and again. The man is dead long before John stops hitting him. There is blood everywhere, splashed on the walls, all over John's legs, arms and chest, and all over the dead man.

But through the hole the horse made comes another man. He runs at John with a sword and a small round shield, but Adam stands up behind a beehive, scarcely able to see over the wicker mound, and follows the man with his bow, just as if he were out hunting. He looses and the arrow jumps across the yard. It catches the man's thigh, whipping his leg away from under him. He spins, trips and lands heavily with a bellow of rage. He spills the sword. John takes a step and drops the billhook down on this second man's head and with three or four more clumsy blows he manages to kill him too.

Thomas doubles back around the hall, stepping through the gap in the goose-pen fence and then out past the wood stack. He thinks there are still two more. Where are they? They will have had time to string their bows by now. He is past the wood stack, into the mess where the privy drains. The smell is foul, but familiar. Where are they? He edges forward. He glimpses something in the orchard, from the tail of his eye. He turns too late to see one of the soldiers among the trees. He has his bow raised and an arrow nocked. Thomas sees him loose the arrow.

Just then his heelless boots slip. His feet go from under him and he falls on his back into the mire with a winding crash. The arrow slaps straight into the wattle and daub of the wall above his head, leaving a neat hole. Thomas recovers his bow, scrambles to his feet and runs ducking around the corner. The last soldier is there, hiding from Adam and his bow. He turns to look at Thomas. He has only a rondel knife, gripped in his right hand, but he is a boy, shaking, and only holding the dagger because he knows he ought.

Thomas stands a moment, looks the boy in the eye, then takes two swift steps and smacks the knife from his hand with the tip of his bow. The boy sucks his breath and clutches his hand. His hat drops over his eyes. Thomas takes another step and punches him in the chest. The boy collapses. Thomas takes the arrow from his belt, nocks it and turns back to the soldier in the orchard.

He is bobbing in and out from behind an apple-tree trunk. He is trying to see who is alive and where his friends are. He calls out. There is no answer. He calls again. It is very quiet when he is not shouting and in the weak sunlight his face is very pale between the trees' trunks and Thomas thinks it would be easy to catch him.

He lifts the bow, then lowers it. He turns around and steps over the boy on the ground who is still gasping for air, kicking his legs in the dirt, and he comes out into the yard where Adam is still by the beehives, with his bow and an arrow shaft gripped in shaking, white-knuckled hands. His eyes are fixed on his father who is standing over two dead men, staring at the blade of the billhook that is chipped and ruby with blood. John is breathing hard with the effort of having killed the two men. He looks up at Thomas. They are listening to the one in the orchard shouting out. Thomas turns on his heel, rests his bow against the wall of the house and goes to fetch the other boy who is crawling in the dirt, still hardly able to breathe. Thomas picks him up under the arm and walks him back around the corner and out into the yard where he drops him next to the two dead men in the thin sunlight.

'Water,' he says, gesturing to the bucket.

Adam puts his bow down and throws the contents of the bucket over the boy, who gasps and sits upright.

'Go and fetch your friend,' Thomas tells the boy. 'Tell him to put his bow down and come and there will be no more of this.'

The boy gets up from the mud. His face is mottled and his breath reedy, and he is sopping wet, and he cannot take his gaze off the dead men as he goes back around the corner and tries to shout to his companion in the orchard. Both John and Adam are staring at Thomas with their mouths slack.

'It is – safe,' Thomas says.

John starts to laugh. So does Adam. Thomas feels himself smiling.

'He speaks!' John laughs. 'He actually speaks!'

Then he throws his arms around Thomas and pounds his back and Thomas can feel the bristles on his brother's chin and the breeze of his breath on his ear. John is laughing so hard.

'By the saints,' he gasps, addressing Adam over Thomas's shoulder, 'by all the saints, we did for them, eh, Adam my boy?'

Now Adam is laughing too, and all the more so when John lets go of Thomas and pushes him away and looks at his hands.

'Jesus, man!' he snorts. 'You're covered in shit!'

They laugh again. Tears are rolling down Adam's face. Thomas's face aches. John can hardly breathe with laughter. But then they hear it. A terrible sound. Someone is crying. It is Elizabeth, in the house, with William. John goes. Thomas waits outside, washing his hands. Then John shouts from within.

'Adam! Thomas!'

Adam goes in first, then Thomas. For a moment Thomas cannot see for the gloom of the house, but John and Elizabeth are gathered on the far side of the dead fire, kneeling around the boy William who is lying on her lap, one leg outstretched, the other bent with the foot tucked up under the knee of the first.

When he can see more of him, Thomas sees there is an arrow dug deep by his sternum, and across the room dust motes and smoke particles swirl in a thin stream of light that emerges unexpectedly from a hole in the wattle and daub. It is the arrow that missed Thomas. It has come through the wall to hit William, who is breathing very fast and has a glossy circle of blood spreading on his shirt while his mother clutches him to her, pressing his body to hers, rocking him as she might have done when he was an infant, only she is moaning a high-pitched constant cry. Next to her the boy's father is on his knees, helpless. He looks up at Thomas and there are tears in his eyes and blood on his cheeks. Adam stands mute.

It doesn't take long and when it's over Thomas turns and goes back out to the boy and the archer in the orchard. They are standing side by side, their caps off. One – the younger of the two, the one Thomas punched – is knock-kneed, the blonde down on his chin catching the sunlight, his pale eyes clear and very frightened. The other is darker, with a faint and ugly moustache above his lips which are curled in a sneer of defiance to mask his fear. They look up at

Thomas when he comes out, and then back at the dead man at their feet, at his wounds where bubbles of blood rise and pop gently.

'Come,' Thomas tells them. Something warns him that these two must not be the very first thing John sees when he emerges from the house. He takes them with him to check the other bodies beyond the fence.

'Stand over there,' he says.

The leader of the band is still alive, but Thomas doubts it will be long before that changes. He is holding Thomas's arrow in his chest, and his horse is cropping the grass next to him. Beyond is another body, with an arrow in the throat.

Thomas crouches next to the first man. He is breathing quickly, his teeth are red and blood is foamy in his mouth. The man snarls and manages to spit blood at him. It is surprisingly warm and Thomas stands and wipes it from his chin and throat and he's wondering what to do next when his brother comes out of the house and through the gateway. He has the billhook clenched in both hands and he is striding toward the dying man. Thomas steps aside. There is nothing he can do to stop this even if he wanted to.

'Look at me,' John tells the dying man.

The man turns away his face. John kicks his cheek.

'I said look at me.'

The man slowly turns. He shows his red teeth.

'God damn you,' he snarls. 'God damn you both.'

'No!' John shouts. 'God damn you!'

John lifts the billhook and he chops it down into the man's throat. It goes straight through the bones at the back of his neck and into the grit below. The horse bolts at the noise. John wrenches the billhook from the ground and the man's head rolls slack and more blood gurgles in the grass. Then he turns on the two boys. He is going to kill them, too.

'No,' Thomas says. 'Leave them.'

John pauses. He looks at Thomas. He frowns.

48

'For Christ's sake,' John breathes. His face is smutted with ash and blood, and tears have made lines in his cheeks. 'For Christ's sake.'

He hurls the billhook across the grass and then walks back into the farmhouse where they can hear Elizabeth howling. The two boys are staring at Thomas. Then they hear the tone of Elizabeth's cry change and they hear her shouting and then she is in the yard and they turn to see her coming at them. She is screaming, her bare feet flying, and now John is pulling at her, trying to hold her back, but she twists out of his grip and Thomas sees she has a knife in her hand. When the boys see it they react like sheep before a dog. They each dip one shoulder and then turn and run, parting so that Elizabeth does not know whom to chase.

She comes instead at Thomas, perhaps because there is no one else there. Thomas stands until she is almost on him, and she pulls back her arm to slash at him, and he can see she is mad. He steps inside her swinging arm and catches her wrist and the knife shoots from her grasp to the ground behind his feet. He tries to hold her. She pushes at him. She scratches his face. He catches her hands and he holds her at arm's length. She is strong but he is stronger still. She has lost her headdress and her face is scarlet, smudged with ashes and snot and tears and blood and her mouth is a rectangle of rage. He can feel how hot she is. She is almost feverish.

'Beth,' John says. 'Beth.'

He wants to say that it is all right, that everything will be all right, but it is not. Her son is dead. Nothing can change that. Her husband stands behind her.

'Beth,' John soothes. 'Beth. Come now.'

Finding how helpless she is, she slumps. Her arms go slack and Thomas releases her. She turns and lets John wrap his arms around her and she sobs against his chest. After a moment Thomas cannot bear to witness the misery and he turns. The two boys are standing a little way off watched by Adam who has his bow nocked again.

49

'What are we going to do with them?' Adam asks.

'They can start by burying their friends,' Thomas says.

Elizabeth stops, turns her head. Strands of wet hair cover her face. Her eyes are already red from weeping. She points at Thomas.

'He speaks,' she says. 'Dear God.'

They are all staring at him, even the two boys who know nothing of his silence. Thomas does not know what to think. He did not realise that he had not been speaking, or that he now has. But he does feel odd. He can hear the river on the rocks of the ford and some birds in the tree crowns. And there is more: it is as if a veil has been lifted. Colours are brighter. Movement is faster.

Elizabeth is still staring at him.

'You,' she says, pointing one long shaking bony finger at him. 'You did this. If you had not loosed that first arrow . . .'

John looks down at her. He loosens his arms as she pushes him away.

'No, Beth,' John says. 'It was not like that.'

'It was,' she says. 'They would have only taken the horse and maybe some bread. My boy would still be alive. If you had not killed that man.'

She gestures to the body on the ground. Blood winks in the wounds and they can smell it. Thomas wonders if she is right. Doubt clouds his mind. When he saw the way the men had been when they'd first arrived at the house, he assumed they were threatening John, and he thought, Dear God. Perhaps Elizabeth is right? John glances quickly at him.

'No, Mother,' Adam says. 'They meant to take everything. You saw them.'

'But they would not have killed my William!' she wails.

'They would have killed us all!'

She turns on Adam with those mad eyes.

'You are on his side,' she says, gesturing at Thomas.

'Beth,' John mutters. 'Not now. It is not about that.'

'Don't talk to me,' she says, stepping away from John. 'Don't speak to me. You know nothing. You stand there while them that murdered my boy still live! And while the man who caused it all stops me from exacting justice. An eye for an eye, the priest says, and he – the simpleton! – he stops you!'

'By the Mass, woman, you have gone too far now.'

'Yes?' she says, turning her livid gaze on him. 'What will you do? What you always do. Drink ale by the fire.'

Now John strikes her. A backhanded blow to the face that sends her staggering. Neither Thomas nor Adam moves. The crack of the blow fades.

'Get back in the house,' John tells her. He rubs his knuckles and she her face. Seeing her expression, Thomas steps on the knife, pressing it flat into the grass. But she goes, and when she has gone, John is chastened.

'I am sorry,' he says. Thomas shakes his head. He is not sure what John is sorry for: his wife's remarks, or for hitting her, or both.

'We'd best get on,' Thomas says.

'Aye,' John says. They summon the two boys to move the dead men, but while Thomas is washing himself he begins to feel dizzy. Pain shoots through his head, bad enough to make him clap his hands to his temples. He has to sit at the river's bank for a long moment. He watches the boys carrying out the bodies and laying them next to one another on the grass. The boys are both snivelling, and he wonders absently about their relationships with the dead men. Sons? Brothers?

His head swims. He wonders if he will vomit. He gets up, reaches his arms deep into the river, deeper than his elbows, then he splashes water on his face, down his neck. After a moment he feels better and he sits again on the bank and watches the river slide past over the rocks. He looks around him. He sees things afresh, as if for the first time, and he wonders why he is here. He stares at his hands.

They are broad and calloused, square-palmed and ingrained with dirt. Questions occur to him. What is he doing here? How long has he been here? Why is he not in Holy Orders?

'Good question,' his brother agrees when Thomas asks him. 'Why aren't you?'

Thomas just cannot remember. He feels leaden, weighed down. He can hardly open his mouth to speak such thoughts that come sluggishly to mind.

'Last I knew of it,' John tells him, 'that is where you were bound. Made yourself unwelcome hereabouts, if you remember, like Adam here, always starting fights, and old Father Dominic thought you might be good for a friar, if I paid him.'

Thomas asks him where that was.

'Lincoln way,' John says. 'Some priory run by canons. He said it'd keep you out of mischief.'

The boys have laid the dead bodies next to one another, still warm, and now Adam is stripping them, taking anything of value. The dead men have come like windfalls, and Thomas's brother is suddenly rich, with horses to sell, clothes and boots to wear, coin to spend. There are bows and arrow shafts, swords, knives, steel helmets and pieces of plate, too.

They set the two boys to digging the grave under the aspens on the edge of the pasture, well below the farm. The ground here is rocky and full of roots and the boys make heavy work of it.

Beth comes out again. She is still pinched with anger.

'We should make them dig room for two more,' she says. 'Three, even.'

John pretends he does not hear. He turns to Thomas.

'What I want to know,' he starts, 'is how you learned to do all that.'

He mimics the action of drawing a bow.

'You were always good with a bow, I'll grant you that, but to kill men, like that?'

52

He blows out.

'And it looked like you've done it before,' he goes on, 'and all those cuts and scrapes and what-have-yous, all over your body when you turned up. And that dint.'

He taps his temple.

'You don't get those writing up the gospels.'

Thomas can tell John nothing. They are silent for a long while, watching the boys dig. Adam climbs into the pit with them to help. The day wears on. When the boys have dug so deep into the earth they are up to their thighs, John stops them. He gets them to roll the dead men – naked now save for their braies – into their grave and then to shovel the black earth in on top. No one is sure about leaving any cross to mark it.

'Plenty of people'd have just swung them in the river,' John says. 'Or dragged them into the next Hundred. Let those bastards over there take care of the coroner. Least we buried them. Will you say a few words, brother? Save us paying the priest.'

Thomas is lost for a moment. He stands over the raised mole of earth and is struck by the sense of having done this before. He asks the Lord to look down favourably on the men they are burying and to forgive them for what they have done, and for any other sins they may have committed in this life and then he asks for their time in purgatory to be appropriate and that when they are cleansed of sin, that the saints and martyrs will be on hand to receive them in heaven and guide them to the new Jerusalem. He crosses himself, and the others except for Elizabeth do likewise, and the crows in the trees above caw loudly as sunset comes.

'Now what are we going to do with these two?' John asks.

The two boys stand in their shirts and hose and linen caps and again Thomas is tugged at from within. Of what do they remind him? Of whom do they remind him? He cannot say, only that while Elizabeth wants them dead and John wants them gone, he feels some sort of responsibility for them.

53

'If you put them out, then you put me out too,' Thomas says.

There is a silence. Thomas sees John glance at Elizabeth.

'Good riddance,' she says.

John looks at her.

'Let them stay tonight, if they wish,' he says. 'Then tomorrow, we'll see.'

That night Thomas does not have nightmares, but the pain in his head wakes him before dawn, before the others are awake. One of the two boys is whimpering in his sleep, having a bad dream, and Thomas nudges him with his boot. The boy shifts, seems to wake, then slips back into sleep.

Thomas goes outside to wash his face in the stream. He comes to a decision, and returns to the farmhouse and shakes the first boy awake.

'Come,' he says, 'gather your stuff.'

Then he wakes the other boy and he, too, gets his coat and as they are leaving, Thomas turns and sees that Adam is awake and watching. He raises his hand and Adam nods and then Thomas takes the two boys to the stable where they saddle their horses.

'Where are we going?' the younger of the two asks.

Thomas doesn't reply.

'Can we take our bows?' the older boy asks. He gestures towards the pile of stuff Adam stripped from the dead men: their clothing, boots, various knives, swords, the seven bows, ten arrow bags, some pieces of armour and an unsteady tower of helmets.

Thomas shakes his head and the boys accept it. They are waiting to be killed, he thinks. They think I will kill them, and perhaps I should. But then he does not, and while they watch he takes a jack from the pile and holds it up only to discover that it is no ordinary jack. Within its usual flax and linen padding are strips of metal. He cannot help but smile: they might not turn an arrow or a point, but they'd stop a blade. He tries the jack on and finds it tight. Still, though. Next he wraps one of the men's bows in oiled cloth and takes that, along with a bag of arrow shafts. Then he picks a sword – rejecting the first, choosing a second – which he unsheathes and taps on a rail in the stable to check its resonance. It is good. Then he takes a riding cloak, a cloth cap greasy with wear and the largest of the sallets, which he ties to the chosen saddle of his chosen horse.

'That is my father's horse,' the younger boy says.

Thomas looks at him, then the horse. The older boy looks on. He must be a nephew or something, Thomas thinks.

'Do you want it?' he asks.

The boy nods. Thomas shrugs and picks another horse. The younger boy takes his father's horse and saddle, and Thomas and the two boys lead their horses out of the stable. Thomas adjusts his stirrups and when they are ready, John appears, sleep-tousled and malodorous. He has a flask and a loaf of bread from yesterday. He hands it to Thomas.

'You'll come back one day?' he asks.

Thomas nods. They embrace. Then when he is in his saddle his brother looks up.

'Thomas,' he says, 'answer me this before you go. It's been nagging away at us all. That name you kept calling. When you are having your dreams. What is it?'

Thomas looks down at him. He can feel his eyebrow cocked. He has no memories of any dreams.

'A name?'

'Aye. It sounded like that.'

Thomas looks down into his brother's hopeful eyes. Then he shakes his head and he is about to say no, when something wells up within him, closing his throat, and he can only nod at his brother. His brother nods back, relieved to have got that clear, and then he says goodbye again, and Thomas turns his horse and he leads the two boys off along the path, heading east. Before he has gone very far, he finds that he is weeping so the tears drip from his chin.

4

The coroner's clerk is bent-backed in his dark coat, a drop of clear liquid quivering on the tip of his long nose, and whenever he fetches ink from his pot he looks up at them over the top of his temporary desk, and Katherine, standing next to the Widow Beaufoy, shivers. It is not just the cold, though that is bad enough to make her ear ache, it is that she feels feared for, just as she used to feel in the chapter house at the priory, when she was made to stand and suffer the inspection of the other sisters while she waited for the Prioress to deliver the inevitable guilty verdict.

'Get on with it,' one of the jurymen shouts. 'We'll catch our deaths out here.'

He is right. It is the second day after the feast of St Agatha, virgin and martyr, and winter still has its hold. They should be up above in the hall of the Guild of the Blessed Virgin, where inquests might ordinarily take place, but the Guild members will not allow Eelby's wife's body to be taken up, and no one really blames them, for she has lain buried in the ground these past weeks, and the rot has taken hold despite the cold. Before the inquest there was talk of leaving her buried, but the coroner says the law is the law; and that he must see the body, or the men of the Hundred must pay a fine additional to all the others they will already incur for having a murder committed in their parish. So this morning, before dawn, Agnes Eelby was disinterred by a couple of men with linen cloths bound around their faces, and now here she is: set out in the open, a little way off, downwind of the Guild house, on a plank and a pair of trestles. A boy stands by with a shepherd's crook, ready to keep the birds off.

The coroner – a foursquare man with a close-cropped, reddish beard and cheeks mottled in the cold – stands with his back turned on the corpse, not wishing to look on the stained and corrupted shroud, and he addresses the jury.

'Fellows,' he says. 'Fellows. We are here to decide if Agnes Eelby, God rest her soul, late of this Hundred, is dead by natural causes, or by misadventure, or by reason of a felony in her own case, or by murder.'

As he speaks, there is a general grumble from the jury. It is a reluctant crowd, about thirty strong, every man over the age of twelve, from the nearest four villages, ordered from their fields and their trades to hear yet another inquest into yet another woman dead in childbirth, and they are not happy. They give off a vapour, like a herd of bulls in the cold, and one of them has brought a dog that whines and strains on its plaited rope leash. Standing in a ring about them are the grey shapes of women and children, spectating, the smog of their breath like pale scarves around their heads.

Finishing his preamble, the coroner turns to address Eelby, who is standing apart from the jury with his brown cloth cap clutched in his knuckly hands and his unshaven cheeks blue with the cold. Katherine thinks he looks unusually meek before the coroner, as if he were afraid of authority, and yet she knows he is not. She wonders what he is up to, and supposes she will find out soon enough.

'And you are first finder?' the coroner asks. Eelby nods.

'I am,' he says.

'Name?'

'John Eelby, of Cornford, of this Hundred.'

At his desk, the clerk records this.

'And the dead woman?' the coroner goes on. 'Is your wife?'

'Was, yes.'

'May God rest her soul. Tell us what you found.'

57

Eelby swallows and begins.

'I heard them calling,' he says, 'and I was worried about my wife, so I came running. They was in the kitchen up at the castle. I found her, with blood all over her dress.'

He points at Katherine. There is a murmuring among the jury.

'And my woman was lain out on the table, all cut. Across here.'

Now he points on his own body, showing a slash from left to right, just above his pubis, though Katherine remembers the cut as being vertical. It is the longest speech she has ever heard him make.

'And when was this?'

'In the week before All Saints, this last year,' he says.

'And you raised the hue and cry?'

Eelby allows that he did, though in fact there was little need since there was no felon to chase down. After he had come into the kitchen, Katherine and Widow Beaufoy and the widow's maid had stood there, gathered around the baby, Eelby's son, whom they had miraculously saved.

'Did the members of the nearest four households come running?' the coroner presses.

'Yes,' Eelby lies. 'Yes, they did.'

'You will name them to my clerk at the end of the proceedings,' the coroner instructs.

Eelby nods.

'And then you called the bailiff?' the coroner continues. He is eager to find any breach of the complex laws that surround any sudden or unexpected death, since any infraction will allow him to impose a fine on the Hundred or on Eelby himself, and so boost his own income.

'I did,' Eelby says, nodding at the bailiff, who gives his name, and the clerk makes another entry in his roll.

'Only he wasn't needed,' Eelby goes on. 'Because them who cut my woman open stood there just as if it right pleased the Lord.'

58

'And these are they?' the coroner asks, turning back to Katherine and Widow Beaufoy.

Eelby nods and the coroner studies the two women again. Katherine tries to see them as he must. She imagines he sees them in good, but old dresses, one, the widow, taller and broader than the other, while next to her she, Katherine, looks if she has been denied her portion of milk and butter over the long winter.

'And which one made the cut?' the coroner asks.

Eelby indicates Katherine.

'It was her,' he says. 'Lady Margaret.'

The coroner reminds the clerk of Katherine's name, and he nods as he writes it.

'Why do you think Margaret, Lady Cornford, cut her?'

Eelby shifts from foot to foot now. There is a pause, almost as if he is coming to a decision, as if he were choosing which path to take in a wood, and the coroner frowns, waiting, until Eelby makes his choice and says: 'Lady Margaret never liked her. Never liked my woman.'

There is an outlet of breath. Men in the jury start murmuring. The coroner raises his eyebrows.

'Lady Margaret cut your wife – killed her – because she never *liked* her?'

There is some muffled disturbance at the back and the coroner looks up, and then over at his clerk who has also looked up, and the two exchange an unspoken sign. Katherine can make no sense of it, but when she looks to Widow Beaufoy for guidance, Widow Beaufoy is determinedly absent, staring away from her, and away from the disturbance, as if it does not concern her. Something is up, but what? After a moment there is silence.

'Go on,' the coroner says.

'She hated her,' Eelby reinforces. 'As is well known.'

He raises his voice, calling on someone at the back of the jury, and someone answers, shouting out: 'That's right! She hated her!'

And, from a different part of the crowd, someone else shouts that Katherine wanted Eelby's wife dead, and now those at the front of the jury are turning around, craning their necks to see, and everyone is murmuring and staring and the clerk has put down his pen and turned and all at once everyone realises that something is up. The jury has been packed, or bribed, just as Richard and Mayhew had warned it might be, and Katherine feels first the flare of panic and then the grim slump of acceptance. They had told her she needed powerful friends in a moment such as this, and suggested she seek help from Lord Hastings.

'Someone might bribe the coroner,' Mayhew had explained, 'or pack the jury. Anything can go wrong. And if the coroner finds the death unnatural, then he will have to record it as murder.'

'But it was not murder,' Katherine had said. 'I did what I had to do to save the boy. The woman was dead! Or so close to it, it hardly mattered.'

Mayhew had been patient.

'It doesn't matter what really happened,' he'd said. 'All that matters is what people say happened.'

'But why would anyone say different?'

Richard had mewed like a cat, or an old woman, and Mayhew had shaken his head.

'Please,' he'd said. 'Please just go to Lord Hastings. Or the Earl of Warwick. He owes you his life. Or his leg at the very least. Send a letter. I'll take it if you like. Explain what has happened and ask them to advise you.'

But Katherine had not. She'd refused. She was certain that if she could see that what she had done was the right thing to do – the *only* thing to do – then others would too. Others would see that she'd had to act, to do something terrible in order to avert something worse. That was all. So she had ignored the advice of her husband and Mayhew and instead she'd thrown herself into restoring the estate, and she'd known that the two things – the saving of the child and the saving of the estate – would soon come to be seen as one and the same thing.

So now the watermill has been repaired by a carpenter from Boston, who's been induced to bring his family and his apprentices, and to pay his rent on one of the houses along the causeway. Others have come, too: a man from Lincoln, two more from Boston, a fourth, an eel trapper called Stephen – a wiry man with wild hair and a prominent tooth – from Gainsborough. Since their arrival fences have been repaired, hedges relaid, hovels and outhouses rebuilt. The sluice gates have been made to work again and water has been diverted, corralled. The fields are drying and there is every chance of a pea and a rye crop in the coming year. There are geese and chickens and piglets in their pens and sties, and there are five cows on the island, and a pair of glossy brown oxen to pull the plough. The punt has been made water-worthy as well, and while one of the new men reaps the broad ribbon of teasels that grow to the west of the castle, the eel catcher Stephen sits with one eye on the weather, and daily adds to the pile of eel traps that he is building up around his house.

More than that, the barber surgeon's assistant, Matthew Mayhew, had arrived after Christmastide, having left the Earl of Warwick's household after a disagreement with the Earl's physician, Fournier.

At the heart of it all though, has been the thought of the boy, Eelby's miraculous son John, named after his father and his father's father, who is still alive against all expectation. He has been the rhythm and the reason for all this: the inspiration and the seed of hope that something is possible. When Katherine thinks of him, her heart feels full, and she smiles. And to think that after the boy's mother had died – after Katherine had killed her – Widow Beaufoy had given him no chance.

'However will you feed him?' she'd asked scornfully.

But Katherine had remembered the newborn in the village, and so she had paid that child's mother to act as the orphan boy's nurse.

She had then spent many precious coins buying the woman mutton and beef and butter and ale from the markets, just to keep her fat and healthy, and so far her milk has kept the boy alive.

And the longer he lived, and the stronger he grew, the more certain she became that the death of Agnes Eelby was tragic, but it was not an act of her doing. Rather it was an act of God's. And with every week that had passed the more surely she placed her trust in others to come to the self-same conclusion.

But now, in this inquest, she can see that she was wrong, that they have ascribed her far darker motives – that she disliked Agnes Eelby, or was jealous of her – and so at last she must react.

'That is not true,' she shouts. 'I wished her only well. Otherwise I would not have fetched Widow Beaufoy or paid for her services out of my own purse.'

Next to her, Widow Beaufoy has taken another distancing step.

'Is that true?' the coroner asks Widow Beaufoy. 'Did she?'

'She did,' she agrees, reluctantly. 'But I would have come anyway.'

'Course she would!' one of the hecklers shouts.

The coroner cocks an eyebrow at Widow Beaufoy and Katherine sees he has understood something, and she feels her own ignorance as a sharp if familiar pain. The coroner nods and turns back to Katherine, and it is as if he has forgotten where he was, or perhaps, no. He has not forgotten. It is something else.

'So,' he asks. 'Why did you hate the dead woman?'

The question makes Katherine feel closed in upon, hemmed, surrounded.

'I did not hate her,' she spits. 'I hardly knew her.'

'But . . . ?' the coroner begins, gesturing to the jury, as if they are proof of the opposite.

Katherine has had enough.

'I do not know any of these men other than by sight,' she counters, 'and I am certain the same is true in reverse.'

'Yet there seems to be some doubt?' the coroner persists.

'Oh, there's doubt all right,' the first heckler shouts and before the coroner can silence him, the second chimes in:

'Yes,' he calls. 'If you hardly knew her, why'd you fetch Widow Beaufoy there? Why'd you pay for her services, eh? For someone you hardly knew?'

'Doesn't seem likely, does it!' shouts the first.

This second man is in the shadows but she thinks he is the one with the tall reddish hat. She does not think she has seen him before.

'I knew her well enough to do my Christian duty,' she states.

'Did you?' the first heckler replies. 'Cutting her open? I'd hardly call that your Christian duty!'

This gets a low laugh. The coroner is content to let the exchange run.

'I did it to save the baby,' Katherine shouts above the noise. 'Is he not alive now, because of what we did?'

'You only saved the baby because you wanted him for yourself!'

This is too much.

'Who are you?' Katherine calls. 'What village do you come from?'

'Never you mind,' he calls back.

She takes a step towards the men. She can feel that roaring in her ears. She wishes she had a knife now, for someone needs to shut this man up.

'That's enough,' the coroner shouts at last. He turns to Katherine.

'Tell us what happened,' he instructs.

She tries to calm herself. She can feel her face flushed and her heartbeat in her teeth. She takes a deep breath. She can smell her sweat rising from the stained wool of her dress.

'Come on!' one of the jurors calls. 'Get on with it.'

'Swarm of lies it'll be anyway!'

'Let her speak,' the coroner demands and Katherine begins.

'The baby was stuck in Eelby's wife,' she says. 'He would not come out in the normal fashion. He was turned, or the womb had moved. Or something. So we cut— No. I cut, with Widow Beaufoy's instruction, I cut Eelby's wife to save the baby.'

'And this is the knife used?' the coroner asks. He is on safer ground here, and he holds up Widow Beaufoy's beautiful knife, and there is a murmur of appreciation. Eelby confirms that it is the knife and the coroner places it next to his clerk's inkstand. It is deodand now, forfeit to the Crown, unless Katherine is willing to pay for it a second time. She glances at Widow Beaufoy, who is turned from her.

'Go on,' the coroner instructs. 'What happened after you cut her?'

'She bled. A lot. We could not staunch the flow of blood. And then she died.'

'There, you see!' one of the hecklers shouts. 'Told you she killed her!'

'I admit she died because of what I did,' Katherine replies. 'But by then she was already dead in all but name. I shortened her life by as long as it might take to say the prayers of the rosary.'

There is silence for a moment, as if this is reasonable, then one of the men shouts: 'That is time she will never have back.'

There is a grumble of assent.

'No one regrets that as much as me,' Katherine says. 'But you did not see her. She was dying anyway, and the baby was too. We wanted to baptise him.'

'You wanted her dead so you could have the baby for yourself!' comes the first heckler.

'That is not true!' Katherine hears herself shrieking. 'That is not true.'

'Then why'd you kill her?' demands the second.

'I didn't!'

'Yes, you did!' the other one shouts. 'Said it yourself!'

The coroner has lost control of the inquest. Katherine looks to him and, for a moment, he seems to be considering trying to recover it, but then he decides against it. After all, it is not his task to get to the truth of the matter. His task is to fine the Hundred for the breach of as many rules as possible, and to establish if it is worth the King's Justices pursuing the case to trial, given that should the perpetrator of the crime be found guilty at that trial, then all their property will come to the King. In this case they all know that Margaret, Lady Cornford's property is extensive, even if it is run-down, and even if it is in the name of her blind husband, so it is certainly worth the Justices' while to hear the trial when they are next in Boston. More than that, though, the presence of the hecklers means that someone, somewhere, is taking an interest in the case, and someone, somewhere, wants it to go to trial, and so it is useless the coroner trying to stop it.

The coroner turns to them and Katherine can see him looking at her with that mixture of pity and scorn, and she can guess what he is thinking: that her husband is blind, and that she is a woman, and so it is not only natural that she is separated from her property, it is inevitable. He is probably wondering, indeed, why it has taken someone so long to take it from her.

So, finally, the coroner gathers himself and holds up a hand.

'Fellows!' he calls. 'I believe there is doubt enough in the circumstances of Agnes Eelby's death to admit the possibility of a felony. So I order the binding over of Margaret, Lady Cornford, to await the imminence of the King's Justices.'

There is an eruption of cheering and of stamping of feet in parts of the crowd, but puzzlement in others, and the midwife takes one further step from Katherine.

'I find further that Widow Beaufoy is innocent of any involvement in this felony, and that she is therefore free to go, though I demand of you in the King's name that you fulfil your duty to God and Man and make yourself available to the said Justices when they should come into the county.'

Widow Beaufoy nods, sombre as nightfall.

'Wait!' Katherine shouts.

'Bailiff?' the coroner says.

The bailiff moves quickly on his spindly legs. He places himself before Katherine and Widow Beaufoy and he has a short sword on his belt, which he touches emphatically. Katherine retreats a step. She will be no trouble. When he is sure of her, he asks the coroner what he wants done with her.

'The gaol?' the coroner suggests as if it were obvious.

The bailiff draws air hissing through the gaps in his teeth.

'Is under water,' he says, spitting. 'Been so these five months past.'

'What have you done with other prisoners?' the coroner asks.

'We have shown them the gaol and one look and they've paid a fine or forfeited some part of themselves.'

The coroner tugs on the short hairs of his beard. His glance travels over her and Katherine feels herself withering within. She cannot help unconsciously covering the blade of her clipped ear, hidden under the felt of her hat, with her fingers.

'Is there nowhere?' the coroner asks the bailiff. 'Some convent perhaps?'

The bailiff shakes his head.

'There is one,' Widow Beaufoy volunteers, 'one that might have her.'

And she looks at Katherine for a long moment, as if she knows, and Katherine feels a terrible crushing weight on her bones.

'St Mary's,' Widow Beaufoy says. 'The Gilbertine Priory at Haverhurst.'

PART TWO

The Priory of St Mary's Haverhurst, County of Lincoln, Lent, 1463

5

Thomas Everingham pays the ferryman a small silver coin to cross the river on Lady Day, 25 March, the first day of the New Year, and then rides south and east through thin drizzle, following a track that he is told will lead him – 'by and by' – to another that will take him south to Lincoln. He rides all morning, stopping only to let his horse graze, at about midday, while he drinks from his costrel under a tree. Afterwards he follows the track through shaded woodlands where pale moths each the size of a child's fingernail rise up at him from the undergrowth.

As he rides, his mind starts playing curious tricks on him, tripping from one thought to the next without ever settling, and as they come, each successive thought or observation feels more significant than its forebear, until that one is itself replaced by another that feels yet more important, vital even, until that too is replaced by another, even more important thought. He sees even the most common object – a pile of rocks acting as a way marker, a winding post by shallow-banked washing pool, a stand of elms – and at first each seems to reveal within itself some previously hidden significance that leads to another and on to another. Each time he is struck by these thoughts he is relieved to have remembered it, but then he realises – these thoughts, they mean nothing. They are irrelevant.

At first the sensation is pleasant, but soon it becomes confusing, then wearying and finally irritating. He starts to ride with his eyes shut, and distracts himself by wondering what will happen to the two boys he left on the west bank of the river. He supposes they will return home to wherever it is they come from and he tries to imagine what sort of homecoming that might be.

In the late afternoon he reaches a crossroads as predicted and he turns his horse south and once again he is assailed by thoughts he cannot control. Only this time, instead of those fruitless associations he experienced in the morning, these insights ring true. They are proper memories: hazy-edged and cacophonous, peopled with face- less men and women, but simple and even sensible: here he once stopped in the dark to let drunk men piss. Here he rode one autumn day with – with – with who? A boy? A boy. No. Not a boy, not a boy like Adam or John, but . . . He feels odd. A warmth fills him, fills his chest, makes his shoulders glow, and again the tears come. Why? He wipes them away with a knuckle.

He shakes his head and rides on. But the memories continue, ambushing him as he comes out of the woods and into the fields from where he can see the great cathedral of Lincoln. He stops for a moment, ignoring the spire, and looks back along the length of the road he has just travelled. He is gripped by the certainty that he is riding away from something, rather than towards it. He turns his horse and it waits patiently while he studies the road that disappears into the gloom of the trees. After a long moment the horse snorts and Thomas shakes his head and turns and rides the last few furlongs to Lincoln just as the purple-edged dusk arrives and parish bells ring out. Lights appear on the city walls, like stars, and at the gatehouse the men of the Watch are suspicious around their brazier.

'Come far?' they ask and laugh when he admits he has, yet he does not know where he has come from, only it has been 'that way'. They direct him to the friary of the Austin Friars by the Newport gate, and he follows his feet, his mind still crowded with memories and associ- ations, so that when he gets there, and after the friars have given him soup and bread, they leave him alone, thinking he might be touched.

In the morning he is up and gone before the bell for Prime, when it is still dark, and he walks his horse out past the cathedral close and

70

down a steep hill where his mind erupts again and he is afraid he is going mad, and he finds his feet tangling as he passes a well-made, jettied house on a steep hill, and he almost falls to his knees. He remembers sunlight and the sound of horses' hooves on the cobbles, and something calamitous, but what? He cannot say. He recalls a woman, but so ghostly is the impression that— No. There is nothing there. Nothing to hold on to. He feels he could bang his head against the ground to clear it of these flickering shades, and he turns with his eyes half-closed and he stumbles on down the hill like a drunk, hanging on his horse's reins while the animal's hooves skitter on the rain-slicked cobbles and the slough of wet straw and dung. At last he is out, through the Broadgate and across the bridge over the turbid waters and he is away, into the flat farmland to the south of the city.

Here the sensations let up, soften, become less urgent, and he climbs up into the saddle as the sun rises and he rides east with the sun before him, a pink orb, flat gold rays filling the mist-softened lands. He seems to know where he is going, but he does not, really, until he finds a crossroads and a man in a rough woven reed hat to tell him that this road leads east, and eventually to Boston.

'After which you will go no further,' he says in a familiar accent, 'on account of there being no further to go.'

Thomas thanks him and rides on, now with his face into the wind, until by midday he sees what it seems he has been looking for, and again, here comes the turbulent riot of uninvited thoughts. He stops his horse and swings from the saddle and drops to the road's muddy surface. He falls to his knees and presses his forehead into the black grit at the side of the track. After a while, his heart slows, his mind ceases its lurching, and he stands and shields his eyes and stares across the wet lands and it is just as he has remembered it: the grey clutch of slate-roofed buildings gathered behind their wall in the shadow of the square-towered church. Nothing has changed. The reeds that fringe the road and the waters' edges are vivid green and lustrous with spring growth, and there is still that smell in the air, of mud and rot, and the sky seems vast, from horizon to horizon, and above float pale winged gulls in the clear grey sky, and that is it. Nothing else.

He is back here again, he thinks, back at Haverhurst.

He walks his horse to the gates, and he feels the weight of watching eyes from about six hundred paces. He walks on, until he stops before the wooden gate, and he pauses a moment, suddenly breathless, as a person is before stepping from a height, and then he gathers himself, and bangs on the gate with the bottom of his fist. After a moment the hatch opens.

'God be with you, my son,' comes a voice. 'What can we do for you this day?'

He is at a loss for words, since he doesn't know why he is here.

'I have come far,' he says.

'We have all come far,' the voice replies.

'I wish to see the Prior,' Thomas decides.

There is a pause and the hatch is shut. Then Thomas hears the locking bar raised and the gate swings open and there it is, the courtyard where he spent much of his youth. Standing before him though, demanding his attention, is a man with his hair freshly scissored in a tonsure.

'You wish to see Father Barnaby?'

Thomas nods.

'I do.'

'Who are you?' the man asks. 'He will want to know.'

'Tell him it is Thomas Everingham,' he says.

The canon frowns, stares a moment too long, then comes to a grunting decision, and nods and turns and walks away through a gap between two buildings through which Thomas can see a stretch of pale spring grass. Thomas slowly turns and looks about him: at the church tower, the almonry, the stables where the ostler in a leather apron is studying him from under furrowed brows, a length of leather, a belt perhaps, held between thumb and forefinger.

All around the other brothers have stopped what they are doing to join in the staring: two of them on a raised platform rendering a wall, another restoring a wicker fence, another with a hammer and a pile of clogs, a line of nails held between his lips. A young canon, ruby cheeks still peachy, stands with a rake at his side, gawping at Thomas as Thomas might once have done himself.

'You are busy?' Thomas asks, nodding at the stilled workers.

'The Prior of All is coming,' the boy says, as if this explains everything. Thomas nods, but it means not much to him. He is distracted by raised voices, one concerned, the other irritated, and then the first canon reappears, leading another man, who frowns at Thomas for a long moment, and Thomas stares back and he thinks he might have known this man, that there might be something there, and then the other man starts with recognition. He gapes and flushes, and lifts a hand, half in greeting, half in repulsion, and it is impossible to read the expressions as they flit across his face, each replaced by the next so fast that Thomas cannot divine whether this man is pleased or horrified to see him.

'It is me,' he ventures. 'Thomas Everingham. Do you remember?'

And then the man decides he must smile, and he does so, and broadly, but there is a note of something else there, Thomas thinks, a flicker of some other emotion, though what he cannot say.

'By Holy Mary and her seven sorrows!' the man cries, and then he bundles forward and throws his arms about Thomas and he presses himself into Thomas's chest and pulls him tight and he smells reassuringly of wine and stockfish and musty cloth.

'I do not believe it!' he continues. 'I do not believe it! It is Canon Thomas, back, back from the dead, and with us here, by the grace of God!'

'Brother Barnaby,' Thomas says, the words coming unexpectedly, as a surprise.

Barnaby pushes him away, holding him at arm's length and looks at him archly.

'Father Barnaby,' he says. '*Father* Barnaby.'

There are filaments of iron grey in his fringe, but his cheeks are still full and ruddy and he looks prosperous, fat even. He takes a step back, allowing the other man, the first canon, who is standing uncertainly by, into the circle.

'Brother Blethyn,' Barnaby says, 'this is Thomas Everingham, our infamous apostate, returned to the fold at last! And Thomas, this is Brother Blethyn, our Dean and infirmarian. We give the good Lord our thanks for his continued presence among us.'

Barnaby is grinning, but he is shifting from foot to foot, and Blethyn stands not facing Thomas, as perhaps he should, but looking at Barnaby, taking his lead from his newly made Prior.

'Peace be upon you, Canon Thomas,' Blethyn says, only his eyes turning to Thomas, 'and may God give you good guidance.'

'And you also, Brother,' Thomas replies.

'Oh, come,' Barnaby says. 'Enough of this. We have wine, and we have some fresh cheese. And a soup.'

Barnaby places a hand between Thomas's shoulder bones and guides him across the yard toward the almonry, but Blethyn knows he is not included, and he remains motionless. When Thomas glances he is watching them, his face pinched.

'Great God above,' Barnaby is telling Thomas. 'You have been playing the archer? You are all thick, here, like some robber, or man of war! I confess, if I saw you on the road I should be terrified.'

Barnaby guides him, ducking under the lintel and into the gloom of the almonry where sensations press in on him from the shadows, but when he tries to reclaim them, to think them into being, they are gone, slipping away to become peripheral again. Barnaby has delayed by the door, and is talking quietly to someone beyond and then when he comes in, he shuts the door and launches into telling Thomas of the winter they have had to endure, of the privations they have accepted, the test the good Lord has sent them.

A boy comes in and sets to work lighting the peat fire with a steel and after a moment thick brown smoke rises in a column from the sod's edge to spread across the blackened ceiling of the room. Then the boy whom Thomas saw with the rake comes in with a pewter jug, the contents of which steam in the cool of the almonry, and two earthenware cups on a wooden tray.

'From the kitchen,' he says, his gaze fixed on Thomas.

'Thank you, John,' Barnaby says. 'Now, away with you!'

When he is gone, Father Barnaby smiles.

'You will have to get used to that sort of thing,' he says when the door is shut. 'You are famous with the brothers hereabouts.'

'Why?' Thomas asks.

Barnaby guffaws.

'Why? he says! Ha!'

He gestures at the bench while he turns to the tray of wine. Thomas sits while Barnaby pours the wine and passes him a cup.

'Feel,' he says. 'It is warm! God is bountiful! And wants us to drink to your safe return.'

Barnaby takes a small sip, and then sits back just as if he is a man at ease, taking wine over a fire, but his eyes are never still, and he is pent up and restless.

'So,' he says. 'Tell me! Tell me all.'

And now Thomas has to shrug. 'I have nothing to tell you,' he confesses.

Barnaby laughs: he still thinks Thomas is joking.

'Nothing?' he says. 'Nothing? When the last we saw of you was your legs as you slid over the wall and out into the world?'

'I have had an injury,' Thomas explains, 'and I can remember nothing, or almost nothing. My brother puts it down to this, to being hit on the head.'

He removes his cap and shows Barnaby the fob of silver hair above his temple. Barnaby stands and comes to investigate.

'May I?'

75

Thomas nods. Barnaby presses his fingers into the well. Thomas can hear them above his ear just as if they were inside his head.

'*Jesu!* What a dint!' Barnaby says, sitting down. 'Where did you get it?'

'I don't know,' Thomas says. 'I am only now trying to discover its hows and whys.'

Barnaby looks at him very closely, very seriously, with narrowed eyes.

'So what *do* you remember?' he asks.

'I remember here,' Thomas tells him, looking about the room. 'And when I saw this place from the road, I knew that it meant something to me, though not what, or how long I was here, or, what I did while I was here. And as for how I left . . .'

He waves his hands in the air and recognises with a mild start that he has made the sign to indicate smoke dissipating above an open fire. Barnaby smiles.

'You remember that at least,' he says. 'But do you honestly remember nothing of your departure? You don't remember the giant? No? Well, perhaps that's just as well. He would only give you nightmares. What about Giles Riven? Do you remember him? No? The name means nothing to you?'

'It sounds – known, I suppose, yes,' Thomas admits. He feels discomfort, a sense of fright even. 'But who is he?'

So Father Barnaby tells him how this Sir Giles Riven, who used to occupy a nearby castle, once accused Thomas of attacking him and his son beyond the priory's walls, and Thomas can feel himself pulling a doubting face.

'I cannot believe it,' he says. 'I attacked a man?'

'So Riven said,' Barnaby tells him. 'But it gets better. Or worse, depending on your view of the matter. He challenged you to trial by combat, and you fought him – a knight – in the garth! Out there. You can't have forgotten that? Surely. Dear God! How unfair. Had I done that, I would *never* have forgotten it, *never* have tired of telling the story! You fought him with a quarterstaff, and you beat him. You had him laid out on the ground. You had him there! He was practically a dead man! We all thought you would kill him for what he had done to you, but no. You spared him.'

'I remember — a stick?' Thomas tries.

He thinks he can feel it in his hands. Light, paltry, missing some weight, and now he remembers fragments of a fight, in the snow, bloodstained, strong-smelling, hard work and painful, a man hitting him with that stick; and then he recalls a cry, or an echo of one, like the alarm of a crow, and he touches his scalp and looks at the fingers, half-expecting blood.

'That's it!' Barnaby cries. 'It was God's judgement, of course, but when you downed him Riven was not happy. His men — the giant. You really don't remember him? *Jesu Christu!* We could not decide if he was Gog or Magog!'

When Barnaby mentions the giant this time there is something, some outline of a memory, something distant in the landscape of his mind; there is also a sort of vast lurking terror, but it will not form, it will not come to life, and Thomas is relieved.

'But then they killed Brother Stephen,' Barnaby goes on, his tone sobering. 'Or that giant did. He nearly chopped him in half. Great God above. I will never forget that. And then they came for you, all of them, and, as I would testify to St Peter at the very gates, you did the right thing. You threw down your stick and you climbed on to the roof of the cloister and then over the wall and then — well. That was the last we saw of you.'

It is like hearing a story about another man.

'And then afterwards,' Barnaby continues, 'Giles Riven and his men came back from the river swearing to do terrible things if ever they found you. Blind you. That was the one thing, because of what they said you'd done to his son, who had his eye out. Then they were going to cut off your stones and put them in your empty sockets — just like that — and set you free to wander the world.'

Barnaby mimes the action. Thomas is aghast.

'Dear God,' he says.

'Oh, there is nothing to fear now,' Barnaby assures him. 'Riven went north to join old King Henry's power when our new King Edward – may God bless his soul – challenged for the kingdom. It was two years ago now, ancient history if you like, but there was a great slaughter, up there, in the north, near York, with so many men dead in the field in that one day, that the angels did not know whether to laugh or cry.'

He takes a drink.

'And among the dead was Giles Riven, for since then we have never seen or heard of him or his giant. None of his other men came back either, not a one, and the estate – the castle, the farms, the manors, the what-have-yous – well, they have not prospered. He should not have taken the serfs and the churls, we all said that, but he did. He needed the numbers, they said, to fulfil an indenture, and so the bodies of the men who once worked the land hereabouts now serve to fortify some field in the north rather than their own, down here.'

Barnaby likes his joke, but when he tails off to watch the flames among the peat on the hearthstone, he does not do so with a softened focus as a man might ordinarily stare into a fire, but he blinks rapidly, and he nibbles the inside of his lower lip, and Thomas sees he is thinking carefully about something, and that he is prey to nerves, or guilt, or something. But what? After a moment he looks up, his eyes bright with some purpose, as if he has come to a decision, or seen the solution to some awkward problem.

'And now Cornford,' he says, 'this castle that was once Riven's, and its estates, has gone back to its original owner, or at least to the man who married the original owner's daughter.'

Barnaby waits looking at him, as if for some reaction, but none of this means a thing, and Thomas can only remain blank-faced. After a moment Barnaby goes on, cautiously, like a man picking his way through a fen, testing the mud before him.

'The original owner's daughter's name is Margaret Cornford,' he enunciates. 'Does this mean anything to you, Thomas? Lady Margaret Cornford?'

Thomas feels a significance, a weight, a resonance, but there is no detail, and no image of a face to fit the name. He feels a quickening of his heart, a tightening of his chest, and he feels he is on the verge of something, but after a moment it stops and so he shakes his head. It is hopeless.

'If I saw her,' he supposes.

Barnaby stares at him over steepled fingers, and then seems to change the subject.

'Do you remember taking the ferryman's punt that day, Thomas? After you absconded?'

Thomas shakes his head again.

'It is as I say,' he says. 'I remember nothing.'

'It was winter,' Barnaby prompts. 'Around Candlemas, while there was still ice on the river.'

He leans forward, waiting, intent. There is a moment's silence, in which they can hear only the flutter of the flames in the peat. And then from nowhere tears well in Thomas's eyes. They brim the lids and plash his cheeks. He wipes them with his palms and his wrists but they keep coming.

'What is wrong with me?' he mutters. 'What is wrong with me? I am weeping like a novice.'

'Let them come,' Barnaby advises. 'Let them come. They will help you remember.'

And as the tears flow, Thomas feels a great stone of misery rising to fill his throat.

'There was a woman,' he says. But how he knows this he cannot say.

'A woman,' Barnaby presses. 'Yes. Do you remember anything of her? At all?'

'Oh, by Christ,' Thomas sobs. 'I don't know. I can't even— Yes.

Yes. Or. Oh, by Christ. But. But who is she? Who is she? Is she this Margaret? This Margaret Cornford?'

And now Barnaby sits back, satisfied by something, relieved even, his hands on his knees. He takes a long breath, a sigh almost, and he seems to be playing a different part — older, wiser, sadder — and Thomas feels he has ceded him some power he did not know he had.

'It is a long, confusing story,' Barnaby tells him, settling into it, and his role, 'and I am as yet unsure of all the details, or of the order in which to relate them, but to make sense of it I must begin with Lord Cornford, who was Margaret Cornford's father, and who was killed in some scuffle, five or six years ago now. He had no issue save this girl, this Margaret, who was betrothed to a cousin, a man called Richard Fakenham. Does that name mean anything? No? They are a small family from the north of here?'

Barnaby gestures and Thomas shakes his head, though the name does perhaps set off a distant peal of recognition.

'No? Well,' Barnaby goes on, 'when Lord Cornford was killed, our Giles Riven seized the castle. I don't know by what right he did so, though no doubt deception and violence played their part, but at the time, Richard Fakenham — who might perhaps have been expected to take it by right of being betrothed to Margaret — was the Duke of York's indentured man, and just then that Duke and all his retinue were outside the King's grace, do you see? But Giles Riven was firmly with King Henry, who was then in the ascendant, so whatever the divers rights and wrongs of the matter, Fakenham was unable to unseat Riven, and the bastard was left to sink his roots into the estate.'

Barnaby wets his throat before going on.

'Of course, that was before the great reversal,' he continues, 'before King Edward drove King Henry from the field at Towton, in the process of which, as I say, Giles Riven met his end, and so now, with him gone, Richard Fakenham is in the ascendant, is he not?' The loyal Yorkist, there to receive his reward, through his betrothed wife, of an estate worth, when old Cornford had it and ran it properly, more than two hundred pounds a year.'

Thomas says nothing.

'Yes,' Barnaby says, 'an enormous sum, a great fortune. So this newly minted Richard Fakenham and his wife Lady Margaret arrive – two summers past, it was now – with a retinue of borrowed soldiers and they took the castle, and all the lands, though in parlous state by now, as if by right. And if it had ended there, then that would have been its end. Obviously.'

'But?'

'But at around All Souls this last year, the reeve of the castle, a man named Eelby, who is a drunk and a thief actually, and who in quieter times might have long since expected to find himself dangling at the end of a rope, had a wife heavy with child. Now, as from cloth comes the moth, so from womankind comes wickedness, as it is written, and as you know, and it has always been, since Eve first corrupted Adam, but still – but what follows, I confess, shocked me. For it transpired that Lady Margaret, the childing woman's mistress don't forget, was herself barren, being married and still without child, and so, filled with such hatred and envy as is unique to her sex, she cut open the reeve's wife to reveal the child within.'

The fire's flames have matured, throwing out more heat than smoke, and the bell rings in its tower and Barnaby glances up, and Thomas knows instinctively what time it is and what the bell means, and part of him is pleased he does.

'So there was an inquest,' Barnaby continues, 'as was right, just this last month, and ordinarily a man such as Fakenham would have packed the inquest's jury with his own men, or he would have paid the coroner some sum, and fixed it that way, so that it was found that there was no felony, and that would have been that. But I have not told you the crucial thing about Richard Fakenham, have I?'

Thomas shakes his head. He supposes not.

'The crucial thing about Richard Fakenham is that he is blind,' Barnaby says. 'Blind, not from birth, nor from cataracts nor any other disease, you understand, but from having had both orbs put out, some time during the recent wars.'

'Do you suppose he ever encountered your Giles Riven and his giant?' Thomas asks.

'I have wondered that,' Barnaby admits, 'but whatever its cause, his blindness undid him, for unable to see, he was forced to leave it to his wife, this Margaret, to fix things, and she – well. She either did not know what to do, or she was unable to do it. She being, of course, a woman.'

'So she was found guilty?'

Barnaby holds up a finger.

'Not quite,' he says. 'It has not progressed that far, if it ever will, because, you see, when this Lady Margaret was brought here, under constraint, in a cart, with no maid or servant, it was discovered a most surprising thing. Can you guess? No? Well, it was discovered that she was not Lady Margaret at all, but another girl entirely, someone else altogether.'

'Who?'

'Well, this is it. The strangest thing! The Prioress recognised her as being a girl who was once in her flock. A girl who made herself apostate on the very same day as you! Do you see? She was the selfsame girl as you allowed on your stolen punt!'

And now Thomas feels his mind slant, like a table being tipped, and all his thoughts rush to one side. His heart lurches, thumps, and it is hard to breathe. He presses his eyes with the heels of his palms, and sees stars within the darkness, and when he takes them away his wrists are slick with tears again.

'Ah! She means something to you now,' Barnaby says.

'Tell me about her,' Thomas manages. 'Who is she? Please. For the love of God.'

'I cannot say,' Barnaby tells him, 'for I do not know.'

'You must!'

'But I don't. There is a further, deeper mystery to her, you see. The Prioress knows who she is, her real identity, if you like, but is sworn to secrecy, and will tell me nothing. When I sent message to the Prior of All, to enquire as to the girl's identity, instead of enlightenment, he sent a messenger by return to say he is coming to see the girl in person, for there are, he says, divers matters at stake. Can you imagine? Did you know that neither he, nor his predecessor, nor his predecessor's predecessor, ever thought to seek us out here in our muddy little world since the third year of King Henry the Sixth's reign? That was nearly forty years ago now! Before you or I were even thought of!'

'Does she have a name?'

'Katherine.'

My God, Thomas thinks, and he whispers her name. 'Katherine.'

But now Barnaby leans forward, staring and intent, the line of his mouth short and hard.

'Do you really remember nothing of her?' he asks.

And Thomas tries to think, but after a while he has to shake his head.

'Nothing,' he says. 'I cannot even remember what she looks like.'

'Nor how she came to pass herself off as Lady Margaret Cornford?'

'No,' Thomas says. 'I remember nothing. If I ever knew.'

And Barnaby sits back frustrated.

'Well,' he says. 'Then that must remain a mystery until the Prior of All honours us with his presence. Then we will be allowed at the truth.'

'Where is she?' Thomas asks. 'Where is she now?'

'She is with the Prioress, well cared for.'

'Can I see her?' Thomas asks.

Barnaby laughs.

'Of course not,' he says. 'She is in cloister.'

'Please,' Thomas begs again. 'Please.'

He finds himself on his feet, looming over Barnaby who shrinks before him, but then as if on some unseen signal, the door opens with a clap and a man with a staff strides in and stands before Thomas. He is broad-chested, red-bearded, a head taller than Thomas, and the quarterstaff looks like a twig in his meaty hands. He looks at Thomas almost sadly; as if he might be a farmer about to reluctantly slaughter a favoured pig.

'Please, Thomas,' Barnaby says from behind him. 'You know we cannot allow it.'

And Thomas subsides. He knows Barnaby is right.

'So we must just be patient,' Barnaby goes on. 'And wait on the Prior of All, and then when he comes, all shall be known. All shall be revealed, and God willing, perhaps you shall see your Katherine once more.'

And now the bell rings in the church tower, summoning the lay brothers in for prayer from the fields and woods and riverbanks. It will soon be time for Vespers.

'Will you join us to observe the hour, Brother Thomas?'

Thomas agrees to, because there is for the moment nothing else to do.

'It will be good to have you back,' Barnaby says. 'We will find you a cassock, and Brother Blethyn will cut your hair.'

Thomas is half-standing and stops, confused.

'No, Father Barnaby,' he says. 'I am – I cannot come back. I am no longer as I was. I feel as if I have – I have done things. I have seen things. I do not feel the same. I do not belong here. I cannot come back. I thought you knew?'

Barnaby hushes him.

'All will be well,' he smiles. 'All will be well.'

Barnaby leads Thomas out of the almonry and over to the cloister where Thomas stands with the lay brothers and waits for Barnaby to vest himself and prepare to read the lessons. The brothers are all farmers with no land of their own. Rough men, unlettered, with chapped faces that are almost never inside under a protective roof or enclosed by cosseting walls, but out in the fields in all weather, and so they look on the observance of the hours as a time of rest, recuperation. He is familiar with them, or their sort, and comfortable in their presence.

But they are all looking at him now. He has removed his cap, but he has a full head of hair, and he wears his plated jack, with a knife at his belt, a heavy purse, blue woollen hose and polished brown leather riding boots turned down to the knee. The way they look at him reminds him of something, but he does not know what, and he sees their envy, and he feels a twinge of guilt, but it does not shift the sense of loss.

During the observance the words come back to him, but he knows he would not be able to say them on his own and they mean nothing to him, and afterwards, Barnaby summons him again. He walks with him along the cloister range to an iron-hooped door which he unlocks with a key as long as his forearm and while he does so, Thomas turns and looks out on to the garth, the small square of grass held bracketed by the cloister wings. He wonders if he can remember the fight Barnaby says took place, but he cannot. His gaze floats over the cloister walls, and he can hear the jackdaws clacking in their treetops and the geese chuckling in their meers, settling for the night in the world beyond, and he can remember nothing.

Barnaby swings open the door and fumbles with a lamp. When it is lit, Thomas recalls that the room is the sacristy, where they keep the altar silver, the transubstantiated hosts, and such coinage as they possess, but there is also the priory's illuminated Bible, a book of hours made in Ghent and there, the smallest of the three, lying on top of the pile on a shelf made of stone, a bound book the size of a woman's palm and as thick as a man's thumb.

Barnaby picks it up and passes it to him.

'Do you recognise it?' he asks.

And Thomas does. It is his psalter, bound before it was ever finished. He opens it carefully. The early pages are filled with tiny, beautifully neat rows of perfectly exacted letters, each page begun with an initial lit with colours not seen in nature, or not at least by Thomas: rich reds, purples, the deepest blues, golds and even silvers. And folded within are scenes from the Bible – here is Christ being presented at the synagogue, here he is at the wedding feast in Cana – each design picked out with startling artistry. It is a marvel.

'The time I must have spent on this,' Thomas breathes. 'But why is it bound? It is not finished. Look.'

Towards the back of the book he finds that in reverse of the normal practice, his former self had saturated the backgrounds to the pictures first, leaving the clothes and the faces of the foreground characters blank. On one page the pale ghost of Christ is betrayed by the pale ghost of Judas while the outline of St Peter looks on, expressionless, in a grey rocked garden bound with grapevines from which hang luscious blue fruits, so cleverly painted that you can see the powdery bloom against the gloss of their bulging flesh.

'It was guilt, I think,' Barnaby says. 'The Prior regretted ceding to Giles Riven his demands – that he kill you – and when the ferryman told us about how his punt would sink, we presumed you drowned, and had gone ahead to heaven. We have prayed for your soul every week since then, do you know?'

Thomas smiles. He turns a few pages of the psalter.

'You might yet finish it?' Barnaby says. 'You could unpick the stitches – like this – and resume your great work. It is good work, isn't it? That glorifies God and Man?'

Thomas smiles again but feels the chill in the room and a shiver creeps over his skin.

'No,' he says. 'That is not me now.'

'But what about the Prior of All?' Barnaby asks. 'He will want to see you. He will want to know what has happened to his apostate Thomas Everingham.'

And now the slither of steel that had been present in Barnaby's wheedling is revealed as a blade. Thomas feels himself becoming stonier still, and is about to say something when his eye is drawn to a worn leather bag that hangs from a peg behind Barnaby's shoulder. He cannot stop himself reaching out.

It is something he recognises. Something he carried with him wherever he went, a comforting weight on his shoulder, something that fitted perfectly under his head when he slept, and now here it is. The pardoner's ledger, in its worn and punctured and patched bag.

His hands are shaking and he cannot draw breath. He grabs the bag desperately, with a drowning grip, a madman's grip, and wrenches it to him. He registers Barnaby saying something but it is as if he is in a gale with a wind blowing around him and Thomas can smell blood and hear the crash and slide of steel weapons and he can hear himself gasping for air. He feels great pain, his ribs being crushed, his back afire.

He cannot stand it. He needs to be free, out in the open, away from here. He stumbles and catches against the cupboard. A plate slides, the chalice jumps, the monstrance in its velvet hood falls with a bang and the host of paper tubes that fill the lower shelves come unbound and slither across the floor.

'Blethyn!' Barnaby is shouting. 'Blethyn! Call Robert. Get the lay brothers.'

He barges past the two men and starts running. His boots slip in the grass and he goes down but he is up and quickly across the garth. He swings the bag around his shoulders, just as he has many times before, and takes hold of the post and hauls himself up on to the low wall and is about to launch himself on to the roofs again when the canon with the red beard appears. He is carrying, of all things, a quarterstaff and he uses it to knock Thomas's legs, and Thomas scrambles and then falls. The bag catches, rips, and the book spills free and thumps to the ground next to him. Thomas gropes for it but the red-bearded canon is quickly across and plants a clog – a great wooden thing made with leather and nails – across Thomas's wrist, pinning him to the ground.

'Now then,' he says, and he holds the staff over Thomas's head and looks him in the eye, unhurried and calm. His beard is thrust forward, like a challenge. Thomas subsides. Whatever took hold of him has passed. He breathes out. He stares at the mud and then inches his gaze across to the book where it lies, roughly bound and carelessly cut, with a dent in it as if it has been stabbed by a madman.

'He is possessed!' Barnaby repeats. 'He is fallen out of his wits!'

Now two more of the lay brethren are in the garth and stand confused to see the new arrival held to the grass.

'We must keep him away from the brothers,' Blethyn says.

'What shall we do with him?'

'Bind him, for his own safety, and ours. You, fetch the ostler. And bring straps.'

One of the lay brothers hurries off. Thomas says nothing. There are tears in his eyes again. By Christ, when will this stop? He does not know how he came to be here. He hears Barnaby and Blethyn talking and then sees their toecaps under their cassocks.

'It is a humoral imbalance,' Blethyn diagnoses, 'brought on by a pernicious enthralment to sin. It is what drove him from us in the first instance, and since then it will only have become worse with temptation.'

Now the ostler is back and he helps the canon and two lay brothers bind Thomas – ankles, then wrists – with leather straps from the stables. They are strong men, particularly the red-bearded canon, and Thomas's struggles only present them with a challenge to which they rise.

'Feel him,' Blethyn tells Barnaby and they crouch next to Thomas and press the backs of their cold fingers to his forehead.

'Saints, he is hot!'

'As I suspected,' Blethyn says. 'The devil finds it easy to take a soul already weakened by sin.'

'He seeks our care,' Barnaby explains. 'He wants our prayers. For a cure. Take him to the stable.'

'The ledger,' Thomas mutters. 'Let me have it.'

The ostler and the canon and the lay brothers hesitate as Barnaby crosses to the ledger and picks it up. He wipes the mud off its surface and holds it open and puzzles over it, just as he must have before.

'Why?' he asks. 'What is it about this book?'

'It is mine,' Thomas says. 'It's mine.'

'Yours?'

He looks back at it again, turning it in his hands. He stares at it and then after a moment he gives up and shakes his head and moves to put it back in its ripped leather bag, and so they pick Thomas up, one at each corner, and carry him across the garth and out into the yard just as if they were bringing in a yule log at Christmastide. Ahead of them the ostler's boy leads Thomas's horse out of the stable and they carry him in and deposit him face down in the horse-pissy straw.

'The ledger!' Thomas calls. 'The ledger.'

Father Barnaby is standing at the door, looking disappointed in something, as if Thomas has not lived up to his expectations.

'Oh, let him have it,' he says and Blethyn, who has taken the book, looks at it in its bag one more time, then swings it by the strap, releasing it into the stable where it lands next to Thomas's head and skids across to thump against the wall.

6

It is Sister Katherine's task to wash the clothes. Not only those of the sisters, but also those of the lay sisters, and the brothers, *and* the lay brothers. She has replaced the three lay sisters who might ordinarily have completed the task in two days, and it takes her seven, so that by the time she has finished her week's work, the cycle begins again.

She does this in the stream, to the west of the sister's beggars' gate, where the banks have been worn shallow by generations of washerwomen, and there are planted three wringing posts, though of course she only uses one. The bed of the river is stony here, hard on the soles of her bare feet, and she sometimes wishes for the soft welcome of mud between her toes, but the water is so cold that soon her legs are numb anyway, so after a while it matters little.

All day she works, watched by the three lay sisters whom she relieved of the task. One stands on the bank nearest the priory, the other two on the far bank, making sure she does not bolt again, and now, two months later, they are yet to be bored of the task, and watch her every movement. They even watch which way her eyes look, and if she stares at something too long, a tree in the distance, say, or the ferryman on his punt, then one of them will get up and come and stand in front of it and tell her that she must not dawdle.

And so now here she is, her nails bleeding from the lye, her hands slippery on the beetle, up to her knees in cold, dark water, beating a pile of ragged linen with a stick, forcing the water through the weave in the hope that it will carry away the dirt as it goes. She has a rhythm, steady and unchanging, and she pounds away until she thinks that the shirt is clean enough to pass inspection. Then she stops beating it and throws it into one rush basket and collects the next dirty shirt from another rush bucket where it has been soaking in the lye that she has made herself from the ashes of the kitchen fire. Then she pounds that. 'She doesn't half hit the thing,' one of the lay sisters calls across to the other two.

And she does. She goes at it with all her strength, all day, every day, and when the tears come, when she remembers what she has lost, and the wrongs that have been done her, she hits all the harder.

'She'll work herself to death,' one of them says.

'Or she'll break the stick,' the other laughs. 'Then she'll catch it from the Prioress.'

But she carries on, just as she has done for two months, beating away so that now her back is corded almost like an archer's and her shoulders are rounded with muscle. They feed her more often than she believed they would, with soup and bread and ale, and they leave it on a rock and step back to watch her eat. They are contemptuous of her, and she is glad, because she could not stand to be shown any kindness, and she knows that if she is not to die here in the priory, she will have to hurt these women, one day, maybe soon.

Each evening, when the mist begins to rise from the water, and the night bell rings, the lay sisters call her in and she climbs wearily from the stream and gathers her baskets and together they trudge back up to the beggars' gate. They wait while Sister Matilda comes and unlocks the gate that she once slammed in the giant's face. Then Sister Matilda admits her, takes her to her cell, pushes her in, and draws the bar of the door behind her.

Sleep always comes quickly. But every night she is woken with the other sisters and is led down the stone steps and across the yard and around the wings of the cloister to the nave, where she joins the community to observe the hour. She stands there with the junior nuns, dizzy with fatigue, listening to the lector read the psalms from

91

the other side of the wall, and if she were not so tired, if she had not worked herself half to death to avoid just this situation, this would be the time she feared most, for this is when she must face the Prioress.

And there she stands, the Prioress, across the tiles from Katherine, a head above the next tallest sister, or she kneels at her prie-dieu with her huge hands clasped tight in that simulacrum of prayer, with that heavy brow lowered and her eyes tight shut, and whenever Katherine glances at her she cannot help but shudder. It is a mixture of fear and revulsion, very powerful, that sometimes makes her gag.

And the Prioress knows it. She plays on it. Sometimes she will ignore Katherine, and pursue this pretence of prayer; then at other times Katherine's gaze will be drawn to her, and she will find herself staring into those eyes that carry such a charge of hatred that Katherine will almost cry out.

On the first day she was brought back to the priory, death would have been preferable. It was the only thing on her mind, but seeing her reaction, they had trussed her hand and foot, and she had been rolled in the back of a wagon like a corpse on her way to the churchyard, lacking the chance to have herself killed. She'd railed and spat at the bailiff and his men. She'd called them everything foul that she could think of. She'd drawn on her time around soldiers' campfires, where ale uncurbed the tongue, and at the cutting table, where pain did the same, and the bailiff's men had been shocked at first to hear such words in a lady's mouth, and one had been provoked as she hoped they all might, with drawn knives, but the other two calmed him and soon indignation gave way to marvel, and they began to laugh at her as she lay there so powerless.

When the cart had trundled past the castle, they had stopped and allowed Mayhew to guide Richard across the newly repaired bridge to say goodbye. He was carrying the baby John, and held him up for her to see, and she had wept then, for him, and for Richard, since he could not, but she would not weep for herself. Then the baby started to cry, raucous, and the girl came and she wept too. Richard had put a hand on her ankle and promised that he and Mayhew would ride to London to find William Hastings, that he would have her freed within the week, the month, and then he had given her the pardoner's ledger, telling her that he knew the consolation it gave her.

When the oxen had pulled on, leaving Richard and Mayhew and the baby behind, the bailiff took the ledger and opened the bag and laughed.

'Thinks it's a book of hours, does he? A romance? Fuck me! It is just a list of fucking names.'

The other men had laughed too, though she was sure they could not read, but they whistled when they saw the hole in its face, and speculated on the cause and then, after a moment, the bailiff had returned the pardoner's ledger to the bag but soon lost interest in it, and had thrown it down next to her, so close she could almost touch it. She focused on it as the cart moved along the potted causeway to the priory. The men had begun talking in that desultory way about Agnes Eelby, and their lack of envy for those who'd had to dig her up and now rebury her. Then they'd moved on to the men who'd appeared out of nowhere to sway the jury. Neither knew them personally.

'But you know who sent 'em, don't you?' one of them had said. There was a silence then, filled with meaning, and she looked up to see the bailiff glance down at her.

'Who?' she'd asked.

There was no reply.

'Who? For the love of God who sent them?'

But the men felt they had said enough, and they turned their backs on her while the bailiff rode ahead to arrange the detention with the Prior of Haverhurst. The wagon lurched and she angled herself so as not to be thrown off and she stared up into a sky that was sallow with the threat of more snow. When they got to the priory the pardoner's ledger was taken from her by two of the lay brothers and a lay sister whom she did not know, and they were apologetic, and promised the book would be kept safe and returned when she left the confines of the community.

Then she was taken through the yard and up the back steps to a cell she had never seen before, and had not known existed. It was large, whitewashed, with fresh rushes on the floor and a raised palliasse, filled with fresh hay that smelled of hyssop, and there were linen sheets and a blanket. There was a window with a shutter to block the night air and a small crucifix in a sconce on the wall with a beeswax candle, and the lay sister was apologetic, saying the Prioress would be with her as soon as the lessons were read. Katherine had sat on a stool and shook, and prayed that the Prioress whom she had known was dead, and that this might be some new incarnation.

But the moment she heard the heavy tread on the steps she knew it would be the Prioress, her Prioress, and so it proved. When Katherine had seen that great prow of a face enter the room and those small eyes turn on her and the realisation dawn, they had simply stood staring at one another. The Prioress had her mouth open ready to deliver some simpering greeting reserved for Lady Margaret, daughter of Lord Cornford. Katherine was trembling, and crumbling from the inside.

What happened then happened as if in a trance. The Prioress shouted something, and advanced towards her with those beefy arms outstretched. Katherine felt herself caught, lifted off the ground. Her legs swung, her feet in mid-air. Then she was pressed against the wall. The Prioress's face was huge, blotchy, her eyes screwed in knots, her teeth bared, spittle everywhere. Her hands were around Katherine's throat and she could feel the pulse booming in her ears. The pain grew. Vision wavered. She grabbed the meaty wrists, could not even get her hands around. Then the other sister was there, pulling the Prioress back by the shoulders. Another joined them, also pulling. A third. There was screaming and shouting, dull in her ears. Until the Prioress had to let her drop. She fell gasping. Her throat burned, every breath a torture.

The Prioress was like a bull, her great jaw thrust out, her body straining at the door, just held back by three sisters.

'I will kill you!' she'd bellowed. 'I don't care who you are, I will kill you this time!'

The three sisters pushed and shoved the Prioress from the room, holding her back as she surged forward, finally getting her out. Katherine was left alone. Then another sister came and Katherine thought it was Sister Joan, back from the dead, but it was not, it was some copy of her, and Katherine felt hands on her, pulling at her limbs and her clothes and even her precious rosary beads and she allowed it to happen and then she was hauled naked from the room and pushed and shoved down the stairs and out into the yard and across it and she was made to stand by the well while her hair was hacked to her scalp, and it fell on her ivory white feet in pale hanks and she was shivering and weeping, but they held her up while the scissors ground through her tresses. She stood there and wept and she had never felt so alone and abandoned as she had then, and in her pain she damned everyone who had abandoned her, everyone who had left her, the dead and the quick. And one of the sisters told her to cease her blubbering mouth for she was cursing aloud, and then the sister cutting her hair nicked her scalp. After that she was put back into the cell in which she had been stretched the night after she had been seen with Thomas. The door was shut and the bar was drawn and she was alone in the dark.

She was there three days. By the fourth she was nearer death than life, and she was better off that way, for at least then they would not drag her out and hang her from some tree. Her waking hours were tormented by thoughts of Sister Joan, writhing under her, her dove-white throat soft under the thumbs, then the thick blood – the colour of damson juice – spluttering to her lips, and then the Prioress's bellows. So when the door was opened on that fourth day, she thought to herself, this is it.

She had faced death before, of course: when the Earl of Warwick had wanted her hanged for running from his army outside Canterbury; when they were caught in the storm off the coast of Wales; when she fell from the horse outside Brecon with the arrow shafts flitting over their heads; and then just before the rout by Wigmore Castle, when the giant and Riven's boy caught them in the trees. And really, what had she left to live for? Almost everyone she'd ever loved, or even known, was dead. Her one regret was Richard, Richard and the boy John whom she'd saved. So she'd stood up. She'd said her prayers, such as they were. She was ready.

But when the door opened it was a bowl of soup, some ale, a piece of bread and a worn linen shift. Then the door was closed again.

'Wait,' she'd cried and she'd run at the door in the darkness and beat on its planks. At that moment anything would have been better than a return to the darkness and silence of her own mind. But no one returned for a day, and when they did it was with the same thing: a bowl of soup, bread, and some ale, and that was it.

More days passed. She lived like a dog, shivering. The cell stank. She stank. Were they going to keep her here for ever? Until she died? But if so, then why feed her? Why not let her die?

This was a question that became more unanswerable by the day. Why had they not hanged her for Sister Joan's murder? Why had she not been taken out and hanged from a tree as she had imagined they might? Then it occurred to her that they were waiting for a judge to oversee the trial. Someone more senior in the Church's hierarchy than the Prior. A bishop perhaps? That would be it.

Eventually they let her out. It was Sister Matilda again, accompanied by three curious lay sisters who wrinkled their noses when the door was opened and one even retched. Each sister carried a washing beetle, a three-foot length of whittled oak with a bulbous hammer-like end, and they escorted her down to the stream she would come to know so well and they stood closely by and watched while she tore her clothes off and threw herself into the water and scrubbed at herself with a handful of bunched linen dipped in lye soap. Then they stood watching her put on clean linen and a lay sister's smock.

''S happened t'your ear, Sister? Never known a girl to have her ear clipped.'

In a moment of weakness she told them.

'I ran away from the Earl of Warwick's army,' she said. They were unimpressed.

'Always runnin' from some place, aren't you?' one of them said. 'If it's not this, it's that.'

The first time she was set to work, she ran straight away. She lifted her cassock skirts and waded across the freezing stream. She was trying to loop back around the priory to find the road to Cornford, but the lay sisters caught up with her easily enough. She turned and lashed out at the first one, a woman with a near-constantly dismayed expression, but the woman was fast, and had been beating laundry all her life. She stepped back to let the beetle swing past, then she struck. She caught Katherine on the ball of the shoulder, knocking her staggering and then sprawling in the mud. The pain was intense, disorientating. It made her helpless and when the other sisters came they did not need to hit her any more. They picked her up under her arms and had to keep her upright on the way back. Then they put her in the cell and that night she had a powerful pain in her head, as if it might split, and she was constantly thirsty.

The next day she tried to run again. This time the sisters were ready for her. They merely held up their beetles and Katherine could hardly run let alone take the pain a second time. She turned and they pushed her back to the washing and they stood on the bank while she stood in the water.

'Why?' she'd muttered. 'Why?'

She had supposed they'd be on her side.

'What do you think'll happen to us if you run?'

Katherine shrugged. There was blood in her nose.

'We'll be beaten black and bloody blue for one thing.'

'And we'll have to do the linen again, is the other. So.'

Katherine understood. She picked up her own beetle and a shirt and began the work, and every day since it has been more or less the same. Now, though, it is the week before Easter, spring, when the water around her knees has lost its iron bite and the hawthorn wands along the far bank are in flower. The working day is longer, and the mist appears later, and at the end of it, Katherine is bone tired. Today she drags her feet and her basket up to the beggars' gate where Sister Matilda is waiting, this time shifting from foot to foot with impatience.

'Quick, quick,' she says. 'Take the baskets up to the dorter. The dorter now. Not the cloister. The dorter.'

Katherine sees there is something up. The yard has been swept and there is meat cooking, despite it being Lent. In the cloister two sisters are at work with brooms while another has an old goose wing and is removing the swallows' nests and spiders' webs from among the eaves, and a fourth is taking down the drying lines. The bustle reminds her of the time the Bishop of Lincoln was due, when they cleaned the priory from dorter to dishpan, all the time knowing that he would never witness their endeavour, and still being disappointed when he did not come to the priory at all, not even to see the Prior over the other side of the wall.

And then it strikes her. If the Bishop is coming, it must be to oversee her trial for Joan's murder. There can be no other explanation. That night she hardly sleeps despite the tiredness. She wonders when he will come. If they are cleaning up that day, then possibly he will come the next? He will arrive late in the afternoon, before Vespers, and having ridden down, or been carried down in his litter more likely, and he will not want to conduct any business that day, but will wish to start the next, surely?

She starts to imagine how any trial might be conducted. In the nave of the church, perhaps? The Bishop might call his questions over the wall, or write them down and pass them through the turning window? But then how will she answer? By passing her replies back through the turning window? Or will she be able to speak in the church as no sister has ever done before? Or will the trial be held elsewhere? But if that is the case, then why is she still here? Why has she been held here when surely the Bishop would have summoned her to Lincoln? Unless he cannot because he needs the infirmarian and the Prioress to act as witnesses to what happened, and he cannot call them out of cloister.

Unless, of course, it is not the Bishop who is coming.

But then, who?

Katherine begins her next day carrying the baskets down to the hovel where she keeps the barrel of lye soap. In a curious way she enjoys the process, since she knows this will be the last time she does it, and that this time tomorrow her life will be shaken out of this routine to hang in the balance once more.

One of the baskets is unusually heavy, as if someone has hidden stone within, and she begins to sort through its linens with a frown. They are from the canons' cloister, and when she lifts a shirt her eye is instantly drawn to the oddity: some odd-coloured cloth, russet, unusual here where every other garment is black or white. She hauls it out and is further surprised by its bulk and weight. It is a man's jack, only so heavy. Then she discovers its surprise. There are metal plates sewn into the lining. A soldier's coat. The faint tang of the metal within the padding, and a pleasant dusty smell. It smells of men, she thinks.

One of the lay sisters – the dismayed one, standing on the same bank as Katherine – has come to see what it is. Having spent so many years washing clothes herself, she too is an expert in linen, and any oddity is bound to be of interest. They hold the jack up together. It is large, with cloth enough for both to make a coat each and more to spare.

'Ain't it heavy?' she says. 'It must belong to him what's touched.'

'Him what's touched?' Katherine asks. 'Who's touched?'

'Him,' the lay sister says, nodding towards the canons' cloister. 'What they're saying all the masses for. What blew in on a horse and is proper frothing.'

Being apostate Katherine is not permitted to attend Mass, so she does not know they are praying for anyone in particular. Studying the jack, though, she feels a chance coming, and her heart beats a little faster.

'How long will he be here?' she asks.

The lay sister shrugs and drops her side of the jack.

'Till he's dead, I 'spect.'

She is about to retire to sit on the old stump when Katherine asks if that is why they are cleaning the cloister.

'No,' the woman says, 'it's not for him, you daft bitch. It's for the Prior of All, isn't it? First time he's been here since any of us've been born.'

Katherine feels a lurch, as if the ground has tilted, and her head feels suddenly full. So that is it. The Prior of All.

'When is he coming?' she asks. But the lay sister shrugs and walks away. Katherine returns to the jack and part of her is able to wonder at the irony of it all. She escaped the priory and spent all those months pretending to be on her way to see the Prior of All to appeal against her unjust expulsion from the cloister, and now here he is, coming to try her for murder.

'Get on with it,' the lay sister calls.

But the jack has given her an idea. A glimpse of something, anyway. She glances quickly at the lay sister, then returns to the jack, examining it for stains; she dips the cuffs and the undersides

100

of the sleeves in the urine and pours some more on the shoulder where the strap of a bag has worn and stained the cloth, and then she puts it aside for that to work while she continues with the rest of the basket. There is nothing odd in here until she gets to the bottom and finds a pair of men's hose, of blue wool. They are badly stained where the man has sat astride a saddled horse, and there is crusted mud on the knees. She plunges them in the lye with everything else and then agitates the brew with her beetle.

It is late morning, nearly time for Sext, and there is watery sunshine and a breeze from the east, so when she has washed and pulverised the laundry, including the jack and the hose, she wrings it hard as she can on the post – awkward with the metal plates – and then pins it on the hawthorns.

Towards the end of the afternoon Katherine finally stops her beating, ostensibly to rest her back. The sunshine has gone and the sky from where the wind blows is grey, louring, and she knows it will rain soon. Good, she thinks, and she begins thumping the other linens, one strong slap after the next. When the rain comes the lay sisters shout at her and she sets aside her beetle and hurries to take down the still-damp laundry. The lay sisters watch her for a moment, then turn and huddle against the rain. Now she moves quickly, practised hands secreting the jack and the hose between various braies and shifts. When she has finished neither can be seen.

Then she returns to the stream and carries on as the rain prickles her back and pebbles the water around her. That day the night bell rings before the mist starts to rise from the stream and as it rings Katherine carries the basket wherein the jack and hose are hidden back up to the priory. Sister Matilda is at the gate, key in hand, shifting from foot to foot, impatient.

There is still more work to be done, which means the Dean of All has not yet arrived. It is a stay of execution, but only until tomorrow. Her heart is quick as she hurries up the steps and as she passes her cell she stumbles and puts her basket down and clutches her back.

No one is looking. No one would care anyway. She snatches the jack and the hose from under the pile and dips into the darkness of her cell. She unrolls the straw mat on which she sleeps and rolls it up again with the clothes inside. Then she is out again and carrying the basket across the yard and up the steps. No one has seen her.

After five trips up and down the steps there is no space left on the lines in the dorter and after more pottage and bread and ale, Sister Matilda quickly shunts her through the door to her cell and pulls the bar across and she is condemned to her darkness once again. But now her heart is beating fast and her breathing is unsteady as she waits the length of time it would take to say the Ave Maria, then she unrolls her mattress and hauls out the damp, heavy jack. She tries it on. Its weight drags across her shoulders, as heavy as a child, she thinks, and its hem reaches her knees and she has to roll each sleeve back halfway so as to be able to use her hands. With a belt around her waist she persuades herself that she will not look too much the fugitive.

But how to make use of it? It is no good to her while she is locked in her cell. She has paced the floors and knocked on the walls and tried to scratch away the mortar between the stones, but nothing gives. Then she has an idea. She takes off the jack and turns it open. Working in the dark, she rips open a seam under what she imagines is the arm and she feels the strips of steel within the padding. Each plate is rough edged, too stiff to bend, and punctured in the middle so that it can be stitched in place. She chooses one, and twists it until the linen threads snap and it comes loose. It is a piece as long as her hand, two fingers wide. It is perfect.

She returns the jack to its hiding place under the mattress and fumbles her way over to the door. It is so dark that she cannot see her hand in front of her face but she feels her way up the door jamb until she comes to the stone into which the bar is set. She wonders whether she can scrape out the cement around the stone, then she wonders if she can't just work the drawbar back? She slides the strip into the gap between the door and the stone and lifts it until it meets the bar. There is perhaps the width of a coin in which to work. She presses the steel into the wood and moves it from left to right. She does this slowly, time and time again, and she presses her eye to the crack in the door, imagining that if someone came, they would bring a light, and she would see that before they saw the bar move in its tiny increments.

She keeps at it and is so long doing it that her hands ache. And then she sees the throb of light through the gap between door and jamb, a tiny muted line, and hears footsteps as someone comes. She throws herself on her mattress and forces the plate under it, and then feigns sleep as the drawbar is pulled back and the door is opened and she will never know how far she managed to work the bar back before it was pulled all the way. Not enough to arouse suspicion anyway. Sister Matilda is there with the rush lamp.

'Come,' she says. Her face is flat and blank with fatigue and she drags her feet in front of Katherine as they descend to the cloister and along its spotless wings to the nave of the church where they stand and listen to the lector read the observances. When it is over and she is returned to her cell Katherine resolves to try the door again. She finds the metal plate under her mattress, though this time instead of going straight at the door, she spends time sharpening the end of the plate against the stone jamb, slowly grinding an edge.

She falls asleep while she is doing it, still kneeling on the stone floor, her head against the door, and is only woken by the sound of clogs outside. She is quick to secrete the plate in the sleeve of her cassock and she walks to the nave holding both elbows.

'What's wrong with your head?' Matilda asks. 'It is all striped.'

After the observance she is too tired to start again with the plate or the door, and she collapses on her mattress and sleeps as if dead until she is roused with a kick at dawn for Prime. She is nervous all day, suffering from a gnawing anxiety that infects everything she does. Any alteration imposed on her routine takes on a sinister potential, but the day passes unchecked. That night she starts to work on the drawbar again, slipping it back a sliver at a time. She moves faster now, conscious that she has only three hours before she is to be woken again to attend Prime, conscious that she has no way beyond instinct to measure this span of time.

On she goes, until her hand aches with cramp and her vision swims. Finally the door's bar leaves its housing with a slight sigh and the door slumps on its hinges with an unoiled creak. Her heart beats faster, but she remains motionless in the silence. Then she pulls the door open. It is almost as black without as within her cell, and she remains kneeling with the plate stretched before her like a knife, waiting, knowing that if someone comes now she will have to kill them.

There is nothing. Not a movement. After a long moment she returns to her mattress, fumbling with it to pull out the still-damp jack. She twists out of her cassock, so that she is wearing her linen slip like a shirt, and her braies. She slips the jack over her shoulders. It is very heavy. She wonders if it will be so much of a help in the long run. The hose are trickier. She pulls them on, still wet, struggling in the darkness, and hoists them up her legs and rolls the hem in a thick coil around her waist. She wishes she had a doublet to keep them up. Then she slips the metal plate back in its slot under her arm and returns to the door. She lifts it as high as she is able so that it does not strain on the hinges and creak as it opens and she steps out into the corridor. She closes the door and slides the bar across. To the left is the way up to the sisters' dorter, to the right the stairs down to the yard.

Cold air pushes up from that way and she turns and feels her way down, letting her hand slide on the stones until she feels the breeze coming from below. She is at the top of the stairs. Then she steps down, slowly, carefully, the stone cold through the soles of her hose. At the bottom the door is barred. She feels for it and slides it back from its housing and then is out into the yard. A moon is up, somewhere behind a gauzy veil of cloud, casting an uncertain light that comes and goes.

She crosses the yard to the beggars' gate. She pulls the drawbar back into its housing and pulls. It stays in place. She pulls again but it does not move. Dear God. She has forgotten the new lock. It is unbreakable. She steps back. The wall is too tall. Then she remembers Thomas and his escape from this same spot, the very first time she saw him. She crosses to the wood stack and hauls herself over its eave. The tiles here are slippery but her wet hose help. She scrambles across them and then catches the parapet and pulls herself up and on to it. It is easy, she thinks. But then she looks down. It is the churchyard where the canons and the sisters are buried. She slips her legs over and then lowers herself down, the rough stone edges biting her palms. She has still a fall to make, and she drops, lands heavily and rolls in the earth. She gets up, hobbles a moment, and then waits for the moonlight to come. The graves are marked with dark stones, each laid flat, simply carved with the name of the dead person. In this light they look like shafts down into the graves. She shudders. Joan must be here, and Alice.

She needs to keep moving. There is a gate on the far side of the graveyard. It must give on to something. She circles around, one hand on the rough-dressed stones of the wall, and when she is at the gate she finds that locked too. But it is low, wooden, and she can clamber over. She pulls herself up and peers over. Beyond is a small yard. She waits a moment. All is still. Crossing it will put her in the canons' cloister and she is aware as she scrambles over the gate that what she is doing, she cannot now undo.

She drops quietly into the mud and straw of the yard and moves across to the shadowy space that she supposes must mark the opening to the garth. She skirts the cloisters, keeping her hand on the balustrade, and then finds herself lost. Where is the beggars' gate? She passes from the garth into the yard and there, in the fleeting moonlight, she stops for a long moment. To the right is the turning house, the other side of the great turning wheel through which all the laundry passes from one cloister to the other, then the almonry, then the chapter house. Ahead is the gate, and to the left are the stables and the buttery and pantry, and then the frater house and the canons' dorter above. She cleaves to the moon shadows and crosses swiftly to the gate. The locking bar is huge, a trimmed tree trunk, normally moved by two men.

She tries, though, trying to inch it back when – footsteps. A canon is awake, walking slowly through the first yard. He is carrying a watchman's lantern. A door is opened. A brief kindling of light, then a voice. Then the door shuts. Then there is only darkness again and silence. She is shaking in her damp clothes and she looks up at the clouds skimming across the moon's face, and there is a wind, and suddenly she is terrified, not of being caught, but of being out in the dark. After her cell, everything is so huge, so open; she is exposed and vulnerable, the prey of any and every thing.

And now she does not know what to do. The walls are all too tall for her to climb, and there is someone awake in the cloister, so that she cannot return the way she has come. She is trapped.

Then the door opens again, a patch of light somewhere in the bowels of the first yard. The door closes but the light stays, flickering as if moving. Two lamps now, and two voices. Men talking, and coming quickly. She runs to the stables. Christ. The door is barred. She slides it open and steps in. There is no comforting snuffle from any horse or mule, only silence within. She is relieved. She pulls the door to and steps into the darkness beside it. Her heart is hammering over the sound of her breathing and there is a rushing in her ears. She sees the light through the crack between door and jamb falling on the straw, and the voices are coming nearer.

By Christ, she thinks. They cannot have seen her. She was too quick. Nevertheless she fumbles for the sharpened plate under her arm and takes it out with trembling fingers. She holds it out in front of her and readies herself to kill whoever comes.

They are coming. Or one of them is, grumbling about something. He does not sound as if he is suspicious or even vaguely alarmed. He sounds more annoyed. She holds her breath. The door is banged against its frame as if to check it and then it is opened. Light splashes across the straw on the ground.

Katherine squeezes back into the darkness.

The man stands outside the door, one hand on the frame. He is very close. She could touch him. He holds the lamp up and a long oblong of light fills the stable. But there is a slice of darkness where Katherine is pressed to the wall.

The man grunts something, some vaguely relieved noise, and then he steps back and closes the door. The drawbar is pulled across and rammed home.

'Some bloody fool forgot the bar,' he calls, his voice muffled, and across the yard the other man grunts something to suggest he is familiar with such incompetence.

'Is he there?' he calls.

'He's all right.'

There is another grunt, and they continue on with their round, the sound of their voices dying with the light until Katherine is left in the absolute darkness, but she does not move. She stays pressed to the wall. The sharpened plate is held before her, shaking. She can scarcely breathe with the fear of it.

Because there is a man in the stable with her.

7

Thomas blinks. He wonders if he is imagining it: a brief glimpse, in the glow of the watchman's lamp, but the details remain vivid even after the man has gone and silence is returned. A boy in a long coat, with strange patchy hair, as quick and quiet as an eel. Thomas shakes his head. He has not imagined it. Such things — you don't just imagine them. He doesn't move. He listens and hears the boy breathing.

'Who are you?' he asks. He keeps his voice quiet. Conspiratorial. His enemy's enemy must be his friend. But there is no answer. So he asks again. Still no answer.

'I know you are there,' he says, but now, suddenly, he is not sure. By Christ, he thinks, I am going mad again. They are right to keep me in here. Strange shapes swirl in the darkness before him. He begins to sweat. He starts the paternoster, silently, and then he hears something again.

'What do you want?' he asks. 'Tell me. Who are you?'

Again there is nothing but the slight sigh of breath being drawn.

But perhaps his enemy's enemy is also *his* enemy?

'If you do not say something, I will shout,' he says. 'Then the canons will come running.'

He feels stupid even saying this. Imagine someone hearing him. The boy still says nothing. There is a long moment. Then Thomas decides something. He slips his blanket aside and rolls off his mattress, and he moves slowly, his eyes fixed on that spot by the door. He controls his breath and takes a step. His vision conjures up strange shapes again. Still, he takes another pace through the straw, stroking the air before him. A third step, then he stops. Shapes uncoil in the darkness. He pinches his eyes closed.

Then he takes another step.

'Get back!' the boy snarls. 'I have a knife.'

Thomas leaps back. He imagines a movement in the dark, a swinging arm, the burn of the blade passing through his flesh.

'By Christ,' he whispers. 'I do not wish to hurt you.'

'Do not say anything more,' the boy says. 'If you call out I will kill you before the brothers can come.'

Thomas wonders if the boy can see him. He can't see the boy, despite the sliver of moonlight. He realises he is standing in it, that the boy can see him, so he steps aside into the darkness. He hears an indrawn breath. Good, he thinks.

'Who are you?' he asks. 'If we are going to share a cell, we should be acquainted.'

The boy does not want to talk. Thomas takes a few steps back. He stretches for his mug on the floor where he knows it to be. It is leather, not quite heavy, but will do as distraction.

'Are you some sort of oblate?' he asks. 'Is that why you are running? Or what? A thief? If so you have picked the wrong door, Brother, for there is nothing of value here, and no way out either. They have taken everything I ever had, even the clothes I stood in.'

Still silence. Thomas listens. He is so familiar with the cell that he knows exactly where to throw the mug, and so he readies himself, hitching the skirts of his cassock around his waist. He plants his feet. Then he draws back the mug. Drops of ale fall down his sleeve, cold in his armpit. Then he throws. And at the same time he springs across the length of the stable and he crashes into the boy. He feels a small hard body in his hands, a wiry shoulder. He strikes down, catches the arm and knocks it away. The boy cries out and something flies out of his hand and hits Thomas's foot. Thomas runs his hand back over the body, feeling the stiffness of the metal plates of the jack, and then has both the boy's arms clamped tight in his.

That is when the boy knees him in the testicles.

For a moment it hurts no more than any other blow to any other part of the body, but then a great green sickness billows up within him. He expels a cough and lets the boy go. He reels away and falls to his knees and then he crawls, scrabbling in the straw, into the corner from where he has come. He wants to die. He vomits softly, a dense bubble of half-digested bread and gravy.

Thomas can hear the boy patting the ground, looking for his knife. He would be happy to have his throat cut, he thinks, happy to die, for it to be over with. He lies on his side with his legs curled up and he gags and swallows. He hardly tries to move his face away from the scalding slick of vomit that smells so bad. The sickness only seems to swell, taking over his whole body.

'God damn you,' he moans, 'God damn you.'

Still the boy says nothing. Thomas lies there so long that eventually he is granted the blessed relief of sleep. The sickness wavers, relents, and he slips into unconsciousness.

When he wakes the bell is ringing and dawn has come. He opens his eyes. Grey light fills the stable. He remains absolutely still, moving only his eyes. He is lying on his side with his knees drawn up, his hands tucked between his legs. There is vomit everywhere. The events of the night before return to him, unreal, and yet there is that hollowness in his gut and sharp stink from the pile of grey stodge in the straw. Once the bell has ceased its toll, he listens and there is a thin buzz, regular and easy. He strains his neck, lifts his head, and peers around. He can see nothing of the boy. Then he uncoils slowly and rolls over.

The boy is asleep, head bowed, slumped in the corner, his legs outstretched and the blade on his lap in loosely curled hands. He is snoring gently. Thomas sees he is wearing a jack such as he himself owns, or used to own, and hose too, identical to his, and that both are too big for the boy by some margin. He stretches his legs, then

110

raises himself, not taking his gaze off the boy until he is crouching. Then he gets to his feet and takes the few swift steps across the stable; he dips and snatches the knife away.

The boy wakes.

Thomas holds the knife out.

The boy looks up.

They stare at one another.

Thomas drops the knife.

Katherine's eyes open wide, then her mouth drops open, and her eyes screw up again. Thomas drops to his knees. Her hands come up. For a moment they cup his beard.

'Thomas,' she says. 'Oh, Thomas.'

And they look at each other for a long while.

'Katherine.'

She takes her hands away and she shakes her head. She closes her eyes, as if she does not believe what she is seeing.

'No,' she says. 'It cannot be.'

Thomas cannot speak. He feels his hair standing on end, all over his body a great rippling, like grass in the wind. He opens his mouth to say something, but can't find any words.

'Where have you been?' she asks. 'For the love of Jesus! Where have you been?'

'I don't know,' he says. 'I don't know.'

He puts his arms out to take her in them, to gather her to him, as he wishes to, but she shies away. He hardly knows who she is, only that he is filled with elation at seeing her.

'No,' she says. 'No. Tell me. Tell me where you have been.'

He lets his hands drop to his sides.

'I don't know,' he repeats.

'We thought you were dead.'

'No,' he says. 'Or not yet anyway.'

She stares at him, examining him while he examines her.

'What is that?'

111

She points to the white hair at his temple. He tells her. She places her fingers against it. He explains. Katherine nods.

'But why are you here? Here in the priory again?'

'I came back,' he says.

'Why?'

He shrugs.

'I had to start somewhere. I remembered here. My brother said I was like a bird returning in the summer: I could not describe where I needed to go, but I knew it when I saw it.'

'Yes,' she supposes.

'Why are you here?' he asks her. She looks at him for a long time, as if wondering where to begin, before admitting that it is a long story.

'But you are not—? You were hiding from the watchmen, last night?'

She nods and shrugs.

'As I say,' she says. 'A long story.'

'And why are you wearing my clothes?' he asks.

'These are yours?' she says with a laugh. She pulls on the cloth of the jack.

He sees she is missing the tip of her ear and he asks her about it.

'You did that,' she says with a smirk, and he denies it, but she tells him how he was made to do it by the Earl of Warwick and just as he is about to deny it again, he stops.

'Shhhhh,' he says suddenly. He holds out a hand. There are footsteps hurrying without. Then someone shouts quickly, a list of instructions. A bell rings, sharp and clear, summoning the lay brethren from their fields and granges. The sun is above the roofline, throwing a barred square of very faint light on the opposite wall of the stable.

'You cannot stay here,' he says. 'They will come to fetch me soon enough.'

He looks around the stable. It isn't the first time he's sought a means of escape, of course, but as with all his other searches, this one yields nothing. Katherine takes the blade from him and approaches the door. She slides the blade into the crack and is about to lift it to the door bar when there are voices without. She withdraws the knife and ducks back into her corner. She clutches the blade by her thigh. She looks ready to use it. But the noise is in the next-door stable, where Thomas's horse is kept. A door bangs and men start calling urgently. Someone coaxes his horse out into the yard and then there are more men coming. Thomas recognises Blethyn's voice.

'She will have gone east,' he is telling the others. 'Towards Cornford. Check every ditch. Every bush. Everything.'

They wait in silence as the horse is ridden out of the yard and with it the men's voices fade.

'You?' he asks.

She nods.

'I hoped I'd be at Cornford by now,' she says. 'I couldn't get out of the sisters' cloister. They have a lock on the door now.'

Thomas peers through the gap between door and jamb. After a while he turns to her.

'They have forgotten about me,' he says. She is still staring at him, as if unable to believe he is back, and still holds the makeshift blade by her hip.

'Will it work?' he asks, nodding at it.

'Try,' she says, offering it to him. He stands listening, his eye back at the sliver of light between door and jamb, then, after a moment, he slips the blade in, just as she had done, and lifts. The stable drawbar is even easier, for the door fits less well, and there is at least the width of a finger with which to work. He moves the bar back, then forward.

'Hah,' he says. 'I could have done that with almost anything.'

Then he looks around. There is nothing.

'It will soon be the chapter meeting,' he tells her. 'We will go then.'

She nods. That makes sense, it seems.

'Why do they keep you here like this?' she asks. Thomas shrugs.

'They say I am an apostate,' he says. 'And Barnaby wants to show someone – the Prior of All, I think – that I am safely back in cloister, not out in the world bringing shame on myself and on them.'

Again she nods.

'And they want me to finish a psalter I once worked on,' he continues, holding up an inked finger. 'Though they do not trust me with it yet. I think they fear I will rip it to pieces, so they give me endless scripture to practise my pricking out and lettering instead.'

She scoffs.

'I have been washing linen since Candlemas,' she tells him, holding up her own hands. They are red-skinned, her fingers almost claws. Then, while they wait, she tells him everything. She tells him about how they met, how Barnaby's Giles Riven attacked her, and how he – Thomas – saved her, and she says that he once told her he fought a duel with the man, though she did not see it herself, and then how they escaped the giant on the ferryman's punt, and how they met the pardoner, and then took a ship to Canterbury to find the Prior of All to explain their case, only to be diverted when their ship was captured by Sir John Fakenham and then sailed to Calais, 'which lies over the Narrow Sea, in France'.

Then she tells him they came back and came to live in Marton Hall with Richard Fakenham, the knight from Barnaby's story, and she tells him they were happy, then, and she tells him of a journey to Wales that they made, and how their friends were killed, one by one, by a giant and the son of Giles Riven, and then she tells him how Margaret Cornford died in the snow one night, and how she became Margaret Cornford in her place.

And he is astonished, but thinks, this could be a story from the Old Testament, from the Book of Kings, perhaps, for all the names and the places she mentions are as distant to him as is Jerusalem.

She goes on, and tells him how Richard Fakenham came to be blinded, and how they went north together, all of them, with a hammer, intending to find and kill this Giant, and Giles Riven, and even his son if they could and he almost laughs. Then she tells him how it was for her during the battle, about how she removed an arrow from the Earl of Warwick's thigh, and then about the days and months after it.

'I thought you were dead,' she says. 'We all thought you were dead. We looked for you. Richard and Mayhew and I. All that night. There were so many of them dead. All those men. You must have seen. And it just became . . .'

She shakes her head. She cannot describe what she saw. The act of remembering almost chokes her and for a moment she cannot continue. He reaches out to touch her, but she pushes his fingers away. Then she gathers herself.

'We thought we'd found you,' she says. 'Someone called out my name. Katherine. It turned out – it turned out it was a Welshman, likewise called Thomas, married to a woman called Katherine too. Richard and Mayhew were confused. Why would I answer to a man calling out Katherine when they knew me to be Margaret? But, that night, they were confused as to why we were there in the first place, to tell the truth. I told them you had saved me from certain death, and it was my chance to do the same for you.

'So we stayed with William Hastings,' she goes on. 'In his household in London and I waited, but all the time I thought, what are the chances? If Thomas is gone this long, then he is gone. Otherwise he would be here by now.'

Then she tells him how she came to marry Richard Fakenham, because how could she not? And then how Richard insisted they take Cornford, since that was what it was all about, and that was what his father wanted, though she seems unsure of this. Then she describes how they left Hastings's household in London and with a few men and a cart full of wedding gifts, they had come east to Cornford.

'And Richard Fakenham thought all this time you were Margaret Cornford? He did not know you were – you?'

She shakes her head in sorrow.

'No,' she says. 'I was caught in the trap of the initial lie, and every moment it bound me tighter.'

Then she describes the day she killed Agnes Eelby.

'I have wondered so often what else I could have done, if I had my time again. Of course I would have gone to find that midwife sooner. I would have sought some advice, but if it was only the day on which it actually happened, then as all the saints are my witness, I would have done the same thing again.'

She says this as if he might doubt it, but he does not, for he can see she believes she did the right thing. Afterwards they both look at different parts of the stable floor. Then, when the bell for the chapter meeting rings, they gather shoulder to shoulder by the door in silence, Thomas's eye at the crack, waiting. He can see the canons making their way to the chapter house, and at length the sounds of hurrying footsteps pass and, except for the sound of the chickens, silence descends.

They are silent for as long as it might take to say the rosary, and all through it, Thomas wants to take her in his arms, but he fears she would try to kill him if he tried, and then he wonders if he can stand it a moment longer, but instead of trying, he takes the knife and uses it to slide the bar back and he gently pushes the door open. The yard is deserted. Even the chickens are elsewhere. They are about to leave when Thomas returns to the mattress and collects the leather bag containing the pardoner's ledger.

'Ha!' she says, pleased to see it. 'Thank God you have it still. They took it from me when they brought me back here and I thought I had lost it for ever.'

Thomas passes her the bag while he slides the gate's huge drawbar back in its brackets. She holds it, and then he takes the bag back and slings it over his shoulder, just as she has seen him do a hundred times, and then he opens one half of the gate and then, like that, they are out of the priory and into the world.

116

PART THREE

Toward Marton Hall, Marton, County of Lincoln, End of May 1463

8

'Run now,' he says, and they do, as fast as they can in their bare feet, along the dusty, rutted and pocked road for a hundred paces or so, down to the mill by the newly built bridge, where the water-wheel has been jammed to stop it turning and water flushes loudly through the rill. The miller is absent, as is the ferryman.

'Looking for you, I suppose,' Thomas says.

It is warm. The sun is on their faces, there are towering thunderheads to the east, and the colours of the fens seem unnaturally vivid. There will be a storm soon, he thinks. He is wearing almost precisely what he was wearing last time he was here, but what is different about him is that this time he is so much stronger; he can flip the ferryman's punt with one hand, despite it being newly made and heavier, and while she fetches the boat pole, he slides the punt down to the river's edge. He stops it there and stands and looks about, as though caught by a thought. She watches him for the briefest moment.

'This is where that giant had you,' she tells him, and she touches her right eyelid. 'I knocked him out, with something like this,' she says, passing him the pole, 'and we should have killed him then and there. We know better now.'

She climbs into the punt and settles herself. He launches it out on to the water and clambers in after her, and once again he stands at the back with the pole and he pushes off, swinging the craft out into the current.

Then they hear the cry.

'Dear God,' she says, pointing. 'It's them.'

Three lay sisters are running down from the priory, across the furrows of the rye field. They are carrying beetles and their skirts are flying. They come fast and the first one hits the water without a pause and is up to her waist before she realises it is deeper here than she is used to, and she cannot swim. The other two plough into the water just as readily, but neither can they swim, and they stop alongside the first. The water stains their cassocks at their waists and together they start shouting at Katherine, demanding she return. Threatening to kill her if she does not.

'Leave me be,' Katherine shouts. 'Go home and leave me be!'

One of them throws her beetle at Thomas. It misses him and hits the far edge of the punt with a dense ring. Katherine stops it going overboard and holds it up in ironic salute. The sisters realise they are losing and they turn and forge back through the waters and up the bank. They are sodden, their skirts heavy, their bare feet brown with sucking mud. The younger one is fringed in dripping bright green weed. After a brief argument she is sent running back to the priory for help while the other two shadow Thomas and Katherine along the river's bank.

'They will not catch us,' Katherine tells Thomas, seeking reassurance. 'We came this way before, chased by the giant, you remember?'

Thomas nods, though he does not, not really.

'Where are we going?' he asks.

'Cornford,' she tells him.

Cornford, he thinks. The castle. After that she is silent, lost in thought. The sisters are still there on the bank, just as the giant was. They have stopped their threats and now are merely calling on Christ and the martyrs to assist them as they clamber over the willow fences and wade through the ditches that drain the fields. Katherine's head is turned and she looks the other away, across the fens towards her castle, and there is a moment of sunlight and in it Thomas sees how pale she is, as a daisy petal, and how sharp and fierce she looks, with that frown and the pointed nose. It makes him smile for some reason, and he feels for a moment fiercely protective.

They come to the place where the riverbanks veer apart and before them is the larger body of water, smooth, brown and even faster flowing, and the punt is dragged away by the stronger current.

'I shall not miss them,' Katherine says, without a backward glance. She pulls her knees closer to her chest, and stares south. Thomas watches her sitting there, the beetle across her shins, and he can see her clipped ear and how fretful she is, but she does not look sorry for herself, which, he thinks, if he were her, he might. After a while they pass a village and Katherine points to a spot on the bank a little further down.

'This is the end of the Cold Half-Hundred drain,' she says. 'We can walk from here.'

Thomas digs the pole into the waters and the punt yaws towards the bank and after a moment they come nudging into a stand of reeds and Katherine crouches in the punt's bow and leaps ashore, conscious now of the value of keeping her hose dry, and then she turns to haul the boat out of the water. Thomas joins her and they haul it through the reeds and leave it with its pole for the ferryman to find. He scrambles up the man-made barrow and at the top finds himself the object of scrutiny of some sheep that stir in among the reeds. They are ugly, muddied things with sad faces and matted fleeces the colour of snow clouds.

She stands looking about them, regaining her breath.

'What are you looking for?' he asks.

'Rabbits,' she says. Then she asks if he has anything to eat. He shakes his head. She hisses a laugh.

'It is always the same, isn't it?' she says. 'Nothing changes.'

They set off, Thomas slinging the ledger over his shoulder as feels comfortable, and they follow the rough track raised on the bank. On one side: the ooze of the marshes, shimmering in the sun, and on the other: the quicker, weed-speckled waters of the drain. Gulls wheel above, and the air smells of mud and rotting things. She walks ahead, huddled into her metal-lined coat, wrapping the still-damp folds about her narrow frame.

'How far is the castle?' he asks.

'Beyond those trees there,' she says, pointing ahead over a stretch of boggy ground that looks impassable, to a broad copse of sappy willows above which he can now see the dark details of a stone tower. Katherine is looking around, frowning at the stretches of reeds and rushes, at the pools of black mud through which long-legged wading birds strut, dipping after worms and things. There is a broken sluice gate letting the water from the drain gurgle into a field of liquid mud.

And she sets off, picking up her pace, slapping the beetle into the mud with every stride, doing it to reassure herself as she guides them through the marsh, her hose becoming heavy and sodden so that he thinks she ought to go bare-legged, but they walk on, keeping the drain on their right, following it to a long stretch of reed-stippled water where there is another silver-timbered punt pulled up on a bank on which sits a duck. He wishes he had a bow with an arrow. They skirt the pool where there is a broken jetty for a fisherman, and they follow a path up through some more greenery to a broad causeway where some houses line a road. As they approach they see none of the comforting sights you might expect, such as hearth smoke, children, dogs, women at work.

'Where are they all?' she wonders aloud.

'Looking for you?' Thomas suggests.

'No,' she says. 'They are my people. Something is wrong.'

Thomas follows Katherine up on to the road, where they have a view of the castle. Thomas waits while Katherine stoops to look inside a cottage by the roadside. There is nothing much to see, no sign that anyone lives there. The next is the same. She looks at

him, seeking reassurance. He can only shrug. She hurries on. Her
eye is fixed now on the castle roofline, above which there is the
suggestion of smoke, as if it, at least, is occupied. Thomas follows.
They emerge into a clearing and he sees that the castle is on an
island, reached by a bridge first to one island on which there are
what look to be stables, then another bridge, turned at a right angle,
to the castle's gatehouse. They cross the first bridge together over
the still, black waters of the moat and find the stable empty, and
there is only old cow dung underfoot, none fresh. They cross the
second bridge, a drawbridge, and enter the cold damp shadow of
the small gatehouse where the gates hang open, one of them broken,
and they come into the courtyard where there is an eruption of
barking, and two dogs fly at them, scrabbling and baring their teeth.
Their chains bang taut bringing them up short but Thomas and
Katherine leap back.

'By Christ!'

The dogs stand on their chains, growling and snapping, saliva
spraying, ugly, broad-jawed, wall-eyed, the sort to bait bears, their
smell enough to make a dyer flinch. Behind them a man appears in
a doorway in the yard. He is barrel-bellied and furtive, a piece of
cooked meat in his hand, grease in the greying bristles on his fat,
wind-mottled face. He is at first cautious, but when he recognises
Katherine he is startled, then seems to recover himself. He takes a
clumsy step down, and throws the meat between the dogs, who
begin to fight.

Katherine turns on him.

'Why are you back here, Eelby?' she asks. 'And where is everybody? Where's my husband?'

Eelby stops and waves his hand airily and talks through pursed
lips.

'His lordship is gone to London,' he says in a voice not his own,
'accompanied by his personal surgeon in search of their old friend
the Lord Chamberlain, Lord Hastings, in the hope that he will look

kindly on your ladyship's plight and bring his influence to bear in the matter of my murdered wife.'

He snarls the last words, and Katherine sighs loudly, as if they have been through this before.

'What about John?' she asks, ignoring his attack. 'What of your son? Where is he? What of the others?'

Eelby does not answer. His face creases, and he folds his hands under his stained armpits and begins to pretend to find something very funny.

'You don't know!' he snickers. 'You really don't know, do you?'

'I've no time for this,' she mutters.

'No,' he says. 'No. You've no time for anything now.'

Thomas can see that Eelby means something, but Katherine turns her back on him. The man continues his laughing, closing his eyes, his whole body shaking with this false laughter, and Thomas senses trouble, but he is too late. Katherine takes a few quick steps, and she has the beetle swinging through the air before Eelby opens his eyes again, but he is also too late. He manages to raise his arm and the blow lands with a crack that makes the dogs jump and begin their barking again. Eelby screams and clutches his arm and Katherine raises the beetle again, but Thomas steps in, and Eelby looks at her with piteous fear. Then he turns and runs.

For a fat man with an injured arm he is startlingly fast. He is across the yard, past the dogs and scuttling up the stone steps to a doorway in the tower before Katherine can set off after him. Thomas runs to catch up.

'Wait,' he shouts. But she is gone, slipping through the doorway and up some winding steps after Eelby. Thomas follows. He hears scuffling footsteps on the turning stone steps above, then a rough-edged bellow. A door crashes open and light spills down. He runs, turning up the steps until he reaches a door out on to the daylight of the tower's enclosed rooftop.

It is a small square, ten paces across, stone-flagged, framed by regular merlons, with an iron brazier rusted vivid orange to one side. Katherine has the man pinned in a corner. His face is pink, sweating, and he is clutching his arm before him, which Thomas can see is bent, as if it were trying to turn a corner without him. Katherine has the beetle raised, but neither is looking at the other: both have their heads turned and are staring through the stonework to the countryside beyond.

Thomas peers over. Men on horseback. Soldiers. He recognises their type instantly, though from where he cannot say. They are in a column, two abreast, winding down the road that passes the priory. With bows across their saddles and many with those long lances stood in their stirrups. There must be fifty or more. A long line of laden carts follows, pulled by pairs of oxen.

'Who are they?' Katherine asks.

At first it seems Eelby is wheezing sibilantly through his teeth, suffering with the pain, but in fact he is trying to laugh again. Despite the pain he is enjoying this moment. Katherine raises the beetle ready to strike.

'Who are they?' she demands.

But now Eelby is braver.

'You have such good eyes, my lady,' he says. 'You tell me.'

Katherine peers into the distance. Then she lowers the beetle and grips the stone merlon.

'Merciful Christ,' she breathes. 'It cannot be.'

Eelby tries to laugh again but his face is wiped blank with fresh pain and his eyes roll in their sockets. He blubbers through thick lips, and the fingertips of his broken arm have turned blue.

'Who are they?' Thomas asks.

She looks at him over her shoulder.

'It is Riven,' she tells him.

'Riven?' he repeats. 'Giles Riven?'

She nods.

'Barnaby said he was dead,' Thomas says.

Eelby is laughing. Katherine turns on him.

'Why is he here?' she shouts. 'Why is he here? He's dead!'

'It's not him! It's Edmund. The son. Look for yourself. Here he comes to claim what's his.'

'But it is not his,' Katherine snaps.

'Try telling him that,' Eelby says, raising his head and nodding at the soldiers. 'Your father tried that once, didn't he? And look what happened to him.'

Instead of hitting him, Katherine meets his gaze and then looks back out at the men.

'What shall we do?' she asks Thomas, who is also peering over the walls at the advancing column.

'Close the gate,' he suggests. 'This is a castle after all.'

'Gate's broken,' Eelby says. 'Wouldn't stop a house cat. No, my lady and whoever you are, you'd best be gone 'fore they catch you.'

He is beginning to laugh again.

'Where have the others gone?' she asks. 'Where's the baby?'

Pain makes Eelby gulp. He is very pale and sweat sheens his fat, green-tinged face. When he has recovered he answers.

'They went with that fool the eel catcher, back up north. He can spend his coin to fill their bellies.'

'You let your son go to another man?'

'Why not? He can have the boy till I need him.'

Katherine lifts the beetle again.

'Katherine,' Thomas says. 'We must go.'

He places a hand on her arm.

'Why do you call her that?' Eelby asks.

'Shut up,' Katherine tells him. 'Do not even talk.'

'Come,' Thomas says. 'Before it is too late.'

Katherine threatens Eelby one last time, for the pleasure of watching him flinch, and then they leave him.

'Farewell, my lady,' he calls, reverting to the high-pitched, twisted voice of before. Katherine almost returns to hit him again, but

Thomas takes her arm and drags her through the small doorway and down the winding steps. In the yard the dogs come crashing at them again, forcing them to one side, and Katherine threatens them, but then they are out through the gatehouse and across the first and second bridges. The soldiers are still a good bowshot away along the causeway, but near enough now for Thomas to see the black badge on the breasts of their white jackets. They are led by a man with what looks like a bandage across his face.

He stops to stare, Katherine at his shoulder.

Then they hear Eelby shouting from the battlements. The horsemen slow to hear him, but they cannot, nor can he point for clutching his broken arm, so by the time the men know where to look, it is too late. Thomas and Katherine are gone.

9

When they reach the ferryman's punt they find the red-bearded canon studying it as if it has somehow come up short.

'Oh, Christ,' Thomas says when he sees him. 'Pass me that.'

Katherine hands him the beetle. The canon looks up at them, then at the beetle. He remains calm.

'Thought it might be you,' he says.

'Leave us,' Thomas says, 'and there will be none of this.'

He lifts the beetle.

'I do not want to stop you,' the canon says.

Thomas lowers the beetle.

'What then?'

'Take me with you.'

'You don't know where we are going,' Katherine says.

'Nor do you,' the canon says.

Thomas looks at her.

'No,' she has to admit. 'That is true.'

'And I have food,' the canon says. He opens his bag to show a quarter loaf of brown bread, and he has a large costrel of ale. Katherine cannot stop herself: she steps forward to take the bread, breaks it into chunks and bites. The bread is gritty with salt. She chews until her jaws ache, and then guzzles the ale, swallow after swallow. Thomas holds his chunk and looks back over the rushes to the distant trees. They should be gone, she can see him thinking. He comes to a decision, and passes her his bread.

'Help me, then,' he tells the canon, and together they shove the punt through the reeds and back into the river's tugging brown waters. Katherine takes the canon's knife and cuts off the feet of her hose and as she is about to throw them away, he takes the woollen socks and puts them in his bag. Then he hitches his cassock, takes off his clogs and throws them into the punt, and steps into the mud to hold it while Katherine climbs aboard.

'Well done, son,' he says.

She hesitates, unsure, and looks at him. He avoids her gaze and waits for Thomas. No one says anything. Does he really *not* know who she is? He gives no indication either way, just holds the boat fast as Thomas climbs aboard. Then he takes the pole, steps aboard himself, and shoves them off. Thomas is for a moment at a loss as to what to do.

'Where are we going?' the canon asks.

And she thinks. Downstream is Boston. But what help might she expect there? None, really. She knows no one save Widow Beaufoy, and she is not like to get help from her. No. There is only one place, really.

'Across,' she says, and she points over the river, to the rough sedge on the other side.

The canon grunts and steers the punt out into the current. He's a big man, solid and strong, with square feet and mud-rimed toes that seem to grip the thwart's edge. He guides the punt expertly through the water, as if he has been doing this all his life, but after a moment he looks down and catches Thomas's stare.

'What he did to you was unchristian,' he says. 'That is what I think Father Barnaby can be – unchristian.'

Thomas lifts an acknowledging hand from the gunwale.

'What is your name?' Katherine asks.

'Robert,' he says.

Then there is a pause.

'And yours, son?' he asks. Katherine squints up at him again. Is he playing with her or does he honestly not know who she is? She cannot tell. He stands there, patient, silent, steering the punt, and the need for an answer becomes pressing. She looks at Thomas for guidance but he does not seem to know either and then, finally, she says: 'Kit. My name is Kit.'

'Kit,' Robert murmurs. 'After the travellers' saint. Well, that is us, I suppose.'

And once again, in a moment, it is decided: she is to be Kit. Nothing more is said. There is only the noise of Robert's pole and the faint throng of the water against the side of the punt and after a while he manages to find a tongue of solid ground among the eastern bank's marshes and they climb out and haul the punt up out of the water to hide it among a stand of rushes.

'Just in case,' Robert says.

And they turn and set off through the marshland, ever careful of the green-crusted mud, and there are insects thick in the air, and strange red-beaked birds scuttle away before them.

'Edmund Riven,' she says. 'Edmund bloody Riven.'

'That was him?' Thomas asks. 'The man with the bandage?'

She growls an affirmative.

'How can he be here?' she demands of herself. 'His family is attainted! I was there in Westminster the day it was done! Richard said it marked the legal death of that family, of every Riven that was ever alive or lived still, or will ever live in the future.'

Neither Thomas nor Robert says a thing. Why should either know?

She will have to ask Sir John Fakenham, she thinks, that is all there is for it, for he is the only man who would ever tell her how it had come to pass, but now she thinks of him, and of Marton Hall, and she feels a roiling mixture of guilt, fear and shame. She thinks how she treated him: how she lied to him from the very start, how she passed herself off as someone else, and how she married the man's son while pretending she was someone else again. And all he ever showed for her – in any of her guises – was charity.

130

But there is one crumb of something, she thinks, something approaching comfort, or hope at least, and she thinks again of the day of the fight at Towton, when she was Margaret Cornford and she was tending to Sir John after he'd been brought down off the field, out of his wits with his head stove in. No one thought he would live, and they'd lain him on the ground and he'd clutched her hand and called her Kit. He'd even thanked the Lord that she – he – was there. And when she had corrected him, told him she was Lady Margaret Cornford, he had said that he knew what he knew, and that she should not be wasting her time with him, but she should go to find Thomas. Go out and be with Thomas, is what he'd said. She did not understand it at the time, or understand what he knew or how he knew, but she went to find Thomas, and it was only later that she tried to divine a deeper meaning in the old man's words. Did they mean he'd known from the very off that she was a girl pretending to be a boy, and that at that moment in the hospital she was the same girl, only now pretending to be a different girl? Or perhaps he thought she was, and always had been, Margaret Cornford, and that she'd pretended to be Kit to get away from Wales? She had struggled with this all that summer after Thomas was dead, endlessly going over it, again and again, watching Sir John's expression for any further clue, but the matter was never raised again, and she had never struck on a happy answer, not even at the altar, when she swore oaths before God and Man, and took Sir John's son as her husband.

So now she nods, and says: 'Marton Hall, in Marton, that's where we must go,' for, anyway, after all that, what else is there? Sir John is all that remains to them. They must seek him out and throw themselves on his kindness. It is their last – their only – recourse.

They pass the first night in a barn where a miller lets them sleep on a platform, reached by a ladder, on which straw is piled on a cradle of hawthorns, above two strong-smelling oxen. In amongst the straw are a few thick-skinned apples that they eat quickly, guiltily, greedily. A moment later and Robert is asleep in his wet clothes, snoring loudly, seemingly spread across the whole space so that wherever they move they must touch him.

Katherine and Thomas sit together, with their backs to a beam, legs hanging from the platform. She has taken off her jack and they can hear it dripping in the darkness.

'It will be cold tonight,' he says.

'We've known worse,' she tells him, and she reminds him of the night on the Welsh mountains, in the snow, the night that the real Margaret Cornford coughed herself to death.

He is pleased he cannot remember it.

'What was she like?'

'Oh, she was very young,' Katherine tells him. 'With much to learn. But that was another strange thing.'

'What?'

'Eelby still thought I was Lady Margaret, didn't he? You would think, wouldn't you, that the Prior would let it be known I was not?'

'Perhaps it is because they do not know who you really are?' Thomas asks, and she grunts. She cannot see how that would affect anything.

Thomas is silent in the darkness. She cannot see him, but she thinks about waking up to find him in the dawn that morning, in the stable, his expression so naked and confused. She'd thought she was dreaming still, of course, and she'd thought this was just another, stubbornly persistent one, from which she could not wake, and she thought for a moment perhaps she must be ill or mad, as they said she was, but then when she'd felt the soft bristle of his beard, she'd thought, no, by God, this is it, he is here, alive, and she had almost wept not with happiness, or relief, as she might once have done, but with the mad confusion of it all.

With this she thinks of Richard, her husband, and she wonders where he is and what he is doing. She thinks of him wandering around in London with Mayhew, shy, anxious Mayhew, frightened by men with power, men with velvet gowns and riding boots, men with retinues and weapons, and she wonders how that will turn out, but already their story feels distant, and their fate, somehow, not her concern.

'So will you continue as Lady Margaret for now?' he asks.

'It is the easiest,' she supposes, and he grunts his agreement.

'We would have to tell Robert here,' he says.

'That is nothing,' she tells him.

'But then,' he says, 'would Edmund Riven not try to kill you, just as he tried to kill the real Margaret Cornford?'

And she thinks about this for a moment, and sees that Thomas is right. Edmund Riven followed them to Wales to do just that.

'But what then?'

'Well, you are dressed as Kit. Robert here knows you as Kit.'

'Kit then?'

'I don't know.'

Thomas has lain down and in a moment he is breathing evenly, asleep. She lies next to him, as she was once used to, and she can smell him, and she means to offer up a prayer of thanksgiving, the Te Deum perhaps, but she does not. Then in the early hours of the morning, when it is darkest and they should be at Matins, she is woken by the unfamiliar, and she feels that Thomas has an arm around her as, again, he once used to. It is comforting, but later in the night, she is woken by something else: an unfamiliar pressure in her tailbone, and she feels him pressing against her. He is still asleep and when she whispers his name, why she does not know, he removes his arm, withdraws his body, and his dream, whatever it was, diverts elsewhere. She is left with only the impression of him, and she does not move until she is woken by the sound of the barn door on its hinges and the shouts of the boy leading the oxen from their pens below.

They walk through the morning under a pale sky, the breeze at their backs pressing the cold cloth to flesh, and they meet not a soul. Before midday they see the spire of Lincoln cathedral and the castle on their hill above the haze, and now she knows she can postpone answering the crucial question no longer: what is she to tell Sir John?

Can she really be Kit again? Will Sir John accept the boy back? All she can cling to is the strange hope that he already knows she is not who she says she is, and that he does not — what? Care? Think it matters? Or is he too playing some unknown game, some sophisticated scheme, the advantages to which she is yet blind?

She almost cries out with the frustration of it. Perhaps she ought not to have escaped the priory in the first place? Perhaps she should have stayed to face the Prior of All, to hang for the murder of Sister Joan? Then at least she would not be bringing her lies into the lives of others.

But then she remembers the Prioress. The beatings. The cruelties. She remembers gentle Alice, first raped, then left for dead, then murdered in her bed by those sworn to protect her. She remembers Giles Riven, his viciousness both casual and calculated. She remembers that giant who wanted to put Thomas's eye out, who blinded Richard, murdered Geoffrey. She remembers the boy Edmund who had once hunted her for pleasure, then in earnest. She thinks of Eelby, and his smirking greasy face, triumphant as she was expelled from the world because she tried to save his baby when he himself had not lifted a finger for his wife. And when she thinks of these people, when she thinks of the harm they've done, she finds she is so angry that she has overtaken both Robert and Thomas on the road, and that she is banging her beetle on the ground with every step and that her body throngs with pent-up fury and the desire to live, to survive, to thrive, if only to beat them, destroy them, and finally see them all dead. By Christ! She will do anything to see that.

When they arrive at the village it is late afternoon. There are pigs and goats in their pens, a few geese, and a boy with a shepherd's crook is slinging stones at blackbirds in a furlong by the churchyard.

'Who is it going to be?' Thomas asks quietly.

She pauses for a final second, then: 'Kit,' she says.

And it is decided.

The last time they surprised Sir John he was barricaded behind his door with a crossbow ready to kill the next man he saw. He was in a foul state, Katherine recalls, smelling like a badger, and the estate was despoiled and Geoffrey lay dead in a field. Already this is better, and as they approach, she sees — with an appreciative eye for having tried it herself — that fences are mended, hedges laid and there is the makings of a new hovel not yet finished among the recently coppiced hazel wood. She smells plum-wood hearth smoke and hears a peal of laughter: a woman's.

As they approach a dog yaps. It is not the full-throated bark of the talbots that used to run here, but something smaller and a moment later a terrier comes racing through the gateway to the yard and stands before them, yapping fiercely, tongue very pink, eyes very black. Robert swings his stick good-naturedly at the dog and mutters some soothing words. A moment later she hears Sir John's voice raised in question. Thomas gives her one last nod as she swallows, pulls her brigandine down and her hose up, exaggerating the empty codpiece, and steps forward.

Sir John is sitting in the last golden beam of the afternoon sunlight, on a log by the step on which they used to sharpen knives. Opposite is a woman in a green dress, likewise on a log, and they are both drinking from mugs and looking up from a chessboard. There is a long moment of silence while the old man holds Katherine's gaze. She feels her bowels liquefy, and tears spring in her eyes. She wants to turn and run. This was a mistake.

'John,' the woman says, 'who are these men?'

Sir John's mouth opens slack, his face is wiped clean, all expression erased by shock. For a moment he says and does nothing, then he whispers: 'By all the saints.'

'Sir John,' Katherine starts, a lump in her throat, tears in her eyes. 'I am sorry—'

'By all the saints,' he repeats. 'It is you. And you. Dear God. Kit. Thomas. I— Dear God.'

He stands. He seems uncertain on his feet, lost, clumsy, like her idea of a bear. His teary gaze is fixed on her, then switches to Thomas, then comes back, and she in her turn shifts from foot to foot, and she wishes she could turn and run, but equally she cannot help but grin, and tears tremble on her lids, then spill down her cheeks and then Sir John gives a whoop of delight.

'Dear God,' he calls. 'Dear Blessed God above! It is you. You! Back from the dead! Dear God. And Thomas! Oh, my boys. I never thought – oh, to see you again. I thought they'd rolled you in some hole in Wales, with Walter and those Welsh lads. And you! We were sure you were dead at Towton!'

Tears leak into the deep creases in his face and drops gather in his newly trimmed beard and now he stumbles forward and envelops Katherine in his right arm and Thomas in his left and he pulls them as tight as an old man can and he smells of some sweet herb and now all three have their arms around one another and all three are weeping uncontrollably.

At last Sir John pulls away. He holds her by the shoulders at arm's length and looks down at her and he is snivelling, but then a frown flickers across his brow.

'What in God's name is this?'

He slaps her chest with the back of his fingers. She flinches and now, dear God, she feels as if she might burn up with shame, but then Sir John's face wrinkles into a laugh.

'A brigandine!' he shouts. 'A brigandine! Great suffering Christ, boy! You've still no beard yet here you are strutting around like a fighting cock!'

Sir John looks over at the woman who stands with her hands clasped at her broad waist, a rosary looped over her belt, and a length of linen wound around her head to form a headdress.

'Isabella!' he calls. 'Isabella! This is Kit, this little one here, and this is Thomas, this big lunk here.'

He thumps Thomas on the shoulder and then frowns again.

'Who are you?'

Thomas introduces Robert.

'May God bring you joy, sir,' Robert says.

'He already has!' Sir John says with a great, shining smile. 'Look! This is my wife. Isabella. My *wife*, do you hear?'

He beams at her, and then at them, plump with pride, and she is smiling patiently at him. She is uncertain of their social rank, and so smiles at them all but makes no move toward them, and why should she, since they appear as beggars, and it is only because of her husband's reaction to their presence that she looks at them twice.

'I have told you about them!' Sir John presses on. 'Do you recall? About our time in Calais? How this one saved first young Richard when he was caught by an arrow, and then how he cut me? I have even tried to show you the – but anyway! Here they are. Alive. Solid in flesh, though dear God, look at them! In parlous circumstance, just as ever they were. Look at you. Filthy as crows. And what in God's name has happened to your hair? Did you cut it yourself? By Christ, I shall love to hear how it has come to pass this time!'

'Sir John,' Katherine says, 'we are mortally hungry. Is there anything we might eat before we tell all?'

Sir John defers to Isabella. She smiles.

'We have some capons,' she says, 'and some pike. Peasecod too. Plenty of ale still, and even some red wine from Gascony.'

'From Gascony!' Sir John echoes, sitting back on his log, rubbing his hands and rolling his eyes. Katherine's mouth floods at the thought of meat. Isabella then retreats to the house, calling for someone as she goes.

'Is she not wonderful?' Sir John says, watching her back as she departs. Then he lowers his voice. 'She is old Freylin's widow, you know. We were married after the Annunciation this last year – sudden you might call it, yes, but I tell you. It was meant to be. And she is rich! As Croesus! Freylin left her manors all over the county – and look.'

He holds out his legs to show them his fine shoes, wiggling their strikingly long toes and laughing delightedly.

'Nor,' he adds conspiratorially, grinning and shooting his eyebrows up and down a couple of times, 'is she unduly observant of feast days after curfew!'

It is astonishingly good to see the old man so happy and well, and the wine is brought by a girl whom Sir John calls Meg and they sit and drink while Sir John laughs and promises them he has had Mass said for their mortal souls, pointlessly as it turns out, and how he has given some of Isabella's money for the painting of a figure of St Christopher in the church and how he and Isabella often walk down there to look at it for luck and he burbles on about the estate and how if it were not for having to keep terriers rather than decent dogs, such as the talbots he loved so, then he might come to believe that he was living in an earthly paradise.

'But sir,' Katherine says, 'what of Richard? Where is he? We had hoped to find him here.'

Sir John stops his laughter and stares at her. Thomas shakes his head minutely, regretfully, as if he already knows more than her, and she wonders what she has done wrong.

'You never did like passing time much, did you, Kit?' Sir John says.

She thinks that if that is all it is, changing the tenor of an evening, then she does not mind so very much, but now Sir John hunches forward, spreading his legs and peering at the ground between his feet.

'Richard is in London,' he says. 'With his surgeon, named

Mayhew. They are seeking help in the matter of his wife – you remember her, don't you? Margaret? Whom you brought back from Wales? Well, she has got herself caught up in – in something. She is something of a leech, this Margaret. A surgeon more like, with a gift almost as great as yours, Kit. She even saved my life after Towton Field.'

He removes his cap, and points to a bald patch the size of a crab apple within which sits a circular worm of livid scar tissue. Katherine cannot help her hands coming up as if to touch it. She resists.

'A tonsure almost as good as yours, eh, Canon?' Sir John laughs before restoring the cap. Robert smiles, but says nothing. He is a comforting presence, like a large dog, happy to sit and listen, just to be with them.

'Anyway,' Sir John continues. 'This last year Margaret cut a woman who was dying in childbed. She saved the child, something of a miracle apparently, but not the woman. So there had to be an inquest, of course. We told her she must seek someone of influence to let the coroner know where his best interests lay, but she is stubborn, this Margaret – even Richard says as much, though he is still so smitten with the girl to find it charming. Anyway, she did not follow our advice. And Richard could do nothing since he is a blind man. Did you know?'

Katherine nods.

'Yes,' Sir John continues. 'So the inquest came and she was caught out. Some other fellow swayed the jury. Packed it, or bribed it, I don't know. So the coroner found the thing – the intervention, the what-have-you, the cutting – to be murder and so they bound her over. She's languishing in some closed convent, some blessed hole in that part of the county, waiting on the King's Justices to troop along and try her case.'

'And who is Richard petitioning for her release?' she asks.

'William Hastings. You remember him? He saved you being hanged that time, the time you had your ear clipped. A good man,

Hastings, but busy. He has gone up in the world, like the lark, by God, almost beyond measure. He is Chamberlain to the King, can you believe it?'

At that moment Thomas looks up and glances beyond Katherine.

'Tell us about it again, Kit,' he says, a little too loudly. 'Tell us how it came about,' and she glances around, sees Isabella standing staring at her, and understands, and she tells them the story of how she tried to run from the Earl of Warwick's camp that time they came from Calais, and how the Earl's men caught her and how the Earl wanted her hanged as an example to others thinking of deserting.

'That's right!' Sir John laughs. 'And Lord Hastings – as he is now – he saved the day! Got the sentence changed to the clipping of Kit's ear, and no one wanted to do it, so Tom here, he did it. With hot shears! I remember. Ooof.'

Thomas rolls his eyes and shrugs as if to say, well, any man would do the same, and then Katherine brushes her hair back to reveal what remains of her upper ear.

'That was a close shave!' Sir John barks. 'Too close. Ha ha! Bella, my love, come. Come. Did you hear that? A joke!'

Isabella's gaze remains fixed on Katherine. This is it, Katherine thinks. This is the woman who will find me out. See my secret.

'May I?' Isabella asks. She has a soft, husked voice that is kindly, and she is like someone who laughs a lot, but she is no fool. Katherine can only shrug, and Isabella bends over her, and Katherine can smell the same sweet herbs that perfume Sir John, and she can see the knobbly texture of the linen of Isabella's dress and apron and Katherine's body shrieks and shrinks as Isabella raises her hand and touches her fingers to her ear's tip, but she allows it.

'Does it hurt?' Isabella asks.

'It aches in the cold,' Katherine mutters, brusque with nerves.

'We all ache in the cold!' Sir John laughs. Then: 'Stop fussing,

Bella,' he says, 'and have some more wine. Kit and Thomas can tell us all.'

Isabella will not sit with them, despite Sir John's entreaties, and she leaves them to it, and Katherine is relieved, and now she is able to steer the conversation away from her made-up story – that she was on a boat that got lost at sea, trying to get back from Pembroke, and they sailed to Ireland, where again she became lost – without any difficulty.

'But has Richard sent any news from London?' she asks.

Sir John actually growls.

'By Christ,' he mutters. 'Richard wrote – or rather his man Mayhew did – a few weeks ago to say that the Duke of Somerset is back in the King's grace. Can you believe it? King Edward has *forgiven* the man who killed his father! He has forgiven the man who killed his brother! The man who put their heads on spikes on the gatehouse in York! The Duke of Somerset led King Henry's forces at Northampton, do you remember? And we beat him then, and he led them again at Towton Field, and we beat him then too, but, by God, only just.

'And each time he slipped away. And now the bastard's done it again. He got caught in one of those castles up north, some hole from which not even a practised rat such as he could escape, so he surrendered. And King Edward accepted! If old Warwick had been there, or Montagu, God forbid, or anyone else for that matter, anyone. They'd have chopped his bloody head off. Right there and then.'

He makes a dusty-sounding chopping motion with his hands and imitates the head bouncing twice. 'Bonk bonk.'

He gulps his wine, bangs the cup down, pours more. Thomas fiddles with a chess piece, doesn't look up. Katherine is suddenly certain Sir John knows nothing of the return of Edmund Riven.

'But not King Edward,' Sir John resumes. 'No. In fact, not only has he reversed the death sentence he passed on the Duke of

Somerset, not only has he restored all his divers lands and titles, he's even – and you will not credit this – he's even taken him as a gentleman of the bedchamber!'

Thomas and Robert look blank. Katherine is likewise in the dark.

'He sleeps with him in the same bed!' Sir John tells them. 'In the same bloody bed! Naked! With neither knife nor sword! King Edward and the Duke of Somerset! King Edward's father killed the Duke's father, and the Duke killed King Edward's father, and now they lie, like that!'

Isabella returns, moving quick and soft. She sits beside Sir John and places a soothing hand on his forearm, and he places his hand on hers.

'He who covers over a transgression seeks only love,' Robert says.

There is general silence for a moment. Sir John looks at him balefully, but Isabella smiles.

'Amen,' she says.

'I know,' Sir John says. 'I know. I know. I know you are right. But I lost friends, and men I admired, and men whose families needed them. Don't you see? All this – this – this pissing about that men such as Edward of York and the Duke of bloody Somerset do – it doesn't affect them as it affects the rest of us.'

Having explained himself, he is calmer, but Katherine needs to know:

'Richard has said nothing of – nothing of Edmund Riven?'

Isabella is suddenly still, wholly alert, head cocked, eyes as wide as pennies: a deer sensing a hunter.

'Dear God,' Sir John whispers, 'that is a name I hoped never again to hear at this table.'

There is a long moment of silence, then:

'What of him?' Sir John asks.

'We heard that he too is – he is back,' Thomas says.

'Back?' Sir John asks. 'Back from where? The dead? Giles Riven

is dead. His family is attainted. There is no way back for him, unless
– what do you know? Why do you say that?'

Katherine hesitates a moment.

Then she says: 'It is Edmund Riven The son. He has come back
with the Duke of Somerset. He has taken the castle at Cornford.'

For a moment Sir John is silent and still. Then he erupts. With
a sweep of his arm, he clears the board of chess pieces and mugs
and the ewer, sending them bouncing over the ground. The little
dog that had settled by his wife's feet is up and yapping and now
all are standing and Sir John is bawling and Isabella is trying to calm
him until Robert steps in and takes Sir John by the shoulders and
holds him steady and starts talking softly to him. After a few long
moments when it seems Sir John remains looking for something to
kill, he calms slightly, and is left breathing heavily, his eyes rolling
and flecks of foam around his mouth.

Isabella takes him in her arms and guides him inside.

Thomas and Katherine bend to pick up the mugs and the chess
pieces. For a moment they cannot find the black king, but then there
it is, lying on its side.

Later, when they are in the hall by the fire, and the bones of the
birds and the fish lie picked on the board, Sir John comes down
again, this time without Isabella, and he sits where he always used
to sit. He looks much older than when they saw him first that
afternoon, she thinks, and he has lost something too; that sheen of
new-found happiness, and she feels shame, and wonders if he'd have
preferred to live in ignorance. Then again, though, someone would
have told him. The old man does not say anything for a moment,
but sits and stares into the flames. Then he stretches a hand to pick
up one of the chess pieces they've brought in: it is the white king.
He begins in a low voice:

'I don't mind that they did this to me,' he says, pointing at his
head. 'I don't mind that they took the castle that should have been

my son's. I don't mind that I have spent my dotage flogging around the country looking for him so that I could see justice done. I really don't. But what I do mind, though, what I really do mind, is that he stole my house. What I really do mind is that he killed so many of those for whom I cared, and what I really, really do mind is that he blinded my son. My only son! That I do mind. That I do mind, do you hear?'

Thomas and Katherine can only nod. It hardly matters that it was the father not the son who blinded Richard.

'So I cannot let this lie,' Sir John continues. 'I cannot just lie back and assume this is some piece of divine providence. My wife says that those whom He loves, He first purifies in the flames of suffering, and I have to allow that this may or may not be true, but I am not so vain as to believe it is all done for me, do you see? I cannot believe that bastard Riven, or his whelp, is God's chosen instrument. I can't believe that family were sent here just to test me and mine, to forge us like bloody arrowheads in the fire, just to make sure we are worthy of our place in the Kingdom of Heaven. I do not think it is like that.'

Now Robert nods approvingly.

'So I am not going to prove myself the saint. I am not going to endure. I am going to get up. I am going to rise up, and crush his serpent's head under my heel, do you hear? I will crush every member of his family, so that the name Riven is extinguished throughout all eternity. Do you hear?'

144

10

Thomas does not know what is wrong with him. He does not know what has happened. He sometimes looks at her and he feels the blood rise to his cheeks, his chest tighten and, worse, most shaming, he gets erections to fill his codpiece and force him to sit for a while. They come all the time, triggered by anything: the sound of her voice, a glimpse of her skin, her smell, her smile. It is worst at night, of course, when she sleeps next to him by the ticking dome of the fire cover, and the sound of her breathing can be drowned out by the noise of his heart beating in his ears.

He cannot recall if it was always like this, if he felt these things before he went away. He thinks not. He thinks back to the moment he saw her in the stable that night and he remembers his feeling for her was – what? Whatever it was, it was not this. It did not involve his loins. It involved his heart.

And now this. If she touches him, however slightly, however accidentally, her heel slipping from one mattress to cross to touch his shin, say, he experiences a jolt through his body that will keep him awake for hours. He cannot help but sigh then, and, turning on his mattress and sighing again and again, he will not rest until she is finally woken, and she will sometimes ask him what's wrong, and he will tell her that nothing's wrong, and sometimes she will murmur something and extend what she supposes is a comforting hand and place it on his shoulder, say, and he will lie with his breath stilled and his heart booming in the darkness, willing her to move her hand and place it elsewhere on his body. Eventually his stirrings will disturb her so much and she will remove her hand and then in an ecstasy of frustration, he will get up and go out into the yard, ignoring the yapping of Isabella's terrier in the room upstairs, ignoring the dark, and he will stand as still as he can and let the night's cold seep into his bones and he will try to reconstruct exactly what the Prior used to say when he lectured the novices about the fruitless spilling of seed.

But by Christ, it is difficult.

He wonders if it would be easier if Katherine were known to be a woman? Would he simply do as he supposes other men do, and ask her to come and lie with him in the woods? He thinks about his brother and his Elizabeth, since that is the only example of courtship he has known unfold. How did his brother get her to marry him? He asked her, he supposes, or perhaps their parents asked hers, before their fathers went off to France, and then, when they were man and wife – well, those two boys, Adam and William, they had to come from somewhere, didn't they?

He cannot ask Katherine to marry him. And by Christ! Even if he could, even if it could be known that she was not Kit but Katherine, and even if she would ever want to marry him in return, she would have to say no, because she was already married. To Richard Fakenham.

He sometimes groans so loudly, standing there under the eaves of the hall, that the dog wakes again and takes up his yapping and in the morning Sir John is bad-tempered and worries about intruders in the night and he suggests posting a nightwatchman and getting in geese, even though he hates them, though they do taste good, and the fat is useful for salves and what-have-you, but do they really need one?

He and Katherine have been at Marton Hall for three months and now it is the week after the Assumption, in the middle of August. In that time they have been fed and reclothed, and they have helped harvest the pea crop, wash and shear the sheep, even start on a new, larger sty for the greater number of pigs that have been bred. Katherine has had to tell the story of her missing months three or four times, each version closely questioned by Isabella, who has also inspected Thomas's own wound as if she does not believe it to be real.

Sir John has been preoccupied. He has sent messages to Richard in London and he has received some back, written by Mayhew, and each time he receives one he reads it aloud and it puts him in such a foul temper that Isabella must spirit him away upstairs and he will only emerge the next day, or the one after that.

'It is because there is nothing he can do,' Katherine says. 'He feels impotent.'

And Thomas strangles a laugh.

When they have not been earning their keep on the farm, he has been practising with a bow, trying to build up those lost muscles, rediscover that technique, but he is also trying to tire himself out.

'Have to get you a proper bow,' Sir John says. 'You can let Robert have that one.'

Then we will have a company of two, Thomas thinks. Since the night he proclaimed his desire to kill Edmund Riven, Sir John has apparently heeded Isabella's caution against action, but the old man is impatient for news, and every day he is out there, glumly pacing the boundary, ready to intercept any message that comes from his son Richard in London. What piece of information is he waiting for? Thomas wonders. He cannot decide whether Isabella is being cautious because she doesn't want Sir John to stick his staff in a wasps' nest, or whether she is more sophisticated than that, as Katherine suggests, and knows there is more than one way to skin a cat.

And in the meantime he and Katherine have made journeys through the country around Marton Hall, looking for Stephen, the eel catcher.

'Why are you so keen to track him down?' Thomas asks, and as the words come out of his mouth he thinks they sound churlish, and he worries that she will think him jealous, and then he thinks how foolish that is because she does not know how he feels about her, so why would she possibly think him jealous? She might just as well think him hungry, or tired.

'It is not Stephen,' she tells him. 'Or perhaps it is, a little, since he was a good worker, but it is the baby, really.'

He tries to imagine what it must have been like, cutting open the woman's belly and plucking out the child. He cannot. Or not accurately. And he is relieved.

They try other villages, in case any there have heard of Stephen, and discover nothing, and then they try further afield, and on these trips Thomas's mind is at its most active, as if the sights he sees set his mind refilling with memories of his childhood and of his brother, and his father going off to France. He recalls his first days at the priory; a year when the waters were so high the crypt flooded to the brim and the coffins rose and tapped against the floor of the nave above. He recalls his early lessons in dull lettering and subsequent discovery of his gift for embellishing the plain page with painted images of animals, plants and even insects. He remembers taking up the feather and he looks at his hands sometimes, half-expecting to see them ink- or paint-stained and is sometimes mystified to find them so broad, calloused and thick with muscle. He buys some paper from a man in Gainsborough and some thin oak-gall ink from a couple of boys who'd made it themselves and weren't very good at it yet, and he cuts himself a simple feather brush, and he begins the faint design of a snail with a striking shell. He tries to hide it when Katherine sees it, he does not know why, but when she does, she smiles at him and he feels the familiar lurch.

It is on their way back from one of their ventures north that they walk through a hamlet Thomas thinks perhaps is familiar.

'This is where Little John Willingham lived,' she tells him. 'He

148

is the only one of Sir John's company that I do not know for certain to be dead.'

And sure enough, there he is, Little John Willingham, outside his family's cot, clutching a bill, back from laying a hedge perhaps, arguing with an old lady who can only be his mother, and when he sees Thomas and Katherine, he flinches and crosses himself as if they might be ghosts, but then when he has accepted that they are mortals, and still alive, and when he has greeted them with a shout of laughter, there is something odd about him. He is thin-faced and pale, with purple-shaded half-circles cupping his eyes. He is twitchy and restless but when they tell him they are looking for a fellow called Stephen, he is grateful, relieved.

'I thought it was because of what'd happened up north,' Little John admits. 'When you came along the road and I saw you, I thought, here we go, they've heard, and they've come for me.'

Neither Katherine nor Thomas knows what he means.

'Perhaps that is just as well,' he says, but she can see he wants to tell them, to confess something.

'What? What is just as well?'

'It is just that I was – I was at Towton Field,' he mutters.

'You were? But with who? Whose company?'

There is a long pause. Little John looks left and right, up and down, but there is no escape. He is skewered.

'Giles Riven,' he admits.

Now neither Thomas nor Katherine knows what to say.

'It was – it was after. Well, I thought Sir John was dead. I thought you were all dead. It is what I'd heard. What they told me. They said he was dead and so was everyone else.'

'So you thought you'd join them?' Katherine asks.

'It wasn't like that. I – it was because I'd been with Sir John in the summer, hadn't I? The wheat here was all rotted – it wasn't brought in properly. The barley was damp, the hay was damp. The ox died too. Everything was fucked.'

He jerks his thumb over his shoulder at his mother, smaller than him, with a bent back, in ragged skirts and bare feet.

'So Giles Riven needed more men,' Little John is saying, 'and was offering sixpence a day for archers who'd wear his livery. He needed to replace some who'd been killed. I thought at Wakefield, but it was all over the place, it turned out, and some of them by Sir John. Anyway. He needed more if he was to meet his obligation to the Duke of Somerset, who was his lord. You know how it is. So I went along. I could hardly say no. I'd no money, no food, and ten or fifteen men with swords and sallets, standing where the mint grows.'

He nods to the front of the cot.

'I had to go,' he assures himself. 'They'd have killed me if not.'

Katherine and Thomas both nod.

'What was it like?' Thomas asks.

'It was – well, we went north from here, over to Doncaster, you know, then south. It was mad. All sorts of us, not all there for the fighting. Scotsmen, some of them. The sort to steal what they could and murder them who'd lost it. Riven's company were better than most. Englishmen, in the main, though they had that Irish giant who was no better than an animal. A dog. Slept where he fell, took food from other men's bowls. Least I think he was Irish. He said nothing ever, and – he carried your pollaxe, Thomas. That was why I thought you were dead. Knew you'd never give that up if you weren't.'

Thomas knows nothing of any pollaxe.

'Anyway. Riven didn't want any of us going off with what we'd found or stolen, and he didn't want anyone to get themselves killed over a pig or what-have-you, so that he'd have to come to the Duke short-handed, so he kept us tight. Kept us in food. Firewood. Women, even. Well, one.'

He winces with remorse, remembering her.

'And so we went down towards London all together, but the Earl of Warwick, you remember him? He came out and lined his men up against us. Outside a place called St Albans, just a bit away from London. Well, it was madness. No one knew what was going on. We thought the bastard was luring us into a trap, and that he had some secret force hidden away in a wood like, and that he was a genius, but it wasn't that. It was – he was – he was just looking the wrong way, wasn't he? And all his archers were in one place, the wrong place as it turned out, and all his men at arms were in another, likewise wrong. Anyway. Anyway. Each time I loosed an arrow I said to myself, that's for Kit's ear, you bastards.'

He smiles uncertainly, and he wants to please, but it grates a bit, Thomas thinks.

'And after that – well. We sent them packing. Bloody hell. It was – odd. They ran. Thousands of 'em, and they left the King – King Henry I should say – just sitting there, under a tree. So we all thought, well, that's that then. We can go to London and have a fine old time. Only of course they wouldn't open the gates, would they? So we hung around for a while, but we were running out of food, and all the Scots had pissed off with what they'd manage to thieve, so we came back. Up here. We had to move pretty quick because there was nothing left to eat by now and the land we were going through was the same as what we'd come through, so it was – you know.'

He gestures to show it was hopeless. Katherine nods. Little John's dark eyes are more evasive than ever now and he swallows hard and rubs his bristled jaw and looks around as if for something to drink.

'And then that day outside Towton,' he says.

'We were there,' Katherine says. 'Though Thomas can recall nothing of it.'

'Oh,' Little John says. 'Why is that?'

Thomas removes his cap and indicates the white fob of hair at his temple.

'I was knocked out of my wits,' he tells Little John.

'And you remember nothing of it? By Christ, Thomas, you are

a lucky man. What I would give to forget that day. By all the saints and martyrs, yes. I would give anything.'

There is a long pause. Little John looks harrowed.

'How did you live through it?' Katherine asks.

He shrugs.

'God knows,' he says, and he seems to want to leave it at that, but Katherine presses. Little John relents.

'We were in the front,' he says, 'lined up and ready, forty-eight arrows apiece, in formation, ready to do our worst, only then the wind changed, didn't it? And your volleys hit us first, carried by the wind, and before I'd loosed one shaft, I got hit, on the sallet.'

He bangs his fingertips on his cap.

'It knocked me right over. Not like you, Thomas, not so that I forgot everything, but I was flat on my back in the snow, blood streaming down my face and then the next moment some great big bastard fell on me with an arrow in his face. He'd been standing in front, and the arrow turned him right around, span him, bang, just like that.'

He slaps his hands together.

'The shaft went right through his chin and into his neck and he came down on top of me like a sack of something awful. We were eyeball to eyeball, me and this dead man, with the fletching in my ear and his and my blood mixing everywhere. But by now the arrows were coming in, weren't they? They made the sky dark. My God. You've never seen anything like it, to be under them when they land. Each one like a smith's blow, but fast as raindrops in a summer storm. As many as that. And you know how much armour we had – just sallets and jacks – and after a minute I could see all the others were being killed and those that weren't were trying to turn and get out of range, but the men behind couldn't move to let them through and the arrows kept coming. They always say it is like a cloud, an arrow storm or whatever, but it was like night. Dusk anyway. And they just kept coming. Everyone was crying out and trying to run but there was nothing we could do. And the noise! Christ alive.

'I huddled under that bloke, I tell you. His blood was all warm all over me, and he'd shat himself and pissed himself, but I didn't care. I buried myself under him. He was like a pavise, you know? Those massive shields those bloody crossbowmen use. I thanked St George for making this bastard so big. The bloody arrows kept coming and one went straight through him and caught in my sleeve, just here.'

He rolls back his sleeve to show them a slip of polished grey flesh that has hardened on his pale forearm.

'And then they started sending our own arrows back. I could see them in the ground and the bodies next to me, with their fletchings all fucked, and they made those sounds as they landed. So I could see they'd run out of their own shafts, and then, finally, the nobs on the Queen's side, the Duke of Somerset it was, finally got the trumpet blown, and all the men-at-arms came down the hill. They had to scramble through all the – all of us, lying around, crying, screaming. Blood was everywhere. It was drizzling blood! The snow-flakes were red with it. I'll never forget it. Never. As long as I live.

'I lay there, praying to God no one would notice me. No one would get me up and try to send me to do anything. I think I'd shat myself too, by then, but who cared? We'd all done it. Or pissed ourselves. And then a bit later, the heralds and the priests and the fucking cutpurses came and one of them tried to steal my fucking bow. I lashed out. Kicked him. And the fucker stood on the dead bloke and tried to drown me or crush me or I don't fucking know what.

'A grey friar pulled him off, thank the Lord. Told him there would be richer pickings later, elsewhere, if he would only let this humble fucking archer – me – live. I am grateful to him, whoever he was. He saved my life, dragged the dead bloke off me, and got his robes covered in blood and whatnot for it. When I was up I saw the ground started steaming with all the blood on it. You couldn't help breathe it in. Christ on his Cross, I must have ale.'

He fetches a wooden ewer and pours himself a beaker and drinks it off as if to wash his mouth out before offering them anything. Thomas accepts the cup, and lets Little John pour him some and then drinks it. It is thin and bitter.

'There was nothing I could do after that,' Little John admits. 'Archers weren't what was wanted, especially one with my arm like this. I stayed with the ale wagons and then I even helped some friars with the wounded, though all we were doing was taking them from one place where they might have died and putting them in another place where they did die. It was as if they were tidying up, really, that was all.'

He takes another vast swig of ale and doesn't bother to wipe his mouth afterwards. The words bubble out.

'By midday we were sure we were going to win, and I was thinking that if only Riven survives, I'll be all right. I'll win my share and I can come back home – come here – a rich man, and I can forget about all this shit. The snow slowed around that time, and you could see how far the King's army had advanced, and all the bodies that were in mounds, piled up everywhere across the field and I thought, bloody hell, there can't be many more men left in England who aren't dead or fighting for us, on our side. And then someone said Edward of March was dead, and there was such a cheer, only then it was proved untrue, and then someone said Trollope was dead, and I cheered inside for that, because do you remember? He was the bastard that switched sides before we went to Calais. Or maybe that was before you came to us. Anyway.'

A donkey brays somewhere unseen.

'Then the Duke of Norfolk's men arrived, just before dusk, and that tipped the thing the other way, didn't it? You could feel it, right from where we were, and suddenly the ale carts were spilling their ale and whipping their oxen to get away, just as if they knew it had

154

already been lost, and they would be too, if they weren't gone soonest. I climbed up on the back of them. I hid in a barrel. Benefits of being small. By the time they found me it was too late. They threw me out on the roadside, but by then the nobs were coming past on horseback. Flying up the road to York, all their weapons and harness gone, horses all mad-eyed, frothing and sweating even in the snow.

'I ran along as best I could, but then there was a river, and turned downstream. I thought if I could find a boat, anything, then I'd be all right. And I did. A little thing. I stole it. Just pushed off into the river and prayed to God to get away before Edward's men came through, or any of ours too. They were killing each other just to get past. Anyway. I fell asleep in the boat, as God is my witness, despite my fright and the cold, and by the time I woke up I was – well. I don't know. West of York, on a gravel bank being watched by two boys and a dog and – well, that was the end of it, really. I got out, staggered on to dry land and slept where I was, and in the morning I could hardly move, my clothes were that stiff with blood.'

There is a long silence. Little John is done, exhausted by the reliving of that day, and he does not ask after them. He is not interested where they have been or how they survived their day. Having spoken for so long he wants nothing but silence.

'Will you come back?' Katherine asks.

Little John starts as if he has forgotten who they are. Only then does he ask after Sir John and the men he's known. When he hears who is alive and who is dead, he is caught between sorrow and relief.

'Is Riven looking for you?' Katherine asks.

Little John is startled.

'I don't know. Is he even alive? Did he live through the day?'

'No one knows,' Katherine says. 'But the boy is.'

Little John is frightened.

'Edmund?' he asks. 'Edmund Riven's alive?'

Katherine nods.

'Oh, good God,' he says, and he might almost cross himself.

'So will you come with us? Rejoin Sir John Fakenham's company?'

'And go against Edmund Riven? No. No. Not likely. Not a chance. I need to be here with my old mum.'

Thomas is dismayed.

'Is he so bad?'

'He is a devil in human form. He has a wound here –' he points to his eye – 'that has not healed and yellow stuff comes from it, with blood in it, and the smell is enough to curdle milk, I swear. It makes you retch. He wipes it with a cloth and the smell clings and even pigs stay away.'

John almost gags at the memory of it.

'And all he talks of is of cutting men – of blinding them, like he is in that eye – and of raping women.'

He shakes his head.

'I am sorry,' he says, 'I will not go against him, not unless there are many of us. He is a vicious bastard.'

When they get back to Marton Hall it is late afternoon and Sir John is out in the yard with Robert. Sir John has a pair of curious brass eyeglasses on his nose, and another letter from Richard in his hand, delivered by the same merchant who then sold him the eyeglasses.

'He also deals in divers objects that he claims to be rich in natural magic,' Isabella tells them, and she nods at a small grey stone lying among the pieces of the chessboard. It is unpolished, the size of the ball of a man's thumb, and pierced with a hole through which someone has thread a loop of bowstring.

'It cost a groat,' she says through pursed lips.

Sir John is looking equally wintry, and he raises the letter.

'It is confirmed,' he says. 'Cornford is to be given to that bastard Riven. The son, that is, as you say, Kit, the boy without the eye. Richard says there has been some initial ruling in council. Lord Hastings is trying his best to overturn it, he has told Richard, but he is gloomy about his chances because King Edward is still warm with the Duke of Somerset, and Somerset is still warm with Edmund Riven. The Duke of Somerset has asserted that with Margaret accused of murder, and Richard a blind man, natural justice should run its course, and the castle and its lands should revert to Riven. Natural bloody justice. By the blood of the risen Christ, what does the bloody Duke of Somerset know of natural bloody justice? If he did he'd have hanged himself long ago, and taken that bastard Riven with him.'

Sir John crumples the letter and throws it towards the fire.

'There is one last, final chance, Richard thinks, and then –'

He makes a pffft noise. There is a long silence.

'What actually is that?' Thomas asks. He points to the stone on the chessboard. Isabella sighs.

'To me it is a wasted groat,' she says, 'but to the pedlar it is a lodestone.'

Sir John picks it up and holds it near Isabella's belt buckle. It swings on its lace and clacks against the metal. Sir John's smile is distracted.

'What's it for?' Katherine asks.

'You tell me,' Isabella murmurs. She plucks it from her belt and then holds it near one of the eating knives. The knife moves of its own accord.

'It seeks out certain metals,' Sir Johns says. 'Attracts them, you see, but the pedlar said it is helpful for finding your way. Something about the North Star and not getting lost at sea.'

Sir John looks at Katherine, and almost laughs.

'You should have it, Kit,' he says. 'Save you getting lost again.'

He passes it to her. She blushes slightly, probably remembering her slim story of being lost in the Irish Sea, and thanks him for it.

'Put it around your neck,' he says, 'and that way you won't lose it.'

Again she thanks him. It is not something she really wants,

Thomas can see that, but it would be wrong to refuse a gift, and she hangs it around her neck and tucks it into her shirt. Thomas cannot stop himself imagining it hanging between her flattened breasts. He tries to think of something else, anything else.

They slump back into a long strained silence that Sir John breaks by swearing at Riven again, and at the Duke of Somerset, and at King Edward for being such a fool.

'When you think of all we've done for him. All the blood we've spilled.'

'There must be some other way,' Katherine says.

Sir John turns to her.

'You were always convinced the wars would start again, Kit,' he says. 'And you were right, weren't you? On more than one occasion, too. But will they come again? Will we have another chance to shake all this up and unseat Riven?'

He gestures at the chessboard where just the two kings and a handful of other pieces remain.

'I know nothing of them now,' she admits.

There is another long, disappointed silence. Sir John sighs and begins toying with the chess pieces, clearing them to leave the two kings at opposite ends of the board. He sits back and studies them with a curled lip.

'Kings,' he says. 'Kings and bloody dukes.'

Thomas leans forward and picks up a piece from the discarded pile.

'Perhaps the Duke of Somerset will prove a false friend to King Edward?' he says, and he places a black knight next to the black king. 'Perhaps he will turn back to King Henry?'

'But why would he,' Sir John asks, 'when King Edward is all-powerful?'

And he returns some white pieces to the board, so that they outnumber the two black pieces five to one, and then he moves the black knight that had been under the black king to a square next to the white king, and he turns it so that the horse's teeth face the black king.

'And,' he adds, 'when all that remains of King Henry's army is banged up in a couple of useless castles up north?'

He places two black rooks on the board, on the black king's side. They all stare at the board as if it will reveal the answer. It does not.

'So if there is no chance of separating the Duke of Somerset's loyalties from King Edward,' Katherine ventures, touching the black knight and the white king, 'is there a way to separate them from Edmund Riven?'

She places a black pawn on the board, next to the black knight, and then draws it away. There is another silence, but one by one they shake their heads.

'I do not see how,' Sir John says.

'If you cannot separate this Riven from the Duke of Somerset and you cannot separate the Duke of Somerset from King Edward,' Robert says, bunching the black pawn and the black knight under the shadow of the white king, 'then you must either suffer in silence, or —'

And he moves a white knight from the white side of the board toward the black side, and he turns it to face the white king.

'Or King Edward becomes your enemy, and King Henry becomes your friend.'

There is another long silence. They can hear Sir John breathing noisily.

'I remember Richard suggesting the same,' Katherine says, 'when the Earl of Warwick awarded the castle to Riven after Northampton. You said you would not change sides. You said you would not turn traitor.'

There is another long silence, and all eyes are on Sir John, to see whether he moves the white knight back toward the white king, and he stretches his hand, and his trembling fingers hover over the piece, and he tries to draw his hand away without touching it, but in the end, he cannot. He moves the knight back.

'I have bled so freely for the House of York,' he says, 'that to turn my back on her now, it seems a betrayal not just of them, of King Edward, but of those I've lost in her service – of Walter, of Geoffrey, of all those bloody Johns. I cannot just switch in a moment of rage, however gross the provocation. So let us see. Let us wait to see if this last appeal to King Edward's good sense brings us Cornford Castle, and Margaret's freedom, and Richard's return. We should pray for those things, and if our prayers are not answered, then we shall have to think again.'

And with that he tidies the chess pieces away, and curfew is called.

11

The haymaking involves eight of them, working with whetted scythes in a staggered line across the field. Thomas is strongest, and goes first, on the right-hand end of the line, then Robert, to the left, and a little behind him. Katherine starts on the extreme left of the line, since it is thought she is the slightest of them all, but she is faster and stronger than she looks, thanks to her months with the washing beetle, and as the morning progresses, she is moved up the line, until she is to the left of Robert. When the first field is done, they sit in the shade of an ash tree on fat stooks and drink ale, and Robert tells them they must stretch or they will be stiff from the unusual strain that the scythes put on a man's muscles.

Later she walks with Thomas down to the river, and they follow a stony path worn by horses along the river's bank, and she thinks they have some of their old ease back again, and are walking as they did before that last terrible winter. Thomas seems less fraught than he was, she thinks, less pent up. Perhaps it is something seasonal? She wonders at him though. The way he gets up in the middle of the night and returns chilled to the bone. If she is awake she will ask him where he has been and he will tell her he has been outside, but his voice will be whispery, as if he is sad, and he will turn his back on her and that will be that. She remembers him pressing himself against her that night in the barn, and once when he got up in the night, she rose and followed him, thinking perhaps he was going to see one of Sir John's serving girls, and she felt a terrible stab of jealousy, and she thought she might scream if it were true, but no. It was not that. Instead he stood under the eaves in the moonlight, so tense and still it was as if he were waiting for a fox to pass. She supposes it is something to do with his memories fleeting, returning to him in dreams, and sometimes she tries to calm him with a touch, but that only seems to make things worse, and she can feel him lying there like a strung bow, vibrating and so hot under her fingertips she has to withdraw her hand. Though it will be useful in the winter, she supposes.

'Richard will come from London soon,' he says.

She supposes he is right, but she does not want to think about Richard. She is just enjoying being with Thomas, when he is happy, and she had supposed he was enjoying it too.

'What will you do then?' he presses. 'When he comes? Will you go to him?'

She sighs. She has been putting off thinking about this for as long as possible, but now Thomas seems determined to be unhappy, and to make her so too.

'I don't know,' she says. 'You know that. I suppose – I suppose I will have to go. I cannot stay and be his wife again.'

'Sir John says Richard is still smitten with you.'

'Yes,' she agrees, 'but he is smitten with Margaret Cornford, who was his wife, not with me.'

'But you are his wife,' he says.

'Am I?' she asks. 'Yes. I suppose I am. But Thomas, it is as I say – I don't know. I don't know what to do. None of this was— Well, I did not plan it.'

She sighs. She knows flight is the only option. To this end she has been saving money, tiny amounts, a halfpenny here and a halfpenny there, driving a harder bargain at the market than needs be, accepting second best from the stallholder and keeping the difference. Isabella has noticed something is not right in the balance of accounts, she is sure of that, but she has said nothing as yet.

She wonders whether Thomas will come with her when she leaves.

Or whether he will stay with Sir John who loves him as a son, and where he is warm and well fed and – except for these odd moods of his – happy.

Suddenly she has to know.

'If I go,' she begins, 'will you come with me?'

He turns on her. He looks haunted by something. Not his usual self.

'Where?' he asks.

'Where? I don't know.'

She can feel herself breathing quickly. She feels hot and very anxious. He takes a solemn step but he says nothing.

'You don't have to,' she says. 'I am sure you have a life planned for yourself here. Without – without all these complications.'

He stops and squints at her.

'What do you mean?'

He is being evasive, deliberately obtuse.

'Forget it,' she says, and she walks on.

He catches her arm. She tears it away.

'Wait!' he says.

'Look, Thomas,' she says, turning back on him. She has no idea what she is going to say. The words tumble out. 'I know I have brought you nothing but trouble. I know without me you would be a – a – a canon, still, happily embellishing your psalter, but I – I – oh, God!'

And now God damn them, the tears fill her eyes and she finds she can hardly breathe and she feels a great heat glowing within her. She cannot bring herself to say that she cannot contemplate life without him by her side. But can she ask him to come with her, to look after her, to keep her from danger as he always has, and in return for what?

He once told her he loved her, but that was then, and this is now, and he is he, and she is she. And that is the problem. She is she.

'I'm so sorry,' she says, sniffing and drawing her sleeve across her mouth.

But now he is looking at her as if she is mad and he steps towards her and envelops her in his arms and she wraps hers around him and she presses her face to his chest and she inhales that dusty smell of his and she can feel his lips pressing on the crown of her cap, and she wishes he would – and then she feels it: the hard knot of him pressing against her and she catches her breath.

She has lain with Richard Fakenham on numerous occasions since the night of their marriage, when she knew what must come, and so forced herself to drink too much wine, and William Hastings was there, among others, and everything seemed preordained. It is to be done like this! Then this will happen, then this. Then the sheet was spread on a broad, feather-filled bed in a private room, something she had never slept in before, and it was sprinkled with holy water and then she was instructed to formally guide Richard to it, but he had had too much wine, too, which one of Hastings's men said was bad for a blind man, especially on his wedding night, and he had made odd, confusing gestures with his hands and fingers, right before her husband's face, so she had closed the door on him and heard him laugh beyond.

What happened then was not as humiliating or unpleasant as she had feared it might be. She undressed and then helped him. He smelled loamy and acidic; not very pleasant, but she imagined she smelled the same. He asked if she wanted to blow out the candle and she did, but not before she had seen his penis protruding from its nest of hair, and seeing it, she had felt not the shrieking revulsion she had thought she might, but the onset of a laugh. So this was what those nuns had spoken about with more reverence and veneration almost than the consecrated body of Christ? This thing?

Richard almost knew what to do. He lay beside her and placed his hand on her pubis, in the wrong place, and then he felt cautiously between her legs. She lay still, her eyes seeing strange shapes in the dark, and he was not so much gentle as tentative and though it was never as pleasurable as Sister Joan suggested it might be, it was not an ordeal. Then when he felt he had done something, or enough of something, though she knew not what, he had clambered on top of her, pressing her into the sheets, his hipbones and frail wand of a penis digging into her body. Then he took some weight on his elbows and he placed his mouth over hers and kept it there, hot and sour, again for what seemed like a pre-planned and requisite length of time – as long as it took to say the Hail Mary, perhaps – and she was sure then that Richard was new to this too, following instructions, or a set of them, as planned as the Mass itself, given to him, she had to assume, by William Hastings. Strange to have him in the room, she thought, almost peering over Richard's shoulder.

Then he shunted her legs apart and after a moment of fumbling – and she unexpectedly knowing to raise her hips and part her knees – there was a sharp jolt of pain, nothing she would care to experience again, but equally, not as painful as a thousand things she had endured, before or since, and he pressed himself into her further, a strange, continually sore experience, a chafing probing sensation, and she felt him breathing very fast and then there was a moment of great tension in the air just above her face, and a grunt and a vast gust of exhaled breath. A moment later his head was on her shoulder and he was murmuring the name Margaret over and over while she laboured to breathe until he rolled off, leaving her with an unknown mess between her legs.

And that was that. Until the next time, the next evening, when the whole thing happened again, though without the solemnity.

It became marginally more enjoyable with the passing of time, but it was never anything akin to the delights the sisters had suggested while they were whispering in the dorter at the priory. It happened quite regularly, and sometimes she looked forward to it, but eventually, after six, seven months perhaps, of him trying to get her with child and her flowering the next month, Richard seemed to turn in on himself, and would rather be left to drink wine than come to bed, and that was the beginning of his decline, and, before all this, she used to worry that it was her fault; that there was something she was not doing, which is why they were not blessed with a child.

Now though, here is Thomas.

She looks up at him through the circle of his arms.

'Thomas?'

And he pulls away, awkwardly with his hips, and drops his arms, and now it is his turn to apologise.

'I am so sorry,' he says. 'I cannot help it. It just happens.'

He is blushing a wonderful colour.

'It is all right, Thomas,' she says. 'I understand.'

'It is just—'

But she does not let go of him. And after a moment, he stoops to kiss her lips. The kiss lasts a moment longer than it might were they friends, and then, finally, an understanding is reached and their hands are on one another and they are pulling at each other's points and laces, while all the time their lips are locked, and both have their eyes open and he is moving her off the path and into the longer grass when the sensation of being touched there by another, sympathetic, hand is too much for him. She sees his eyes widen and roll and he breaks away, gasping as if he is being strangled.

'Thomas!' she says. 'What is it? What's wrong?'

He is shuddering, hardly able to stand upright.

'What is wrong? Christ! Shall I get help?'

'No!' he says. 'No! Just. Just. A moment.'

There is a pause. Then she realises.

'Oh,' she says, and she cannot help but laugh, but she is also, unexpectedly, furious.

'Yes,' he says. 'Sorry. I – well, I am not used to it.'

'I thought you were dying. I thought you had stood on a blade, or one of those caltrops.'

He laughs.

'No, no,' he says. 'It was – God.'

'Let us sit,' she says. She begins to retie her points, hoiking the hose up to lace them to her pourpoint. He does the same. When it is done, she sits on the bank, with her shoes above the sliding brown waters, and she feels a twinge of sorrow. She hardly knows what to say. But he does not seem sad. He sits next to her, closer than he might usually, with his shoulder against hers. She smiles at him. He puts his arm around her. Well, that is nice, she thinks. He laughs.

'Is it always like that?' he asks. 'I mean, does that happen all the time?'

'I don't think so,' she says. 'But perhaps everyone is different?'

He sighs.

'Did you – did you ever . . . with Richard?' he asks.

And she is silent for a moment, sad.

'I did,' she says, after a while. 'I was married to him, so of course we had to.'

'But you never had a child?'

'No,' she says. 'No. I used to wonder why. I used to tell myself that it was because, because it was not right. Because I was not who I said I was, and so God did not smile on us, Richard or me, or bless the union. I did not mind. Really. Though I sometimes thought, I thought it would be nice. To have a child. I would have called him Thomas.'

He grips her to him.

'I'm sorry,' he says.

'Mmmm,' she agrees.

Birds call, a single woodpigeon, and the water flows by, and she is not sure if she understands this thing that she is feeling – this intense emotional sickness – as if her heart is swooping and falling, swelling and shrinking, but she knows it is to do with Thomas.

'But I am glad, too,' he says.

'Why?' she asks.

He looks at her, puzzled.

'Because – because don't you know?'

But she does, really, and she sees that his hose is bulging, and she feels she too would like to press against something, and she places her hand on his thigh, and stretches to kiss him again and then once again they are in a rush to get their laces untied, and as she is hopping to remove one shoe, and pull her hose and braies off, he says something about how it would be easier if she were dressed as a girl, and then she is on her back and he is on top of her and this time it is better, and she cannot help gasping with the pleasure of it, and while it lasts it is golden, but it does not last long and he cries her name out as he shudders, and afterwards, while he is lying on her so heavily that she can hardly breathe, she cannot help smiling as she sees a flying wedge of geese pass high overhead, and she feels not just the great warmth of what they have done, but an absence of coldness, and despite his weight pressing her down, she feels lifted up, and that she might like to do that again, very soon.

But then they hear a cry from the river, and he lifts his shoulders and turns, and now she can see a sail on the water, and Thomas is about to leap up and run, but she holds him tight with her arms and legs, and she looks into his eyes where the sunlight catches them, and she keeps him there, and he smiles down at her and then bends to kiss her and – my God! – they ignore the boatmen who sail by with shouts and jeers and there is something thrown, and he keeps at it and a moment later she feels she might burst with it all.

When it is over, finally, and they are retying their hose, she asks if he remembers that first time they stood on a riverbank and he smiles.

'"Two are better than one,"' he quotes, '"because they have a good reward for their labour for if they fall the one will lift up his fellow."'

'"But woe to him who is alone when he falls,"' he carries on, '"for he has not another to lift him up."'

Then they turn and they walk together, never not touching one another, and he has a fat smile on his face and she feels that they should have done that long, long ago, and she feels simultaneously full and empty, and for a few blissful moments she does not care who she is and where they are, and what is to come. It is enough that they are with one another and that at last she has made Thomas happy.

Richard's second letter arrives a few weeks later, when the hay has been taken in, and there is the first hint of autumn in the air. Sir John stands in the yard with a cup of warmed wine. He is wearing a jacket over his doublet and he has given up the extravagantly piked shoes in favour of polished riding boots, which he wears turned down to the knee, and he is now never without his eyeglasses.

'What have we here, eh?' he asks, breaking the seal and unfolding the letter. It is short, though not written in any haste from London, but rather composed, considered, and contains three pieces of news: the first of which makes Sir John laugh until tears meet his beard, the second that makes him bellow with rage, and the third that creases his face in grief.

'The people of Northampton rose up and tried to hang the Duke of Somerset!' he laughs. 'Dear God! They have not forgotten what he and his men did before the battle there that summer! Do you remember? They fired the place! Just as if it was France! Their own town! Well, I suppose some of them were Scots, so they can hardly be blamed, but oh, my Lord!'

'Apparently the townsmen were only persuaded to desist from hanging the bastard by some soothing words from King Edward himself, and a cask of wine opened in the marketplace! Now Somerset has been sent to some castle in Wales where King Edward hopes he will be safe. I hope he's wrong! You can at least trust a Welshman to do that properly!'

The second piece of news contained in the letter is the one they have been waiting for, and it is as bad as they feared: Lord Hastings's final attempt to have ownership of Cornford Castle revert to Richard has failed. Edmund Riven, his family's attainder reversed, is now free to enjoy the right and title of the said estate, unentailed, and is at liberty to assign it to the heirs of his body or anyone else he chooses.

Sir John puts the letter on the log where the chessboard is carved and he removes his eyepieces and rubs his face with both hands.

'So,' he says. 'It is over. We have been royally fucked. I mean that, Isabella, and I want your girls to hear me say it. We have been royally fucked. Fucked by a royal. Do you see? A royal has fucked us. For his own narrow self-interest, King Edward has gifted our property – *our* property – to that conniving, murdering, treacherous little shit Edmund bloody Riven.'

He gestures at the chessboard, recalling their earlier conversation, though today the pieces are put away.

Isabella sighs.

'Never mind,' she says. 'We do not need the castle.'

Sir John is angry.

'It is not about the goddamned castle,' he says. Then he apologises and admits that it is about the castle. Isabella forgives him and asks what else the letter says.

Sir John picks it up. He adjusts his eyeglasses.

'Let's see, let's see. Oh, dear God. Listen. This is Mayhew writing on his own behalf. "I have saved the worst news for last," he writes. 'Our dear Margaret Cornford is dead. The Prior of St Mary's has sent message to say she was killed trying to abscond from the priory and that the boat she had stolen was later found drifting, empty, on the river as it runs through the town of Boston in the county of Lincolnshire. He enclosed a bill for the costs incurred housing her, for food and other divers needs, and for the search subsequent to her departure. Richard is inconsolable, and mourns her more than he mourns the loss of Cornford. I am keeping him under close watch, for he is more miserable than a worm, and right likely to take up weapons against one and all, including his own body."'

Sir John lowers the letter. He is weeping openly, and Katherine too cannot stop the tears filling her eyes when she thinks of the harm she has caused, and she feels guilt press down on her shoulders like a physical weight. Any happiness she had been feeling dwindles into nothing.

They sit in silence for a while.

'So what will Richard do now?' Thomas cannot help asking.

'Come home, I suppose,' Sir John says. 'Christ. It will be good to see the boy, but I wish it were in other circumstances. I wish — well, Isabella is right. There is no point going over all this again. It is as it is. There is nothing we can do, nothing we can bring to bear on the situation, so.'

At that moment Robert returns from the woods where he has been walking. His tonsure has grown out and he has settled into Sir John's household without a ripple. He is wearing russet from top to toe, and he is carrying a stick and a bag slung over his shoulder. He takes the bag off and opens it to show them a haul of glossy chestnuts within, but Thomas is on his feet instantly.

'Why have you taken my bag?' he asks. 'And what have you done with the ledger?'

Robert is surprised, but then he remembers Thomas's attachment to the thing.

'I am sorry, Brother Thomas,' he says. 'I did not think you would mind me borrowing the bag. I put your book quite safe on the coffer within, where the dogs cannot get at it. I needed a bag, is all.'

Sir John snorts.

'You didn't touch his sacred ledger, did you, Robert? He won't like that.'

'It is safe and sound,' Robert protests.

'Good thing, too,' Sir Johns says. 'He was never separated from it, were you, Thomas? Took it into battle at Towton, didn't you, though why I never knew.'

Thomas has no proper idea why either. Robert takes the chestnuts to the kitchen and returns with the empty bag and the ledger. He fits the one inside the other and passes it to Thomas. It sits between them and Sir John frowns at it.

'It was your old master's, wasn't it? Old Dowd the pardoner? And he felt it valuable?'

'He hoped to sell it for a fortune in France,' Katherine says. 'Though we never knew who to, or why anyone would pay for it.'

'A mystery then? May I?'

Thomas lets him. He takes the ledger and opens it. He holds it up to the fading afternoon light and peers at it through his eyeglasses.

'It is just a list of names?' he says. 'Men who served in France. Some I know. Yes. Yes. Hmmm. Yes. All their movements for those years. But why should it be of any value to anyone at all?'

'We don't know,' Katherine admits with a shrug. 'Red John once said it must prove someone was somewhere they shouldn't have been, or wasn't somewhere they should've.'

Sir John looks beady. It is the first time he has ever been interested in the ledger. Perhaps because there is almost nothing else left in which to take an interest.

'But you said old Dowd thought it would make him a fortune, didn't you? So, think on it. There will be nothing of any value in finding that, say, this fellow – Thomas de Hookton – was here, say, rather than there, will it? No one would pay a farthing to discover the whereabouts of a simple archer from Hampshire.'

Katherine groans. It is so obvious. Of course it could only be someone of wealth! She feels utterly foolish.

'The Duke of York,' she says. 'King Edward's father. He is mentioned.'

Sir John nods.

'Well,' he says, wrinkling his nose, 'he is dead, of course, so your book may be of little or no value now, but let us have a look anyway.'

And he starts the book at the beginning.

'So where was he then, that he should not have been? Or where was he not that he should have been. Let us begin at the beginning, St Edward's Day—'

'That is the eighteenth day of the month of March,' Robert intones. They all look at him. He smiles slightly.

'Father Barnaby made us learn them,' he says. '"Knowledge of the lives of the saints and martyrs is what separates us from the pagans and the beasts in the fields."'

They stare at him a moment, wondering if this is true. Then after a while Sir John continues.

'Anyway,' he says. 'St Edward's Day, of the nineteenth year of old King Henry's reign. So, now, what is our old friend the Duke up to then, hey?'

He reads, moving his lips, but in unnerving silence, and Thomas's shoulder touches hers and she nudges him back.

'Aha,' Sir John says after a moment. 'Here he is. It says the Duke is in the garrison at Rouen, with Sir Henry Cuthbert of Gwent, three companies of men-at-arms and four of archers from Cheshire and other divers parts of the realm. He celebrates Mass with Cecily, Duchess of York.'

He turns the page and reads its reverse.

'And he is in Rouen until – yes. Here he is there all that month, until here – on the first Thursday after St George's Day.'

'Which is the twenty-third day of April,' Robert says.

'Yes, yes,' Sir John agrees, slightly impatient now, 'when the Duke leaves for La Roche-Guyon – I remember La Roche! Anyway, he doesn't stay long, because he's back in Rouen for Mass to mark the Finding of the True Cross—'

'Which is the second day of June.'

'—at the cathedral, again with the Duchess, and he's still there until – until here, the last week before the Feast of St Peter and St Paul?'

'The twenty-ninth day of June.'

'After which he goes to a place called Pontours, is it? Yes. Pontours. That is in Aquitaine, I think, quite small. Never went there myself. But the Duke is there, why? Ah. "To resist the King's enemies", or as we call it, fighting the French. Anyway, he is there in the company of Gui de Something – can't read that word – a gentleman of Gascony, with one incomplete company of men-at-arms and two likewise of archers, and he's gone until . . .'

Sir John turns some pages and then adjusts his brass-cupped eyeglasses.

'Until here,' he says. 'The week following the feast of the Assumption.'

'That is the fifteenth day of August.'

'When he is back in Rouen five days later, bringing with him, "by the grace of Almighty God, two thousand four hundred best arrows, twenty-two men-at-arms and forty-three of the King's best archers".'

He turns the pages and continues to describe the Duke's movements all that year. He returns to Rouen on St Luke's Day ('the eighteenth day of October,' Robert says), and remains there for most of it, sallying out now and then, but seemingly without much incident, and he is mostly within the castle walls throughout Advent into Christmastide until he leaves for England after Candlemas ('the second day of February'), '"trusting himself with God's blessing, to the dread perils of the Narrow Sea at his port of Honfleur, or thereabouts".'

'He returns three weeks later,' Sir John goes on, 'and he is back in Rouen for the start of Lent and, yes, look here. In April, a rose, in the margin – white, of course – to celebrate the birth of his son on St Vitalis's day.'

Thomas leans forward to look at the rose and is unimpressed by its quality.

'That is King Edward?' Katherine asks.

'Edward? Yes,' Sir John says. 'I remember he was so sickly when he was born they didn't think he'd make it through the night, so they baptised him at a rush in one of the side chapels of the cathedral. My God! You'd never think it to look at him now, would you?'

Sir John laughs. Katherine remembers Edward: a great giant of a man, taller and broader even than Thomas, bulky with muscles from the training ground, but with the sort of skin you kept only if you were lucky enough to be able to take shelter when it rained.

'Anyway,' Sir John says. 'The Duke is there for a month. He's present for the Duchess's churching, then he is off again, with all these men, look at them, returning to . . .' He frowns again at the page before saying: 'Pontours again. Quite a trip. Must say I don't remember there being so much action down that end of the country, not then anyway, but it was a while ago now.'

After that the list runs on. The Duke was active in those months, ranging over English France, seldom in one place for more than a week at a time.

'And that is it,' Sir John says, closing the ledger on itself. He looks around at their blank faces and sighs.

'I don't know,' he says.

There is a long pause. How can any of that be of value? she thinks. Yet there must be something in it. She tries to look at it the same way Sir John had: who is the wealthiest person mentioned therein? The Duke of York. What would matter most to him?

Katherine asks to see the ledger again. She can feel a rushing thrill. She knows what it is. She knows it now.

'Edward was born in April,' she says, pointing to the white rose in the margin. 'St Vitalis's Day.'

'The twenty-eighth of April,' Robert reminds them.

She turns the pages back to the beginning of the ledger. Her hands shake, and the others lean in, waiting.

'Where is Pontours?' she asks, pointing at the ledger.

'Aquitaine,' Sir John says. 'As I say.'

'Is that far from Rouen?'

175

He looks at her, having forgotten that she knows almost nothing.

'Two weeks?' he supposes.

'So the Duke is there from the end of June – and he is not back in Rouen until the week following the Assumption, so about the twentieth, let us say, of August.'

Sir John agrees.

'And where was the Duchess all this time?' Katherine asks.

Sir John looks as if this might be a trick question.

'I don't know,' he mutters. 'She must have been in Rouen. She would not have risked travelling to Pontours with him, however many men he took. By road would be awful and by boat, well, that coast was infested with pirates, always has been.'

'Could it be proved she stayed in Rouen?' Katherine asks.

Sir John shrugs.

'I dare say,' he says. 'There will be household accounts.'

'Then that is it.'

The men are blank.

'It is not about the Duke of York,' she tells them. 'It is about the Duchess. You have to count the months, you see? Look. Backwards, from April, when Edward was born. Nine months, which is how long a woman is reckoned to carry her child, and so you come to July the year before.'

Still the men are blank. They look at her, waiting.

'It means,' she says, 'that Edward was conceived in July. But where was the Duke in July?'

'Pontours.'

'And where was the Duchess?'

'Rouen.'

They look at one another in the gloom. Sir John is aghast. Thomas places his hand over his mouth.

'Merciful Christ!' Sir John breathes, his eyes round with astonishment. 'The boy's a bastard.'

PART FOUR

The North,
After Michaelmas 1463

12

The path rises steeply at their feet, over rough sheep-cropped grass and through bent and broken bracken, where the wind is loud in Thomas's ears and pulls at his flapping cloak. Blue-black clouds race from west to east, low enough to touch, and the rain stings and claps his cheeks.

'How much further?' Katherine shouts from behind.

Her hair is loose on her forehead under her cap, and raindrops cling to her eyebrows and the tip of her nose.

'To the top,' he calls. 'Then over, and down.'

He points. Each movement allows the rainwater into the warmth of his skin.

'And then over and down again?' she calls back, and he has to nod.

They are five days' walk from Marton Hall, and they have still as many to go before Thomas imagines they will be anywhere near the castles wherein they hope to find anyone who might bring them before King Henry so they may show him the ledger. Five days' walking, from dawn to dusk, through five days' solid rain, but at least they have been alone, unwatched by Canon Robert, or Isabella, or even Sir John, and on the first day they even found an inn wherein they were given a bed to themselves, in a room to themselves. To begin with they were shy, but by the morning, waking up with their skin pressed together, they wished they might stay another two, three, four nights.

'We should have asked for a kirtle and smock,' he'd said, watching her lace her hose to her pourpoint. 'Then we might travel as man and wife at least.'

She had agreed.

'But whatever would we have told Sir John and Isabella? That we'd wasted their money on women's cloth instead of these things, and that I was really called Katherine?'

'We must tell them one day,' he'd said.

'I know,' she'd mumbled. 'I know.'

Thomas prayed they would find another inn that night with a similarly empty bed, but it was not to be. After another ten hours trudging north, they arrived in the dark at the Friary of St Nicholas, by a bridge over a broad river, and they'd slept in a cold dorter with five or six other travellers, every one of whom snored. In the morning, when they were woken for Prime and were guided along the cloister to the door of the chapel, more memories had returned to Thomas, and he'd found himself gripping Katherine, almost crushing her wrist.

'More,' he'd told her, with his gaze fixed on the grass. 'I remember more. I remember the fighting now. Christ. A man with a stick. Christ. He had some rosary beads. And he'd done something to – was it you? Or? No. It was another sister. Dear God. He'd killed her. Yes. I remember him. Was that Riven?'

Afterwards they had followed the road north, toward Towton, retracing their steps of nearly three years previously, neither speaking a word. Thomas had been aware that Katherine was watching to see if he recalled anything more, but for a while nothing came to him other than an intense sadness that seemed to leach into his new-found happiness. He does not want any more grim memories to stain the delight he feels just walking with her, without really having to pretend anything to anyone.

Then the memories begin to return. When they'd crossed a bridge among some willow trees, they'd stopped and said their prayers at a little chantry chapel that was pitted with the distinctive marks of arrowheads, and Thomas had found himself shuddering and moved to tears he could not explain when he looked down into the frothing waters below the spans.

They'd passed Towton Field a little after noon. The autumnal sun threw their shadows very far before them and there had been little there to remind him of what he had done, and what had been done to him. Some rough heathland, a tree on the skyline. They'd stopped and stared but nothing had come.

'Perhaps it is for your soul's protection?' she'd wondered.

York Minster had broken the horizon a little after that and they'd passed through the city gates and under its castles' walls in a deepening gloom, but they'd been brought up short when they'd seen the minster in the full, and had stood in silence, stilled, not just at the building itself, or the windows then being lit from within by a hundred candles, but at the number of people abroad. They could see more in one glance in one street than they might in a whole month at Marton. Then they'd been accosted by a boy who wanted to show them the new crop of heads on the Micklegate Bar for the price of a farthing, but they did not take him up on it, and that night they had to share a bed with a lead dealer from Gloucester. When they woke up, Thomas and Katherine had become intertwined where she had turned to him in the night, and the lead dealer gave them a curious look, and they hurried away through the town's North Gate without breakfast.

Since then they have seen Durham with its cathedral and castle raised up so prominent and uncompromising it could only inspire awe, and then reached Newcastle, where it was easy to believe the walls and gates had been built by giants, as men said, and they'd stood rooted, staring so long that the men of the city Watch began to take notice. They were hard-looking men, Thomas thought, old soldiers, in red-and-black livery coats with what looked like a winged dog for a badge.

'Lord Montagu's men,' someone had told him. 'Best make yourself scarce.'

The same sort had been there the next morning, on the West Gate, warming their hands over a brazier filled with glowing coals. Archers, Thomas had guessed.

'Where are you going?' one of them had asked, and Thomas knew to tell him Carlisle, and not Alnwick or Bamburgh. The man had grunted and said no more.

The rain set in just as they left Newcastle and it followed them as they double backed east, to find the road that would take them up to their destination, and now here they are, with the land rising before them, and every heavy step taking them nearer winter. Thomas is pleased Sir John has provided them with new clothes – bought with Isabella's money from a tailor in Lincoln – and boots that fit and are oiled against the rain. He also bought them a sword each – 'A falchion, Thomas. A proper archer's sword' – and Thomas walks with a quarterstaff.

They also have ale and bread, and in the shelter of a small wood through which an old stone wall runs, Thomas unstoppers the bottle and passes it to Katherine. When she has finished and has wiped her mouth she asks him, as if it has only just occurred to her, how he intends to even get an audience with King Henry.

He shrugs.

'Surely he will want to see us when he knows we have something so valuable to his cause?'

He pats the ledger. She supposes this is so.

'But you cannot just talk to a king, can you? Even if he is in exile. We'll need to go through all sorts of retainers and courtiers, surely? And they will try to steal the ledger from us. Make it seem it is their find.'

This had not occurred to him. It had not been mentioned when the plan was first devised, that evening after Richard's letter had come from London to break the tidings that King Edward had sided against them. It was just after this terrible moment that they divined the ledger's secret, and as soon as he breathed the words, Sir John had slammed the book shut and hurriedly put it back in its bag.

'Christ, boy!' he'd said. 'You've been carrying that around with you all this time? Showing it to people?'

Thomas had nodded.

'Is it really that dangerous?' he'd asked, though he must have known the answer: just to think King Edward might be illegitimate was treason.

Sir John had leaned forward on one elbow and kept his voice low.

'If it is known we have it,' he'd explained, 'they will burn our feet until we tell them where we got it, and who else knows about it. Then, when we have given them any and every name we can think of, they will round them up and burn their feet, and get everyone they know, and do the same to them. Then we will all meet up again on the scaffold where we will be half-hanged, choked almost to death, you understand, but just before we die, they'll let us down, and then they'll cut our bellies open, and our guts will be pulled out and burned before our eyes, or wound around a sharpening wheel until we swallow our own tongues, and then, and only then, will we be chopped into pieces with a blunt axe, and we'll have those parts of us doused in hot tar and sent to Devon and York and Kent and bloody Wales to be hung on gates to remind others not to even think such thoughts, so yes, you could, young Thomas, *you could* say it is pretty dangerous.'

They'd sat around the fire in the gloom, and they'd drunk more wine while the dogs chased rabbits in their sleep. All were silent for a while, each with their own thoughts, Sir John drinking with quick hands. Frowning, Isabella told them she was going to bed.

'But first I will pray for Richard,' she'd said, 'and I suggest you do the same. Prayer and faith in the Lord led to all being well with my boys, and I am sure it will be the same with yours.'

Sir John stood to kiss her, but she turned from him, and after a moment's hesitation he wafted his hand, and sat down with a heavy sigh. He took another long drink of wine, and all the time his eyes above his cup were fixed on the ledger. Then he banged the cup down.

'I am sick of it,' he'd begun. 'I'm sick of it, d'you hear? I'm sick of seeing others prosper at our expense. It is not just Riven, it is the whole crowd of them. The Earl of Warwick, the Duke of Somerset, all of them, all scheming, all getting ahead, rubbing two coins to make three. By Christ! They said King Henry and his advisers were like fleas on a traveller's buttocks, sucking the weal for all its goodness, but I tell you, these new men are worse, for they are the hungrier for being the emptier. By Christ, when I think of the blood we have spilled for them, and for what? For nothing. No. It is men like us who have suffered, and I say we have suffered enough. It is time we shifted for ourselves, since no one else will do it for us.'

'So what to do?' Thomas had asked.

And Sir John had gestured at the chessboard, brought in from the yard, and had the pieces not been put away, he might have moved the white knight back across the board to the black king and his two black rooks, and he might have turned the knight's horse so that its teeth were bared at the white king.

'Providence has placed a powerful weapon in our hands,' he'd said. 'If it is known that King Edward is a bastard, no man in the realm will stand by him. All his earls and dukes and lords of this and that, they will turn on him and drive him from his palace, where he would no doubt be in bed with some guildsman's wife anyway, and they'll take his crown and sceptre and that will be the end of Edward Plantagenet, so you take King Henry your ledger, Thomas. Take it up to Alnwick or Bamburgh or wherever he is. Show it to him and I imagine even he will be able to do something with it. If not, the Queen will. But by God, this time we will see to it that no service of ours goes unpaid, d'you hear? This time we will not be scorned!'

And so, leaving Robert with Sir John for mutual safekeeping, Thomas and Katherine set off almost that next day, first to Lincoln, where they bought these new clothes, and then up the road north, and now here they are, in the wind and rain, somewhere, he believes, in Northumberland, sodden through, dog-tired, too lightly armed to fight off a badger, should one come calling.

More than that though, they do not know precisely how to do it.

'We must wait to see who is whom before we offer the ledger to just anyone,' she says.

'They will wonder why we are coming to join them, though,' Thomas tells her.

'We could say we are coming to join the rightful King, like those men who attacked your farm?'

He nods.

'We'd best buy a pie, then,' he says and she looks at him anxiously, as if he might be mad. He does not explain. They walk on. After noon the rain passes east and the sky turns pale and they find the north road running through deserted furlongs and over gentle countryside, and they walk until Katherine's hands and feet are numb from the cold, and gradually the day fades and the moon rises, a perfect star-bright crescent in the violet-tinged evening, and they come to a village where a blacksmith is prepared to let them stay for a price. They sleep together with him and his boys in his workshop, huddled against the stones for warmth, and in the morning they wake up observed by three goats, a dog and a cat, there for the same reason.

The smith says they are a day from Alnwick, where the castle is.

'I'll not ask your business,' he says, and his dark-eyed boy watches them leave, pumping his bellows without a word. They walk all morning, until a little after noon, when they find a brewster with her broom set out to proclaim she has ale, and she finds some bread too, and she tells them there are no men left in the village.

'All gone,' she says.

'Where?'

She points upwards.

'You two should stay,' she says. 'Many a young widow aching for a man.'

But they carry on, along the road, over another series of ridges and valleys, until they find their way blocked by a looping river flowing east, its current so sluggish in parts that its brown water might be ale in a barrel. Unable to cross they turn upriver, and follow it until they find a ford where the water froths amid jumbled rocks. They remove their boots and roll up their hose and he helps her across, hopping from rock to rock. Then when they are dressed again, on the northern bank, they follow the track until they find a deserted hamlet where the houses have been ransacked and pulled apart for firewood.

'We must be close now,' Thomas supposes. He loosens his sword in his scabbard, and she does likewise.

'Remember,' Thomas reminds himself, 'it is King Henry, not Henry of Lancaster. King Henry. King Henry. Remember that.'

And that is when they hear the horses. They look at one another one last time. He takes her hand.

'We can always just run, you know? We don't have to do this?'

But he thinks, we've come this far . . .

She squeezes his palm.

'No,' she says, 'because then, what else?'

He nods. There really is nothing else for it.

The riders, soldiers all, come down the road ahead, and they pull up and spread out across the road on their shaggy-coated ponies. It is not easy to see their livery, since they wear a mismatched motley of begged and borrowed coats, with scarves around their faces like bevors and wool caps pulled low over their ears. Their leader – a thin-faced man, not shaved for a while – wears thick mittens, one of which he removes to flex the pale fingers beneath.

'God give you good day,' he says.

Thomas takes a breath. Here we go, he thinks, and he walks forward, the slightest swagger in his step.

'Who are you?' he asks, brimming with a feigned confidence. 'I don't recognise the livery.'

The captain is slightly taken aback.

'I am John Horner,' he says. He fishes in his coat and pulls from it a flap of cloth on which is a silver badge. He holds it up to Thomas, who cannot see it.

'I am captain of the Watch at Alnwick,' Horner says, 'and serve Sir Ralph Grey of Castle Heaton, who also serves King Henry. Who are you, sir, and whom do you serve?'

'No one,' Thomas says. 'Or no longer, anyway. We used to serve in the retinue of a gentleman of Lincolnshire, whose name I will not repeat, who was of the Duke of Somerset's affinity, but he – like the false Duke – has since gone over to the treacherous Earl of March, now calling himself King Edward the Fourth.'

One of the men spits, but another spurs his horse forward to Horner's side.

'I know this man,' the second rider says.

Horner looks at him. So does Thomas.

Oh, Christ, Thomas thinks, it is him. That boy, the one from the farm. The one who hid in the orchard. What is he doing here? He should never have let him go. He should have killed them both. Is it too late to run?

'You do?' Horner asks. 'Who is he?'

'I don't know,' the boy says. 'Never gave a name but he is useful with a bow, I will give him that. He killed five men before one of them managed to loose a shot or lay a glove on him.'

'I – it was in defence,' Thomas says, his confidence destroyed, the part he is playing much changed. He tries to signal to Katherine to run.

'One of them was my uncle,' the boy goes on.

Thomas can only repeat it was in his defence.

The boy gets off his horse. They look at one another, eye to eye. There is a long moment. Thomas stares at the boy, but is counting the others. How many are they? Ten. Too many for any one man.

But then the boy extends a hand.

187

'I hated my uncle,' he says.

And Thomas can only take the hand. He feels a ripple of surprised hope.

'And you saved me from that woman,' the boy adds.

Thomas smiles. So does the boy.

'My brother's wife,' Thomas says, shaking the hand. 'You had just killed her son.'

It is the boy's turn to look abashed.

'I was aiming at you,' he says.

Thomas almost laughs.

'I slipped in shit,' he says.

The boy laughs too.

'God damn it!' he says. 'I thought you had some God-given power! I'd've never given up if I'd known it was *shit*!'

The men smile. Tension dissipates, slowly like smoke in a still room.

Then one of the men at the back speaks.

'You got any food?' he asks.

Thomas has the pie, bought to ease exactly this sort of situation, and Katherine acknowledges his foresight as the men – even Horner – dismount and cluster about to break it up. When it is shared out and crammed into grateful mouths, Horner remembers his purpose.

'So?' he asks. 'What is your business here?'

'We are come to join the real King,' Thomas says, resuming some sort of authority.

'We?'

Horner glances at Kit.

'This is Kit,' Thomas says. 'He is a surgeon. Able to patch any wound.'

'Save those that are fatal,' she adds.

The men look at her doubtfully. Thomas's grin is fixed. She is not good at this kind of thing. After a moment Horner says:

'Really? Good. Good.'

188

Then he turns back to Thomas.

'Our surgeon – he ran off. He knew his astral charts and the healing properties of divers stones, all right, and he was a bugger for taking urine, but he was cock-all use in a pinch.'

'He can have a look at Devon John,' one of the men says.

Horner agrees.

'You'd best come with us then.'

And they remount their shaggy ponies and let Thomas and Katherine walk beside them. Thomas sees that the horses are not in good condition, and when he looks carefully at the men, they are pinched, scrawny even, and their clothes are worn and their metal-work matt with rust.

'What is your name?' the boy asks.

Thomas tells him.

'Yours?'

'John Bradford, of Dorset. My friends call me Jack.'

'I'm sorry about your uncle,' Thomas says.

'He was a bastard,' Jack says. 'No one mourned him. Not even his dog. I'm sorry about your nephew.'

'Yes,' Thomas says. 'Well. And what about your brother? Is he well?'

Jack shakes his head.

'Dead,' he says. 'Just the other day. May God rest him. We had a run-in with some of Montagu's men.'

'Montagu?'

'Lord Montagu holds Newcastle for the false King Edward. He is the Earl of Warwick's brother, did you know? And no friend to King Henry, or us.'

Thomas thinks of those men on the gate at Newcastle. He would not like a run-in with them.

'I'm sorry,' he says.

'There is much to be sorry for, isn't there? These days.'

They walk up through a forest of spindly ash trees above which they can see dark crenellated towers and a little while later they come out on to moorland bearing traces of past camps, where trees have been hacked down for firewood and where the grass is yet to grow back through the sooted circles of old fires. Ahead is the mass of the castle, hulking in the distance, filling the skyline.

'Christ,' Thomas says.

'Yes,' Jack says. 'Welcome to Alnwick.'

Katherine is staring at the standard that flies from the keep.

'There is no royal standard,' she says. 'Is King Henry not here?'

'King Henry?' Horner says. 'No. King Henry is in Scotland.'

As they enter the shadow of the castle walls, Thomas looks about as if for an escape route, but there is none, and behind from the forest comes another picket, the leader of which raises his arm in salute, and is recognised by Horner and his men, and so it is too late. The castle's drawbridge is down and in a moment they are on it, their footsteps ginger on the slippery spars, and the great gates are opened and they are drawn into the gloom of the barbican, and the men of the other picket ride in behind and join them as if in a queue for something, and Katherine looks up to see they are being watched through the arrow slits and the murder holes and over the crenellated walls by four or five pinch-faced men in helmets. Behind them the gates close up again with a deep boom, sealing them in.

After a long moment the next set of gates opens before them, and they process out into the broad spread of the first bailey where miserable-looking sheep are penned in and guarded from thieves by poorly shaved men you would not think were Christians, carrying billhooks. Large parts of the rest of the bailey are given over to the frilled tops of root vegetables, and they get hungry stares from the few sallow-faced wretches and their desperate women and children. Dogs are chained to walls and the place smells of wet stone, frowsty clothes, rotting meat, unclean garde-de-robes.

'You think this is bad,' Jack mutters to Thomas. 'They're already eating toads in Dunstanburgh.'

Ahead is the mass of the keep. It is huge, like a cliff, raised above them on a flattened motte, breasted with crenellated towers on which he can see only one guard resting his elbows.

'Who is castellan here?' Thomas asks Horner.

'Sir Ralph Grey,' Horner says, nodding to the multi-towered keep. 'He is my lord.'

Horner has left his horse with the ostler, and he now walks with his coat open to reveal a pale jacket quartered by the red cross of St George, and on his belt a ballock dagger and a purse that is obviously empty. The soles of his riding boots clack with each step as if he were on his way to the cordwainer.

'Is he the man who deserted at Northampton?' Katherine asks.

'No,' Horner answers. 'That was Grey of Ruthyn. This is Grey of Castle Heaton. He didn't swap sides until last year, and he swapped the other way – from Edward to King Henry. Some slight, it is said. He was overlooked for a command and couldn't stand being in the other man's shadow. So. You'll see how it is.'

'Hmph,' Thomas grunts.

Horner leads them through a muddy gateway and into the second bailey where more of the grey-woolled sheep graze on the sparse grass. A few men traipse around the muddy acre, but there is no sense of urgency, or of multitude.

'Sir Ralph will be in his chamber,' Horner says, looking up at a sweep of glazed windows that must be the keep's solar. 'Never likes to stray too far.'

'You do not seem to have many men,' Katherine says.

'No,' Horner agrees. 'There are more at Bamburgh. And we have other castles, too, along the way.'

He opens a door on shrieking hinges and stops in the malodorous gloom of the stairwell.

'A warning,' he says. 'Sir Ralph Grey is – well, he can be unpredictable.'

He believes he's said about as much as he dares, and now he leads them into the darkness and then up some turning stairs from which they emerge into a solar, occupied by a small barrel-bodied man, fierce-looking and dressed in black. He stands – slightly unsteadily – with his back to a small greenwood fire hissing in a chimney, holding a small earthenware beaker. He looks up, his eyes blazing.

'Horner!' he cries. 'Where in God's sainted name have you been? And who for all His love are these with you? By Christ! Beggars? Beggars! You dare bring me beggars?'

'Sir,' Horner replies. 'These two have come to join our company.'

'Oh, they have?' Grey scoffs, as if this sort of thing happened every day. 'Well, I don't want them, do you hear? Take them away. Though not that big one. He looks useful. Ever loose a bow? Course you have. Course you have. But what about the runt? Damn you, Horner, can you do nothing right?'

'He says he is a surgeon,' Horner ventures.

'A surgeon, is he? Looks like a stable boy. Bet he's had his ear clipped.'

Katherine restrains from touching her ear.

'He's saved many a life,' Thomas says.

'Has he?' Grey says, slightly mollified. 'Has he now?'

Then he takes a sip from his beaker and crosses to the board under the window where he places it clumsily and pours into it something from a jug. My God, Katherine thinks, he is drunk. Now he advances crabwise across the rushes, kicking at them impatiently, until he is a couple of paces away. He smells strongly of something sweet, and flammable, too, and there is an unsettling brightness in his eye. He looks at her for a long moment, then smiles as if he has a secret, and taps the side of his nose.

'Ahah,' he says, and Katherine tries to shrink, to make her body pull away from the shell of her clothes. He will see, she thinks. He will see. Not because he is clever, but by accident, because he is a drunk. He grins at her sideways, his teeth crooked, his eyes sky blue, watery and red-rimmed. He has been poorly shaved.

'So,' he says with a smile to suggest he knows her game. 'A surgeon, is it? A surgeon. Hmmm. Now. Tell me. What does a surgeon actually do, eh? I mean. A surgeon, eh? Saved lives, you say? Lives of men? Men I might know?'

Katherine stares ahead. It would be dangerous to catch his eye, she thinks.

'I have, sir, yes. I am not sure if you—'

'Well, look,' Grey interrupts. 'Look here. I've an idea. An idea. How is this for one?'

They remain silent, waiting. She can hear him breathing. Then he looks away, and turns to Horner.

'Horner,' he says. 'Horner, Horner, Horner. What are we to do with you, eh? Look. I tell you what. Let us – you and me – have a little wager.'

Horner rolls his eyes.

'I've got nothing with which to wager, sir,' he says.

'Oh, it needn't be much,' Grey says. 'It needn't be much. No no no. Not much. A noble?'

Horner swallows. A noble is a lot.

'On what are we to bet, sir?'

Grey holds his finger up and beams craftily at Horner for a moment. Then he stumbles back across the room, through the rushes to the board under the glazed window, and finds some scrap among the papers spread there.

'Who was that boy?' he asks over his shoulder. 'The one wounded in the run-in with Montagu's men?'

'John, his name is,' Horner tells Grey. 'John from Devon.'

Grey is still for a moment, head cocked in thought.

'John from Devon,' he mutters. 'John from Devon. John *of* Devon? John *de* Devon? Either way, a name to conjure with, eh? John from Devon. Still alive, is he?'

'Far as I know.'

Grey turns and sits back against the board.

193

'Good,' he says. 'Now. Take this surgeon to him, will you? For me? Take him along to this John. This John of Devon. This John de Devon. And, well, let us put it this way – if he can save the boy's life, then he is a surgeon, isn't he? Hmmm? Bloody good one, I daresay. Needs to be.

'But if the boy dies, well, then, perhaps this surgeon of yours, perhaps he is not a surgeon after all? Did you ever think of that? Perhaps he's some sort of spy, sent by Montagu? It's just the sort of thing that bastard might do, isn't it? What do you think? I don't know. I don't know. D'you know? Eh, Horner? D'you know? No? No? Of course you don't. No one does. You see? That's the thing. No one *knows* anything. But if he isn't. If he isn't a surgeon, I mean, then we'll – what? – I tell you what! If he isn't a surgeon what we will do with him is we'll hang him! *Can* we hang him? I don't know. But we could do, couldn't we? They say hanging's too good for them, you know, don't they? But I don't know. I don't know.'

'Kit is not a spy,' Thomas says. 'For the love of God. We came here to help.'

'Yes, yes,' Grey says. 'Of course you would say that. *I'd* say the same, in your place. If I was standing here. Any Christian man would, wouldn't he? But look. Forget all that. Go on, Horner, make the wager. We said a noble, didn't we? Even if nothing comes of it, eh? It'll be a little fun, won't it? You and me? A wager? Why not? It'll be fun. And – and don't we, you know, don't we *need* a little of that? Around here? Now? We do. We do. Don't we?'

He screws up his face, looks imploring. Then he takes another drink.

'Let's say, if the boy lives to see what? All Saints? Or wait! All Souls? No. You're right. All Saints it is. If he is alive for All Saints then we'll assume you know what you're doing, that you're a surgeon, as you claim, and I shall give you, Horner, a noble. How does that do? Eh? Seems fair, doesn't it? More than fair, that, I'd say.'

Horner nods. His face is a mask.

'Go on then,' Grey says. 'Scuttle off. Scuttle off and do whatever it is you do.'

They leave the keep and recross the outer bailey, along muddy paths between the sheep pens, past the hawk mews, which smells grim, toward an isolated guerite in the northern wall.

'Is he serious?' Thomas asks.

'Well, he has a point,' Horner says. 'You have turned up as if from nowhere. And he likes a wager, too.'

He indicates the gibbet to one side of the bailey.

The door to the stubby stone-built tower is heavy on its hinges, and within it is dark, but there it is again: that stench. It seems to slide out, cold and pungent and thick enough to coat your tongue, so they all three take a step back, and they all clap their hands across their faces.

'By Christ!'

'He's started to smell a bit strong,' Horner admits.

A guard laughs from the parapet above.

'Won't be long now, poor old bugger.'

The guerite is one room, square, about ten paces wide, with no windows, but a wooden ladder leading up through a hatch into another identical room on top, save this one has two arrow loops on the hugely thick outer wall, and two doors on either side opening on to the parapet walkway of the crenellated curtain wall. There are four or five of these towers on the walls here, each placed between the corner towers, in which guards might shelter in very poor weather.

This John of Devon has the whole of the lower room to himself. When her eyes become used to the dark Katherine sees, in the light from the door, that he is on a pile of straw and, despite the cold, he is wearing only his braies and yet his skin is dewed with sweat. He has a linen sheet bunched over his face, and by his side his left arm

195

lies as if it is not his, but the property of someone else. The wound – just above the wrist – is tied with a bandage crusted black with dried blood, but above it, the boy's arm is swollen, the skin tense, and it is dark red, almost black. It extends to the elbow.

Oh Christ, she thinks, I will have to cut it off.

'What do you think?' Horner asks from the doorway.

Katherine says nothing. She holds her breath and touches the arm. It is scalding to the touch. She lifts it. The boy moans. There is a connective string of something between it and the stained linen sheet below, and a thin gruel of watery pus dribbles on to her wrists. She lets it down. She hurries to the door and pushes past and vomits on the grass. She hears men laughing as she retches. After five or six heaves, the retches turn dry and painful. Jack arrives and offers her some ale from his bottle.

'I'll need more light,' Katherine announces. 'And air. We'd better bring him out.'

'Should we not wait until tomorrow?'

'No,' she says. 'It must be soon, if we are to save him. This evening.'

Thomas and Jack exchange a look, then they wrap cloths around their mouths and go back in. They bring him out. Jack has his ankles and Thomas his armpits. The boy's arm lies across his pale belly. They lay him on the patchy grass. The sheep watch in silence. The boy is breathing very quickly. She bites her lip and returns to the wound. Using her own knife she lifts the bandage. It is a gash, black now, drying at the edges, something wet within. It hardly matters what that is like though, for now she sees the swelling has extended beyond the elbow. She will need a saw.

'When did it happen?' she asks.

'Three mornings ago,' Horner says. 'It was one of those things. Montagu's men. They were too far north. We were too far south . . .'

He shrugs.

'It will have to be cut off,' Katherine tells them. 'Here.'

She points to the upper arm, a finger's length above the tidemark of the discoloration. She lifts the sheet off the boy's face. He looks half dead already. Men are gathering on the parapet above.

'Kill him now,' one of them calls. 'You'd be doing him a kindness.'

'Do you have any tools?' she asks Horner. 'A knife. A saw. A needle. A curved needle if you have it, and a good length of horse's tail. And I'll need plenty of linen. Clean, mind, and a good new bowstring. And wine. And urine, fresh.'

'I absolutely know we have no wine,' Horner says. 'That was all drunk months ago, but we have some of Sir Ralph's spirit. The friars at Hulne make it for him. As for urine, you can have any amount of that. Right now, if you please.'

She recalls Mayhew cutting a bone after Towton.

'And I'll need a beeswax candle. It must be beeswax. And a fire in a brazier.'

Horner nods.

'Very well. Let us try the kitchen first.'

He guides her down to the keep's kitchens. It is gloomy down there, with high windows letting in a little light and air, and it smells strongly of mutton grease, but at least it is warm and Katherine finds what she is looking for: a sharp-enough knife, though without the curved blade, and even a butcher's saw. There is a pair of powerful scissors, blunt enough for her purpose, and she takes a stirring spoon. She waits for some water to boil on the fire. A large-eyed boy – an underemployed spit turner – watches her glumly from the shadows until the water is frothing and she is about to plunge the implements in the pot when Horner asks why she's washing them.

'They're only going to get dirty again,' he says.

She looks, puzzled, at the blue-black blade, the crusted snags of the saw's teeth. Why does she clean them? She really doesn't know. It just seems right. She plunges them and swirls them around, then wraps them in clean linen. She takes a small iron poker by the fire's side, too. Meanwhile Horner organises the urine.

'Come on, everyone! Into the pot.'

He collects half a gallon in a green glazed jug.

'Not bad,' he says, holding it up and shaking his other hand dry.

They go up and out into the thin autumnal sunshine to where the boy is laid out. She glances up at the keep to see the blurred shape of Grey at his window, and sees clouds in the reflection, scudding fast, west to east, and the sun goes in again.

Thomas is looking at her.

'How do you feel?'

She is not sure. She doesn't have that feeling she once had – of certainty. She holds up her pale hands. They are still, but feel heavy, as if – dead. For a moment she doubts herself.

'I don't know,' she says.

'Will it hurt?' Jack asks.

'Course it will, boy,' Horner says. 'Though we might first stun him with a cup of Sir Ralph's distillation?'

He holds up an earthenware flask. Thomas takes it, removes the stopper, breathes it and coughs. His eyes water.

'Strong stuff,' Horner laughs. 'Shall I send for more? Or a priest? Or both?'

'No,' Thomas says, stoppering the flask. 'He won't need a priest. He'll live.'

Thomas smiles at her. He is proud of her. Christ, she thinks, I hope this goes well.

'Come on then,' Horner says.

Men are gathering round, joining those on the parapet above, though some drift away again when they catch the stench of the arm. It has a coating miasma.

'Don't breathe it in,' one of them says. 'It'll kill you as sure as a headsman's axe.'

One of Horner's men brings a small perforated brazier in his cloak-wrapped hands. It lights up his face as he places it down next to her, and for a moment the smell of the burning coal masks that of the boy's rotting arm. She passes him the poker.

'Get it good and hot,' she says and he slides it in among the coals and starts blowing on them. Sparks rise.

Now that she has started, Katherine finds herself doing things without thinking. She first lets Thomas pour some of the distillation between the boy's cracked lips. It makes him cough, but they hold him down, and they give him more. And more still. She wishes she had some of the dwale that she had for operating on Sir John, or some of that midwife's soporific, but this will have to do. Besides, she is becoming sure that speed is of the essence here. She kneels next to him on the grass and she sees at once that the skin above the blackened swelling is gaining a rosy hue, and she imagines it a harbinger of the blackness, as if it is spreading up the limb from the wound. She wonders what it is that will finally kill the boy. Does the infection get into the blood and from there to the heart? Is that it? Does the heart then turn black like the swelling limb? Either way, she knows she must cut the arm well above the rosy fringes of the swelling if she is to prevent the boy's death, and she must do it quickly.

After a while the boy seems unconscious again. He begins long racking snores. Good, she thinks. She first loops the bowstring around the arm, above the bulge of his muscle. It goes around three times and then she ties it off and inserts the spoon under it and twists it within the bowstring, tightening it so that it bites into the flesh. Then she stops and feels the arm. She knows she must first find the artery. That is the biggest blood vessel. She has seen that cut and blood leap from the wound to splatter the ceiling. She presses her fingers into the muscle. There. She feels the throb of it. Good.

'Thomas,' she says. 'Twist the spoon.'

Thomas leans forward and does so. She keeps her fingers on the artery.

'Again,' she says. 'And again.'

The jump of the boy's pulse lessens, its kick diminishing. Finally it stops.

Thomas is watching her closely.

'All right?'

She nods. She reaches for the knife and she makes an incision, shallow, cutting the skin above the elbow, above the blackness. It is below the heft of his arm, where the muscle is biggest. She cuts right the way around and thinks, this is why Mayhew's knives are curved. Then she cuts upwards, towards his armpit. The boy writhes.

'It is all right,' Thomas says.

'Don't let go of that spoon!' she snaps.

He returns to his duty.

Now she peels the skin from the flesh of his arm and the boy really bucks.

'You aren't supposed to flay him,' Horner says.

'Give him something to bite on,' Jack says. 'Can we use this?'

He has the strap of the bag holding the ledger.

Thomas shrugs. Why not?

'Give him some of this first,' Horner suggests, and he tilts the bottle so that the boy must swallow another slug of the liquor or drown.

When it is swallowed and the boy is slack again, Jack places the leather strap between the boy's teeth.

Katherine is unaware of anything else now going on around about. It is just her and the boy under her knife. She pours some urine into the wound, rinsing away the blood. She saw Mayhew do this after Towton. She is looking for the artery, the thick one that carries the blood under pressure. She cuts down, very slowly. Slice by slice, pass by delicate pass, the blade's edge sliding through the meat of his arm. And now there it is, the artery, limp now. Next to it, nestled in the pink flesh of the muscle, is the other vessel still plump with blood. It is springy under her fingertip.

'Undo the spoon, one turn,' she says, and Thomas slackens the noose. Immediately the fat artery swells, and there is blood in the wound. Good, she thinks.

'Tighten it again,' she says. Thomas does so. The artery subsides.

Now she gets the curved needle Horner took from the saddler. She passes it behind the artery and makes a tight loop around it. She ties it off, then does the same thing again, a finger's width lower. She does the same with the thick blue vein next to it. Those are the two you must watch for, she thinks.

'See?' Thomas asks Horner. 'He really knows what he's doing.'

Horner grunts.

She takes the knife and slices the flesh around the vein and the artery. The boy is rigid with pain. Now she bites her lip. This is it. She cuts in two swift tugs up through both vessels, between the knots. There is a thimbleful of blood from each, but no more. She stares. Thanks be to God.

'Urine,' she says, and she slops more into the wound. Now she cuts quickly, through the muscle and the hard white ligaments, right down to the bone. There is more blood. Too much? She does not know. The smaller vessels need to be sealed.

'Pass the poker,' she says, and the man by the fire does so. It is a gleaming red tip. She takes it and presses it to the flesh. There is a hiss and a meaty smell. They lean back to let a curl of smoke rise up and vanish in the sky.

'Bacon!' someone says.

'Shut up,' another mutters.

She reheats the poker and passes it over the pink flesh again, turning it grey and brown. The smell is now disgusting.

'Loosen it,' she tells Thomas. He untwists it one turn. There is still blood from one or two of the vessels. She takes the blunt scissors, and she teases them out and then ties them off with the horsehair. It is tricky, fiddly, with the blood and the urine.

'Need three hands for this job,' Jack mutters. He is stroking the boy's head, absent-mindedly keeping him calm, not realising that he has already fainted.

More urine.

The flesh is cut all the way through now, and all that remains is the bone.

'Where is the candle?' she asks. Horner holds it up.

'The last good one,' he says.

'Light it, will you?' she tells him. He puts it to the brazier.

And now, here is the saw: a long blade with a curved wooden handle. She moves the arm so that it is at full angle from his body.

'Hold it, will you?'

Horner looks at her.

'I'm not touching that.'

'Just stand on it.'

He does so, gingerly, and when he steps on the hand watery pus bubbles through the broken and blackened skin. The smell is very strong, almost overpowering, and Horner gags and retches. She lets the saw run. It cuts on the pull. She goes quickly. The boy is awake again, screaming, bucking against Thomas and Jack. It takes about ten saw cuts before she is through, and the limb is detached into a shallow pool of dark blood. Something steams on the saw teeth.

'Get rid of it, will you?'

Horner kicks it scuffling across the grass, the fingers flapping. Some in the audience laugh but others groan. She takes the urine and pours it over the stump from which blood is running freely. She balls some linen against it. How did Mayhew do this? How? With the knife blade.

'Bring the candle!' she calls. 'Hold it above. Tip it now, so it drips.'

The wax drips onto the side of the knife where she holds it under the bone. It is burning fast, the wax dripping quickly. When enough wax has built up and it is beginning to harden, she presses it into the marrow and then presses the linen back over the hole.

'Carry on,' she says.

It takes four goes of pressing the wax into the bone before it begins to clog among the filaments of marrow. She stares at it another long moment before she exhales. It has stopped bleeding.

'Fuck me,' one of the men mutters. 'Bloody well fuck me sideways.'

But it is not over yet. She tells Thomas to untie the bowstring. He does so. She stares at the wound for the length of time it might take to recite the Credo and she waits a moment longer too before she nods. He removes the bowstring entirely. Jack takes the spoon. Katherine is sick with nerves. She fumbles for more horsehair and the needle again, and then she pulls down the flaps of his skin and folds them over, and then she begins to stitch them together. Before she finishes sealing the wound she stops.

'Blow it out,' she says, nodding at the candle. Horner does so and is about to tuck it in his purse.

'No,' she says. 'I need the wick.'

He grumbles but breaks the candle for her, and he holds the two pieces apart so that she can tug it out. She folds the wick and places the folded end into the wound. This is something she saw Mayhew do. It is supposed to draw out any malignant humours. She places a final stitch in the skin to hold the wick in place and she gives it the gentlest tug. It gives grudgingly. Perfect, she thinks.

Then she forces some linen into the jug of urine, soaking it up. This she presses to the wound. A dribble of pink fluid fills the waxy wick, and drips to the ground. But there is no blood.

The boy strains still.

'Not dead yet,' Thomas encourages.

She wads up more linen and presses it to the wound. She remembers the chaos of Towton, and the day before the battle, when she removed an arrow from the Earl of Warwick's thigh, and thought she had cut the main blood vessel. Mayhew had stood by her, his hand on her shoulder it felt like, until the blood had ceased and they knew the Earl would at least not bleed to death on the beaten earth of the barn floor. She wonders what those standing around now would think if she told them she'd had the Earl's life in her hands, and had saved it.

Some of the other boys are playing with the limb, now. They've dragged it off and are hitting it with sticks and screaming with delight. Then a dog comes and seizes the arm and drags it away with the boys cursing after him, but before they can retrieve it more dogs come, and there is so much snarling and snapping, the boys forget it, and come back to watch.

She stands there, her hands covered in dried blood and fat, and she looks around at the men who are ringed about her and the wounded boy. Grey is still at his window, a candle lit behind him, throwing his shape against the glass. She watches him raise his hand and take a drink.

'Bloody hell,' Horner says. 'I'd've never believed it if I hadn't seen it.'

'Told you,' Thomas says. 'Kit's a surgeon. Best surgeon.'

'Let's get him in,' she says, nodding at the boy. He is deathly pale, his hair sodden with sweat, his breathing lively and irregular. His eyes are pressed closed.

'Bit lighter than he was,' Jack notes as they pick him up.

The guerite chamber still smells of rot, but they are permitted a few rush lamps and soon the smell is mixed with tallow.

'Even worse,' Thomas says. 'Are there any herbs we can burn?'

'Herbs?' Horner laughs. 'This is Northumberland. Listen. Sir Ralph wants you guarded day and night, and so I will leave Jack here with you. You can talk about old times. How you killed one another's family.'

When he has gone, Jack asks if the boy will live.

She doesn't know.

'Well, he's not dead yet,' Thomas says.

'Not yet,' Jack agrees, 'but how many days until All Saints?'

13

The first few days after the operation are the worst. Katherine
and Thomas are confined to the chamber of the guerite, and must
take turns sitting up with the boy. She sniffs the wound almost
hourly and removes the dressing every day to tease the dribbling
wick from the sutured skin in tiny increments, letting the wound
heal behind it. The boy is in pain all the time, delirious with it,
screeching with it, writhing with it, and there is nothing they can
do except hold him down, stop him wrenching at the dressing, and
try to force some of Sir Ralph's spirit into him. If they can get
enough of it down, it seems to place him somewhere between life
and death.

'Is he in purgatory?' Jack whispers.

And Katherine places a hand on the boy's neck to feel something,
then shakes her head.

'Not yet,' she says.

Jack is still with them, and she has been surprised to find she does
not mind, or fear his company as much as she'd think. He has even
been protective of them, sending others away, including one man
who wanted her to come with him to cure his brother who has
leprosy. He is cheerful, usually, and if there is anything to be overcome, he always knows of somewhere it is worse.

'Scotland!' he'll say. 'Oh, Christ! You should see the women
there,' or 'Scotland! They eat bats there. Bats!'

When they need something – more of the distillation – or they
get hungry, they send Jack to find Horner and Horner might come

to check on the boy, bringing a hard loaf of bread and some watery ale, and he usually has some new tale to tell about Grey:

'He wants me to find him a woman,' he tells them. 'Not just any woman – a negress.' Or: 'He wants green ink.' 'A live turtle.' 'Someone to teach him Genoese.'

And they'll shake their heads and sympathise. Sometimes they hear Grey shouting in the night. He goes up to the battlements at the top of the keep with a flask and his hawk and he rants all sorts of comical obscenities, usually about the Earl of Warwick, or the Earl of March, sometimes about Horner, often about someone called Ashley. And the next morning a pallid Horner will appear with rings under his eyes.

'What's it like in Bamburgh?' Thomas asks.

'Better,' Horner admits.

One morning, when it is cooler and looks set to rain, Grey makes his way across the bailey, unconvincingly steady on his feet, a feverish rosiness in his cheeks, smelling of his distillation and with Horner trailing in his wake. It is the first time they have seen him since the cutting, and he has come to see the boy, who lies on his damp bed in the gloom, having taken a turn for the worse. Grey prods him with a toe.

'Looks like I shall win my wager,' he tells them. 'Though by the Mass you do put on a fine show. If you're alive at the end of all this, do you know I've half a mind to make you my own? How would you like that, eh, boy? Surgeon to the most powerful man in the whole of the Northern Marches and beyond? It could happen, you know? Hmmm? It could.'

And Horner closes his eyes and Katherine looks over at Thomas and Thomas knows just what she is thinking: they really cannot show Grey the ledger. He will lose it, burn it, drop it down the chute in the garderobe. Or, worse, he will fumblingly understand it for what it is and take it to King Henry himself and claim some advantage for himself alone, forgetting Katherine and Thomas and Sir John Fakenham, if ever the scheme to proclaim Edward illegitimate were to come good.

'My confessor tells me today it is the feast of St Luke,' Grey continues, clapping his gloved hands together. 'So we have but two weeks until the big day, after which we will learn if Horner will owe me a noble, or I him, and whether or not you two shall be hanged for spies.'

The next day all are there to see the boy open his eyes, and hear his few stammered words. He swears and bucks with the pain, pulling at the stump as if he means to tear it off, and Thomas and Jack are quick to throw themselves on him, pinning him down while Katherine forces him to drink some of Grey's spirit.

When he is sufficiently stupefied, they relax.

'He will live,' she announces.

'My God!' Thomas says. 'You are a miracle worker.'

He cannot help beaming at her, and Jack looks unsure, as if he is intruding on something, and he leaves them to it.

She has missed being alone with Thomas, but though Devon John is unconscious, she still feels anxious when he wraps his arms around her.

'If anyone should catch us, Thomas . . .' she says.

'I cannot help it,' he says.

And she tries to imagine what would happen then. She is certain that the gibbet would come as a mercy.

He lets her go and steps away to pace awkwardly.

'We did not come here for this,' he says. 'We didn't come to rot here with Grey. We must get out. Find King Henry.'

She nods.

'But how?' she asks, looking around them at the damp curtain walls. 'It seems as easy to break out of a castle as to break into it.'

The gatehouse is always closed and guards armed with nocked bows patrol walkways, there to deter deserters as much as intruders. Their only hope is to be sent on a patrol with Horner, and attempt to slip away as opportunity affords, but so far they have not been permitted out of the castle's great encircling wall.

'And even if we managed it, we should have to go to Scotland.' Scotland sounds horrible, and impossibly far.

But just then the church bells start ringing and Horner approaches, striding across the bailey, looking purposeful and pleased.

'Finally,' he calls from some distance. 'Finally! King Henry is coming to Bamburgh.'

They look at one another. It is uncanny.

'Why?' she asks.

Horner is nonplussed, because why wouldn't King Henry come to Bamburgh? But Katherine wonders if it means the Scots have ejected him, as was threatened, and so there will be no more help for Henry's cause from that source, and what few supplies they have, well, they will soon be used up, won't they? And after they are, what then? But Horner is not interested in that.

'Now all we need is one spark!' he says. 'Just one little thing to set the country alight, to get it to rise up behind King Henry and oust this usurper Edward of March.'

There is a moment of silence. Thomas cannot help but glance at the pillow on which the boy is out cold. Horner looks down too.

'Christ, he looks drunk,' he says. 'Will he live?'

'I believe so,' Katherine says.

'Sir Ralph will be pleased,' Horner says.

'Why? I thought he was looking forward to hanging us as spies.'

'That's all changed now,' he says. 'One of King Henry's gentlemen of the bedchamber is carrying a wound that has so far defied his physician, and Sir Ralph has been boasting you are a miracle worker, and can cure him.'

Katherine is instantly nervous.

'Me?' she asks. 'I cannot just—'

Horner laughs at her predicament, then leaves them.

And Katherine sits suddenly, exhausted, there on the foot of the pile of filthy straw, her slight frame hidden in overlarge hose and pourpoint, an old-fashioned linen cap covering her ears, her fine fingers on the tip of her pointed chin, deep in anxious thought.

'At least we will be near King Henry,' he says.

And she looks at him and at that moment she is caught in a waft of the thin autumn light from the door, and she is so ethereally, delicately beautiful, to his mind, that he almost laughs.

'But Thomas,' she says. 'Should we still give King Henry the ledger?'

'Why not?'

'Because – because if this place is anything by which to judge the health of his cause, then I cannot imagine him ever prevailing against King Edward. You have forgotten, but I will never forget that army coming up the road to Towton. It took a day to ride from one end to the other, you know? And look at what Sir Ralph Grey has here. Two hundred men? Three hundred?'

'But King Henry might have a great power in Bamburgh?'

'Yes,' she says sadly. 'He might.'

There is a long silence.

'Well, let us see,' Thomas says. 'See what manner of army he has, then decide.'

She nods.

'And in the meantime,' she says, 'we have this wounded gentleman of the King's bedchamber.'

'He might prove a more reliable conduit to King Henry than Sir Ralph,' Thomas supposes. 'We might show it to him, and he in his turn might show it to King Henry, and then that's Horner's spark, the one that will light up the country in favour of Lancaster.'

He says it to reassure himself, but she nods.

'He could not be worse,' she says.

And then it is, finally, All Saints.

They have found some fresh straw and a clean blanket, and after Mass, Devon John, the boy, is sitting up, shirtless, waiting for Grey to come and pass him as alive. He is unable to stop looking at his stump, which he holds up like a fish's flipper, but he is definitely, defiantly still alive. He is swearing almost constantly – about the stump, about the pain he still feels, about the man who hit him with the billhook – in an accent you only hear in parts around London, and he keeps demanding more of Grey's distillation, on which he has developed a reliance.

Eventually Grey comes, approximately sober, and he peers at Devon John's stump and closes his eyes and mimes a shudder of revulsion.

'Dear God,' he says. 'Nevertheless, it is as fine as anything King Henry will have seen in Scotland these past months, of that you may be sure. So. Get him up, dressed and ready to ride before midday.'

'Today?' Katherine says.

'Yes,' Grey answers. 'Today. This morning. King Henry commands it. And you are to come too. And you, whatever your name is. And you too. Help make up the numbers.'

'He is not yet strong enough to walk much further than the privy. How will he cope with a ride in the rain?'

But Grey has turned and he waves his arm airily as he stalks away, just as the chapel bell is ringing again.

It is only a few hours later, just after noon, that they ride out on borrowed horses, under a scudding slate-grey sky. Devon John is slumped on a sag-backed pony between Thomas and Jack, his face the colour of goose fat, and Katherine watches him anxiously. He is well topped up with Sir Ralph's distillation, but even so, a trip like this could be the end of him.

'Is he all right?' Thomas asks.

'Doesn't matter anyway,' Jack calls. 'It's past All Saints. You've won your bet.'

They ride out through the barbican's mossy walls and over the bridge and below them the moat is stippled with raindrops and a boy is trying to fish for something in the pungent waters. Before they have ridden a bowshot, Grey stops the party while he uncorks his costrel and takes a nip of the spirit. Is it Thomas's imagination, but does the air waver over the bottle when it is uncorked? It seems so. They ride on, three abreast. Despite himself Thomas finds there is something special about riding in a party like this. He feels watched, feared, and very serious. He finds that his jaw is set and his gaze fixed in the distance. He supposes he would soon get used to it though, and come to find it boring.

The sea appears again at their right hand, restless and grey and scored with heavy foam-frilled waves, and that's where they first see Dunstanburgh Castle, sited above the sea on a skirt of black cliffs around which gulls wheel.

'D'you ever see such a spot?' Horner mutters. 'Wouldn't want to be there when the wind blows, mind.'

Thomas has never seen anything quite like it before. On one side is the sea, beating against vertical black stone cliffs, while on the other is a long slope down to three or four broad lakes through which a narrow road must twist to arrive at the turreted barbican. It must be impregnable.

They ride past and then come down through scattered black boulders on to a beech of fine sand where the waves thunder and throw up clouds of spray. They follow that, curving around, blown by sea spray, and then up again through broken dunes, and in the distance is another great pile of turrets and a square tower behind curtain walls.

'Bamburgh,' Horner tells them. He is just as proud of it as if he had built it himself, and it is possible to see why. Hard by the seashore it is a perfect succession of stone battlements topped by the massive tower of the keep. It seems huge when they first see it, and it takes the rest of the afternoon to reach it.

By the time they are there, it is late evening, time for Vespers, and Devon John is practically dead. Whether it is the cold or the lingering shocks of the amputation, Katherine does not know. Grey is quite drunk, too, chattering incessantly, and he sends a rider ahead to announce his arrival. As they come under the castle's lower barbican, the gates open and they process as usual into its court, and the gate is dropped with a boom behind them, and they are kept trapped in the dank yard while many eyes assess them. Thomas always hates this bit: sitting there, scrutinised, waiting not to be killed.

'Get on with it,' one of Horner's men calls, and after a pause the chains start their slow grind as the inner portcullis is raised and after a moment the huge gates beyond are drawn open. Thomas kicks his horse on, past some steps up to the keep, and into the inner bailey, sunk in gloom now, but crowded with men about the business of getting bread and ale, and finding themselves somewhere warm and dry for the night.

No one pays them much attention. They ride up to the great door of the keep where lanterns illuminate a knot of guards gathered on the steps, and Grey dismounts successfully, clings to his saddle a moment longer than he ought, then rights himself and sets off up the steps very deliberately. After a moment he stops and waits for Horner, who has removed his cloak to show his colours, to catch up. Thomas can hear the challenge, the reply, the muttered conversation that follows. He hears a note of peevishness from Grey, then a deep authoritative murmur. A message is sent. There is a moment of waiting. More men come from the doorway. A slim figure appears in better clothes than the others, and they step back respectfully. Explanations are offered, a misunderstanding cleared up.

Meanwhile Katherine swings off her horse, and Jack too, and they help Devon John down from his saddle. He is mute and limp, his face very white in the gloom, his eyes fast shut.

'We need a fire,' she says. 'Somewhere to warm him.'

Horner comes down the steps alone. King Henry will not see Grey today, but he is to be found space on a mattress in the keep, and is invited to dine in the same room as the King, if not at the same board. His men meanwhile are to be billeted in somewhere called the great outward postern gate, just about as far from the keep as they can be while remaining in the confines of the castle, and they will have to find food for themselves. There is a long moment while Grey's baggage is extracted from the mules, and then they remount, and ride down through the bailey again, following a slow-walking steward in pale livery who guides them to the inner postern gate, and then through it and into the outer bailey where now there are sheep – guarded especially at night by men with bills and bowmen – as well as the ruins of hovels and stables, pulled down for hearth wood. It is a bad sign.

'And we are to be given duties,' Horner admits. He is depressed. He had hoped for a flourishing garrison, ready to sally out to retake England for Henry of Lancaster. Not this.

The outward postern gate is shut and barred and there is no one in the lower guardrooms, where there are puddles and rotting straw on the flagstones and the walls are glossy and green with running water. Horner wrinkles his nose. It is like a cave, Thomas thinks. Up the circling steps there is the mechanism of the portcullis winch, two great piles of rusting chain links and a long iron bar with hand spikes. The wind whistles constantly in the murder holes. Up the next set of steps and the reason for the abandonment of the lower storeys is clear: there is a broad circular bread oven that dominates the room, of the sort in which a man might easily fit, three men even, and there are that number sitting on a ledge around it, with their backs against it now, legs outstretched, ankles crossed, one of them asleep, the others playing a form of dice. Their weapons – a billhook, three unnocked bows, a sheaf of arrows, and a short tapering sword – are a long hand-stretch away.

'Thanks be to God,' one of the dice men says when they tell him he is relieved of his post, and he wakes his companion. 'Come on, John,' he says. 'We're set free.'

While one goes up the steps to break the news to their colleague in the tower's top, the others pack up their few belongings, taking their weapons, their mugs and bowls, a sheet of waxed linen, and slinging the rough rolls of their mattresses over their shoulders.

'God's blessing on you,' the returning sentinel says. He is sodden through, his face as pale as parchment, and he stops to press his palms against the declining warmth of the oven's stones. 'You'll need it, here,' he adds.

When he is gone, Thomas and Jack help Katherine bring Devon John up the awkward steps and lean him against the oven, just where the other men were slumped. Thomas unblocks the door of the oven. Inside it is deep with grey ash, winking embers and the bones of yesterday's fire. There's no bread, that's for sure.

'Well,' Horner says, and he holds out his hands over the non-existent fire. Thomas already misses the guerite at Alnwick.

At dawn the next morning it is Thomas's watch, so he wakes and rises and climbs the steps up and pushes open the iron-bound door against the wind, and emerges on to the long rectangular space, with the wind fresh in his face, and he claps his hat to his head and looks about. Horner is there, looking tired. He turns and studies Thomas over his shoulder for a second, grunts something and then turns back. The stones of the wall are green with moss and lichen and caked in seagull shit. Underfoot, men have also relieved themselves in a gutter and despite the wind, the smell is clammy and strong. Beyond the wall, where the wind is coming from, is the broad ribbon of dunes and then the beach of white sand, leading to the sea, grey-green now, mist-shrouded and rising and falling as if it is breathing. There are seagulls everywhere, shrieking, floating in the air, their din louder than any clapped bell. To the north is the dwindling stretch of unworkable moorland, and to the west, more or less the same thing, save for a small village hard by the castle walls among the blackened ruins of a larger one in

which at least the church tower has been spared. Funny to look
down on it, he thinks.

Horner joins him, his fingertips green with lichen from the stones.

'Scots did that last year,' he says, indicating the burned walls of
the old village. 'Or maybe it was the Earl of March and his men the
year before?'

'Pity,' Thomas says.

'Yes,' Horner mutters. 'Christ. What a place. I'd imagined, you
know – more, more men. Less, less shit.'

'Yes,' Thomas says.

It starts raining. Both adjust their cloaks.

'We could find some wood?' Thomas suggests.

'I'll send some of the men out,' Horner moans, 'but the place has
been gone over a thousand times already.'

'Why don't I take Jack and see if we can't find anything in the
way of bread and ale?' he suggests.

'You can try,' Horner agrees, 'and get bread if you can. Not
oatcakes. D'you hear? If we're on oatcakes already then you know
things are worse than we thought.'

Thomas finds Jack by the oven and leads him down the steps and
out, trudging back up through the muddied paths of the outer bailey,
watched by the sheep and their armed herders. There are a few tents
to one side, from which oily smoke billows, and at their openings,
their inhabitants, dirty-faced men and women, a few children, are
hostile. Beyond are a few stalls such as you might find in a market,
where there are feathers and linens for sale, shoes, old clothes,
bundles of rushes and mattresses already made up, and candles.
Thomas can smell vinegar, rotting meat, wet stone, the cesspit.

And now he can hear the rhythmic tonk of men practising their
fighting, something Jack enjoys, both participating in and watching,
and next to him the boy picks up his pace, walking on his toes, since
someone told him this is how fighting men walk. They pass through
the inner postern gate, and then up into the inner bailey, where sure

enough they find men in various livery jackets going at one another with various weapons, and the noise and the smell reminds Thomas of some days before – before when? Something comes back to him, another fragment of time: in a small castle on a hill above the sea, and loosing arrows endlessly, all day, every day, falling asleep over supper with his back knotted and aflame. He remembers being shouted at, forced to run, forced to loose his bow. But he remembers laughter too. And something else. Something that leavened it all. A lightness like sunlight, something like that first moment when you realise from one day to the next that spring is really here.

'You all right, Thomas?' Jack asks and Thomas returns to the here and now.

'Yes,' he says. 'Sorry.'

Jack pats him on the shoulder. Thomas is grateful the boy is there, is grateful that he did not kill him in his brother's orchard all those months ago, grateful that he saved him from Elizabeth's vengeance.

Around them billmen are being drilled in companies, small groups of men-at-arms in harness are making elaborate and simultaneous moves across the worn grass of the bailey, past others fighting with weapons swabbed in cloth. Others crowd around, shouting the combatants on, and there is a pack of archers gathered at the far end, taking it in turns to send their blunts into targets pinned to butts set against the curtain wall. Horner would be happy to see this lot, Thomas thinks, but who are they all, in their various liveries?

'Them is Lord Hungerford's men there,' Jack tells him, 'and them belongs to Lord Roos. That one is Lord Tailboys. Them I don't know. But look. There are the King's men.'

And Thomas looks over. They do not look that different from the other men there, but in their buff coats with their St George's Cross badges, they hold themselves slightly apart, as if they may be special, and again, they feel slightly familiar and he has to shake his head to invite further revelations, or clear it entirely.

They walk on, hard-packed earth under their feet, into the shadow of the keep, its lower facade pierced with arrow loops and narrow windows, a spitting guard peering down through the merlons at the top. They pass the keep and enter a service yard where the kitchens are and there is a hubbub of raised voices, and a crowd of men is gathered, all in their various livery coats and badges, many more of them than before, many of whom Jack has never seen, all of them waiting with their backs turned, waiting impatiently for something to eat. And as Thomas walks towards them, he sees something and his heart starts thumping, and his ears roar. He stumbles.

'By Christ,' he mutters.

'What's wrong, Thomas?' Jack asks.

Thomas is breathing as if he has run a hundred paces. What is it? What is it? His eyes are fixed on the backs of the men in the crowd, and then there it is. He recognises it: a flash of something pale, white, with a pattern of dark shapes. He knows what the shape is: it is the rough approximation of a bird, a crow. But no, now that he knows more of these things, he knows that is more properly the rough approximation not of a crow, for who would have that? No. Instead it is a joke, a heraldic witticism, a play on words, for the bird is not a crow, but a raven.

Riven.

'Thomas? Bloody hell! What is wrong with you? Oh, Christ! Come on.'

He feels Jack's hand on his arm, and shakes it off.

'No,' he says. 'No.'

There are two of them in the livery, more besides.

Part of him is terrified. He knows he must get away, knows that these men will harm him, but part of him is thinking, calculating. Jack has a pail for the ale and a probably blunt eating-knife. Thomas's eating-knife is definitely blunt. One of the two men in the raven livery carries a bill with a polished blade, the other has a sword bound to his hip, and though he cannot see them, Thomas supposes each must have a dagger too. No, part of him thinks, this is not the time for fighting, and nor are these the men to fight.

They carry on up towards the knot of men, Thomas sidling towards the two in the livery, though now there are more of them, definitely a gathering. Christ. He feels they are closing in on him, trapping him, as if they know who he is, but his steps seem to be taking him towards them. He cannot stop himself. He starts to feel faint. He had not expected this. He looks for ways out, means of flight, but still, on he goes. And now all around him are armed men in that white livery with the black birds: some full jacks, others sleeveless tabards, grubby, travel-stained, and they are weary-looking men, too.

'It's all right, Thomas,' Jack says. 'It's all right. All we're here for is the bread, eh? Bread and ale. That's all. Then we'll get you back to Kit. He can see you right. Bread and ale, eh?'

Thomas finds himself in the queue with the other men. They have not noticed him. Jack is there, talking still. Thomas ignores him. He wants to hear what the men are saying. They want meat and ale, and are complaining to someone, then they are given something, and they step aside, only grudgingly. There is an obscure threat of sudden very bad violence. Thomas's hands are shaking. Breathing is hard. Standing upright seems more difficult than falling flat. He concentrates on the grit under his scuffed toecaps. And now, a few shuffling paces, and there is a half-door, as in a stable, and behind it, a woman, thickset, rough green dress, white head-dress, brown apron, and behind her a man, could be her twin, her husband, both, neither given to suffering fools, though fools them-selves, probably. The woman speaks. Asks a question. But the words are at a remove, as if from a distance, not meant for him, and he cannot stop himself turning away, staring at the two men, five paces away now, turned back towards the woman behind the door, and beyond them, there are others likewise dressed. One of them has a disc of something brown that he bites with bad teeth. The other has ginger hair under a felt hat just as flat as his oatcake. Thomas cannot look away.

Jack is at his shoulder. He leans across Thomas, getting between him and the men, and he holds out the bag to the woman behind the door, and says something, and the woman replies with something sharp and dismissive and throws handfuls of the brown disks into the bag's depths. Thomas cannot help but keep staring at the men. And then the first man turns. He catches Thomas's gaze and jerks his head back. He says something Thomas does not understand. A challenge. Within a moment he is stepping up to Thomas, chest out, chin jutting, hand on the hilt of the knife Thomas can now see, and there is probably another one he can't. The man barks the same phrase, a question, to which Thomas does not know the answer. The second man, ginger, face leaner than a blade, moves forward. He too has a knife, hanging from a leather strap across his chest, and the sword. His eyes are uncannily blue, even in the wet grey light of late afternoon, like one of those dogs. Other men drop back instinctively, delightedly, forming a loose ring, eyes lit up with anticipation. The woman behind the door swings it shut with a bang.

Thomas is still, unable to move, but Jack turns and manages to get between him and the two men.

'Whoa! Whoa! Whoa!' he calls. He has his arms outstretched, holding them apart. 'We're just getting bread, sirs,' he says. 'That is all. My friend, he means no harm. He has had a bang on the head. Look at him. Look at the white patch. There is a hole behind there through which you may touch his brains, if you've a mind to pay. He looks at people funny. Sometimes he is out of his wits. Come. Come, for the love of St Columba, let us calm ourselves, eh? Reserve our passion for our real enemies.'

Another man appears. A captain.

'The boy's right,' he says. 'Stop pissing about. First man to draw his blade'll have his neck stretched before the sun sets.'

There is a tense moment. Still Thomas cannot speak, nor help staring at the two men. Very slowly, Jack turns and guides Thomas away. There are disappointed groans from the crowd and some entreaties to stay and fight, but Riven's men are silent, staring, recording, and their hands do not stray from their knives.

'By Christ, Thomas,' Jack breathes, 'what are you doing picking fights with men like that?'

Thomas briefly wonders where Jack learned about men like that, living on a sheep farm in the middle of nowhere, but the boy is quick, and without him, he knows he might well be lying bleeding to death in the yard while men stepped over him to collect their oatcakes and ale.

'We must get back,' Thomas says. 'We must tell Kit.'

When he tells her, she can scarce believe it.

'No!'

'But I saw them,' he tells her. 'They are here. In the castle.'

'But Riven was in Cornford! He cannot have come up here! He would not.'

Thomas shakes his head. She is right. Why would he?

'Unless he has men in both camps?'

'Is that possible? Did you see any captain or vintenar with them? Anything to suggest they were here in someone's retinue?'

Thomas shakes his head.

'But there were enough of them,' he says, and he tells her about how he felt when he saw them. 'It was as if I was suffocating.'

'He went proper pale,' Jack adds. 'And he was staring at those two – by Christ, you should have seen them, Kit. They were fierce as ferrets. Scotch I reckon.'

The day wears on. Horner sends some men – not Thomas or Jack – out to comb the beach for driftwood, and others with a few pennies to buy more ale, since without it they will parch and wither to nothing. Both parties return with meagre success: the ale is thin and the few sticks and the length of silvered trunk will not burn without throwing off a fat cloud of black smoke and a foul stench. So they sit and they eat their oatcakes and they drink their ale gathered around the smoking bread oven while Devon John sleeps on, alive but senseless. They hear nothing of Grey, and Thomas imagines him in the keep at the board with King Henry and his earls and lords and so on, and all of them talking as if they are like to win this war, but after a moment his mind returns to those two men in Riven's livery, and what they are doing here. Across the room, sitting hunched in her cloak next to Devon John, Katherine is pressed to the warm stones of the oven, and she too is frowning in thought.

In the evening the bell in the church tower rings time, and it is their turn to go up the steps into the night to take a watch around the tower's top. They have a bull's-eye rush lamp to guide them, and when they emerge on to the tower, there is a strong cold wind off the sea that smells good and there is nothing to be seen except the glimmer of lights from similar lamps in the castle's other towers and faint glints from the windows of the keep.

'They are as desperate as ever we've been,' Thomas says. 'They cannot afford to feed themselves, let alone their horses, and there is little or no wood for watch fires . . .'

Katherine grunts. She is in no mood to speak, but remains deep in thought. Thomas shines the light out to sea. Pointless. Someone signals to him from another tower. He signals back. They are just as bored. He wanders the tower. Some parts are more malodorous than others. He peers into the night. Then, quire an hour later, Katherine clears her throat and he turns the lantern on her, its ochre light revealing chin, nose, cheekbones and brow, leaving her eyes in darkness.

'Thomas,' she starts, 'what if those men you saw today weren't Edmund Riven's?'

'But they were,' he says. 'I promise. I did not know the badge, or I didn't know that I knew it, but when I saw it again, I knew who they were. I knew they were Riven's men.'

'I'm not saying that,' she says. 'I'm not saying they weren't Riven's men.'

'Then — what?'

'What if they weren't Edmund Riven's men? What if they were *Giles* Riven's men?'

'Giles Riven's men? The father's, you mean? But how could they be? He is dead.'

'Is he?'

'You told me he was.'

'I know,' she says. 'I know. But — but only because we thought it so. We did not see or hear of him surviving that day at Towton, and so many were killed, it was natural to assume he was, too. But, but what if he wasn't killed? What if he survived the day?'

'You mean, what if he is alive?'

'Yes,' she says. 'I know you went up there to — to make sure he was killed, Thomas, but you are one man and there were many thousands there that day, weren't there? And you can remember none of it. I think we assumed that because you were dead, or so we thought — I mean, it is absurd, but that is what I thought — we thought he was dead too. I don't know why. It made it easier to accept, I suppose. But what if you were knocked down before you managed to kill him? What if that happened? I mean, that is more likely, isn't it?'

He says nothing. He sometimes gets flashes of snowflakes in the dusk; of lying face down on a jawless man with a beard of gore thickening into a glaze on his ripped steel plate. He feels cramps of pain, too, in his back and on the side of his head, and sometimes he wakes with his ears ringing with screams, and the tooth-jarring din of steel edge on steel edge.

'You are saying that because I am not dead, nor is he?'

'Well,' she says, 'I do not put it like that. All I am saying is that it could be that neither of you is dead.'

Of course this makes sense. Why should it be otherwise? But it does not explain why there are men wearing his livery in the bailey below.

'But then, why are they here? They should be with Edmund Riven.'

'Unless, unless they are with Giles Riven.'

'But that means,' he says, 'that means, what you are saying, is if those men are Giles Riven's men, then Giles Riven is here. In this castle. He is in the keep even now, with Grey and with King Henry?'

And she nods, and he feels a warmth come over him, despite the coldness of the wind and of the stones that surround him, and suddenly he is sure of it. My God, he thinks, Giles Riven is here.

14

They are on watch at Prime, standing to in the grey dawn, listening to sheep bleat and gulls cry, witnessing the world emerging through the murk of cloud out to sea, watching light fill the castle and reveal its contained world: a tented village from which hearth smoke whispers in trembling ribbons. A thin rain persists. Soon the bell in the church in the village rings the angelus, sounding hollow in the morning's cold, and Katherine cannot stop herself shivering, like a greyhound, and Thomas tells her it is a good sign.

'It is when you stop shivering you must worry,' he says.

It is all right for him, she thinks. He seems immune to the cold. She wonders if it is because he was brought up on that farm, in those hills, or because he is so big? Surely it is no accident that you only see thin people – and thin dogs – shiver? Thomas is solid with muscle, and always, even in the direst circumstances, he looks to be thriving. He is almost impossible to feel sorry for, in that regard at least.

Of course, he looks miserable now; they both do. They have spent the night awake, pacing the walkway, wracking their brains, trying to remember what happened that day at Towton, trying to envisage a set of circumstances that might place a dead man alive at the centre of the court of an exiled king. In the early hours she persuaded herself she must be mistaken about him, and that Riven must be dead, must be interred with all the others who in the weeks that followed the battle were rolled into huge stinking pits, just as he deserved, but now, at dawn, she believes she is right: that Riven is alive, and that she – and Sir John and Richard Fakenham – have lived these last few years in a fools' paradise, basing their belief that he was dead on flimsy hope and wayward supposition, on an absence of proof rather than a presence.

She watches as a couple of oxen pulling carts of steaming night soil are lashed through the inner postern gate; there are lines of men on the walkway pissing over the curtain walls, and she looks for any in white livery with that distinctive spread of black birds, but sees none.

'But if Giles Riven is alive,' Thomas starts as if in reply to something she'd said, 'he would not be here, would he? He would be with his son. He would be at Cornford.'

It is a question they have gone over again and again, all night, and yet they remain incredulous.

'But then what are those men doing here if he's not?'

'Perhaps that livery is all they have left to them? It looked worn.' She nods.

'It is possible,' she supposes, 'but surely they would have taken up with another lord? One who would look to their welfare and give them his livery to wear in return?'

Now Thomas nods.

'But if Giles Riven is here, that means he is with King Henry, while his son is with King Edward. A father against his son? It is unnatural!'

'But perhaps,' she says, 'perhaps they are not against one another? Perhaps they are waiting to see which way the tree will fall?'

Thomas considers this and shakes his head. It is too cunning for him.

'No,' he says, 'that is too much, surely? And would King Henry trust the father while knowing the son stands with King Edward? No. Nor would King Edward trust the son while the father stands with King Henry. They can only have – have taken up arms against one another, however unnatural that seems.'

225

She tries to imagine how that might come about, and remembers the moment the father and son attacked her, in the snow, years ago now, and she thinks that such men might easily fall out with one another and if they did, daggers would soon be drawn. Perhaps Thomas is right?

'We will hear when Jack gets back,' she says.

She looks down now and watches Horner crossing the bailey, leaving a track in the dew. He is leading Jack and another man carrying the ale bucket and the bread bag towards the kitchens. They no longer trust Thomas to get the right thing without causing a fight. Thomas meanwhile is staring out to sea, from where the rhythmic thump of the waves rises, and he is lost in thought, introvert and distant again. Every moment they have alone together is precious, so this time feels wasted. She joins him at the wall, and puts a hand on his shoulder, conscious that someone – anyone – might see them. He slides a hand around her waist.

'Even when he is not here, even when he is dead, or might be dead, he ruins things for us,' Thomas says.

They stand for a long moment. She rests her head on his shoulder. Despite it all she feels soothed, warmed by him, and she breaks away only very reluctantly, very late, when Jack comes up the steps with a costrel of ale and some oatcakes.

'Well?' Thomas asks.

Jack nods.

'They are with this Giles Riven fellow,' he says, 'as you supposed. They are not rightly amicable company, either, I have to say, but listen, Thomas, those two you crossed in the yard – they are out for you, the others said, meaning to cut you from groin to gizzard, so do not wander off down there in search of a game of chess or chequers.'

And though the confirmation comes as no surprise, Katherine feels a heavy press of sorrow and hopelessness. She closes her eyes momentarily, and turns away.

'Where are they billeted?' she hears Thomas ask Jack.

'In the main gatehouse,' Jack tells them, gesturing up the hill. 'But he is not with them. He is with King Henry and the other nobs in the keep. His company are mostly Scots, in it for the money, of course, some Lincolnshire men and a few Frenchies, too, with guns.'

Jack takes a bite of his oatcake and a long drink of ale. Then he leaves them, going back down the steps and off to watch the exercises in the inner bailey, hoping some of the Burgundian gunners will be there to give a demonstration, and Katherine and Thomas linger, since they have nowhere else to go.

'By Christ,' she murmurs. 'It never gets much better, does it?'

Thomas says nothing and after a while she puts her hand on his arm, just as she has seen Isabella do with Sir John, and he places his palm over it, just as Sir John did with Isabella, and for a moment they are both still, and she feels a curious melancholic contentment, a curious return to how it was. They watch Jack walk back up to the inner bailey.

'I will have to find him and fight him again,' Thomas says. 'Riven, I mean, and this time, by Christ, I will – I will kill him.'

'But how?' she asks. 'He will be surrounded by his men, or if not his men, then King Henry's. You will never get close.'

She tries to imagine Thomas challenging him to some sort of trial by combat, or sticking him with a knife while they are out walking, but he will never get close enough to do that, not with Riven in the keep up on the hill, and besides, she can't imagine it. That is not Thomas. He is not a murderer.

'If I see him with his men, in the bailey say, I might knock him down with an arrow?' Thomas suggests, miming the action of loosing a bowstring, though only half-heartedly, knowing he never could.

There is that, she supposes, but again, no.

'There must be a way,' he says, though he is at a loss.

'It will come,' she says. 'It must.'

There is a long silence. They watch the comings and goings in the outer bailey. There is a strange atmosphere in this castle, she thinks, and wonders whether it is usual of all castles or unique to this one. Despite it not being under attack or under siege, it feels beleaguered, parlous, and even the men practising their fighting, she sees now, seem to be going through their motions with little conviction. And how many men are here? Hundreds? Thousands, perhaps. But how many thousands? One? Two? There are others in the other castles, of course, but enough to make an army? And what of all the others needed to people an army? The cooks and brewers to keep the men alive, the ostlers for the horses, and all those others? The smiths, the armourers, the bowyers, the fletchers and the stringfellows? What about them?

'It is not how I imagined it when we thought of handing King Henry the ledger,' she says. 'I thought he would have a proper army, something with which to challenge Edward.'

Thomas grunts.

'Yes, but you know what this means now, don't you?' he asks. 'With Giles Riven here, on King Henry's side, anything we do to benefit King Henry benefits him. While anything we don't do – if we don't give King Henry the ledger – that benefits the son.'

Their thoughts are circular, repetitive, always coming back to the same thing.

'Yes,' she says. 'Either way, we lose.'

He sighs again, and so does she.

'They have a foot in each camp,' he says, 'waiting to see which way the wind blows.'

They are silent for a while, each wrapped in the same thoughts.

'But – but what if,' she begins, 'what if we could provoke them to remove a foot? Get one of them to jump into the other camp?'

'How?' he asks. 'And which camp do we want them both in?'

'The ledger,' she says. 'It is all we have. And it only weakens King Edward, and strengthens King Henry, so we must use it to lure Edmund Riven to join his father.'

'Here?'

They look around. It is not encouraging.

228

'Yes,' she says, almost despite herself. 'The ledger will turn the tide, Thomas. You'll see. It will attract new men. That is all that is missing. It is as Horner says.'

'And once Edmund Riven thinks King Henry will win, he will jump into his camp?'

'Yes,' she says.

'And then we hope both Rivens take the field with King Henry, and then King Edward beats them, as he did at Towton?'

'Yes,' she supposes. 'But if he does not, and if King Henry wins, he will naturally reward us for providing him with the ledger.'

'With Cornford?'

'At the very least,' she says.

She thinks of all the men who will lose their lives if this scheme comes to fruition. She thinks of another battle of Towton. Dear God, she thinks. Dear God.

Now they hear Horner's feet hurrying up the steps.

'There you are,' he says. 'Sir Ralph's been boasting to King Henry about you, Kit, and about Devon John's arm, and so now King Henry wants to see it. Or what's left of it. So clean him up, will you? A clean shirt, at least, and we're to present him to King Henry in the great hall before the bell is rung for Sext. They'll have a decent fire going there, at any rate, and we might find something to eat.'

So they wash themselves in water that is painfully cold to the touch, and then Horner gives them each a tabard coat of Sir Ralph's livery, never before worn, and saved for a moment such as this. They pull on the woollen cloths and tie them at their waists. It is pleasing to be wearing something, to touch something, that is actually new and unworn. She is happy to see hers is too long, and hangs below her crotch.

'You do not need to shave, Kit?' Horner says. It is half-question, half-observation.

'No,' she says. 'Or not often. We don't, in my family.'

'Lucky,' Horner grunts. Nothing more is said.

'Well, come on, then,' he says, and he turns, but now there is a moment's pause.

Katherine feels her heart beating, and she is aware of the import of the moment. Thomas looks at her, and she looks at Thomas. Will they do it? Will they take the ledger to King Henry? Will they cast the dice? Set the ball rolling?

She opens her mouth to say something – she is not sure what – but Thomas has already bent and collected the ledger in its bag, and he has slipped it over his head so that it hangs, as usual, between his shoulder blades. And then they take an armpit each and they haul Devon John to his feet. His legs are very weak.

'Ha!' Horner laughs. 'He's like a foal.'

But they get him down the winding steps and support him all the way up through the inner postern gate and up past the men who are back in the inner bailey, back at their fighting practice, the rippling clang of their muffled instruments competing with the shouted instructions from the vintenars and captains and the thick twang of bowstrings. Katherine sees no men in Riven's livery until they reach the kitchens, though, where four of them are menacing a boy over the price of a pig with bristles as red as a squirrel. She feels herself breathing more quickly in their presence, as if she is somehow there to be found out.

'What will you do if he is there in the room?' she asks Thomas quietly. 'If he is sitting at the board with King Henry?'

'I don't know,' Thomas admits. He looks anxious. She tries again to imagine Thomas killing a man as he sits at his dinner board, but she cannot. Thomas is not that sort of man. Riven would have to attack him first, and then she thinks, my God, what if Riven recognises Thomas? He would attack him, surely? Riven is just that sort of man.

'I don't know if he would,' Thomas hazards. 'He last saw me five years ago, when I was a canon with a tonsure—'

'Still, though,' she says. 'You fought him, didn't you? You were eye to eye. And you let him live. That will – he will never have been able to forget that.'

'In that case . . .' Thomas says, and he opens his brigandine to remove her the blade she herself sharpened while she was in the priory, tucked into the wadding under his armpit. She exhales. Christ, she thinks, if Riven recognises Thomas, and that is all he has, then we are all dead, one way or another.

'We are like Daniel,' she says, and he nods.

'Yes,' he says, 'though these lions are armed with swords.'

The walk up to the great hall becomes a sombre affair, more like the approach to the headsman's block, and Horner asks why they are so glum. They don't answer. Thomas is stern and mute, his face clenched, supporting waxy-faced Devon John who is silent, concentrating on not falling, or not being sick, it is hard to tell. At the steps up to the hall, the captain of the Watch stops them. Having heard of Devon John's cutting, he is as interested in the wound as might be any man with cause to fear the same fate.

'Did it hurt?' he asks before he will let them pass. Devon John admits he does not remember anything of it. He has a low burr that makes him seem a simple soul, but Katherine has heard him swear and burble in his sleep and call out for someone called Meg, and also for someone called Liz, and she knows there is more to him than he lets on. Devon John shows the guard his stump, which both delights and repulses him. He leans forward to prod it with an extended forefinger.

'By the rood, man! That is disgusting. Put it away. And come on. You're late. King Henry will be at prayer before long.'

He turns and leads them hurrying up the steps, along a dark passageway, and through a side door where they are faced with a broad stretch of some blank cloth on a wooden frame. A musician in green sits on a stool in the shadows, glumly chewing a crust with his instrument propped against his knee. He watches with a puzzled frown as Thomas reaches over and gives Katherine's shoulder what is meant as a reassuring squeeze, and then, without a moment to hesitate, Horner shunts them from the darkness behind the screen and into the space of the hall itself, where their shuffling appearance silences the whispered conversations, and the hurrying servants are stilled, and twenty pairs of bored eyes turn their way.

She searches quickly. Where is he? Where is Riven? Which one is he? Will she recognise him? Or will he recognise her first? Her gaze flicks from face to face. She knows what he will look like, she is sure of it, but no. None match, and beside her, Thomas, who perhaps will recognise the face of the man he once fought almost to the death, sighs a long plume of relief. Riven is not here. Thank Christ in His heaven. She breathes, and sees Thomas pull his coat together to secrete the unwanted blade more thoroughly.

The boards are arranged in a horseshoe, and down each length the men stare at Katherine and Thomas and Horner and Devon John with careless hostility. They are mostly men of a certain age, though there are one or two youths among them, and they are mostly of a certain type – pursed mouths in the broad unchapped cheeks of those who need not spend their days beyond the threshold – and, save for the priests, they are dressed alike in elaborate hats, and their shoulders are extended by the padded cut of their gowns.

And sitting raised on a dais, half-hidden behind a golden salt cellar the size of a child's head, is the man who should be the centre of it all: King Henry. But of all present, including the two priests at his sides, he is the least impressive. The face above his supine shoulders is soft and long, and he appears tentative, as if he feels he need seek permission to do this or that, and he is never still, but he fiddles with the rings on his fingers, with his linen cloth, with the collar of his simple linen shirt, even the gold circle in his hair.

The great hall is enormously high-roofed, elaborately beamed, with vast woollen tapestries on all four walls and tapering windows, fully glazed, above. There is place for a fire as big as some houses she knows, and in its depths the flames sullenly consume an unseasoned log that hisses and steams, but throws out no heat. The boards along each wall are covered in very white cloths that hang low, and on them are various pots and dishes and trenchers piled with pastries and greenery, and what look like small loaves.

Sir Ralph Grey is at the end of the left-hand board, ruby-cheeked with drink, and now he leaps up and prances into the space between the two table wings with his skinny shanks and his belly that bulges above his belt like a cooking pot. He bows low to King Henry, who smiles uncertainly back.

'Your grace!' he begins. 'Sirs! Allow me to share with you this marvel of the surgeon's craft!'

He introduces Devon John, or rather Devon John's stump, since Devon John himself is of no interest to the assembled company, and then he goes on to make extravagant claims as to his role in the cutting. Then he demands that Devon John exhibit his stump, and Devon John does so, pulling up his sleeve to expose it like the crowning head of a baby. There is a clatter of knives and spoons and a pushing away of bowls and trenchers and the man nearest the stump mutters something about the love of God. But King Henry is interested.

'May we see?' he asks. He looks around, as if seeking permission from the priests and the courtiers, and Grey pushes Devon John toward King Henry. Devon John walks the few paces, his stump leading the way. King Henry's expression over Devon John's head is hard to interpret. If he weren't the king, Katherine might think he was trying to empathise with Devon John, trying to imagine what it might be like to lose a limb. After a moment, he speaks.

'We have a physician,' he says in a fluttering voice, 'who knows the movement of the planets, and can tell the balance of our humours by the smell of our urine alone.'

The priest with no beard claps encouragingly and smiles at King Henry as if owning such a thing is a great accomplishment. The others on the boards are silent.

233

'We have been ill,' King Henry continues, confiding in Devon John now. 'They tell us that we did not move a muscle for a year. As if we were made of stone, they said, like the carved image of a saint or a martyr in one of our cathedrals. Except we were soft. Our wife, the queen, may God keep her safe, prayed for us, and we came back to her, and to our miraculous son Edward, may God also cherish him. But they are in France now, do you know? Undertaking their great task. We wish we were with them. Or they with us. Or we all in Windsor, together.'

The beardless priest is delighted by this eloquence. Elsewhere the silence persists.

'Would you like to meet my physician?' King Henry asks Devon John. 'His name is Master Payne. A good name for a physician, don't you think?'

Devon John turns for guidance to Grey, who clenches his stained teeth and nods enough so that the tassel on his soft cap dances long after he is still again. Devon John says he would. King Henry raises his eyes to a nearby servant as if they hurt him, as if he has the 'flu, and the servant departs. King Henry returns his gaze to Devon John. He smiles almost apologetically, but says nothing, and the silence persists. Not even Grey says anything.

After a while there is a shuffling, the noise of a musical instrument hitting the ground, and then, from behind the tapestry from which they themselves entered earlier, comes a tall man in a soft blue gown, slightly patterned, with a grey-furred collar. He is tall, broad-shouldered, with a close-trimmed beard that suits him, and a lively 'what now?' expression on his handsome features. His cap, a tall red thing, obviously expensive, probably a gift, is perched just so on his fine black hair that hangs longer than the other men wear theirs, almost to the fur collar, and he moves quickly, unencumbered by harness, or the weapons that seem to weigh other men down. The wool of his hose is very fine-spun, and his shoes are wonderfully piked, and have never met mud.

'I am sorry, your grace,' Payne says. 'I was attending to the patient.'

He has a fine voice, carefully enunciated, and King Henry beams at him forgivingly, but there is a stiffening of spines around the table, as if these men approve of neither the patient nor the physician.

'How fares he today?' King Henry asks, blind to their reaction. 'Is he in good spirits?'

There is a moment's hesitation before Payne replies:

'Thanks to your prayers, your grace, and God's ever-continuing mercy, of course, he is tolerably comfortable.'

King Henry bows his head to accept the praise. It is not, Katherine thinks, intended as pure praise, but, rather, has a weariness about it.

'You are too modest, Master Payne,' he says. 'It is in part your skill that keeps him with us, of that I am sure, and with God's great blessings he will make a recovery, and return to us ever more determined to serve. But, as we speak of wounds, pray take a look at this. A stump, where this man's arm once was. I know nothing of these things, but they tell me it is cunningly done?'

Payne glances across at Devon John, then down at his stump. He looks again. His eyes sharpen.

'Ha,' he says, coming to cup the stump in his palm. 'It is. It is cunningly done, indeed. No burning, no dipping in tar, just stitched. Exemplary.'

'Yes,' Grey intervenes. 'My surgeon cut it off, with a silver blade blessed by the Pope himself.'

'Thought you said it was the Bishop of Toledo,' the man at the head of the board mutters.

'I said that was the saw,' Grey says.

'And who is your surgeon?' Payne asks.

'Here,' Grey says. 'Step forward, if you please, master.'

And now the blood floods to Katherine's cheeks. She has not thought this through. She did not expect this. She cannot stand examination by all these men. Someone will say something. She does not move. But Grey is insistent.

'Come, master,' he prompts. 'He is modest, your grace.'

And King Henry smiles as if to say that is as it should be, but he waits, and they all do too, and Payne cocks an eyebrow, and so now she must step forward. She feels naked, as if she were one of those women in the marketplace, and she withers within, wishing she did not fill her clothes at all, wishing she could now be set loose to run. But she can't and Grey is smiling furiously. She steps forward. There is a muttering of incredulity from the men at the boards.

'This boy?'

'This scruff?'

'No, surely?'

But Payne studies her and cocks his head to one side.

'Hmmm,' he says, and she waits for it to come, for him to say something, for she is sure that this is the one, the man who will see straight through her stupid costume, and part of her – dear God! Part of her wants him to! But instead he folds his arms and taps his lips with one finger, and says nothing more, but there is a smile on his lips that will not go away.

King Henry too, says nothing, but she can see he is just as surprised, and as well he might be, she thinks, for she is dressed even worse than King Henry. She is in an old linen cap to cover her ear, an overlarge tabard that hangs loose to below her codpiece, and her hose sag at the knee. Only her boots are good. She stands and is unsteady in them and she can feel the sweat dripping and tingling on the lodestone that she keeps around her neck, and she wishes to God she were anywhere else but here.

She bends her head to King Henry.

'Your grace,' she says.

And King Henry smiles uncertainly again but Grey is going on.

'I assure you, sirs,' he says. 'I saw it with my very own eyes. The boy cut the arm, first with a knife, around, then with a saw.'

'A marvel,' Payne says. King Henry turns to him.

'Sir Ralph Grey of Castle Heaton begs us to allow his surgeon to see the patient,' he tells Payne, and Payne closes his eyes for a moment, more in sorrow than in anything else, and she sees that he is in fact sensitive to the slight, though, she thinks, used to that sort of thing, as if he had, indeed, been expecting it. She is treading on his toes, she thinks, and wishes she weren't.

'May I ask the master a question, your grace?' Payne asks.

King Henry checks with the bearded priest if he might allow it, and the bearded priest nods impatiently through his eating, and so then King Henry allows it. Payne turns to her. She can hardly swallow for the lump in her throat and she blushes warmly. Here it comes, she thinks, here it comes. What will she do? Run. Back out into the bailey and then – she has no idea.

'Under whom did you train?' he asks.

She can barely croak an answer.

'Well?' Payne persists.

'I did not train under one single master,' she says. 'But I have read. Widely. And I have worked in numerous hospitals.'

'Hospitals,' he says. 'Where?'

She is about to answer when at the last moment she sees she has set herself yet another trap. If she answers Hereford, where she believes she learned the most, treating the wounded after the battle of Mortimer's Cross, then the men here will naturally know that she was saving the lives of men who fought against King Henry, and now, she sees, that she cannot say Towton either, for the same reason. But Thomas has seen the danger too.

'You said you would only ask one question,' he intervenes, using that confident voice.

Payne glances over at him.

'And who are you, sir?'

'Only one question,' Thomas repeats.

Payne appeals to King Henry.

'But, your grace,' he says.

King Henry chuckles. The beardless priest laughs.

'It is as you asked, Master Payne,' King Henry says. 'One question.'

Payne says nothing. He closes his eyes and takes a step back. King Henry is childish, she can see this is what he thinks. He makes a mock gracious bow. Katherine turns to King Henry again. She must speak now, she thinks. She must show him the ledger. She will never have the chance again. She holds out her hand for the ledger that Thomas begins to swing from his shoulder.

'Your grace,' she begins, 'if I may—'

But then a bell rings above the distant chapel, and there is a moment of perfect stillness in the room while everybody makes sure they are hearing what they think they are hearing, and then King Henry stands and a moment later there is the scrape of the benches being pushed back as everybody joins him, and then they turn to their right, and the King proceeds out of the room through a door towards the tolling bell. The priests follow him, and then the other men who'd been at board. They file into a line behind King Henry, each face a character study of impatience, or frustration, or resignation, except for Sir Ralph who glares at them as if they have somehow let him down, and the servants – mostly young men who look as if they will develop into the same sort of men as those who are just now trooping out after King Henry – wait until the last back has filed through the door and then there is a sudden flurry of violent action as they fall on the remains of the meal, snatching bread rolls and bowls of dense-looking stew from the table and the victors guard their spoils and back away, retiring to different points of the room to gorge on their rewards.

15

The summons from Sir Ralph comes after Katherine and Thomas have just finished the food they stole from King Henry's board and the taste of the gravy-soaked crust and the white bread has barely faded from their lips. They are sitting by the hardly warm oven again, when Horner comes up the winding steps.

'Sir Ralph is after an audience with you, Kit,' he tells them. 'Something to discuss. Sorry.'

Sir Ralph Grey meets them in the great hall where they were presented to King Henry earlier in the day. The boards have been cleared, dust motes whirl in the wan autumn light from the long windows, and the fire has died in its place. Grey, who has been celebrating the success of his audience with King Henry, is sitting on a coffer, smiling warmly at a long-nosed dog busy with a beef bone.

'Ahhh,' he says when he sees them. 'Aaaahhhh.'

He stands and sits again, so that his head is slightly lower than theirs, his rheumy eyes peering up not unlike the dog's, and he smells strongly of his spirit.

'Boy,' he says, addressing Katherine. 'I mean, ahhh, master. I want you to see to this patient of the King's. I – to tell the truth, and this is absolutely. No. No. I want you to cure him. Do you see? Cure him. Why? Why? Well. I've never met him. I can't speak for him. He may be a good Christian. He may not be. As I say. I don't know him. Never met him. I am not one to judge. But the thing is, now, I need you to – hmmmm?'

She has to remain calm.

'What is wrong with him?' she asks.

'Wrong with him?' Grey says. 'Wrong with him? There's nothing wrong with him. He is as stout a Christian who ever walked God's earth. I daresay. As I say. I know people say things about him. How he turned his coat and betrayed his king, but I'll fight the man who says there is something wrong with – with – with him.'

He puts his hand on his dagger handle but doesn't draw it. Then he switches character, becomes confiding.

'No,' he says. 'The truth is, I mean, forget about him. The truth is, I've made a little bet. With Tailboys. You know him, hmmm? Moneybags, I call him. Always got gold. Keeper of the King's Purse. Or is he? I don't know. You tell me. Anyway. But. As I say. If you can cure the patient, get him on his feet, strong enough to mount a horse – unaided, mind, unaided. No easy task at the – ah – best of times. Then – well. I stand to gain a lot. And I mean rather a lot. Of money.'

He draws the words out and taps the side of his nose. She is absently surprised at this being true. There does not seem like an awful lot of money about the place.

'But Sir Ralph,' Thomas begins. 'What is his illness? Kit – Master Kit – cannot cure him if he is – I don't know. He cannot cure everything. Some things cannot be cured.'

'Say no more!' Grey interrupts, holding up a hand. 'Say no more. Quite understand. Quite understand. Can't cure everything. Not a miracle worker. Absolutely. Understood. But. But there is this thing, I should say, that the piss-sniffer physician made me think, and it is that you aren't a real surgeon.'

There is a moment of silence. She forgets to say she is, because for God's sake, she is not.

'And I was remembering,' Grey goes on, 'how you two blew in, to the castle, in Alnwick. Telling some story about how you were knocked flat at Towton, weren't you? No livery and no one to maintain you save a tale of some gentle no one'd ever heard of. I mean, I can't – remember, can I? Can you, Horner? No. You see? And so we are left wondering if you really are who you say you are? Or whether you are, what? Spies. Sent by that bastard John Neville, the so-called, hmmm? Lord Montagu. Yes. So. If you are. And I am saying nothing. I don't judge. I don't judge. Do I? But I was wondering. If that were the – ah – case. If you were spies. If you were not the surgeon you say you are, then we might be calling on the hangman, right here in Bamburgh? I believe they have a gibbet already set up.'

He nods to indicate somewhere out in the bailey.

'But Kit cured the boy!' Thomas says. 'He cured Devon John! Surely that is proof enough?'

'Oh, pish!' Grey swats away the objection. 'Might have been luck. Boy might have lived anyway. His arm could have fallen off. Ha!'

They say nothing.

'So you must prove your skills afresh,' Grey says. 'Get the bugger strong enough to climb into a saddle, eh? It is all for which King Henry most fervently wishes. Yes. You see? Then we'll be in funds, or I will, at any rate, and we can – well, I'll tell you what. I will pay, and I mean pay, a priest. No. No. Fair enough. You are right. I will pay two priests to say Mass for your soul, should you ever need prayers said for your soul, for all eternity. How's about that?'

'A generous offer,' Horner adds.

'But—' Thomas starts.

'Isn't it? Isn't it?' Grey interrupts. 'So it is agreed. You will see this malingering wretch. You will get him up on his horse. Cure him, I mean, of whatever is wrong with him and then. And then we'll, we'll see what we shall see, eh? Hmm? Hmm?'

How can she avoid this?

'I lack any tools,' she tells him.

'Knives and so forth? I thought you had them? No. No. I shall provide them. Have no fear. I shall ask what's-his-name? The piss sniffer?'

'Master Payne,' Thomas tells him.

'Master Pain?' Grey laughs. 'Is that his name? Master Pain! D'you see? Master Pain! Master Pain the piss sniffer. Oh, very good.'

When he is done laughing he shouts for a servant who comes after a moment and waits with no pretence of patience. Katherine sees that already Grey has set everybody against him. He tells the servant to ask – in King Henry's name – the piss sniffer Payne to lend Katherine his tools.

'Master Payne is with the patient now,' the servant tells them.

'Is he? Is he?' Grey says, his eyes lighting up. 'Well then, lead on! There is no time like the present.'

'Wait,' she says. Only now she can't think of anything to say.

'What for?' Grey wants to know. 'By the Mass, boy! Get on with it. We can't hang about all day. Fellow might die before you make up your mind to save him, and then where will we be? Dangling from a rope with no Masses for your immortal soul! That's where you'll be. Could spend the rest of eternity in purgatory. More than that, my purse will wither and we'll be stuck here for ever. Be the death of us all, that.'

'Kit needs food, sir,' Thomas says. 'He cannot perform without sustenance.'

Grey tuts, then turns to the servant.

'Bring things, will you? Ale and so forth. That is what you most like, you people, isn't it, eh? Ale?'

By the end of their conversation, it seems Grey is almost sober, and she wonders how drunk he was to begin with. They follow the servant from the room and along a stone-floored passageway, past small cells with open doors where men are sprawled, or huddled over fires, not up to much, or playing dice, and then first up and then down some steps until they are deep within the keep. He takes them up a spiralling set of steps worn uneven over the years, where it is so dark there are rush lamps alight in sconces.

'At least it's warm, eh?' Grey says over his shoulder. 'Horner pointed out your billets. Should not fancy them myself. Especially not this time of year.'

The servant is silent until they reach the third storey, when he leads them from the steps along another passageway, and then another tighter, danker, with rougher, undressed stones, and there at the end in the deepest gloom is a blur of something pale – a man, turning to them, in a white jacket – and Katherine is seized by the sudden absolute certainty that she does not want to go down there. She finds herself backing away, and Thomas collides with her, and then he sees what she has, and he too draws a breath. Neither says a word.

Grey and the servant block the passageway until she cannot see the man, but he is there, she knows, and she knows what he is wearing. He is in Riven's livery, and with a sudden rush, she is certain without a doubt, at last, just who the King's patient is.

'My God,' she says. 'It is Giles Riven.'

And Thomas's eyes widen in the gloom and he gasps: 'No!'

And as they stare up along the passage a terrible thought comes to her mind. What if that man is the giant?

'Come on!' Grey calls. 'By Christ!'

And now Horner is there behind, pushing them forward, and it is as if he has never trusted them either. She wonders whether she can turn and get past him and just run, back to the tower, and then, somehow – though she knows it is not possible – somehow, away. But she can't get past Horner, and Thomas is blocking her way too, fumbling in his brigandine to find that blade, and now he is trying to get past her, to get to the giant, and she knows the giant will kill him if he tries, and so she is then caught between them all, and she grabs his arm.

'No,' she tells him. 'No. Don't try. Don't try. Just pass him by.'

And he tears his arm free, and he is breathing fiercely, and he looks mad.

'Thomas,' she says. 'Thomas.'

And he seems to snap out of it, to subside, and after a moment he nods and returns the blade to his jack, and Grey is calling them and Horner is looking at them as if they are both mad. So she turns, and she gathers herself and takes a deep breath and tries to stop the shaking, and she steps forward and as she walks the passageway seems to narrow, closing in on her, her view constricting as if entering a hole, and her pulse booms and she can hardly breathe, and then there he is, only, thank God, it is not him: it is not the giant. It is another man. Not as big, though still too tall to stand straight in the passageway, and he looms over the small forms of the servant and of Grey and they are talking up to him, demanding he open the door, but he will only do it once reassured that they are on the King's business, 'come to save his lord and master'.

He opens the door and grey light seeps into the passageway. The guard steps into the room beyond, then the servant and Grey follow and she hears two men speaking and she stands there, and in that moment, her mind seems to go blank and she finds herself concentrating on the incidentals, the things that don't matter, such as the construction of the door, which is thick and studded, with crude iron hinges and a locking handle, when she knows that she is mere paces from the man who once tried to kill her, and has done more harm to her than any man alive, the man whom she hates more than she loves her own life, and she finds she cannot move, she can hardly breathe. He is there. In the chamber, not ten paces away. She can probably smell him.

'Come on, come on,' Grey calls from within the chamber. She can hear Thomas breathing quickly behind. She does not want to go in, but now it is Thomas's turn to calm her down, and he places his hand on her shoulder. He does not push her, but just keeps it there a moment, and his palm's warmth is enough. She draws breath, and enters the little chamber.

And, after all that, there he is. Giles Riven. On a mattress, raised on a carpented wooden bed frame. He lies on his front. With his head turned away, facing the wall, but still, she knows. She knows it is him. He has blankets pulled up to his waist, and a linen sheet to his shoulders, but from it his right arm is thrust out awkwardly, over the bed's edge, resting on a milking stool. His hair is brown, unclean, cut above the ears, as if he were wearing a woollen cap. He does not move. He could be asleep.

Thomas is beside her, behind her, likewise staring, likewise stiffened, open-mouthed. She glances at him, and after a moment he at her. Christ, it is absurd. The man they have been looking to kill for so long, the man whom they have both promised to kill, lies helpless, with his back to them, naked as a worm, and Thomas has that blade hidden in his brigandine. But Payne is there, holding up a glass jar to the thin window's wan light, and the guard, with a short sword and his knife, and Grey and the servant, too, and the room is so crowded that they are nearly touching one another and outside Horner waits with his head ducked, trying to peer past, to see the King's patient.

'Ah,' Payne says, 'so here he is – the famous barber surgeon of the outward postern gate.'

Katherine says nothing, but she cannot help smiling slightly. Thomas frowns. Grey likewise, and he is probably about to say something when he hears the servant addressing Riven as if he were deaf, or stupid.

'Sir Giles?' the servant says. 'Sir Giles? King Henry has sent his surgeon.'

So now Grey turns on him. '*His* surgeon?' he shouts. '*His* surgeon? He is *my* bloody surgeon! D'you hear? God damn it, man! What's your name? He is *my* surgeon. He belongs to *me*. To Sir Ralph Grey of Heaton. D'you hear? I will not tolerate this a moment longer. By all saints! I am overlooked at every turn! Wherever I go.'

The servant waits for the storm to pass, with one eye on Grey's belt where his knife hangs, though Grey is more a shouter than a stabber, but the outburst has woken Riven, who slowly turns his head. Katherine's heart beats in her throat and she cannot take her gaze from him, though she knows she will give herself away, and now she sees his face and she cannot help but gasp. It is almost exactly as she imagined it would be: skeletal, drawn, his lips peeled back, teeth clenched through long-endured misery. He does not even look at her. Nor Thomas. He looks only at Grey through half-closed eyes.

'Grey,' he whispers. 'Grey.'

Sir Ralph is taking a breath to continue shouting, so he hears the quiet voice, and he stops, looks down at the bed.

'What?' he asks.

'Shut up,' Riven says. Then he turns back to the wall, presenting his skull. There is a moment's silence while Grey grows scarlet and comes to the boil.

'You!' he shouts. 'You! You goddamned whoreson! You goddamned turncoat! You don't tell me what to do. You don't tell Sir Ralph Grey of Castle Heaton what to do. No one – no one tells a Grey of Castle Heaton what to do. Do you hear me, turncoat?'

Riven is still. The only sound is Grey's breathing, the faint creak of Payne's boot sole, a distant bell. After a moment, Grey looks up. He catches her eye and she sees the doubt in his. He does not know what to do. So he turns and marches out of the chamber, leaving them in silence, listening to his departing footsteps, a scuffle, some muttering, and then a slammed door. A drop of water drips behind another smaller door that leads to the garderobe. The servant coughs.

'You may leave us now,' Payne tells him and when he is gone, after raising his eyebrows once or twice at them, Payne says he supposes she would like to see what there is to be seen of the wound, and when she nods, still unable to speak, he bends and folds back the sheets that cover Riven. She can see the muscles of his back flex as he breathes. His skin looks too big for him, as if he has withered from within, but there is the wound, a whorl of thickened skin, as

246

if someone has taken a stick and stirred a hole in his back, as big across as the mouth of a drinking cup.

'There it is,' he says, gesturing with an open hand. 'Do what you will.'

And she stands there next to Thomas and they continue to stare. Do what you will. Do what you will! How many times has she wished she could do exactly that? When she thought about Walter, Dafydd, Owen, Geoffrey. When she thought about Goodwife Popham and her daughter Elizabeth. When she thought about poor blind Richard. When she thought about Riven attacking her that time, all those months ago, outside the priory in the snow. When she thought about Alice.

But still she stands, her hands trembling at her sides, and she closes her eyes and lets out a deep breath and she knows that it is already too late. She cannot do it. She opens her eyes and turns to Thomas. He is pale, aghast, his hand over his jaw, and it looks as if he might cry, and she knows that he too has discovered he cannot just kill a man lying in his bed.

They should have done it in a rush, she sees. They should have come straight in, closed the door behind them, and stabbed him then. Cut his throat. Put the blade between the ribs. There would have been a fight with Payne. They would have had to kill him, perhaps, and Christ, the others too: Horner, Grey and that guard. And then they could have covered Riven's body with the blanket and left, telling anyone they met that he slept, and then – well, they would have been caught and hanged, but at least they would have done it, at least they would have done it! And the future be damned.

'Well?' Payne says. She takes a breath, swallows, steps towards Riven. Her nerves are stripped and raw. She can feel everything. She can see her hands shaking. She bends to touch him, touch his naked skin, something she never thought to do with anything other than a length of steel, but now here she is. He is cold under her fingertips, and she pulls back. He is part corpse already, she thinks, and she remembers how Richard changed shape after he had given up all that sword practice, how the muscle had withered and he had become padded with fat, cold to the touch just like Riven, until that had melted away for lack of vittles.

Payne says nothing. He is staring at her.

'Is this the wound?' she asks. Her voice rises and cracks. Payne merely stares at her. It is obviously the wound. And then Riven turns his face on the sheet again, and he looks at her through those half-closed lids as if he is interested in anyone so stupid as to ask such a question, and she cannot meet his gaze, and finds herself looking away, down at the floor, back at his wound, then quickly back in his eyes and then away again.

'Who are you?' he asks. His voice is softer, and weaker of course, than she remembers it that one time she heard it, but there is something about it, some grim power that makes her feel she must meet his gaze.

'My name is Kit,' she answers. 'I have had experiences of wounds such as this. I have cut men, saved their lives. King Henry asked me—'

'Kit what?' Riven asks.

She falters, and says nothing, for she does not know. She has no surname. She looks around for inspiration. The room is bare save for a coffer on which sit various dishes, two or three stoppered pots, a knife for the bleeding and a spray of dried herbs she does not recognise. There is a bag on the floor – Payne's instruments, she supposes – and a rolled-up mattress where perhaps Payne sleeps. Through another door she imagines the garderobe, with its hole down to the cesspit, and Riven's and perhaps Payne's all-too-immaculate clothes on their pegs.

'Kit what?' Riven repeats, and she turns to look down at him, and as she does so, she almost misses it. But no. There it is, too distinct a thing to overlook or ignore. She jerks her head back and is fixated by it, propped in the rounded corner of the room, a thing of singular purpose and value, if not beauty, and despite his gaze on her, she gasps when she sees it and she cannot help clap her hand to her mouth. My God, she thinks. My God.

It is Thomas's pollaxe. She shivers to see it, the steel beak; the hammer, the spike on the poll. She remembers it so clearly, how it always seemed to have a life of its own, she thinks, some force within it, and she remembers the men Thomas killed on that boat, almost as if he did not want to, as if it had done it itself, and she remembers levelling it at the other physician, at Fournier.

Riven follows her eyes.

'You like the pollaxe?' he asks her. 'How strange. There is a story behind it, you know? I lost it, once, but it came back to me. Things. They have a habit of coming back to me. People, too—'

'Where did you find it?' Thomas interrupts. He is also staring at it, confused. He will remember it better if he picks it up, she supposes. She hopes he doesn't, or not for the moment. Riven switches his gaze to Thomas, and Thomas looks back and there is a long moment as they hold one another's stare, until Riven blinks.

'Who are you?'

'Thomas Everingham.'

'Thomas Everingham? Hmmm. No. I do not know that name, but I do know you. But where from, Thomas Everingham?'

Thomas cannot help glancing at her before answering. Riven lies there, looking Thomas up and down, measuring his precise worth and station.

'You do not,' Thomas says.

'Oh, but I do,' he says. 'Yes. And someone such as you would remember someone such as me, so you obviously do not want me to remember you. So. What can that mean?'

Thomas says nothing.

'You have changed, haven't you?' Riven goes on. 'Yes. That is it. I knew you as someone else, perhaps? Who, though? Or – more like – what? No. But it will come to me. It will come to me. By and by.'

And then he closes his eyes and he turns to face the wall again. Thomas looks down at her. What should he do? He stands there with his hands at his sides. All the advantages he has over Riven are gone, precisely because he has so many, and so will not use them. This is the difference, she thinks, between a man like Riven and a man like Thomas. A sudden image comes to her: of how it would be if it were the other way around and Thomas was lying there, and Riven had come to kill him. She can see it eerily clearly: Riven walking fast, on light feet, Thomas not given a moment to cry out before a knife comes down. Or he would have that pollaxe. Dear God. She can so easily imagine the noise that would make, and the blood on the sheets and the walls perhaps. She clenches her eyes shut.

'What are your thoughts?' Payne asks, nodding at the forgotten wound. She starts and looks down at it again.

'An arrow wound,' she says.

'Never?' Payne laughs.

'But it is not diseased?'

'Ah, no,' he says. 'No gangrene. That is a miserable death, and afterwards, did you know, when the patient is dead, you can remove his liver – which will be quite black also – and place it on marble, and it will seethe, like a wet cloth being wrung?'

She cannot believe what he is saying.

'You have – cut open a man to look at his liver?' she asks.

'In Cambridge,' Payne says, quite as if everybody has done this. 'And then again in Bologna.'

She rubs her chin, looks at the wound again, and then glances back at Payne. He is boasting, or lying. The Church would not allow such things, surely? And what or where is Bologna? She dare not ask. There is something very unusual about Payne, she thinks. It is as if he has some other life, a parallel life of which she knows nothing.

'But is there nothing you can do for him?' she asks.

'Oh, I keep his humours balanced,' Payne tells her, gesturing with the flask of murky liquid at the bleeding bowl on the coffer and at the dried greenery, 'and King Henry has ordered Mass to be said, twice daily.'

'Mass,' she says.

'Yes,' Payne replies, turning with a questioning smirk. 'Prayer is most efficacious, don't you find? Our Lord Jesus is the heavenly leech. He can cure all and with enough prayer I am certain the arrowhead will free itself.'

'Have you ever known this to happen?' she asks.

'No,' he allows. 'But that is not to say that it will not happen in the future.'

'Then why cut a man open to see how he is constructed, if faith is all that is required?' she asks.

'Indeed,' he says. 'But let us talk of that later. We must discuss this patient. King Henry has been swayed by Sir Ralph Grey's unusual eloquence, and has ordered me to assist you in what he believes will be the removal of the arrowhead and the restoration of Sir Giles to bodily if not spiritual health. He expects you to succeed. He has been promised you will.'

'Have you examined the arrowhead?' she asks.

Payne shakes his head.

'The wound was healed before he came under my hands,' he says, coming around, unable to resist flaunting his knowledge. 'It is an interesting case, however. The arrowhead is still within his flesh, caught in the bone, perhaps. I believe it was bent when it was loosed, reused perhaps, or is of some curious design, or was perhaps loosed at great range, and so instead of killing the patient, as the bowman might have wished, it broke the scapula – here.'

He places his hands on Riven's back. He has long elegant fingers, tapering to fine, spotless fingernails.

'I suppose if Sir Giles had chosen to seek help then, from a surgeon, perhaps he might have had the arrow removed with little

251

anxiety, but things being as they were, he could not, and since then the bone has, I believe, absorbed the arrow. It is as if it has grown back, and healed around it, do you see? Or perhaps the arrow skipped across the bone, and is dug in below or even above it, or perhaps to one side, or perhaps to the other. I can't tell. Wherever it is, it has pinned his limb in this position – look, he cannot move it, or at least not without great pain.'

He tweaks the joint and Riven stiffens. After a moment he lets out a long sigh and relaxes.

'To remove it now might require the breaking of the bone, which is not within my purlieu as a physician, but then again the arrow's head may be lodged perilously close to the blood vessels that congregate near the lungs or even the heart? Were you to cut those, the patient would bleed to death in mere moments and it would all be over.'

She listens carefully. Such things are beyond her, she knows that, but then when she looks at the wound, looks at the flesh below it, she can almost sense the arrowhead, see it in its pouch of scarred flesh, and she can imagine slicing the skin and extracting it, and proving to those bastards in the hall, the men who'd almost jeered at her, that she could perform what is, or will be anyway, a miracle.

'With your assistance, Master Payne,' she says, 'I should like to try to remove the arrow.'

Payne blinks.

'I did not think you had any choice,' he says.

252

16

The operation is set for the second week after All Saints, when Payne tells them the planets' positions will be most propitious for an operation that may touch on the heart and the lungs.

'But it is Giles Riven,' Thomas repeats. 'Giles Riven! All the time we've wanted nothing but his death and the moment we have the perfect chance, we falter, and worse. You must now save his life or lose yours in the trying!'

'I know,' Katherine says. 'I know.'

They are back in the tower, staring across the bailey to the keep.

'He would have done it like that!' Thomas says, and he snaps his fingers. 'If it had been me or you on the bed, and Riven had meant to kill us, he would have come in, and simply—'

He mimes a stabbing.

'But we are not murderers,' she says almost sadly. 'Besides, we would have been killed had you even tried. You saw the guard. Master Payne says he is there day and night to prevent any man whose father or son died at Northampton coming for vengeance.'

But still Thomas is disgusted with himself and so the next day, while Katherine is closeted with Master Payne, he goes to the beach with Jack and the rest of Grey's men and he takes his turn to send sheaf after sheaf of arrows across the dunes, thumping them into the mounded sand butts two, three, four hundred paces away. Bows have not been easy to come by, and those they have are not good quality. More than one cracks and breaks in the cold, setting everyone, especially Thomas, on edge, but they carry on. He has discovered that most of Grey's men are poor archers, able to loose a bow, but unable to gauge distance, and so they cannot land their shafts in groups such as archers from the other companies do. Horner maintains a cheerful disposition, but he is too kindly, or his expectations are too low, and Thomas finds himself shouting at the other men, making them loose their arrows all day, and sending the slowest to run through the sand to collect the shafts and then run back.

He hears them grumbling about him, wishing he'd never come, but he does not care. He feels a peculiar ferocity. He wants to work himself into exhaustion so that he does not have to think about the cruel trick God has played upon him and Katherine, so in the morning after a sleepless night of near fruitless speculation, they are at it again, in the rain, the same thing, and by the next day improvements are noticeable despite the blustering wind. Horner has yielded command of training to him completely now, and on the third day, to his order they can land their shafts in a neat line a hundred paces away, then a hundred and fifty paces, then two hundred paces, and the first time they do it in sequence, they are delighted with themselves, and Thomas runs to collect their arrows as a reward. Then they do it again. And again. And when the evening bell is rung Horner comes down from the gatehouse with three loaves of rye bread and a bucket of stew he claims Grey has given him to distribute among the men.

Horner walks back to the outward postern gate with him. They see Katherine in the tower, watching over them. Horner waves. She waves back.

'Small, isn't he? Kit?' Horner starts.

Thomas mumbles his agreement.

'Still, though,' Horner says, 'if we carry on like this, we'll make such a company of archers that we will be in London before Christmastide.'

Thomas says nothing. Their boots are loud on the sandy soil.

'All we need is one spark, Thomas,' Horner goes on. 'One spark!

And I truly believe we can return King Henry to the throne. We can drive out those bloodsucking Yorkist fleas and restore the rightful king.'

But Horner does not know where this spark will come from and Thomas thinks of the ledger, lying up there, rolled in among the straw of his mattress, and it strikes him that he must find a better place to hide it until they can find some way of showing it to King Henry, and they must find someone to help them bring it before him. Payne is a possibility, it suddenly strikes him. Perhaps if they showed it first to Payne, and explained it, he might be the one to effect the connection? Thomas becomes more buoyant. There is a way to do this, after all.

But Horner has dropped his voice, and is confiding now.

'The thing is, Thomas,' he says. 'The thing is we lack a natural leader. King Henry is – well. You have seen. He is – we need someone more martial for what is involved in this. The others, Lord Hungerford and Lord Roos, they are – well. I don't know. They lack the vital spark. And I do not wish to speak ill of Sir Ralph Percy, or our own Sir Ralph Grey, it is only that – well. I should say no more. It is only I wish we had men such as they.'

'They?'

'The Yorkists. They have an embarrassment of leaders. King Edward himself, of course. He has led men in battle, and has won them too. And if he weren't enough, they have the Earl of Warwick.'

Thomas remembers the Earl of Warwick, a little bit.

'And then if *he* weren't enough,' Horner goes on, 'they have Lord Montagu.'

'Lord Montagu keeps Newcastle, doesn't he?'

'Yes,' Horner agrees, 'for King Edward. He is the Earl of Warwick's brother. Mean as a marten, and his men tougher than boiled leather.'

Thomas remembers the Watch outside the gate at Newcastle. Proper soldiers, they were.

'And that the Duke of Somerset has also joined their ranks is just yet more salt in the wound. He was once a fast ally of King Henry, you know, and a fine leader of men, but now – pfft. He is become King Edward's gentleman of the bedchamber. They sleep together, in the same bed, naked as the day they were born, but he still hasn't bothered to kill him.'

Thomas grunts.

'No, the truth is, Thomas,' Horner continues, 'we need someone to take this – us – by the scruff of the neck, to take what men we have and do something with us. But where will that man come from? Around here?'

He holds his arms out and turns on the spot so that his heels dig into the sand. Seagulls wheel overhead in the pale grey sky. There is nothing for miles.

In the gatehouse chamber, Thomas is peculiarly and unexpectedly relieved to find the ledger where he left it: in its greasy leather bag hidden in the rolled straw of his mattress. He takes it out and slings it around his shoulder. He wonders where Katherine is, and then hears Devon John coming quickly up the steps. The others have changed Devon John's name, since it turns out he has never been to Devon, but comes from Essex, and now they call him John Stump. He is breathing hard and carrying a pot pressed to his chest with his one good arm, and from it comes the smell of cooked pork, and something else exotic and sweet that Thomas has never smelled before.

'Wherever did you get that?' Thomas asks.

'It was just lying around,' John Stump says with a grin, and he slops the pot forward to reveal a stew that glistens with oil. 'I got it for Kit. Thought he looked a bit peaky. You too, if you've a mind?'

'Christ, yes,' Thomas says. Devon John places the pot on the oven's ledge. A wisp of steam rises.

'And it is still hot,' he says. Then he winces and flaps at his missing arm.

'Christ!' he says. 'I can feel my arm.'

'But that is impossible,' Thomas tells him.

'Nevertheless,' John Stump says, 'I can feel it. I can feel my bracer is pointed too tight. It aches.'

He moves his stump as he would to hold out his arm to show Thomas where the strap of leather intended to protect his wrist from the bowstring's slap would be. He thinks Thomas will see what he means.

'Let us take this up to Kit,' he suggests. 'He is on watch.'

'Again?' John Stump says. 'You two are always on watch together. Don't know how you stand it, nights.'

Thomas hides his blush, but he is pleased no one suspects them of anything, pleased that no one imagines them wrapped together in their cloaks, sleeping alongside one another, or lying atop one another, his feet against the door's planks so that it cannot be opened. These moments alone are stolen and intimate, terrifyingly risky, but – what else can they do?

The cutting of Sir Giles Riven takes place just after the angelus bell, when it is scarcely light, and while Riven's now crowded chamber is still thick with night-time effluvium and the stench from the garderobe blows strong from under its door in the corner. Servants with candles stand by and the room quickly warms with their heat and mingled breath. Payne is here, and Grey too, who has yet to go to bed, and another man, William Tailboys, with whom Grey has made his bet. There is no sign of King Henry. Katherine has hidden the ledger in the garderobe, on a peg under some of Payne's many hanging clothes.

'It is the perfect place,' she says.

But now here is Grey, pushing his way to the front.

'Will he live? Will he live?' he bleats. 'To hell with you! Why won't you answer me! Should've hanged you the moment I saw you. I knew it! Look at you! Can't even grow a proper beard, let alone cut a man. Will he live?'

Katherine ignores him, and turns to Tailboys, who is sleek in very dark wool, almost black, unstained and obviously finely cut. He is freshly shaved, fragrant of some herb or other, with a faint and complicit smile haunting his eyes.

'Barber surgeon, hey?' he asks.

'Not a barber,' she replies.

Riven is where he always is, face down on the bed, utterly still, apparently careless of all the people in his room. She can't help her gaze being drawn to the scar on his back. Payne's servant has washed him, and the sheets are stained and ripe with fresh urine. They have also pulled up the coffer next to the bed, and filled the jug with more urine collected that morning, to which she gleefully contributed. There are dishes with warm wine provided by King Henry from the last of his stocks, egg whites and rose water. There is a selection of horsehair and human hair, a long iron probe, three silver needles, one of them curved, and also a curved blade such as she wishes she'd had when cutting Devon John, and two straight razors wrapped in fine linen, of which there is also a large supply. There are scissors and a pair of blacksmith's pliers.

'That is all?' Payne asks. 'You need no salve? No dwale?'

She hesitates.

'You have a dwale?'

'No,' he says. And that is that.

She looks at Riven.

'Well,' she says. 'So long as I can have another to hold him down?'

Payne raises his eyebrows to indicate one of King Henry's men, an archer by the looks of him, stripped, like Thomas, to his pourpoint and hose. Both men have their sleeves rolled up to their elbows and their heads bare, just as if they are going into a bout of wrestling. To one side is the bearded priest. He has sprinkled holy water over Riven's back, and the tools she is about to use, and over the backs of her hands, and he has anointed Riven's temples with a sharp-smelling chrism, and the paternoster has been said, and is still being said outside by the beardless priest, sent and paid for by King Henry, and now there really is nothing left to delay her.

But still, she does not feel right about it. Perhaps it is Payne's presence, in blue velvet, and of all things, a woman's apron of sacking backed with fine linen. She has been with him for the last five days, trying to draw information from him of the sort he has been unwilling to divulge, on matters such as his dissections of the human body, on the spread of gangrene, on the movement of the womb of a woman, while he has concentrated on batting away her questions with long explanations as to the movement of the stars and the influence they bring to bear on the various organs of the body, and on how best to balance the humours with bleeding and the application of poultices, and on the properties of the various herbs and spices of which she has never heard, such as cumin and sandalwood. He claims that a brown bark called cinnamon floats down the river from the Garden of Eden.

'Do you believe this?' she'd asked, and he'd smiled at her.

'But of course,' he'd said, feigning shock, and she'd begun to see that perhaps he believed in nothing of the sort.

After that glimpse though, he diverted her to talk about something else, mostly in Latin, a language she recognises but does not understand, before going on to explain the efficacy of certain prayer cycles for certain complaints: the Ave Maria for this, the paternoster for that. At length though, glancing around as if to check he was not being overheard, he began to share his knowledge of the body's internal organs, of how they are arranged, and of the theories as to each one's purpose. And once he started, once he had given in to it, he spoke with an urgent desire to share his knowledge until she asked about women, and about how they differed from men, and then he became agitated, and when she returned to the subject of the womb, and tried to draw him on childbirth, and in particular the cutting of poor Agnes Eelby, it had been too much. He'd gathered his books and stood and left the room, and Riven, whom they had ignored but who had been listening all this time, turned his head and looked at her in that slow way of his, and she'd forced herself to stare back at him until he'd closed his eyes and turned back to the wall, saying nothing.

And then for the first time, though she could hear his guard shuffling his feet and hawking on the floor outside the door, she was alone with him. It was almost as if he were presenting her his back, naked, pink, mottled, there to be stabbed, almost as if to say, here, kill me now if you have the stomach for it. And she'd begun pacing to and fro, up and down the chamber, plucking up the courage to do just that. Payne's bag was on the floor. She could pick up the razor and cut Riven's throat, or she could merely walk the few steps, take up the pollaxe and bring it down on the back of his head, just as she'd seen men do on the fields at Towton. She could imagine the pollaxe in her hand, its smooth shaft in her palm, that weight that seems to pull its spiked head where it ought not go. Just the thought of it had made her heart jump and she could feel the blood frothing in her ears. Do it, she said to herself, do it. Think of all the things he has done. All she'd need to do was drop it on him, just place it by him and stand back, let it fall and kill him. And she was going to do it. She was.

But then Riven let out a long sigh in the bed. It was one of such pitiable loss and resignation that he was instantly human again, a thing of flesh, and she'd had to close her eyes, stay her hand, and walk away.

And so now, here they are.

'Get on with it,' Grey calls. And there is nothing for it. She crosses herself as they expect her to, and then takes the proffered knife: a bone-handled thing, well-balanced, with a tapering blade so sharp it sings in her hand, and she dips it in the warm wine and she nods to Thomas and the wrestler who stand by to throw themselves on Riven, and she approaches that stretch of bared and washed skin. The priest begins his prayers. Suddenly there is incense in the air, and through its whorls, Grey smirks at her.

260

'A failsafe,' he says, with a leer at Tailboys, who is disapproving. She places the knife above the wound, and Riven stiffens. A drop of wine fills the dip it makes in his skin, and then she presses. Riven flinches. Blood wells before the blade's stroke. Riven's head comes up, unused muscles ripple under the skin of his back. He grips the sheets but does not cry out. She continues with the slicing, willing herself to think of poor dead Alice, of poor blind Richard, of Geoffrey Popham, of Elizabeth Popham, but it is hard not to concentrate on what she is doing. When she reaches it, the scar tissue is tougher; more like thin leather after the easy give of the skin above.

Riven is arching his back, and the wrestlers stand by to press him down and keep him still, but he straightens himself and returns to lying flat, merely gripping the sheet again. He is breathing very fast, and a clammy shimmer blots his skin.

'Linen,' she says, and Payne is there with a swab of the stuff, first rinsed in – and then squeezed dry of – wine. She mops the blood away and in the moment before it comes back she can see the second pale layer of fat beneath the skin, though the latter is twisted and folded and then hardened like a knot in wood below the scar. She passes the blade through it again, moving slowly this time, and at any moment she expects to feel the tink of the blade against the arrowhead. It does not come. She must cut deeper. She damps the blood away again and looks up to the wrestlers, who await their orders. She nods. They lean in, ready. She cuts. Riven stiffens but makes no further move. There is still no sign of the arrowhead.

Payne is peering over her hands. They exchange a glance. He is worried too.

'It should be there,' he says.

She will do one more pass. Blood is flowing freely now. She asks for some urine.

'Quickly now,' she says.

It washes the blood away, turns the sheets pink. This time she imagines she will see the dark plug of the arrowhead sticking from

261

the bone, but again, it is not there. She cuts again, deeper, and Riven lets out the slightest noise. By now it is a large wound, and there is a lot of blood.

'What are you doing?' Grey asks. 'It's only a bloody arrowhead, the size of my bloody thumb. Not a – not a – what? A foot? By the Mass!'

'Sir,' Payne says.

'Oh, it's like that, is it? Tell me what to say to my own surgeon? Damned piss sniffer. Good mind to piss on you now, see how you like that.'

But he is silent after this.

Payne leans over.

'Deeper?' he asks. 'You'll be on the bone. It cannot be deeper than that, surely?'

She nods. She wishes she could scratch her nose but her hands are slick with blood, right up to her wrists. Riven is thrumming like a bowstring but he is still, has made no sound, and the wrestlers are impressed.

She cuts again. This time into the pink meat, running the end of the knife against the flat bone that backs it. She feels faint ridges and nodules interrupting the blade's otherwise smooth passage, but nothing like an arrowhead. She stops.

'Pass me that, will you?'

Payne hands her the probe. She washes it and then uses it to examine the cut she's made. There are some of those hard white cords running crosswise. She does not cut them. Riven is pouring with sweat now, his brown hair sodden black, his neck red and engorged with the effort of not screaming. How does he do it? How can he stand the pain? She should be taking some pleasure from this, she knows, but she is not. Instead she is working as fast as she can.

It is not there. There is no sign of the arrowhead.

'Well, then – where is it?' Payne asks, peering forward. His eyes are round, peering in, genuinely concerned, genuinely puzzled.

'Are you sure it was ever there?' she asks. 'That it was not some other kind of wound?'

'He told me –' Payne straightens to tell the room. 'He told me it was after the disaster at Towton. He said he'd managed to cross that river as the rout began, and then he was knocked down by an arrow loosed from the scarp above. He said he managed to break the arrow shaft himself. But he could not get the head out, and then he could not find any physician or doctor or even a barber to treat him, not until he got to Scotland, by which time the wound had healed, and he did not trust any of those ginger-haired butchers to open him up.'

'But where is it now?' she asks, almost rhetorically. 'Could it have hit the bone and not broken it? Could it have slid off?'

She pours more urine over the wound, washing it clean so that she can see the grain of the meat. There is nothing singular, no one divot or dent in the bone's pink surface to suggest it has been marked by an arrow's passing. Riven is breathing heavily.

'Just find it,' he says. 'Just find it, and get on your way.'

The spectators are crowding around her, fascinated. She imagined some of them would find this sickening, but then they have all lived lives, some of them have fought in battles. They will have seen worse.

'Cut across?' Payne suggests.

And she looks up at him. She remembers cutting across Eelby's wife. She remembers how that ended. But if she lingers, hesitates, then Riven will die. And Grey is looking at her as if he will hang her himself, so she does. She cuts across, firmer now, slicing through the fat and meat in one slice. She makes a cross. With that, Riven, at last, faints, and only the panting, the constant flex of his back, the push and pull of muscles under his bloody, urine-soaked skin tell her that he is alive.

'More urine,' she tells Payne, who splashes it into the wound.

For a moment she thinks it is there, a dark roundel of metal snagged in red flesh, but no. It is something else, a clot of something that is washed away by the urine. The arrowhead is not there. Payne is wrong, or lying. She is sweating now. It is too hot in the room.

'This boy's no more a surgeon than I am,' Tailboys announces. 'Grey, old man, let me tell you – I think you shall end the day losing your money!'

'If I lose my money then this boy'll lose his bloody head, let me tell you that!'

Tailboys laughs a sort of hoohoohoo laugh, like an owl, but she looks up and she can see Grey means it. His little face is sheened with sweat and clenched and she wonders how much money he has put on her doing this. But she is at a loss. She cannot cut the whole back open, can she? Or can she? She has already cut a large cross in his skin and peeled back the flaps, exposing almost the whole shoulder blade. She supposes the arrowhead might have skidded off this bone, and gone around it, further into the body, and that it is now lodged somewhere in the muscles that—

That is not the way to do it. So the arrow must have gone deeper, that is the only possibility. But where? Can she just cut away until she finds it? No. That would be to cut through all the bonds that hold this part of him together.

And now Payne is stepping back. He is stroking his beard, aligning its filaments, and when he catches her gaze, he cocks an eyebrow. Has he given up hope? It makes her more determined. Right, she thinks, I will show you. But by Christ, it is hot in here. She wishes she were wearing just a shirt and no pourpoint, though then her hose would fall around her ankles, but she can loosen her collar. She dips her fingers in the wine, then dries them on a clean piece of linen and opens her collar. Her fingers touch the leather strap of her lodestone.

And she thinks.

My God. My God.

And she slips the stone from over her head.

'What in God's holy name is he doing now?' Grey asks the room. 'A lucky bloody pendant won't help either of you now, boy, even if it's been blessed by St Gregory himself.'

She clenches her eyes and tries to still her hand. She holds the stone a finger's width above the spread flesh of the wound, and she concentrates. There is a warm thick silence in the room as every man bends in, or stands on toes to see over shoulders. Christ, she thinks, will this work? She has no idea. She holds the lace still, allows the stone to settle. It takes a long moment and then it is utterly still. There is nothing. She breathes slowly. There is sweat in her eyes.

She can hear Tailboys laugh sibilantly, and Grey tuts loudly.

She lowers the stone, so it is almost touching the skin. Still nothing. She holds her wrist in her other hand to steady it. Still nothing. A faint wobble perhaps. A slow rotation. Then it settles again. She moves the stone to cover a different spot, lower down his back and – what was that? Was there something? She does not know. She would not be able to describe it, but there was some unnatural tweak on her fingers. Very slight. She moves the stone away. There. This time. A definite tug.

There is absolute silence in the room now. She can hear Payne breathing. Hear Riven breathing. She moves the stone. Again. The string seems to straighten. The stone is pulling over to one side. She moves it to the other side, nearer his armpit. The stone pulls back. She moves it down. The stone swings in a tight circle and stops unnaturally fast, as if it is straining towards something. It is below the cut she has made.

Payne lets out a low gasp of amazement.

'Jesu Maria,' he whispers.

He is the only one who really understands what has happened. He passes her the longest of the needles. She stabs it into Riven's skin below the wound she has made. A bead of blood appears. She presses the needle in, through fibrous flesh, with her heart loud in her ears and sweat stinging her eyes, and nothing happens, until – yes. There it is: a dull, buried chime.

'Great God above,' Grey says. 'He's actually found it.'

And she has. She cannot help glancing up at Payne, who seems ashamed of himself, but he was right, in what he had said, that Riven must have been standing upright when the arrow was loosed, and that he must have been at the very end of its arc. It would have hit him as it was coming down, and its momentum would have taken it skidding off the bone. It would have embedded itself in the tangle of muscles below.

And here it is. Just there.

She puts aside the lodestone and takes the knife. She extends the cut, then she slices another cross in the meat under the skin's fat, and she slides the iron probe to part the muscle fibres, separating them one from the other, and she finally sees it, a dark twist of iron, embedded deep. She takes the pliers, dips them in the wine, inserts them into the small cavity and clamps their jaws into the dark plug of the arrow's end; she spreads them so they hold, and she eases the arrowhead free. Riven stiffens, even in his sleep. Out it comes with a final reluctant plop. She holds it up for all to see. It is a finger-long spike, two barbs like the wings of a diving seabird. She drops it in a dish and tosses the pliers aside. Blood comes thickly behind it, as if the arrowhead had been acting as a block in some vessel. This is not over yet.

'Linen!' she says.

And this time Payne is fast. He passes her a wad, and she presses down on the source of the blood. It soaks through the first and the second and the third wadding, but by the fourth, it has slowed. She gets Payne to hold it down while she pours more urine on to the cloth and again Riven stiffens. The linen turns pink. Payne frowns.

'Keep pressing,' she says.

And he does, and some time later she lets him lighten the pressure, and then, later still, she begins to stitch the wound back together again. She splits a candle lengthways to extract the wick, and leaves that like a mouse's tail, trailing from the row of stitches. When it is done, she looks up. Most of the men have gone, and it is just Payne, and Thomas, and the other wrestler, and King Henry's priest. The guard is by the door. The others have left.

'Will he live?' the priest asks.

She looks down at him again, lying there among his foul sheets, at the double cross of her neat stitching that stars his back, at his purple-edged and already bruising flesh, and she thinks that, yes, barring the vapours, barring that creeping, swelling blackness of the flesh, he will live. She has saved his life. Saved Giles Riven's life, and now it is late afternoon, and the thin winter sunlight sifts through the aperture and falls in a lopsided cross on the chamber's far wall, reflecting the one on Riven's back, and she wonders again just what it is that she has done.

17

'We have been stuck here for weeks on end,' Thomas tells Katherine, 'and we are no nearer our aim. Further, if anything.'

A week has passed since the cutting and they are in the tower's battlements again, looking across the bailey at the keep. It is perishingly cold. Ice glisters on the black stones and their breathing creates clouds before their faces. Beyond the walls, all is still, frost-bound, and the mist rises early in the pink-skied evenings.

'King Henry has not been to see Riven,' she soothes him, 'that is all. The moment he does, I will show him the ledger.'

'But what about Payne?'

'I have not told him,' she admits. 'It is not that I do not trust him, or think he would not help. It is that he is just another person to overcome and, anyway, he himself cannot speak to the King without first going through an intermediary such as Grey or Tailboys.'

'So where is it?' Thomas looks panicked. He did not want to give it to her in the first place.

'I have hung it on a peg in the garderobe, secreted under his clothes.'

'And that will suffice?'

She nods. He is still unsure.

'I promise,' she says, and she smiles and she slides her hand under his arm and they are very, daringly close to one another.

'Please,' he says, suddenly crooked with anxiety. 'If someone should come . . .'

She laughs.

A bell sounds, tinny and distant.

'I must go and change his dressing,' Katherine tells him.

'Can't Master Payne do that?'

'He can, but he won't, because he is a physician, and besides, he says King Henry may come today.'

'Today? Should I come? Should I be there?'

'Do you not worry Riven will recognise you?'

'It would force the point, at least. It would be done, then, one way or the other.'

Most likely the other, he knows, but still.

'But we are close, Thomas,' she tells him. 'All I need do is see King Henry, and then . . .'

She shrugs. He knows she is right. But saints, it is difficult. All day long in this castle, hemmed in by towering granite walls, never out of their shadow or the sight of other men, all the time knowing the chances of Katherine being discovered as a woman increase daily. Soon it will be inevitable. One little slip. Christ!

'What will you tell him?' he asks.

'King Henry? It is still as we have agreed. I will only tell him we have something that proves King Edward is illegitimate. Then when he asks to see it, I will tell him you have it hidden, and that we must be promised reward, and recompense for our losses.'

Thomas nods sharply.

'Still,' he says. 'I wish I could be there.'

'I know,' she says, 'but with Riven there too?'

And once more he imagines himself a cornered rat with Riven's men coming at him and he can almost feel the burn of their knives in his belly.

'Anyway,' she says, 'we must go. Mass is over, and King Henry may come straight away.'

So they leave the tower's walkway and descend the winding steps.

'Does Riven talk?' he asks.

'A little, but he is still in pain.'

'Good.'

He leaves her at the steps of the keep and then makes his way down to the stables. There are some of Riven's men there, and he cannot help but stiffen when he sees them, and he stands and watches them, waiting to see if the two who offered to cut him from groin to gizzard are there, but he is in luck, they are not, and he slides past with a ducked head to find Horner, who is already mounted alongside Jack and three other men of Grey's company.

'Thomas!' Jack calls. 'Thomas! We are allowed out. Come. We are riding a picket, just as if we are prickers.'

Jack is wearing a long coat and scarf and a hat that he has pulled down over his ears, so all that can be seen of him are his eyes, which are bright with excitement at the thought of being out from under the castle walls. Horner next to him makes an impatient gesture and Thomas is given his own horse, a pony with a shaggy coat. They ride out, through the main gatehouse, and south, towards Dunstanburgh. The horses steam in the frigid air and the meres are hard frozen and a man might perhaps skate on them. No one says a thing. They ride for an hour. No one sees anything. Christ, it is good to be away from the castle, from its smell and anxious jostle and the constant fear of discovery. Thomas breathes deeply until he sees the others looking at him strangely.

They are about to turn around, half-dead with cold and hunger, when they see three men on horses. Two bowshots' distance.

Horner holds up a hand. The men are only half-dressed, unarmed. They look desperate.

'Christ,' he says. 'Just what we need. Another lot of beggars.'

'Should we just leave them?' one of the others asks.

'Perhaps you're right,' Horner says. 'Look at that one. Shouting at us. By the Mass, we should just run them down.'

The man at the front looks barelegged. He is certainly bareheaded, and he is waving and gesticulating, and kicking his horse on just as quickly as the knackered old thing can manage.

'He will want to sell us something,' Horner says. 'But what? What can he have? He does not look overly encumbered.'

They do not even bother to draw their swords. The man is still shouting at them as he comes, and he is laughing, too. He is delighted to see them. They see from a distance that he has a rough blanket over his shoulders, and his legs and feet are swagged in cloth, but as he approaches there is something about him that tells them he is no mere beggar.

'Sirs! Sirs!' he calls. 'By the grace of God and happenstance! Thanks be that you are come.'

And there is something about the man's voice, Thomas thinks, that confirms the impression he is not a beggar. It is sharp and clear and commanding. And the way the man's companions look to him makes it clear who leads whom. Horner does not smile.

'God keep you this day,' he says, addressing the leader. 'You seem ill-prepared for this weather?'

The man barks a laugh and turns to his two companions.

'Ha! That is funny! Ill-prepared! Ill-prepared!'

They laugh too. They are only marginally better dressed than he.

'Is that – a nightshirt you are wearing?' Horner goes on.

'This? Indeed it is. Finest lawn. It was all that I had on when I was woken in the night and forced to flee the inn where I was staying. I had to leave through the window.'

'You could not pay your bill?'

Again the laughter.

'It was not that, though that is true – I could not pay. No. It was that a company of archers belonging to my Lord Montagu had come from Newcastle to arrest me and take me before their lord who would in all probability have had no hesitation in separating my head from my shoulders.'

More laughter. Horner is impressively impassive.

'Why would he do that?' he asks.

271

'Why? Why? Dear God, man! I have just realised. I have not introduced myself, have I? Nor asked your name. I shall go first, and then you shall follow.'

His companions are very pleased at something, and the man opens his mouth as if he is about to begin to say something wonderful and then shuts it again and looks at them and they snigger and smirk obediently, and Thomas wonders if they have time for this, when the man finally tells them who he is.

'I,' he says. 'I am Henry Beaufort. I am Henry Beaufort, Earl of Dorset, Duke of Somerset. I am a man who once betrayed his king, but shall do so not one moment more, and now, for the love of the great Lord above, who are you? And do you have anything a man might reasonably eat?'

They do not believe him at first. Knowing what they know, they cannot believe that the Duke of Somerset would give up the comforts of King Edward's court in favour of the bleak prospects held out by King Henry. They do not believe that a man's conscience would trouble him so, and it takes long moments before Horner is satisfied, but when he is, he leaps from his horse to clutch the Duke's hand and he gives him his own coat, which the Duke happily accepts, and his hat and scarf, which the Duke likewise is pleased to slide on.

Then they turn for home, Horner pushing his horse in a frisking trot. He wants to be the first to tell King Henry that the Duke of Somerset is here, repented of his dalliance with the House of York, come on bended knee to seek the grace of his dread sovereign anointed by God, come to lead them out of their castle and take them south, back down to London to eject that usurper the Earl of March. And the Duke wants to evade Montagu's men, too, of course, whom he supposes might have ridden this far north in search of such an astonishingly valuable prize, and he wants to be somewhere with a roof over his head, a fire at his feet and wine in his belly before the snow that threatens falls.

'It is the Duke of Somerset!' Horner whispers to Thomas as they ride. 'It is the very thing we need. The very thing to light up the country and help us out of here. By this time next year King Henry will be in Westminster, and the bloody old Earl of March will be dead, or rotting in the Tower, and all his men will be there with him. Vanquished! By us! And all those who perished at Towton Field will be avenged and we will be back in our solars, rich men, with rich wives.'

They pass Dunstanburgh, and then see Bamburgh in the distance.

'Horner! Horner, there!' Somerset calls, and Horner is plump with pleasure as he slows his horse to interpose himself between Somerset and his two silent companions, one of whom is a servant, and who has the better clothes for having been sleeping in them when they were disturbed at the inn, and the other, perhaps a lesser knight, a gangling, serious youth with a Welsh accent. Thomas slows his own horse, and is there a pace or so in front of Horner when Somerset asks after the disposition of King Henry's forces, the provisions of the castles, and the morale of the troops. Horner lies fluently and Somerset is delighted.

'And I have the assurances of twenty of the chief men in Wales that they will rise up against the false king,' he says, 'and there are others in the south and the west who are with us, too. And Bellingham will come, he says, and Neville of Brancepeth, of course, though his presence is more penance than providence. Oh, it is all wonderfully hopeful. If only we can now get support from elsewhere – from France or Burgundy or even those bastards in Brittany, and I have not yet given up on Scotland yet – then we will have them still, tcha!'

Thomas cannot take his gaze from the man. He is dark-haired, broad-faced, with quick blue eyes, and he's very muscular across the chest, and very abrupt, just as if he is going to be called upon to fight, or perform a tumble, or to leap on to the back of a horse.

But what has he just said? There is something in there that alerts

273

Thomas. That is it. Others in the south and the west. Men who would rise up against King Edward. Dear God! Edmund Riven would be among them, surely? If the Duke of Somerset has changed his allegiance, then surely Edmund Riven will change his too. His loyalty was never to King Edward, only to Somerset. If that is the case, then he will have already jumped from one camp to the other. They no longer need show Henry the Ledger. In fact, dear God, they must not on any account show Henry the ledger! To do so now would only be to help the Rivens, and secure them in their prestige.

'And once the commons see this,' Somerset is saying, 'they will rise up across the country, d'you hear? They will rise up as one to drive out the false king and restore the House of Lancaster.'

He bangs his fist on his saddle and his horse increases its pace up the hill.

'Not a bad little horse, this,' he says.

Can Thomas ask Somerset? He cannot see a reason why not.

'Edmund Riven?' Somerset says. 'You want to know if Edmund Riven is among those who would now stand for King Henry against the false King Edward? Can you think of a reason why he might not?'

That hardly answers the question, Thomas thinks, but before he can press, Somerset has turned back to Horner and is telling him of his scheme to attack King Edward at both ends of the kingdom at once: here in Northumberland and also in Pembroke.

And again he bangs his saddle and is delighted that the horse can still trot.

'Ha!' he says.

They reach Bamburgh just as the curfew bell is rung, but on hearing Horner is without, and that he has the Duke of Somerset with him, they drop the drawbridge and throw open the gates, and the garrison breathes life into the covered fires, and word is passed back that the Duke of Somerset is here, come to lead them out of the north; the chapel bells are set ringing again, and men line the walls to look down on them as they wait to be let through the gates, and everybody is laughing and waving and shouting: 'A Somerset!' and 'A Beaufort!' and then they are let through into the bailey which is crowded with more men waving their arms and shouting the Duke's name, and Somerset gets his horse to stagger and prance, then he brings it under control again and he stands in the stirrups and bows and then he rides on up the hill toward the keep, touching men's outstretched hands as he passes and Horner looks on with a smile as if he is witnessing – or even responsible for – some great thing.

'He is our spark, Thomas, our spark!'

He is like the Messiah, Thomas thinks, come to lead them to the Promised Land.

18

Despite Payne's promise, King Henry has not come to see his gentleman of the bedchamber, though Payne supposes he might the next day, and so the next day Katherine arrives at the keep just as the bell is ringing for Sext, with one thing on her mind: the recovery of the ledger.

'Looks like snow,' the captain of guard says. He is the same man who was first so interested in Devon John's stump, and he is there again, stamping his boots, rubbing his hands, looking up and inhaling deeply, and she tells him she does not doubt it, and he steps aside to let her through and she carries on up the steps, through the doors and along the various passageways she's come to know reasonably well since she started treating Riven. As she passes the second guard in the passageway, he greets her and asks if she has any news of the outside world.

'Looks like snow,' she repeats, and he sucks his teeth.

'Poor bugger,' he says. 'Wouldn't like to be travelling in that.'

'No,' she agrees, not quite understanding his point, and she opens the door. It scrapes on the stones and the room echoes unfamiliarly, hollow and empty. Payne is there, standing in his riding boots and a travelling coat. He is very tight about the face, and she knows he is angry about something.

'There you are,' he says.

She thinks she might be late for an appointment but she does not think they have made one. Behind Payne his various things – his dishes, herbs, bags, his jars and ewers, his roll of knives – are packed away and his two coffers are one atop the other. There are some large bags, too.

'You are going somewhere?' she asks.

'Yes,' he says. 'Somewhere my skills are appreciated and my belongings not searched and objects stolen.'

He gestures at Riven, asleep in his bed, face turned to the wall. His dressing needs changing.

'What has been stolen?' she asks.

'That hardly matters,' he says. 'It is the fact of it.'

Then it hits her. The ledger.

'A moment,' she says.

She opens the door of the garderobe, and it too scrapes too loudly on the stone-flagged floor. His clothes are all taken down and the row of pegs on which they used to hang to take advantage of the ammoniac stink is empty. The ledger is gone.

She goes back into Riven's chamber. Riven has turned over, but his eyes are still closed.

'Have you seen a book?' she asks Payne.

'A book? I have two.'

'A particular book. Hung on a peg in there. It was in a bag with a hole in?'

Payne shakes his head. No.

'Are you sure? It was about this size.'

Again, he shakes his head.

'I'm sure I would remember seeing that. What was it a book of?'

'Of – well, it did not have a title. It was a – a list of things. Names mostly. But it had a hole in it. That is what you would remember most.'

She cannot help but glance at the pollaxe in its corner as she says this. She wonders, bets, imagines, knows for certain, that the pick of the axe made the hole.

'The book had a hole? Or the bag?'

'Both.'

Payne pulls a face.

'And you left it here? Why?'

'For – for safekeeping,' she says.

'Ha,' he says. 'More fool you. I have lost a cup – of silver – and a knife that I was given by the Duke of Devonshire, as well as a cap lined with marten fur, and – and – and other, divers items the whereabouts of which this villain is unable to pinpoint, despite lying here when the thefts occurred.'

But why the ledger?

And, Christ! What will Thomas say? She feels sick with it. Faint. As if she might fall over at any time. First Payne is going, and now the ledger is gone! The ledger. Oh, dear Christ. She tries to concentrate. Think about Payne.

'Where are you going?' she asks.

'South,' he tells her. 'To Bywell in Tynedale. A case of the pissing evil.'

'The pissing evil? Is that serious?' she asks. It sounds it.

'Of course.'

'Will you come back?'

'When the illness has run its course, and if King Henry wills it, yes, but not if it is to treat this man.'

He curls his lips at Riven. And now she looks over at Riven, only to see him not looking at Payne, who has just insulted him, but at her, and she knows – she knows – he has the ledger.

Payne says his farewells. Two of the King's men come for his coffers and bags and there is some good-natured badinage between them and Riven's guard. When they have gone, and she has said goodbye and thanked Payne for all he has shown her, and he has clasped her to him in a moment of strained emotion, she returns to change Riven's dressing. His eyes are shut again. She works quickly, tugging the wick a little further from the wound. Her hands are shaking.

'A book, hmmm?' he asks.

She pauses for a moment.

'Yes,' she says. 'Do you know where it is?'

He says nothing. She exposes the wound to the air. It is healing nicely, she thinks, and the wick is drawing clear. She rests her thumbnail on the flesh where it is rosy, and she wonders, for a moment, for a moment, if she could just – cause him pain? Get him to talk that way? But no. She remembers how he faced the pain when she cut him. And besides – it would be pointless. He is lying with his arms by his sides today. They moved the limb down in the week after they had made the cut, and since it had been positioned such for so long, it hurt him enough to make him faint, but he never cried out, except once, to emit a tiny squeak, like fresh rush under foot.

'What do you want with a book?' he asks.

'It is – it belonged to my father.'

'Your father?'

'Yes,' she says. 'He is dead.'

'Ah,' he says. 'Your father is dead. What was he? A barber surgeon likewise?'

And she is briefly caught out. She has never even wondered what he might have been and done.

'Yes,' she says. 'Likewise.'

'And how did this book come by its hole?'

She claims not to know.

'Have you seen it?' she asks. 'Have you taken it?'

Riven sighs.

'It is as I told that bore, Master Payne,' he says. 'I sleep. I do not notice men coming and going. And if they take things to sell to buy food—'

'But you have a guard!'

'He, too, must eat.'

'But why a book? Why take that? It is of no value.'

'Yet you seem exercised by its absence?'

'It is as I say,' she tells him. 'It was my father's.'

'Odd,' he says. 'I wonder if my son would be so sentimental about such a trifle were it mine?'

'Your son?'

'I have one.'

She hardly knows what to say.

'Tell me,' Riven goes on, 'your assistant. Was he ever a monk? A friar or some such?'

'No,' she says. 'Not one of them. Now, listen. For all I have done for you. Where is that ledger?'

'A ledger, is it?' Riven says, but in doing so, he closes his eyes and turns his head away, and just then, as if summoned by a secret signal, the guard shunts open the door and waits for her to leave. He is a very big man, she sees. An archer, probably, with those wrists. She can only obey him, but when she has left the room and the door is shut behind her, she asks him about the thefts. He feigns ignorance, but they both know.

'Look,' she says, 'I do not care about the knife and goblet or whatever, I am only concerned for a book.'

But now he is genuinely puzzled. He really knows nothing about it.

'And has – has Sir Giles been out of bed?' she asks. 'Walking and so on?'

'Oh, yes,' the guard says. 'You cannot keep a Riven down, is what he says. He does not go far, mind. I see to that.'

She finds Thomas standing lookout on the tower's top again. He has his cap pulled very low over his eyes and he is almost shapeless with the clothes he wears under his cloak.

When she tells him, he is unable to believe it.

'Riven has it? Are you certain?'

'I am sure.'

He rubs his jaw and looks away into the distance. She cannot hear his palm against the bristles because of the wind and the seagulls that shriek while they play in it.

280

'Christ,' he says. 'Christ.'

'I know.'

'What will he do with it?'

'I don't know,' she tells him. 'I think he only knows that it is of value to me, so far, and he'll not necessarily discover its significance, will he? Because — because, well, why would he? He thinks it belonged to my father, which is why I want it back.'

Thomas nods. His eyes are watering in the cold wind.

'How do we get it back?'

'I don't know,' she admits. 'It was not there in the chamber, so I cannot simply take it when he's asleep. And if I show him how much I want it, it will only make him more determined that I shouldn't have it. He is like that.'

'But we must find it. Can you imagine what Sir John would say if we were to turn up having lost the ledger, and saved Giles Riven's life?'

And she looks at him, distraught, since she can see that it is all her fault.

And then he starts to laugh, and he puts his hand over hers.

'It will be all right,' he says. 'Put your trust in me, says the Lord. It will not be what we want, or think we want, but it will be all right.'

And now hearing him talk such reassuring nonsense makes her want to cry.

'God's plan?' she asks.

He smiles again, more broadly still, a row of white teeth in his dark beard, and puts his arm around her shoulder and he pulls her to him, and though at that precise moment snowflakes drift to settle around them, she feels, my God, he may just be right.

The snow does not settle, and the next week it is the feast of St Thomas, when the day is shortest in all the year, and most of those in the castle not called John are celebrating their name day. Horner allows Thomas to come with him and a few of the others and they go out of the walls and after a day searching the countryside they drag in a man-high, man-wide length of green log. They shove it in the bread oven, but they cannot get it to burn, or to give off any heat, and it smoulders wetly, hissing for three days and nights until they finally give up on it, and drag it out and chop it up and burn it with some beams they've stolen from a cottage in the village.

'You all right, Thomas?' Horner asks as they are sitting by the flames. 'Only you look – haunted. Like someone is out to kill you?'

'Well, they are,' he says. 'All of Lord Montagu's men. Christ. Most of England.'

'Yes, yes, but we're safe behind these walls,' Horner reassures him. 'Unless someone within them is trying to kill you?'

Thomas shakes his head, but Katherine thinks of the two that are after him to split him gut to gizzard. They are the reason he has not been down to the main gatehouse, where Riven's men are posted, to see if there is any sniff of the ledger.

'Unless it is burned, used as a splint to start a fire, then that is the only place it can be,' he has told her.

But as the week goes on, and there is no sign of it, and Thomas isn't able to go to the gatehouse to find it, the strain begins to tell, not helped by the privations of the Advent fast during which they have lived on briny soup and almost equally briny ale. The thought of its end, and of Christmas itself, is almost too much to bear and when they wake on the morning itself, it is to discover that the first heavy snowfall of the winter is in the process of settling outside, sealing them into their already shrunken world. Nevertheless, despite its flurries, the men and few women of the castle gather in the bailey after the first Mass of the day to watch the candles lit, and their light shine through the chapel's windows and they are there to cheer King Henry when he grants them licence to go out and hunt the migrant swans that have settled on the mere below the castle walls, and any other fish, or fowl, they can find besides.

'I've been eyeing them all month,' Jack says. 'Watching them get fatter by the day while we wither to nowt on this stinking fish stew not worth a louse.'

But neither Thomas nor Katherine nor Jack is among the appointed hunters. Horner commands them to keep watch from the top of the outward postern gate, where one of the men has entwined ivy through the merlons, while seemingly every other man in the garrison is out roaming the country below.

Thomas takes the chance to approach the main gatehouse, and she watches him sidle away through the bailey, keeping to its edges, and already he looks suspicious, like a thief, and she wonders if he ought not to go straight at the steps as if he belongs there. She waits, her gaze fixed on the gatehouse, and she finds herself shivering as she mumbles the prayers for his safe return. At the end of the afternoon, he comes, empty-handed, just as the hunters troop back on new-made paths embroidered in the snowfields, converging on the gate with their haul: most of the swans, all sorts of duck and goose, a fox, three herons, a string of puffins, and even a bulbous seal Tailboys's men killed among the rocks on the headland to the north. They carry this oddity slung from a long pike held on their shoulders and everybody reacts to it in their own way.

That night they sing songs and their bellies are filled with rough meaty pottage and sour beer made with what tastes like nettles brought by an Easterling ship, sent from some French duke somewhere that also brought with it iron bars for the smiths, wheat and salt for the King's bakers. One of the boats unloading the ship sank in the choppy waters while laden, taking with it its oarsmen, and it is not known for sure what it was carrying, though some say malt.

Katherine continues to tend to Giles Riven all through Christmastide. King Henry, through Sir Ralph Grey, has provided her with more linen, wine and rose oil; urine, of course, she can get almost anywhere. The scar is healing, though she still does not know whether he will be able to move his arm.

One morning he is asleep when she goes in, and she believes he remains that way, so she looks again under the frame of his bed, where Payne used to store his mattress, but the ledger is not there, and when she looks up, he is awake, staring at her.

'Where is it?' she asks.

But he wants a different conversation.

'You have not brought your assistant,' he tells her.

'Nor will I,' she says, 'until you return my book.'

He scoffs.

'You know where I know him from, don't you?' he asks. 'But you won't tell me.'

On the morning of the Epiphany she goes to see him again, and she is surprised to find his guard absent, and she opens the door with care to find him standing in the middle of his chamber, wearing only his braies, waiting for her. He is very, very pale, a great rack of ribs and a tilting pelvis, with his belly sunk in, and his skin loose, and swagged like cloth, and his limbs, especially the right arm, withered to sticks, to twigs. He grimaces at her with his brown teeth and his face is waxy and beaded with sweat. His brown hair is damp with it.

'What do you think?' he gasps through the pain. 'You cannot keep a Riven down.'

His guard is within, it turns out, behind the door, waiting to catch him should he fall.

'You look like one of the Horsemen of the Apocalypse,' she says.

He hisses a laugh. She can smell his breath. How coffins must be, she thinks.

'Am I Famine?' he asks. 'Or War? Or am I just Death?'

'It hardly matters,' she says, because, after all, he is not one of them. She will not show fright. She will not.

'Tell your assistant that I am nearly ready,' he says. 'Tell him I am no fan of mummery, that I am not misled by disguises. Tell him I will soon remember.'

284

Katherine ignores him. She is all business, and asks to see the scar, but he will not turn, wisely since he is so unsteady on his newborn colt's legs, and so instead she must go in and stand behind him. Her hands are shaking. It is seeing him upright, she thinks, that brings his presence home. She removes the linen. It is dry, and the skin is pink, puckered and silky. She knows there is no need for her to look at it ever again.

'Cold hands you have,' Riven says.

'It is snowing,' she says.

He says nothing, but after a long moment lets out a sad sigh, and she can only guess his thoughts. He says no more until she is finished with the dressing and is about to go.

'Leave the door,' he says.

But she does not. She closes him in, and she hurries away, and she will not come back.

The snow lasts all month, falling, melting, freezing, falling again, night after night, day after day, and the icicles that hang fast under the drains in the castle walls and from the mouths of the gargoyles in the keep become steadily more grotesque. The walkways and tower tops are scattered with sand from the beach, and the whiteness of snow serves to emphasise the filth that accrues under the castle walls.

'Why you need a moat,' Horner supposes.

All around the castle walls the few patrolling sentries move like heaps of clothing under their heavy cloaks and worsted hats that soon become solid with damp. Below them the bailey is deserted save for the sheep in their folds, eating rationed hay and turnip tops, and bleating constantly through the short grey days.

And there is still no sign of the ledger, or of Edmund Riven.

'He will wait until the spring, surely?' Katherine says. She remembers Sir John Fakenham refusing a summons to spend the winter in Sandal Castle years earlier, a decision that saved his life, as it happened. Why would a man want to come and freeze to death in an ill-provisioned castle in such a bleak spot when he could be at home by his own hearthside?

Thomas agrees that is probable, but still. It would be better to know for sure, one way or the other, and in the meantime, they are stuck in the castle, and nerves and tempers begin to fray all around them.

'How long is this going to last?' Jack asks. 'Herding sheep is more fun.'

He has managed to persuade a woman in the tents below to knit him an oily scarf that smells more of goat than sheep, and it has brought him out in a rash under his chin that he keeps scratching. Katherine is with him now, staring south, over the bailey, over their little world, watching the armed shepherds huddle in their tent trying unsuccessfully to burn dung, and beyond, the ghostly lights in the keep windows, where she imagines the ledger is even now.

'It all depends,' Horner tells them, 'on whether the Scots treat with the false King Edward. If they do, then we'll have them coming at our backs from the north, and Lord Montagu coming at us from the south. We'll be caught, you see?'

He demonstrates by scraping a gloved finger in the ice. It is perfectly obvious.

'I thought the Scots and King Edward had already made a treaty, which is why King Henry had to leave there, and come here?'

'Yes,' Horner admits, vaguely, since his information is patchy and his understanding thin at its fringes. 'But that was just to get them to eject King Henry from Scotland. This treaty is to get them – those Scots – to join Montagu in hounding us.'

'So what to do?' she asks.

Horner tells them that the Duke of Somerset has decided the only way to stop a treaty between the Scots and the Earl of March is to ensure their negotiators never meet, and that he is trying to discover the negotiators' whereabouts, so that he can capture them, or kill them, no one knows quite which.

'Would it be a good idea to kill the Scots?' Thomas ventures. 'Won't they then become your enemies?'

'Our enemies,' Horner corrects, but agrees.

Patrols are sent out into the snow. Sir Ralph Grey does not volunteer his men.

'Pointless exercise,' he says. 'We aren't going to just bump into the bastards, are we?'

But information is acquired and tidings come back. The Scots are sending their negotiators south from their capital to wait for an escort of Montagu's men at a place called Norham, on the River Tweed. It is a castle to the north of Bamburgh, held by men loyal to King Edward. Lord Montagu is to ride north from Newcastle, through this area controlled, although only loosely, by King Henry, to collect the Scottish negotiators and bring them back down to Newcastle, through the same lands again, to negotiate with King Edward's negotiators who in their turn are coming up from London to meet them there.

Meanwhile, worse tidings are confirmed: King Edward is also treating with the French and the Burgundians, who in the past have been friends of King Henry, and if he manages that, then it is all over: all hope is lost to Lancaster. It is not just a question of the long-term promises on which they have banked these past months, years even, that they will lose: it will be the day-to-day necessities – wheat, oats, ale – and without them . . . Well, as for the men of Bamburgh and Alnwick, of Dunstanburgh and the many little fortresses that litter the Northern Marches – not even toads and bats will sustain them. They will have to give up their resistance and make terms with the same Yorkists who killed their fathers and their brothers at Towton. Knowing this, King Henry sends out letters and messages to his wife, his wife's father, the same Duke who sent the supplies at Christmas, to the King of France, to the Duke of

Burgundy, to anyone who will accept his letters and might have '*un peu d'argent*' to spare, imploring them not to treat with the House of York, not to abandon the House of Lancaster. It is, more or less, all he can do.

And instead of the rush of men hurrying to join King Henry's side that Somerset had promised, if anything the number has dwindled. Two or three a day, and none of them with many in their retinue, and the longer it goes on, past Candlemas and into February, the more certain Katherine becomes that Edmund Riven will not join his father, but will remain at liberty, enjoying King Edward's grace. Knowing the parlous state of King Henry's world, it is the only thing a sane man might do.

When the newly arrived see what it is they have come to join, their faces fall, and she can see them itching to back out, to return to wherever and whatever it is they've left, but the Duke of Somerset, a terrific escapee himself, has tightened the security, and now all the old soldiers who've been loyal to King Henry in exile, men who have nothing left to lose, stand gaolers over the newcomers.

'By all the saints,' Jack says, banging his fist against the wet stonework. 'When? When? Fuck me! We'll never get out of this bloody place!'

PART FIVE

South, to Tynedale, Northumberland, Before Easter 1464

19

The company vintenars are with their men in the butts, and out in the dunes, morning till night, come rain or shine, and in the bailey there is always shouting, and the constant ripple of men practising with bills and hammers. Thomas watches them for a while, and sees how quick and supple the best are, constantly twisting one another's wrists, changing their angles of attack, using their weapons in unexpected ways, and getting through their enemies' blades to strike them. Now that they have shed their coats, it is possible to see their livery colours, and Riven's men are among them, Thomas sees, and their comings-together – 'fights' is too grand a word for such swift couplings – are models of brutality and merciless economy: one man thrusts, the other evades, twists, turns and brings his hammer's fluke around to ring against the first man's helmet. It might just as easily have been in his eye.

'They don't hang about, do they?' Jack volunteers.

'Hmmm,' Thomas agrees, 'but who are all these others?'

'Those in the red and green are Lord Hungerford's,' Jack tells him, 'and those in the blue and yellow are Roos's. They should be all right, though? Surely? Don't look too bad?'

Thomas is not so sure. He shrugs.

'I suppose there is still time.'

But there isn't. Or not much. Word goes out that Sir Humphrey Neville of Brancepeth is to lead a party down south, to try to intercept Lord Montagu as Montagu rides north on his way to collect the Scottish negotiators. Humphrey Neville's lands are to the south of Newcastle, and it is supposed he knows them, so that is where he intends to spring the trap, and he and his men take as many arrows and as much of the remaining oats as they can to keep themselves alive in the field.

'What a relief he's gone,' Horner tells them, 'for he makes Sir Ralph seem moderate in his whims.'

Meanwhile the rest of the garrison, along with almost every other man in the north who is still loyal to King Henry, are to be gathered in Bamburgh, ready to sally out in support of the many small uprisings that are reported all over the land. Horner is delighted.

'This is it,' he says. 'It is now or never, do or die. This is the time when King Henry will count on his loyal friends, and in the future, he will remember us. You should hear Sir Ralph talk. He thinks that by the end of this not only will he be castellan of Alnwick, Bamburgh and Dunstanburgh, he will be the Earl of Northumberland, rising higher than the Percys and the Nevilles! He has great plans for a new livery the like of which – well, it sounds fantastical, that is all I can say.'

And still Edmund Riven does not come.

'Where is he? When will he come?' Thomas keeps asking Katherine, but she does not know.

'And where is the ledger? Why has that not surfaced? Do you believe he can really have it still?'

He knows he is letting his frustration grow, but after the long hibernation through the winter, the Duke of Somerset is preparing his army to fight, and Thomas's vague anxiety at the thought of it, of going to fight Montagu's men, solidifies into fear. He does not want to go anywhere, not just with these men, who do not fill him with any confidence, but with *any* men. More than that, he does not want to have to ride out and fight anyone, least of all Montagu's men, whom he vividly recalls manning the gates of Newcastle. He does not mention this to anyone, not even Katherine, lest she thinks him a coward, but he never came here to fight alongside men he

292

might even have fought in the past, and he values his life more than he values this cause. Christ, he thinks, he values his bootstraps more than he values this cause.

But they are caught, still, again, as ever they were, in the same trap that has held them fast since they arrived at Alnwick, months ago. It is not just the question of getting over the walls, though that is hard enough, nor is it merely the question of finding horses when they've done so, though again, that would be hard enough too. It is really the question of getting past the patrols Somerset sends out, ridden by men who are more like the men they call the prickers, who roam a battlefield's rear and whose job it is to strike more fear into a man than his known enemy, whoever that enemy might be.

'What are we going to do?' Katherine asks, divining his unspoken thoughts. 'We can't join this lot in their fight, can we? I mean, do you want to? I don't. I don't want you to. I know I will be left at the rear, and I will do my best to stitch men up, but look at them. They are not good archers, even I know that. They are farm boys, pretending. That one. Look at him. He has no bracer. He will be shouting with pain after he has loosed ten arrows. And that one – he has a hunting bow! You will be against trained archers, equipped with proper bows loosing proper arrows.'

He gets Horner to call the men to the butts once more and they spend the next few days there, loosing, collecting, loosing, collecting, sending the arrows in precise waves, each time faster and further than before. But it is only his men he can make do this. The others – Hungerford's men and Roos's men – watch from behind, and they admire or laugh at their exertions, but that is it, until one of Horner's men gets into a fight with one of theirs and has to be dragged off while both are still struggling to free their daggers from their belts, and that is depressing in its own way.

And then Humphrey Neville of Brancepeth returns from setting his ambush for Montagu with not a single casualty and it is possible to imagine how, for a moment, the guards on the gates might have thought he had set his ambush so cleverly that he must have annihilated Montagu's men, but then it emerges that Montagu's scouts disturbed the ambush, and that consequently Montagu went around it, and reached Newcastle unmolested.

Somerset is said to be furious, and so now he has decided that they must risk everything, and so St Ambrose's day, in early April, is the appointed day, and they gather in the bailey in their companies, in their livery coats, ready to march out of the castle to intercept Montagu on his way north, and there is great excitement and even a sense of purpose and for the first time Thomas is able to see this beleaguered little army as a fellowship, one forged by the common endurance of hard times, and he can see that they share a feeling of togetherness, camaraderie even, when most suspicions are laid aside and men in red-and-black livery might stand happily with men in yellow-and-blue, or even white with clumsy approximations of ravens on their chests, and there are mentions of King Henry's father, who took his own beleaguered little army through France, and, in the thin spring sunshine, one might almost think anything were possible.

But this camaraderie does not include Thomas. He is thinking of only two things, the first of which is the chance this venture will offer to send a stray arrow where it should not be sent: into the back of Giles Riven. And the second, that must necessarily follow on the first: escape. He does not know how or when, but he knows the chance will come. He will seize it, when it does, and loose the arrow and then ride, just as he should have done months ago. He has spoken to Jack and John Stump about leaving – he did not call it deserting – and they will come with him and Katherine. Four are better that two. It is true he is giving up on the ledger, but realistically, what chance is there that it has not been burned? He cannot imagine why anyone would ever steal it in the first place, let alone keep it, other than for lighting a fire. Nevertheless he watches Riven's men now piling their wagon high with all sorts of odd-shaped sacks and bags and boxes.

Could the ledger be on there? Or would they leave it behind?
'Is Riven himself coming?' he asks.

'I don't know,' she says. 'I have not seen him for a month. I doubt
he could have become so strong as to ride a horse, though, let alone
fight.'

He thinks about Sir Ralph Grey's bet with William Tailboys: how
many nobles was it if Riven could mount a horse?

But then there is a thin trumpet blast from the merlons of the
keep, and from its doorway come, of all things, two columns of
Sir Giles Riven's men. They emerge from within to part – ten men
going one way, ten the other – until they form a line, a backdrop,
either side of the doorway, and then, after a pause, King Henry
comes out, wearing a helmet with an open face and a coronet
attached, studded with what look like gemstones – red and green.

'He could sell that,' someone mutters. 'Buy us all a round of ale.'

King Henry acts as if there ought to be a cheer now, but there
isn't, and Thomas can see from the King's expression that he is
merely following orders from – probably – Somerset, whom Thomas
can imagine is waiting inside, barking through the doorway, and
that King Henry would rather do anything but this, would rather
creep quietly to prayers.

Apart from the helmet, he is wearing what looks like a monk's
cassock, and the men in the bailey are struck silent. They are not
complicated men, Thomas supposes, and all they need to see is something they think worth following. King Henry is not that something.
He looks miserably uninspiring, and he knows it, and he mumbles
something apologetic that can only be heard at the front of the crowd,
and there is a limp sort of cheer and then from the keep comes Sir
Giles Riven, and even so diminished as he is by his wound, he still
exudes something, something King Henry is lacking. It may not be
what the men in the bailey want, though, since there are hisses when
he appears, as when Beelzebub appears in a mummers' play.

He glares at the crowd below him, looking to find someone to dare to stand up and say something, but no man catches his eye, and once the hissing has died down, silence resumes, grows, and King Henry shifts from foot to foot and then says something again and a ruddy-faced Grey is there at his shoulder, as well as that beardless capering priest, and they both laugh as if neither has heard anything so funny and Riven turns slowly to them and in a moment they fall silent.

Riven stands waiting, neither patient nor impatient, more tolerating what must be tolerated, and under his travelling cloak he has a sword belt wrapped around his waist, and he is in riding boots, folded down to the knee, and gloves and a hat pulled down over his ears, and it seems he has been within for so long that he is unused to the cold, and that his eyes are watering in the chill breeze.

So he is coming too, Thomas sees, and he watches his fingers grip his new bow, just as if it were they who hate Riven, just as if his body remembers why he hates the man so, even if his mind has forgotten, but he knows this time he will have a chance, and this time, it will be easy, and at least when they return to Marton they will have achieved one thing. An arrow. In that moment of chaos, if they manage to find Montagu's men, and if they manage to draw them into a fight, and if not, then – some other way. But a chance will come, he is sure, out there, and he will save an arrow for that moment. He has a sheaf of the best with his few possessions on a cart, guarded by John Stump, and he can almost see the one he will send flying into Riven's back. He thinks it is even slightly funny, that he will be replacing one arrowhead with another, but as he is laughing, he unearths a different image, a memory, of standing on a hillside in the falling gloom, and of bending a bow to loose an arrow across a snow-filled valley, and of hitting a man, and knocking him down, and feeling he'd somehow missed. He shudders as if at the cold, and then finds Katherine's hand on his shoulder blade, and she is concerned. Others have turned too. He must have cried out.

But now King Henry is talking again, saying something Thomas cannot hear for King Henry does not have a voice that will carry.

But as he speaks a steward emerges to lead a saddled horse up the steps to where Riven stands with a curled lip, and a mounting block is brought up made of a broad log, and placed beside the waiting horse, and for a moment no one can see what is happening because King Henry and Sir Giles Riven are hidden behind the horse, but it seems that King Henry himself is helping Riven to step up on to it, with a servant and the steward nearby, their hands ready to catch either if he should fall. Nearby all the King's men look on with mixed expressions. Grey is there, grinning and hopping from foot to foot, while Tailboys is thunderous.

'Hope the fucker falls off,' one of the men next to Thomas mutters.

When Riven is mounted he turns to the crowd, and stares at them as if he has done this to spite them, and then uses his heels to nudge the horse forward, and with that, Grey has won his bet, and Tailboys lost his, and John Stump looks around for Katherine.

'Kit!' he shouts. 'It was Kit!'

And Katherine looks over from her place by the cart and a frown pinches her forehead but John goes on shouting about how she – he – was the one who should take the credit. Horner interrupts and calls that they were lucky to have such a God-gifted surgeon to ride with them into battle, and that if by any ill luck they should find themselves wounded or injured, then they know that they will have the services of the man who taught the King's physician a thing or two, and what could be better than that? Did Montagu have such a resource? No!

It is hardly stirring, Thomas thinks, but the men seem mildly reassured, even if they are reassured more for their friends, for no man goes into a fight thinking he will be the one to need a surgeon, and it shows that Horner is at least considerate, not just of his men, but where credit was owed. Katherine flushes, even up to the point of her half-ear.

And so, led by King Henry and Sir Giles Riven, and then by the Duke of Somerset and the other lords – Roos and Hungerford – and Sir Ralph Percy and Sir Ralph Grey, and Sir Humphrey Neville of

Wherever it is, they march out through the dank shadows of the barbican and then finally into the spring sunshine, and the Duke, who has found some newish harness, lets the sunlight catch on its polished parts, and his horse is good, and eager for exercise, and the King's long banner is made to stir by his standard-bearer and they ride down the hill and away from the castle and the long trail of marching men unwinds behind them, with every man there wishing he had a horse of his own.

They walk all morning, moving at the speed of the slowest cart, and though no one except Somerset seems to have a very clear idea where they are bound, or how long it will take to get there, they all agree it had better not be too far, and it had better be well-provisioned, for they are not over-encumbered with baggage. There are a few carts carrying barrels of ale, a few laden with sacks of oats that do not look wholly dry and give off the taint of spoil, and each company has a cart piled with arrows and personal baggage and weapons, but that, more or less, is that. It is not enough to keep them in the field for very long, however few they may be.

'Saints,' Horner says, 'it is good to be out, isn't it?'

It is that. Castle walls begin to loom up over you after a while. Their shadows are long and cold and deep, even on a spring day such as this, but now they are out in open moorland, following a gritty track through rolling plains of heather, sedge, gorse and broom even, and men take sprigs of it and put them in their hats like the first Plantagenets, but as they walk on, the relief of being out of the castle fades, and Thomas's anxieties begin to bloom.

He looks around him at the men he's walking with, and all he really wants is to be away, to duck into the trees at the side of the road, to take Katherine with him and to return to a normal life, the one he imagines he is owed, with a house by a stream with some acres to call his own, with oxen, sheep, beehives, a pond. Christ! A spinning wheel and a few pigs.

A man begins playing a flute and another joins him, and then one takes up a song that suggests a plaintive desire to be elsewhere, and it speaks of home fields as the summer comes in, and of sweethearts, and of warmth and plenty, and pretty soon others have joined in, until the word comes down that it is to stop, and there are vintenars on horses threatening men to get them to hold their tongues, and the boys are told to get drumming, and so they do, and their tambours or whatever they are, are beaten in a driving rhythm and the home fields and sweet-hearts are all forgotten as men pick up their pace and forge ahead.

'Is it always like this?' Thomas asks Katherine and she shakes her head.

'When we came to Towton, it was the grimmest thing you ever saw. Every man was set, and it was so cold you wouldn't believe it was nearly Lady Day. And there were thousands of us. Thousands. How many are we now, do you suppose?'

'Horner says nearly five thousand but they expect more to join them as we go.'

They move south, past Dunstanburgh from which a small contingent joins them.

'Were you really eating toads?' Jack asks one.

'Not toads,' he says. 'They're poisonous. Everything else, though. Seagulls are the worst, but we had a lot of them, so.'

They march all day, until it is coming on to night and they pitch camp on moorland that is reasonably flat. There are exactly eight tents, and they gather enough wood and bracken and heather for a large watch fire and the men sleep around it, as close to the tents as they can. The best place is under the carts, where they will be dry if it rains, nor will the dew soak them where they lie. Riven's men are the other side of the camp, likewise gathered around their own cart, but Riven himself is to sleep in one of the tents, alongside Sir Ralph Grey and others. Horner goes to report and comes back impressed.

'He is a cold fish,' he says, 'but he can silence Sir Ralph with a single look.'

Thomas sits awake, watching the tent in which he supposes Riven to be, and he watches Riven's men on the far side of the camp. They keep themselves to themselves, he notices, and he is pleased, but he wonders if their doing so means anything. He wonders if he can walk over there and just look to see if the ledger is there.

Katherine seems to read his intention.

'Do you think it'll be to one side of the tent, by the door, nice and neat in its bag, ready to be collected?' she scoffs.

And he admits it is unlikely. He's becoming sure it is burned now, since why otherwise would they keep it?

In the morning it is cool again, and scouts are sent out while the King's priests lead the remaining soldiery in prayer. They say the Ave, the Credo, the paternoster and the De Profundis before they eat their oatcakes and then dismantle the tents and get on their way, winding westwards now, the sea behind them, the breeze in their faces, stiffening their flags, tugging at their sleeves.

'Always easier to come the other way,' Horner tells Thomas, 'but at least King Henry can ride without having to breathe us all in.'

He is right. Thomas thinks. They do leave a trail, like rats migrating from barn to barn in autumn, and it is better to be upwind of them and their frowsty clothes and unwashed bodies.

All day they potter westwards under racing clouds and the drummers are not so enthusiastic when the showers come, and they remove their skins, and the men trudge through the gathering mud with their heads down and raindrops ringing on their hats and shoulders. The thing is, they do not seem to have a destination. They seem to be wandering around, moving from west to east, east to west, waiting for something to happen that might not happen.

Then King Henry leaves them, riding for better quarters, and he is to be escorted by a company of Sir Giles Riven's men, and so Thomas and Katherine stand in the rain and watch them go.

'Christ,' Thomas says. He almost wishes he were riding with them.

For two days in a row they stay in the same camp, stripping and despoiling the countryside around, until the morning of the third day, when they break camp and retrace their steps. Scouts come and go, bringing conflicting reports. Sometimes Montagu is still in Newcastle, and the Scots have returned to Edinburgh. Sometimes Montagu is riding westwards, via Carlisle, and the Scots are moving that way too, on their way to meet him in Kelso. Sometimes Montagu has many men with him, a great power with bombards, and a force of archers many thousands strong; sometimes he is moving quickly in a party of no more than forty horsemen. No one can be sure of anything. Morale is sapped. Fights break out. The rain comes down.

More days pass, and they are now west of Bamburgh, north of Alnwick, in rough stream-fissured moorland offering little shelter under stunted, wind-sculpted hawthorns. Birds shoot overhead, bundled by the gusts from the west, and the steely grey sky suggests more rain. Sir Ralph Grey comes stalking through the heather, seeking out Thomas and Horner.

'Can't bloody well stand this much more,' he says. 'Shouldn't have left Bamburgh. Christ! Shouldn't have left Alnwick. And that goddamned traitor Riven has slipped off with King Henry so he doesn't have to be out in this. So Riven is gone and with him goes Thomas's best hope for a chance to kill him. Christ, he thinks, if this task is a God-given, God is not making it easy.

'Still,' Grey continues 'There we are. Cowardly bloody bastard. But never mind that. I want you to ride to Hulne for me. The Prior will have had time to distil some more of his – his – his whatever the stuff is called. Actually, while you are there, ask him what it is called, will you? Find out if it has a name.'

'Can I take Kit and Jack?' Thomas asks.

'No,' Grey says. 'They must stay.'

So not only has Riven slipped away, they are still not trusted.

He and Horner and two other men ride out the next morning. It is the first time he has been away from Katherine since that day on the river's bank in the summer, and he feels his departure like a

301

physical pain, and thinks of himself as a stone being pried from the flesh of its plum. They find a few moments alone while Thomas pretends to piss, and they stand side by side by the river, and he tells her it will not be for long.

'What if you run into Montagu?' she asks.

'We won't,' he says. 'Horner says Montagu has looped well to the west, to Carlisle.'

So Thomas and Horner and the four others mount up and are southbound on one of the old roads, paved with large flat stones, centuries old already, that leads south to Morpeth, Horner says, when ahead of them they see a great party of horsemen clustered together, possibly all in black and red.

'Christ!' Horner shouts. 'It is them! It is them! Get back! Let's go.'

And they turn their horses and dig their heels in and they gallop back up the track. Montagu's men do not give chase.

'Did you get it?' Grey asks when they ride into the camp and throw themselves from their horses. When they tell him what they know, Grey is disappointed, but Horner is taken before Somerset.

'Just told him what we saw,' he tells Thomas when he returns.

Trumpets are sounded. Drums pick up. Vintenars are among them again with their sticks and cuffs, shouting, harrying. There is some trouble among Lord Roos's men: a fight, some sort of mutiny, quickly overcome. More patrols are sent out. Thomas finishes his ale, and the remnants of his oatcakes. He wishes they had made it as far as Hulne, where he might have found some food, even if it was only fish soup and bread. The scouts come back. They estimate that Montagu has four thousand men, a number only slightly smaller than their own. As many as a thousand archers are among them.

Preparations are made.

'Dear God,' Thomas says. 'We are going to have to fight them!'

'We mustn't,' Katherine whispers. 'You mustn't. You must get away. Today. This moment.'

302

But the prickers are already there, mounted, in pickets, waiting for any to try just this. He feels he has been asleep and has now woken up to find himself joining the line, bow clutched in hand, getting ready to fight for men he hardly knows against men he hardly knows. And she looks at him with tear-filled eyes and he cannot pretend that everything will be all right and that nothing will happen to him, because anything could happen to him, and it might not be all right. Katherine touches him on the sleeve.

'Kit,' he says and she looks at him and realises what he means – that she is Kit not Katherine, even now – and she withdraws her hand.

And Katherine stands. She is very pale. He looks at her and vows to himself that he will remember her like this, whatever else happens. She is in a long jack that reaches mid-thigh, baggy hose, good boots still, and she wears her linen cap under a simply made fulled wool tube that she has curled over. She has a belt on which is her purse, where she keeps her rosary and her knife. Over her shoulder she carries a pale linen bag that is, just now, half-filled with oatcakes.

'So,' she says, and she extends her hand and he takes it. They hold one another's gaze longer than they ought, and he feels, Christ, we have said these sorts of farewell before. His hand lingers. He is breathing quickly. He wants of all things to pull her to him.

She seems to know, but there is nothing to be done, and then there are the usual parting wishes, of going with God, and of God guiding hands, and of God delivering to safety and finally Thomas has to let go of her hand and look away and Horner is still there, turned, staring up to where men are gathering on the slight crest above. The King's banner is there, though Thomas supposes King Henry himself is not; as is Percy's, on the right, though the others – Somerset who came in just his nightshirt – do not have theirs, and so linen has been painted with the Beaufort colours, and it flutters in the breeze. Above, a skein of geese passes, flying spread out in the shape of an arrowhead, northwards for the summer.

20

The bearded priest calls them together and from the bed of a cart he leads them in a cycle of prayers that few can hear, during which there is an appeal for intercession from the Virgin Mary and from St Edward in particular, to uphold the divine right of King Henry to rule his people as his own, and then another cycle of prayers begins, before they are permitted to disperse to their own carts and their own little encampments, to follow their own routines, to find their own consolations and seek their own encouragements, and now those that have harness put it on, and servants and women start to bustle about the place while men grow still and silent.

Grey has provided his own men with his livery coat and a helmet each, all in the same style made by the same armourer, as well as a padded jack apiece, though Thomas does not need one, and he pulls his livery cloth over his brigandine, and his helmet is close-fitting, good for loosing a bow, but it makes hearing hard, and for some reason it is difficult to judge space and distance around the camp, and then he ties on his bracer, finds the short sword he has acquired and ties that to his belt, and then the buckler that Grey has also given out, and last he picks up his bow and two sheaves of arrows.

And now there is nothing more they can say. On Hedgeley Moor the drums are beating constantly and everyone is shouting for one another and there are bugles and horns being blown and horses are being led to their riders to take them up towards the line. The prickers are riding in packs of four or five, long spears resting on bootcaps, looking for men in the shadows, under carts, down by the

304

river, in among the heather, anyone who might be tempted to drift away.

Then Horner arrives, breathless, pink with pleasure at his attire. He has plate on his arms and legs, good steel gloves, a fine helmet with a face-piece he can raise and a bevor. He has plate under his livery coat, and, with his pollaxe, to Thomas's mind he looks like a boy dressed up to fight, and he remembers thinking that of someone before, but whom? He does not know. He wonders for the first time how old Horner is.

'We are to be in the centre,' Horner tells him. 'On the road itself. Somerset is to lead from there, with Percy's men in the vanguard and Hungerford and Roos on the left.'

'What about the King?' John Stump asks and there is a moment of embarrassed silence.

'Archers will be to the front,' Horner continues. 'Facing south, wind from the west as usual. Whatever happens if Montagu is to survive the day, he knows he has to get past us, and we will stop him here, and then the day will be ours.'

But those flags. They are pointing to Roos and Hungerford's men, in their red-and-green and blue-and-yellow, and Thomas cannot help thinking he would not like to be where they are, on that wing of the front. He sees Riven's men among them, though, and he is pleased. He imagines the men who'd wanted to kill him will be under the drifting arrow cloud when it comes. He remembers Little John's tale of being under one of them, and he is suddenly dry-mouthed with fear. How did it come to this? he wonders. He looks for a way out, an escape, but there is none. He wonders exactly when it became too late. The moment he encountered Horner, he supposes, six months earlier.

Thomas takes his leave of Horner with a quick clasp of his metal hands, and then he edges through the crowd of men-at-arms and their attendant billmen to the front, to find Jack and the others, the archers, his archers, who stand well spaced for the loosing of their bows, some with their arrow shafts in the ground, others with them in their belts. They are confident, it is obvious, and ready for this, and for a moment Thomas is reassured to be among them, since he knows they are good and well trained, and that they will do their best. He takes his place among them behind the man who always came last in the arrow-shooting competitions, having chosen this because he'd rather be behind him than in front of him. His name is John, a cutler from Sheffield. A good man, well-meaning, but as simple as a cow.

Jack is further along the line, craning to see the enemy, still so boyish despite it all. Thomas leans forward to catch his eye, and when he does, Jack nods back, but he is distracted. Thomas hopes he will be all right today. He thinks of him the first time he saw him, bobbing in and out of the trees in his brother's orchard, and he realises how fond of the boy he has become. He watches him tell another man a joke, or something that makes him laugh anyway, and he feels curiously proud. He is like a what? Not a son. Jack is only a few years younger than Thomas, but he is definitely like a nephew perhaps. Like his brother's son; the one who lived.

Thomas turns to the front, and peers over John the Cutler's padded form, and he sees for the first time the distant line of Montagu's troops. At moments like these a man sees his enemy and thinks that if he is to survive he will have to kill every single one of them, that it is him against them. And right now, this does not, at first, look possible. Montagu's men move in a solid block, with what look like archers to the front, as is usual, and then a great mass of men-at-arms behind. At the centre are the polished figures of Montagu's captains, moving up quite quickly, Thomas thinks. Then they stop. There is a short moment while they reorganise themselves. A trumpet brays. They carry on.

'This is it, boys,' someone says. 'Say your prayers.'

There is a susurrus and a murmuring among the men, and Thomas joins them in a mumbled paternoster, and then there is a flurry of arms crossing chests. One or two of the older men bend a knee and mark their place with a cross in the dirt under the heather roots, and some of them take a small piece of this earth and place it in their mouths, but the younger archers don't bother. It must be something from France, Thomas thinks, when the English fought the French, rather than one another.

Another trumpet. Distant shouts in the cold grey afternoon.

Now Somerset propels his horse through the ranks and he rides out a little way, before turning to face them. He has his helmet raised and his bevor undone, and he is carrying a horseman's hammer, but it is for show, since they all know he must dismount and send his horse back, and fight on foot like a proper Englishman. But for now, it is a good thing, something to wave, something to emphasise his rhetoric.

'Men of Lancaster!' he begins, raising the hammer. 'Men of England. On this day, in this hour, now, the fate of the kingdom – our kingdom – hangs in the balance. If we let past this mob of false traitors sent by the treacherous Duke of York to seek the succour of the enemies of our dread liege King Henry, we will lose. Not just the day, but everything. We will lose our names, our lands, our lives. And all the hardships we have shared over the years, all the privations, all the sacrifices, all the time we have been denied our lands, our hearths, our dogs, our wives – they will count as nothing. All the blood we have shed. All the blood our fathers have shed, all the blood our sons and brothers have shed – it will count as nothing. But if we stop them here today, if we send them back whence they have come, then news of this day's work will resound throughout Christendom. We will turn the tide, and we will show the world that we, we men of the north, we are equal and greater to anything they might throw at us, and that we remain loyal. We remain steadfast where others falter, and that we are the true beating hearts of this our land.'

Somerset's oratory is undercut by the sight of a similar-looking man in similar-looking harness riding out to address his own troops across the moor. It might be Montagu, Thomas supposes, and it is easy to imagine him saying the same sorts of the things. At length Somerset finishes with an appeal to St George to send them safe and victorious, and there is a rousing cheer, echoed a moment later by a distant cheer from the ranks opposite, and while Somerset gallops along the front of his army, so does Montagu, and then both men ride through gaps that have been left open for them in the ranks of the men-at-arms and now there is nothing left to do but wait for the signal to get on with it.

Thomas wishes more than ever that he had ale. They all need it, really, to face what they are about to face. It gives them bodily strength, the energy to do what they must, and it gives them the spirit to do it, too. He peers ahead. It is perhaps the middle of the afternoon, and the sky is still moving quickly, still west to east, but it does not look as if it will rain, and Montagu's men are moving forward, quickly, and Jack is on his toes peering over to see if Riven's gunners will soon open up.

Thomas tries to control his breathing.

'Let them come,' he says. 'We have the height.'

Though he knows this advantage is almost negligible and is perhaps reversed by having so few men with good bows, it is something to say. His mouth is so dry. Sweat slips from the leather lining of his helmet. He distracts himself, fiddling with his arrows. He leaves one linen bag of them on the ground at his feet, though he makes sure to open the string, and he takes the other and shakes out his arrows and puts a dozen point first in the ground and a dozen through the loop in his belt. He steals a look around, towards Hungerford and Roos's men, where Riven's men are, and though he knows Riven is not there, he remembers those other two, so he slips a couple of shafts around his belt so that they are at his back. They are both weighty, with long tapering bodkins, and he will keep them, just in case. Next he nocks his bow. It is hard. He needs his whole body to get the wood to bend enough to slip the string over its end, but when it is done, the thing is alive in his hands, singing with its own taut energy. He picks his first arrow, and nocks that on the string. Good fletching, he thinks. Grey goose feathers. Green-tinged bindings. Lots of glue. A heavy shaft, aspen, bulbous toward one end, and a rough iron bodkin to top it off.

Now Montagu's men are within five hundred paces. They are impressively trained, keeping order as they come, moving as one. Thomas has seen this before somewhere. Men moving like this. It was snowing though, then, and were they on a bridge? He cannot recall. They negotiate a stream, a rivulet really, with no bunching, and they come on up after it with no hesitation. They are spreading wide now, along a front just as broad as Somerset's. It is as if Somerset has invited them to something – a dance – and they have accepted the invitation. So strange to think of so many men marching so far, as if by appointment, to come and try to kill one another.

But then something odd happens, and for a moment every man falters, even Montagu's, and some stop, and murmuring spreads along the front, and men lower their weapons, because between the converging ranks some large hares have emerged in the heather and gorse. They are racing around, springing up at one another as if fighting, a strange comical impression of what is to come, and it is so good to see, they are so careless and free, that there is a pause, and one old man calls out that he would put a groat on the one on the left winning the doe, and there is a moment of speculation, and then hearing them, the hares stop and turn and it seems as if they are sniffing the air, and then, as one, they are gone in an instant, and after a moment of silent contemplation, the men in the two armies seem to sigh, and the drums pick up and the men-at-arms lower their visors where they have them, and take a step forward.

'Nock!'

This is a moment easily orchestrated. Everybody knows how to nock an arrow. Thomas's is held loose in his right-hand forefingers, its foreparts resting on the bridge of the knuckle of his left hand where it grips the bow shaft. He squeezes his shoulders, rolls them up to his ears. Here they go. A deep breath. Murmured prayers. Nervous laughter. Something Jack has said. Then a moment of profound tension until:

'Draw!'

And now they lean forward, weight on the left leg, then haul their bows back, balancing their weight, and up, hauling back on the string, letting it cut into the fingers despite the leather tags, pulling, pulling, pulling, the muscles on his back instantly warm, his view down the foreshortened shaft of the arrow and the string coming to his eye, and then from the tail of his eye he notices without seeing, seven or eight hundred pale wood bows, their curved lines cross-hatched by the straight lines of the arrows, and then before anyone has time to shout loose, they loose.

The bowstrings boom and snap against bracers and the shafts leap into the sky, merging into a slate-coloured band, like flocking starlings, and they pause in mid-flight at the top of their arc, and if the archers weren't already nocking and hauling on their strings again, they might have time to stop and admire that moment, which lasts as long as the time between two heartbeats, when the arrow shafts seem to dither in the sky before they begin to drop, gathering speed again as they plummet to thunder on the heads of the men below.

But it is not all one way. Montagu's archers have sent up their own shafts and there is a noticeable darkening of the sky where the clouds of arrows drift through one another and there are some that collide to knock one another down, to fall to the ground like dropped lines.

'Here they come!'

And suddenly the arrows thicken the air around him, pale slashes before his eyes, thumping into the ground. There are cries and sudden thrashing movements. It sounds like a busy smithy. Some men stop loosing and hunch their shoulders. They try to turn themselves into as narrow a column as possible under their helmets. These are always the men with those wide brim helmets, the old kettle helmets, since with such a hat, the temptation to do this is too great, which is why anyone with a retinue of his own will not issue these helmets and why they have become unpopular, for they are like a badge of future cowardice, and only the bravest of the brave can wear them, and continue to loose, and no one is that brave.

Thomas draws and looses, draws and looses, and the bow is becoming easier as he warms, but all around him there are men being struck by Montagu's archers' arrows. They are knocked backwards, or skewered, and rarely fall silently. There is screaming, not so much at the pain, since that is known to come later, but in anger at seeing your arm stuck through, its bones broken, or at being thrown on to your arse or your back, or at being hit on the helmet and having your ears ring and your vision waver, and at being made to stagger like a calf and loose your bowels, or at having a shaft stuck in your thigh and seeing your blood suddenly everywhere, unstoppable, in your eyes, and it so hot!

The pain of loosing the bow builds slowly across his back and his arms. His fingertips sting, his wrist is bruised despite the bracer. He has loosed twenty arrows. He has seen five of his own men knocked to the ground; two of them are dead, but John the Cutler is not among them, nor is Jack, who is sweating and red-faced from the effort, but he wears a childish grin, and his teeth show, and his eyes are so bright, and he seems to imagine that he can see exactly where he is aiming his shafts.

The wind is dragging the arrow cloud wide, he sees, curving them in flight, so that they fall from a three-quarter angle, and he sees that Montagu's arrows fall that way too, as predicted, and that the cloud is converging on the men to his left, on Roos's and Hungerford's men, on Riven's men. Part of him celebrates it. Part of him laughs. Riven's men are there. They are bearing the brunt.

Taking casualties. It is possible to know without knowing that some-thing worse than usual is happening on a battlefield, to know without knowing that someone somewhere is having a worse time of it than you, and everybody knows that the left flank is suffering, while the right flank is yet to engage.

He has four arrows left.

He looks along the line. Jack has already loosed his quota, and thank God he is gone. He is fast, Thomas thinks, better than me. He bends his back again. One more arrow, then another then another, until, finally, the last. He has done all he can be expected to do, and if he is caught between the two lines of men-at-arms, he is a dead man, so he does not look around among the dying on the ground for more arrows. He has ridden his luck. *Ave Maria, gratia plena. Ave Maria, gratia plena.* But stupid useless John the Cutler is still the slowest. He has six more arrows tucked in his belt.

'John!' he calls. 'John! Leave them.'

John the Cutler looks around and later Thomas will wonder if he does not laugh at him, but when the boy turns back to his own business, an arrow hits him on his chin, the bit that used to stick out, and that shatters, and it is through his throat and a black tag appears between his shoulder blades with a spit of dark blood, and he drops, as if from a height, with his feet and hands thrust forward and the bow spilling for a moment he sits upright and then he throws himself back on the ground at Thomas's feet, with his head banging and his arms thrown up, so that the nock of the arrow in his throat is presented to Thomas, offered up as if he might want to pluck it out and nock it on his own string, and above it, or below it, John's eyes are still open and they even move, and they seem to focus on Thomas as if he has said something wounding, and then they swim and roll like something turning in the water, and then John the Cutler is dead. Blood gurgles from the wound, bubbling around the shaft of the arrow, staining it and his scarf as he makes a strange cacking sound.

Thomas can do nothing. He turns and runs. He pushes past the men-at-arms and the billmen who are now snarling and trying to steady themselves for what they next must do, and he emerges out of the back of them, through the few lines of the naked men, to where there should be ale carts, for the archers to slake their thirsts before collecting more arrows that ought to be piled here, and sending them over the heads of the men-at-arms and into the ranks of the closing enemy. But there are no arrows. Some archers are standing around, rueing the chance that is going begging, while others are no longer capable, and are spread about the ground, some of them blood-splattered, others stained shamefully, walking with spread legs and weeping. Some are dazed, while others sit by and watch and among them the wounded cry out as they drag themselves in search of help, or ale, or expire in the thickness of their own blood. Others stand with hands on knees, steaming from their efforts, while yet others are stretching their backs, groaning with the painful pleasure.

Some women are there, chunky camp followers in aprons and caps, as tough as the men they follow, but there is no ale, only water from the stream, and they are doling that out, or helping men on the ground, until, after a moment, it is clear there is something else going on. The women stop and straighten their backs and they look up and over to the left flank and Thomas turns to look and he sees men running. Can it be their lines have broken already? No one can credit it. There is a shocked murmur that swells into shouting. It is almost unbelievable. The left flank is disintegrating. It has broken. Men are running although they are yet to engage with Montagu's men.

But there they are: Hungerford and Roos's men in blue-and-yellow, and red-and-green, have turned their backs on Montagu's men and are streaming away from their lines. Not in ones and twos, not in wounded dribs and drabs, but all of them, in their hundreds, casting their weapons aside and running.

And they are being led by Riven's men, who are fleeing faster than anyone, able to outpace them, and it seems they are hardly encumbered by their weapons or any of the usual accoutrements of the battlefield, and there is something about them that makes Thomas think this is organised, planned, intended.

'Sacred Christ!' a man shouts. 'They've broken!'

And everyone who sees this knows what must happen next, and they too gather up what they can and they turn and run. The dead and the wounded are hurriedly robbed of anything valuable – coins, rosary beads, rings, anything instantly portable – or anything useful. Any decent bow, bill or blade is snatched from weakened hands; a pair of boots, a cloak, a good helmet, a costrel filled with ale. Farewells are said. Wounded men beg to be taken. Toward the rear of the camp men push women aside who trample boys who fight girls to get away. Everyone runs, round-eyed with panic.

Thomas thinks of Katherine. He starts running. He is shoulder to shoulder with fleeing archers and the naked men who've seen what is happening too, and they are scattering in their hundreds. He trips on the heather, staggers, rights himself, has to leap over a dead man, slip the grip of a wounded one, and then he is by the stream and where is she?

Where is she?

He finds her where he left her, wearing only her blood-smudged hose and pourpoint, with her jack cast aside and her linen sleeves rolled up and her legs sodden to her knees. She has a knife in one bloodied hand, and a broken arrow shaft in the other, and there is a man lying on his back on the stream's bank, screaming while his friends hold him down and press some of that urine-soaked tow on to his wound. She and John Stump are ignoring the screaming, and are staring down the stream at the men who are running from the field, watching them rip off their livery coats, cast aside their helmets, cut the straps to the pieces of plate they spent so long tying on. They come running, splashing through the stream around them,

314

sprinting for the woods. She steps aside before she is knocked over.

She starts when she sees Thomas, drops the bloodied arrow.

'They've broken!' he shouts. 'Come!'

And John Stump does not need to be told twice what this means. He has seen a rout before. He throws the soot-blackened pot he is holding into the stream and turns and runs.

'Come!' Thomas shouts, and he means to run past her, to snatch her hand and drag her away from this, into the woods to begin their escape, but she stands, tears her hand from his grasp.

'Where is Jack?' she shouts. He stops.

Christ, he thinks. Jack. Where is he? Where is Jack?

John Stump is paused with one foot on the far bank. He turns to look back at the field where the din is increasing as Somerset's remaining men, those who have stayed, those who are yet to break, shout their final challenges and roar at the enemy, and the enemy roar back, and at any moment the two lines will meet with that sliding crash of steel on steel.

Can Jack still be fighting back there? Oh, Christ!

Thomas looks at Katherine, and she at him, and John Stump at them both, and no one says anything, but Thomas feels the light fade, sadness seep in.

'Go through the trees,' he tells them. 'Get as far as possible north. We will come and find you.'

'No,' she says. 'We'll wait.'

John Stump looks at her as if she is mad, and she is a fool, they all know that, but Thomas knows he must find Jack and he knows she will not leave, so he does not bother to argue. Besides, now here come the prickers, thundering down the slope from the right flank, on the far side of the stream, riding to try to stop those fleeing the disintegrating left flank. Thomas can feel their horses' hoofbeats through the soles of his boots, and one of them has an ox whip. He is lashing at the fleeing archers and the camp followers from his saddle, but he is not stopping to send them back, because he must be there to cut off the fleeing soldiery, and the archers and the camp followers hang back to avoid the whip, to let him and the others pass, and then they press on, and Thomas watches them for a moment as they scramble up the bank and run on, their backs bobbing like rabbits in the heather, making for the stand of pale fluttering-leafed trees.

He wishes Jack were among them, but he is not. He turns and watches those coming past him. He does not try to stop any. They are too afeared and are likely to lash out at anyone in their way with whatever weapon they have to hand. None are Jack. Where is he? Can it be that he is still there? He tries to think. When he looked over, Jack was gone. He was not hit, Thomas is certain. But is he now?

And where does he even start looking? There. Where the wounded are dragging themselves through the heather, where they lie strewn behind the backs of the men-at-arms. He draws the short blade from its scabbard, and he has the buckler. He has never used one before; a small round shield hardly larger than his fist, but he can see its use. A man grabs him.

'Help me!'

Thomas cannot but the man won't let go. His fingers claw at Thomas's face, his collar. He won't be shaken off by anything other than a sideswipe of the buckler. He sobs as it hits him, and he rolls to his side and carries on mewling. Thomas leaves him to step among the others. There are a few in Grey's livery. Most of them are recognisable, or identifiable; some sit, stunned by arrows on their helmets, others are bleeding all over themselves and some are already dead and abandoned by their friends. He peers into cooling faces. None of them is Jack. What about over there? A body splayed in the heather, face down, thrown as if tossed away. He turns him over. A splintered arrow shaft dug in the cheek, one eye open, broken teeth like pale chips in the dark blood. He is almost unrecognisable, but he is not Jack.

He stops and looks up. To his left the tide of fleeing men has proved too strong for the prickers. The man with the whip has been dispossessed and thrown from his horse, while the others have done no more than kill one or two of those fleeing as they pass, before they too have been pulled from their saddles and it is not difficult to guess what has happened to them.

And now, inevitably, the men in Somerset's division are beginning to turn too, before they have even met Montagu's line. Those at the left edge, the fringes of the centre nearest Hungerford and Roos's scattered companies, have suddenly found themselves on the very extremities of Somerset's left flank, and are already being outflanked by Montagu's right. All Montagu needs to do now, if he could but see it, if he could but believe it, is send his men forward to wrap up the whole thing. And seeing this, and knowing this, the men in Somerset's command have started to turn, and with the prickers dead or otherwise engaged, there is nothing to stop them.

Thomas watches it happen.

The centre begins to fray.

Christ!

And now men are really running at him. Trying to get past. It is dangerous to even stand facing them for any one of them will hack at him for fear he is there to stop them. But what can he do? He must find Jack. He steps forward. He punches a man out of the way with his buckler. Then has to use it to block a sliding blow from a bill. He fends men off. He is the only man moving forward.

After a moment he is utterly isolated, alone, a single detached figure, and he watches the gap between him and the nearest of Somerset's troops widen from ten, to fifteen, then twenty paces as each man realises he has been deserted by his neighbour, and he too must run.

But Thomas must go forward, into the ground where the archers were, where the dead and dying are scattered among the feather fletches of arrow shafts. The smell is strong here. He is

317

watched by Montagu's men, he supposes, and he imagines them coming running up the slope toward him and if he is caught between them and Somerset's he will be cut down in a moment, metal plates in his jack or not. But they do not seem to be moving fast, certainly not as quickly as Somerset's scattering division. An arrow lands with a resinous puff nearby, a pretty good shot from Montagu's line, he cannot help notice, and he ducks his head, but he still must move forward, coming back up to where he last saw Jack.

'Jack! Jack!'

He hardly expects an answer and every step reveals something he would rather not see. But then he finds where he thinks Jack was and he sees the heather is beaten down and there is Jack's bow on the ground and then he finds him lying on his side, his foot scrabbling a circle in the dirt, kicking at the snarls of heather. His teeth are clenched and he is seething with pain and glaring in furious disbelief at the arrow shaft that sticks from his thigh, from the wool just above the left knee.

'Thomas!' he shouts when he sees him. 'Look!'

And he points as if Thomas would not have seen it. There is blood, a lot of it, but Thomas has no idea how much is too much and it doesn't seem to be pumping in that way it can. Another arrow lands with a thump.

'Where's Kit?' Jack shouts. 'Where is he? By Christ! Look. I need him.'

Thomas throws aside his buckler and the useless blade he's been carrying and he kneels to slide an arm under Jack's back. He glances over to see how long he has before Montagu's men arrive. And now he frowns. Montagu's men have not moved forward. Why not? They are not pressing their advantage, but rather they are regrouping, reorganising. They are turning to their left, turning towards Percy's division, slightly up the slope. Why? Why have they not pressed their advantage? Thomas cannot guess, but it is a relief.

318

He helps Jack to his feet. He wonders about trying to carry him but Jack can walk or hop.

'Here,' Thomas says, and he bends to break the arrow shaft, but it is thick and strong, and he cannot break it cleanly and it pulls in the wound and blood flows fast and Jack growls with the pain. Then it snaps and Thomas discards most of it.

'Come on,' he says. 'Put your arm around me.'

And Jack does so and he half-drags him, hopping, back towards the rear. No more arrows land, but the ground is uneven, the heather catches Jack's one foot, and they stagger, and they must negotiate the dead bodies and then the wounded man is there again and he shouts something at Thomas and Jack shouts something back at him.

'Keep your strength,' Thomas mutters.

Jack growls again. His lower leg is glossy with blood, his boots red with it. He keeps his leg out straight and he gasps with each hop. A man collides with them, but they do not fall, and instead he blunders on. They are being left behind, Thomas thinks, and soon surely Montagu will bring his horsemen up.

Nearly there, Thomas tells himself. Nearly there.

He does not think about what might be happening behind. He tries not to imagine how a horseman's hammer will feel on the crown of his head, helmet or no helmet, or how an arrow will feel when it knocks him from his feet, and instead he concentrates on getting Jack to Katherine, and the belief that she will save him.

He sees Katherine's pale face peering up at him above the heather where she still stands by the stream. She has lost her cap, and her hair hangs free. Her forehead is smudged with blood and a bruise is developing under her right eye. John Stump is there. He has a sword in his hand and he is shielding her.

When she sees them she scrambles up the bank to help.

'No,' Thomas tells her. 'Let us get him to the trees first.'

John Stump helps them down and together they carry Jack

through the stream and across and under the leaf canopy to almost the precise spot they'd hoped to gather before their escape. They let him down and sit him against a pale trunk and Katherine is there very quickly, bent over him. Thomas removes first his helmet, then Jack's, and he tosses them both into the heather. The boy is sweating and waxy now, but Katherine is swift. She puts her bowls and bags down on the leaves, then she takes the knife John Stump has been sharpening and she cuts Jack's hose from his knee. She inspects the wound. Picks something out.

'Can you move your foot?' she asks, and he can, though not without a deal of pain. Still he looks up at them with wet eyes, like a dog who thinks this may be his time.

'Good,' she says. 'Hold him, Thomas, will you?'

And they exchange a look. This is going to hurt. She has a jug of urine. She pours a great splosh of it over the broken arrow shaft and the wound in the top of the knee, then when Jack is already pushing back with the pain of that, she makes the quickest incision under his knee, a little slit in the skin that makes him roar with pained surprise.

But she ignores him.

'It has gone good and deep,' she says just as if he has done something clever. 'It is nearly out the other side.'

Jack frowns up at her through his tears. How can that be a good thing?

'The barbs on the arrowhead,' she says. 'If I remove it this way . . .'

He knows about the barbs. He has loosed many a barbed arrow himself. They are designed to stick into whatever they hit.

There is still much blood, Thomas thinks. It is still dripping in spools, but Katherine does not seem worried. She trims the arrow's splintered stump, breaking off the longest piece, levelling it as much as possible, and then she widens her eyes at him and he knows to take a good grip of Jack's shoulders and John Stump comes very

320

close to Katherine to be ready to take hold of Jack's foot when the time comes and now Katherine takes the earthenware ewer she has of urine, empties it on the wound and then lifts it and bangs its base down on to the top peg of the arrow and Jack screams and writhes, but Thomas has him and John Stump has him, and now Katherine reaches under the leg and pulls out the arrow. There is a spray of blood. She drops the arrowhead in the leaves and grabs two handfuls of the piss-sodden tow and she presses one into the wound behind his knee and one into the wound above.

'Hold them there,' she says.

And Thomas does so while she cuts up the linen of the jack she has already destroyed and she makes two or three strips that she quickly knots together to form one long one and this she wraps around the leg twice, covering Thomas's blood-soaked hands, and then when she gives the word he pulls them out while she pulls the bandage tight over the tow and she keeps pulling until diluted blood flows down his leg from both wounds. Then she wraps the bandage around twice more and then twice more again and she looks up.

They are in a huddle in the gloom of the trees and while they have been looking to Jack, the two remaining lines have joined, a little further up the hill where Ralph Percy's division has held, and Montagu's men, instead of giving chase after Somerset's, have canted around to address them. Now that Thomas has removed his helmet he can hear the rolling din of the engagement. From this distance there is no clue as to its real nature: the many blows and the screams are become as one, blending to make a noise no louder nor more threatening than waves washing on a shingle shore. Katherine looks up and there is a long moment of silence as they listen to the rattle of arms. After a moment she shakes her head and looks again at Jack.

'Will he be all right?' Thomas asks.

'I think so,' Katherine says. 'He was lucky. Does it hurt?'

321

Jack is surprised.

'Not really,' he says.

'It will,' she tells him.

'That was – incredible,' Thomas says.

'I have done it before,' she says. 'To the Earl of Warwick.'

'No,' they all say.

And she cannot help smile.

'What now?' John Stump asks.

They look around. The fighting continues sporadically in the open, but in the woods, there are many shadows moving in its depths. Men are returning shamefaced, and now Thomas sees they have an audience. Some of Grey's men have crept back, as well as Tailboys's. There is even one who has thrown away his livery, but is wearing Hungerford's badge. None of Riven's.

'Why hasn't Montagu come after us?' one of them asks. 'Don't make no sense.'

'They come chasing after us,' another, older, man answers, 'and they'll be all over Northumberland then, won't they? Never get to Scotland like that. It is good discipline, that is.'

They are impressed now, and they watch in silence as Montagu's men round on Percy's division and they pity him and his men then, and each man there feels he has cause to look shamed.

'It was those bastards in white who started it,' one of them mutters. 'With the crows. Who are they? They ran as soon as the arrows came. As if they'd bloody planned it.'

'Riven,' another spits. 'Never bloody trust them. Never. I was at Northampton. He turned his coat then. Probably did the same thing now.'

It does not last long. Montagu's army swamps Percy's little force – all that is left of Somerset's larger army – and though a few men can be seen running from its rear, and there are horses being brought up to help the escape, there can be only one outcome.

'Christ,' one of them breathes and then there is a restless silence in the woods that will only end when the last man offering any resistance is killed in the field, or the last man has run. No one among the trees can see who it is. Katherine, who has good eyes, does not want to watch. She has seen this before. And she is with Jack, who is very pale now, as if he has faded, and he wants to sleep. She is keeping him warm with all their cloaks and she has given him the last of their ale and she is trying to keep him awake. Still he shivers.

'Are you sure he will live?' Thomas asks.

'I think so,' she says, 'but he cannot ride. He is not strong enough.'

And Thomas nods. He feels sick. He extends a hand and squeezes Katherine's shoulder and she shrugs and turns back to Jack and so after a moment Thomas returns to the end of the wood where men are still gathered, watching, and the rattle of the fighting diminishes, then becomes inconstant, and oddly all the more terrible for that, for it is possible to pick out a single particular noise – of a hammer falling, say – and imagine the ferocity behind the blow, its intent, and what it does to the man below. A father, a son, a brother, a husband. Eventually it stops.

'We'd best be off,' an archer says. 'Look.'

He points to where Montagu's squires and boys are bringing up their masters' horses.

'Once they get on them, they'll be after us.'

But they stay to watch a moment or two longer as Montagu's camp followers arrive on the field from the road south and begin scavenging among the dead, and Thomas supposes there must be scant pickings today, since so few of Hungerford and Roos's men stayed to be killed, nor did Somerset's command acquit themselves as they might have wished, and he imagines that apart from Percy's dead, most of the few bodies left on the field must be those of unlucky archers, with little on them of much value beyond their bows.

323

'Where are the nobles?' Thomas asks. 'Where is Grey? Where is Somerset? Did anyone see them go?'

'They ran just as quickly as us,' one of the men mutters says, 'and further too.'

'They'd've only stopped to collect their gear and to give King Henry the glad tidings.'

'He will be sore depressed,' another says.

'If there was ever a man used to being told that kind of thing,' John Stump says, 'then that man is King Henry.'

And they gather what they can in the falling gloom, and they help Jack to his feet, and they creep away, darting across the track and into the trees on the other side as best they can. They carry him almost a mile, following the tracks they made that morning, unmolested by any of Montagu's prickers, until they are met in a dip by a picket of Roos's men, and there is some ill feeling and some muttered accusations, but there is nothing anyone can do, and a fight, they all know, will just be a fight.

'There was nothing we could do,' one of them says. 'It was those bastards in white, with the bloody crows. As soon as the first arrow landed they just – they just packed up and ran. All that bloody training they did, d'you remember? This and that. Ooof. But when it came to it, they just fucked off, left us dangling on the flank, and we just – well.'

He ends with a shrug.

They enter King Henry's camp from the west, and must make their way past Riven's men, who it seems have had the time to hunt a deer, and they are roasting it on a spit over a bed of flames, and the smell is heavenly, and there are ale mugs in their hands and though they are silent, the men seem not as abashed as Thomas supposed those who have broken and fled from a battlefield might. They look like men who have completed something together: the shearing of a flock, say, or the building of a wall.

'Bastards,' one of Roos's men mutters, but very quietly.

They find Horner, sitting on their cart, looking very sad in the light of a low fire. He has discarded his harness and is more familiar in riding boots and travelling coat. He is pleased to see them.

'Is there any news?' Thomas asks.

Horner shrugs.

'It was not a complete disaster,' he lies. 'We still hope to have enough men to catch Montagu and his Scots on their way south back to Newcastle.'

'What about Percy?' someone asks.

Horner tilts his head.

'There was nothing we could do,' he says, repeating what he has obviously been told. 'And besides, if anything, his death will stir up the North.'

21

There are some wounded to tend the next day: men who have limped into King Henry's camp, or been carried in by their friends, and if they have lived this long, then there is a chance they will live longer. And so Katherine is busy during the morning with the needle she has learned to sharpen, and the tow from another jack she has had to cut up, but there is not very much she can do for their wounds other than clean them and get the men to keep them clean and get them to pray they do not start giving off that foul smell or weeping the watery pus. She finds tears in her eyes when one boy dies of a stab in the stomach, some time before noon, though the end is a mercy really, and a friar has come and he is able to offer some spiritual consolation, for what that is worth.

By the end of it, she thinks Grey has lost five men dead and if the black pestilence does not strike those she has stitched up, then that will be all.

'Not too bad,' Horner says.

'Will we go back to Alnwick?' she asks him, 'or Bamburgh?'

'Neither,' Horner admits. 'We are to keep moving.'

She is disappointed. She has become bone weary of sleeping on the ground, of waking with aches and pains beyond the usual stiffness, to begin again the daily competition to find enough to eat before nightfall. And though every day they send out patrols of scurriers to find fresh supplies of bread and ale and oatcakes, they have scoured the land of more or less anything edible, and it is only the sea that provides sustenance now: endless fish soup which they must reinforce with handfuls of alexanders and nettles, and it tastes so bad she can hardly hold it down, though the others manage, and laugh at her, telling her she is as fussy as a merchant with a choice of meats on his board, but really: the stuff makes her gag. One advantage of this poor diet is that her monthly flowering has stopped again, and she is grateful. A rough camp such as this is no place for the subterfuge needed to hide that.

The scurriers must also keep a lookout for Montagu and his army, which will soon be coming back from Scotland with the Scottish negotiators, though she cannot imagine what they will do if they manage to find them, since King Henry's army is now much dwindled after that day in the field at Hedgeley Moor, with some men being, as John Stump puts it, 'too dead to fight', while others have managed what they could not, and have melted away in the course of the nights that followed the day. King Henry has left the camp, of course, though is said to be close by, and Somerset has taken the precaution of sending the rest of Riven's men away to join him wherever he is, so they do not fight with the rest of the men who think they are cowards for running at Hedgeley Moor and blame them for its loss.

The Duke of Somerset has stayed in camp though, and the others who were gathered around the board at Bamburgh, whom she supposes now have nothing left to lose, including Lords Roos and Hungerford and their men who spend so much of their time blaming Giles Riven for their having run at Hedgeley Moor. Tailboys is there, too, though he has a tent of his own, and he keeps his own company close by.

The others huddle on sawn logs around the charred circles of last night's fires, and since they are unused to sleeping on the ground, even in late spring, and they suffer and have become beleaguered and discouraged. The lower orders, the humbler men-at-arms, the archers, the billmen and the women and children who service them, seem to fare better, for they are used to this sort of hardship, having

327

spent long weeks in the open, and rather than merely trying to remain still until time has passed, they confront the misery as if it does not exist.

Even so though, they are all waiting, waiting for something.

Thomas is waiting for Jack.

'When will he be strong enough to ride?' he asks her.

And she can only say she does not know. The boy is still not right. He is still hot to the touch and sometimes he lapses into garbling.

'Montagu will come back soon,' Thomas says, 'and there will be another attack.'

'Can we not put him on a cart? Take that?'

'We would get no further than the top of the hill before the prickers came for us,' he tells her, gesturing to its brow where two men wait on horseback, sentries looking both ways.

'Others manage it,' she says.

'Not on a cart.'

So she looks down at Jack, who lies under their cart, covered by a mound of cloaks, with his head resting on a log, his skin dewed with his own sweat, and she shakes her head.

'We can't leave him,' she says.

'No,' Thomas agrees, though it is through set teeth.

She wishes she knew what was wrong with him. She wishes the physician Payne were here. He would know what to do.

Three days later, on the day when the bearded priest appears among them to lead a celebration to commemorate the finding of the True Cross, when Jack is no better but no worse, Montagu's army makes its reappearance, just as Thomas had predicted. It is some of Roos's men – led by Roos's own brother – who discover it, or traces of it: a great furrow of hoof- and footprints in the mud on the road, and the marks left by wheel rims. But by the time word is sent back to Somerset, Montagu and his army and his Scotsmen are gone, disappeared south, down to Newcastle to meet King Edward's negotiators. It is easy to imagine them laughing as they go.

Some pretend Montagu's unimpeded passage is a bitter blow, and they talk of rueing their missed chance, but Katherine is becoming certain it is only the Duke of Somerset who really wants to fight Montagu's men again, and if the others were truthful, they would admit to wanting to make peace with him, and to seeking King Edward's grace, and to giving up on all this, and to wishing they were able to go home again.

Home, she thinks. And she thinks of nothing. She has no home, she remembers, and nothing to tether her, and she discerns a flicker of regret for the second passing of Lady Margaret Cornford.

Thomas comes back from the makeshift stabling. He looks grimly purposeful.

'We are moving,' he says. 'South.'

Moving south means that they will try to bring Montagu to the field again, and so the next morning, the mood in the camp is odd, shifting, uncertain. It will be good to be away from here, Katherine supposes, where they have been too long, licking their wounds like dogs, and where morale has withered to nothing, but knowing they are going south to fight an enemy that seems unbeatable means that she, along with many of the other men, lacks the energy to go about the business of breaking camp with any real enthusiasm, and it only gets worse when later that morning Thomas returns, looking grimmer than ever, with the news just brought by messenger that King Edward is moving up from London with a huge army and what he calls 'ordnance'.

'Ordnance? What is that?'

'Guns,' he says. 'Huge guns on wheels. He is bringing them up from the Tower of London.'

Then at least it will take him weeks to come, she thinks.

'The Earl of Warwick is coming, too,' he goes on, 'and William Hastings.'

William Hastings. That is a name she has not heard in a long while. She feels another twinge of sorrow, of mourning for something gone.

With men like that coming, she thinks, it means this will have to end, one way or another, and looking at the men around her, she knows that it will really only be one way, and not the other. It is curiously depressing. All these men, she thinks, will be dead soon, and in the most terrible ways, unless they do something about it. She has been so long with them, they have become so familiar, they have become her family, but now that she can feel the world closing in on them, now that she can feel it all coming to an end, she feels a pitiful nostalgia for these weeks gone by.

She gets Thomas to help load Jack on to the cart.

'How long will we be?' she wonders. She does not want Jack to have to jounce over the roads for many days. Three days, he supposes, and she cannot help but worry. The carters have only one ox left, the other in the team having been killed in circumstances that are both mysterious and obvious, and the remaining ox is pining for its teammate, and it has ceased to eat and has lost patches of hair on its hide. Nevertheless they whip it until it takes the strain of the cart and begins to tow it, grinding along the track toward the road that cuts across Hedgeley Moor. They find this, and the site on which they mostly ran from Montagu's men, and they walk south all day. The road is smooth but at every hole or shifted flagstone, the cart throws Jack in the air and he groans and shudders. Katherine walks by its side, with her hand on his shoulder.

Horner comes to announce that they have found somewhere to camp for the night. He seems quite excited at something, and is about to tell her what it is when he sees Jack and he looks very doubtful.

'Will he live?'

She nods.

'Good,' he breathes. 'Good. We'll need him. There have been risings in Tynedale. The people there. They are with us.'

'Tynedale?' The word is familiar. 'That is where Bywell is, isn't it?

'Do you know it? Not much of a place, is it? Half-built. And damp?'
'It is where Master Payne was sent.'

She explains about wishing that Jack might see Payne. Horner looks at Jack in his cloak.

'All this marching around,' she says. 'It is not good for him.'

'It is not good for anyone,' Horner says, 'but we cannot spare either of you, for we will be busy, if what we hear is true.'

It isn't true, of course. It takes them three days to get there – first down that road south, then west along another drovers' track, and then south again, on one more of those old Roman roads, grinding along over the dressed stones until they meet another one to take them westwards again.

But the fact of it is that when they arrive at the grey stone-walled town of Hexham, where they are promised they will find bread and ale and possibly a great force of Scotsmen come to help them against Lord Montagu, it is to be told that there are none of these things, and that in addition, any small rebellions that may have flared up in favour of King Henry have been quietly put aside in the face of the news of King Edward and his nobles and guns coming north, tidings that have been enough to send most men back to their halls and fields, and it is instantly apparent that the townspeople are merely waiting for them to go, so that they might resume their normal lives.

'By all His saints,' Horner says.

But there is nothing to be done, so they wind past the abbey and out through the east gate and down the hill and across the bridge to set up camp on the far side of the fierce little river the men call the Devil's Water, though none there knows why, and so, as evening falls and the mist rises, they resume their habits of before.

The next day is the feast of the Ascension, and Katherine wakes feeling nauseous. She is sick. Brown vomit. A small puddle. She has a headache, too, and is bone weary.

Thomas is frightened. He finds her some ale.

'Is it something you have taken from Jack?' he asks.

She doesn't know, but Christ, she feels rotten. She throws the ale back up, cursing its waste. All she wants to do is lie down and shut her eyes. She is at sea again. Swirling, tipping, swooping. Thomas holds the mug of ale to her mouth. It smells of old leather, unwashed, and it tastes slimy. She pushes it away and dry retches a few times. He sits beside her and tells her things. She wishes he would not. She wonders if her humours are imbalanced. The bells in the abbey are ringing and men are going up the hill for Mass.

'Will Jack be all right?' Thomas asks. 'He doesn't look too good.'

She looks over at the boy. He is pale, almost blue. Christ, she thinks. What is wrong with him?

'We must see Payne,' she says.

Thomas is happy to be given something to do.

'Could I fetch him? Bywell is not far, Horner says. And we could take you to him? Why ever did he go there, anyway?'

'He was to see to a girl with the pissing evil.'

The pale light is falling slantwise through the haze of fresh green buds on the leaves, striking Thomas in the face where his beard is getting fuller by the day. It is a very dark red, she thinks, like a squirrel's tail. She is grateful he is there, grateful for his protection again, and wishes she might show him some of the same care herself, but this is no place for that, and the soft comings and goings, the little considerations a man might show his wife, and vice versa, they are for another time, another place, and she feels, perhaps, possibly, even other people. Besides, if she moves she will vomit.

A little later she is sick again anyway.

That decides him. He gets to his feet.

'I will ask Horner,' he says. 'That is it.'

She rolls on to her side in the long, wet grass and half-hopes to die. When Thomas returns he is pleased with himself.

332

'I told him you might both have leprosy,' he says.

She does not react.

'So he has told me to take you away, both of you, to find Payne. We are to go now. He says Bywell is but half a day's ride downriver. We are to see Payne, take his advice, and then ride back. He says we are not to be gone more than a day. And if we are, then I am to ride back alone.'

'What about Jack?' she murmurs. 'He cannot ride.'

'It is the best I could do. Tailboys won't even spare a mule.'

Is it worth the risk? She cannot say.

Jack is silent when Thomas and John Stump gather him up.

'It is all right, Jack,' Thomas soothes. 'Come on, I'll walk beside you.'

And, watched from a safe distance by Horner and the rest of the men, they ease Jack up into the saddle of Horner's horse, and they tie his good foot to a stirrup and his bad leg, held out straight, is lashed to the straps of his saddle.

'I will hold him,' she says.

'Good job you're so small, Kit,' John Stump offers as he helps her up into the saddle behind him, but the horse smells very, very strong and she cannot stand it and she slides back down and vomits bile on her own bootcaps. The others watch in alarmed silence. After she wipes her mouth, she says goodbye, and they leave the camp following the road east and then turn left at the crossroads and walk north towards the town of Corbridge. Thomas leads Jack ahead, she follows behind. It is sunny, coming on to noon though early in the year, so their shadows fall long ahead, and as the day wears on, she starts to feel a bit better. Perhaps it is the walking? Perhaps it is being out of the camp? Away from Grey and Horner and the others?

They pass through common land at the road's side, rough pasture where there are a few fat sheep with oily coats and crooked faces, and there are many plump rabbits. The gentle hills are capped in

333

trees, the valleys tilled in parts, red earth hazed in green shoots of a pea or rye crop, and there are a few boys out, keeping the rabbits off with shepherd's crooks, and in the distance, there are smoke-softened houses and farms and it all serves to remind her of Cornford, and she feels a spurt of anger and loss, and she finds her fingers have tightened on the reins.

They find the bridge where Horner had suggested it might be, and they do not stop to say a prayer in the chantry chapel at the southern end, but press on over its flagged spans towards the little town at its far end where they are made to pay pontage by a man in a greasy linen apron who smells like a tanner but has a bill and a sword and a hammer and two daggers and a decent-looking bow with a sheaf of arrows with him in the small wooden shelter in which he stands.

'You are well arrayed?' Thomas comments, and the man grunts. Beyond him, the little town of Corbridge is well shuttered up and every house looks like a tiny castle. They buy some ale from a man who serves them through a small aperture in the thick wall of his house at the crossroads, but there is no one to sell them bread, so they drink their ale and find the mugs are filled with tar or wax at the bottom and they have been given half-measures, but there is something about the place that deters them from complaining.

'Is Bywell Castle far?' Thomas asks.

'Follow that road,' the man says, pointing east, and so they do, leaving the town on another of the old roads, through common land where there are more sheep cropping the spring grass and the sky is filled with clacking jackdaws until they see what they think must be it: a grey, foursquare stone tower that might once have been intended as a gatehouse, if the builder had only gone on to build the thing it was supposed to be the gate to. Instead it is left, standing isolated like a tree's stump, hard by the river.

'Strange,' Thomas says. 'I expected it to be half-deserted.'

There is a knot of men at the gate and two or three in each turret.

334

And there's a flag in one, tied to the weathervane, lifting and falling in the wind. It looks like King Henry's.

'Can he be here?' she wonders.

'We'll find out soon enough,' Thomas says as two horsemen come riding out towards them.

'Oh, dear God,' she says. 'Look.'

They are Riven's men.

'What in the name of God are they doing here?'

The men are in helmets and bits and pieces of plate, as if they expect something to happen soon, or fear it might, and they come well armed, with swords at their hips, hammers and bows across the backs of their saddles, and their livery coats are fresh and clean, so that it is easy to see the rising ravens against the white cloth. The contrast with Somerset's grey-faced, down-at-heel divisions is stark. The two horsemen come to a stop with a rattle of harnesses. One gets off. The other stays in the saddle. They are pretty typical: big, blunt-faced men, of the sort to frequent inns looking for fights or women or work, or just something to do. One of them has the flat-tened nose of a man who has spent too many mornings in the stocks. They recognise her, but not Thomas.

'God give you good day, Master Surgeon,' the one on the horse says. 'What brings you here?'

She indicates Jack, who is slumped in his saddle, and explains what they have come for.

'Master Payne is with King Henry at Mass,' the horseman says, gesturing south to a square tower of a church among the bulbous treetops.

'King Henry is here?'

The horseman nods.

'Aye,' he says.

'And is Sir Giles Riven here?' Thomas asks.

'No,' the one on foot says, 'he is moved on.'

'Where? Do you know?'

335

'I'm sure I don't know,' he says. But she is sure he does.

'Still,' he says. 'Your physician will be pleased you've arrived with a new patient. His last one died not two weeks ago.'

Katherine asks to be directed to a fireside unless they would like the blood of Jack on their hands, and though they don't seem to care about that, they lead Jack's horse across the cobbles and into the yard where another of Riven's men emerges from the stables to help Thomas with Jack, while yet another emerges to take the horse away to be brushed and fed. It is better here than out in the camp.

Together with the other man, Thomas helps Jack up the steps and into the hall where there is a fire newly lit in the hearth, though the room is not yet warm. A servant is placing dishes on the boards in readiness for the King's return from Mass, while another lights candles against the gloom, and there are smells emerging from behind the screen that make her gag. The worst is the smell of the tallow candle, though. She seems to vomit air deep in her throat when she catches its smell and every man in the room turns to look at her.

'Christ, boy!' one of them says. 'You are *green.*'

She slumps on the bench next to where they have lowered Jack, and she sits with her arms across her knees and stares at the ground between her feet and thinks if she is utterly still, she will not vomit again. But when they hear King Henry returning through the doors and into the hall, Katherine knows she must rise and wait for an audience at the dark, cold end of the hall, and she can barely stand. He comes in, looking well, she has to admit, even if he still does not look regal, or even anything much more than clerical in his brown robes. Behind him come some men she recognises from the hall at Bamburgh, various attendants of the bedchamber, she supposes, as well as the beardless priest. Payne is there, too, in his blue jacket, very tight woollen hose and tapering shoes, and when he sees her he starts, and he diverts his steps toward her, careless of protocol.

'Master,' he says.

'No,' she says, shaking her finger. She means for him to understand that she thinks he is the master, not she. He is the one who has been to Bologna.

'But you look terrible,' he says.

He sits her down. He touches her forehead, murmurs something. He smells clean.

'It is not me,' she says. 'It is Jack.'

Payne looks Jack over, and taps the binding on his leg to see if he reacts, and then he frowns when Jack does not, but now King Henry is showing concern and he calls Payne in his quavering voice and Payne approaches the board where King Henry now sits, and he explains, and asks to be excused. King Henry is gracious, and sends them away with a servant carrying a rush lamp and a ewer of warm wine, which Payne says they will need for the patient.

The servant leads the way, out of the hall and up the tight circle of stone steps that twists up one of the towers in the corner of the castle. Master Payne helps Thomas with Jack, while Katherine follows behind. When they reach the next floor, the servant opens a heavy door with a loud locking mechanism and guides them into a solar. He crosses the rushless floor to light a candle and the smell of tallow hits her and she gags, and she has to beg him to blow it out, and Payne looks at her in the glow of the single rush lamp and she sees his eyebrows rise. The servant finds another rush lamp and lights that, and she can see from this that they are in a solar, with a hearth in the middle of the floor, its fire unlit, and in the corner, a pile of straw mattresses on which two black cats are curled, watching, and it reminds her of Cornford and she could weep.

'I have no chamber of my own,' Payne says with a shrug. 'King Henry sleeps above with his gentlemen, and – well.'

He tails off. Thomas clears the cats and pulls a mattress down and flops it next to the fire. They settle Jack on it. Payne gets Thomas to hold up the lamp and he pries open one of Jack's eyes, then smells his breath and wrinkles his nose.

337

'Do you have a sample?' he asks, nodding at Jack's nethers.

She shakes her head.

'We can get some in the morning,' Payne supposes. 'Meanwhile I have something for him, I think, and perhaps for you too.'

He takes the lamp and crosses to his coffer and takes out some things – his bleeding bowls, his roll of knives, his urine jar. The physician finds a clay bottle of something and brings it over. He returns the lamp to Thomas and in its light he lets a few drops fall into a bowl that he then tops up with the wine. He tells her it is meadowsweet and fennel and some other things.

He holds Jack up and gets him to sip the concoction. When he has done so, they lay the boy down. They watch him for a while.

'He will be fine, I think,' Payne says. 'He needs food. Better than he has been getting. Wheat bread is best for this sort of thing. And capons. Meadow birds, too, of the sort with narrow beaks, rather than ducks, though duck eggs would be good. Boiled in their shells. And he needs rest. He needs to stay still for a few days. Not be carted around the countryside.'

Then Payne sits back. He looks at her.

'So,' he says, 'what do you want to do?'

'About what?' she wonders.

'About you,' he says.

'Oh,' she says. 'It is just one of those things. A fever. Something I have eaten, perhaps.'

She has lied like this a thousand times, but this time she feels awkward, and she blurts the words, and when she looks up, he is staring at her very carefully.

'Nevertheless,' he says, quite slowly, very carefully. 'I should like to see your urine.'

She makes some dismissive movement, but he is insistent.

'In fact,' he says, 'I should like to see you urinate into this jar. To watch you do it.'

He returns to his coffer, finds his famous urine jar and offers it to her. Thomas is standing on tiptoe, neck craned to look into the box, hoping to see the ledger, she supposes, and he does not see what is going on.

'Come,' Payne says. 'Come.'

But now Thomas hears and he turns sharply, and Payne is staring at her, challenging her to lie again. He gestures with the jar. She hears her heart beating very loudly and she feels too tall to stand, and she thinks she might faint. Payne holds the jar out, one eyebrow raised, waiting.

She tells him she has just passed water and has none to offer. He sighs as if he has heard this sort of thing before. He puts the jar back on top of the coffer. He cannot make her piss in the jar, they all know that. But now there is a long silence. And she knows, suddenly, but with absolute certainty, that this is it. Her time is up. Her race is run.

She looks at Payne and Payne looks back.

And then he asks, very quietly, a direct question.

'So who are you?' he asks. 'I mean, really?'

Thomas coughs. He starts to say something, something he hopes might distract Payne, but Payne does not take his gaze from her. She sighs. She knows, and has done for some while, that he has divined her sex.

'My name is Katherine,' she says.

Jack grunts on the mattress. They all glance at him. He is like a dog chasing rabbits in his dream. Payne returns to her.

'And?' he asks.

'I am – well, I am not a man, obviously. You have divined that.'

'From the moment I saw you, I believe,' he tells her.

'Then why did you not say anything?' Thomas asks.

Payne glances over at him, then looks back to Katherine.

'We all have things to hide,' he says. 'All of us.'

She does not try to imagine what he means, though she can see it counts a great deal to him. She is wondering whether she feels relief to have told someone, but she doesn't, not especially.

'So what will you do?' she asks. 'Will you tell the King?'

'Why should I? He won't care. He won't even— But tell me. Why? Why are you going around like this? Are you in some danger? Is that it? Are you – what? Being sought by someone? Do you have a husband? Well. I can see you have. That much is obvious. But why did you ever come to Bamburgh, passing yourself off as a man?'

'It is a long story,' she says.

'What is it?' Jack mutters from his mattress. 'Tell us.'

'Yes,' Payne says. 'Come. Tell us.'

But now she is bone weary. Too tired to care very much, and all she wants is to sleep, to be away from these men.

'Sit,' Payne says and he drags a stool from the shadows and places it against the wall next to the chimney. She sits with her back to the stone and wishes she had some ale, or even just water.

'Will you tell them, Thomas?' she asks.

And Thomas scratches his head.

'Christ,' he says, 'where does a man begin?'

Payne looks at him.

'And who are you in all this?' he asks, and then his face clears. 'Ah,' he says. 'Of course. You are the father.'

22

Thomas does not sleep that night. Nor, he thinks, does she, though he cannot be sure, because she lies with her back to him.

'Thomas?' Jack whispers.

It is a surprise to hear his voice after all this time, and he takes it as proof of Payne's skill.

'What?' Thomas asks.

'Is that all true?'

He sighs.

'Most of it, I think,' he says.

But he does not want to talk about it any more. He has talked all night, and so he turns over, the straw sighing under him, and he sees in the cold light of the moon that strikes through the half-open shutters that Payne is awake too, looking at him as if he has done something wrong. Thomas sighs and turns to lie on his back, and he looks up into the night and wonders what in God's name he is supposed to do now.

He thinks about being a father. Men usually give good cheer when they hear another is to have a son for the first time, but that is when they have a name and something to pass on, and that is when they have a wife who wears their ring and lives under their roof, but what, of these, has Thomas? None. Instead, he has what? A woman – an apostate – who is married to another man, albeit under a different name, disguised as a boy who is, Payne has guessed, three months pregnant. She is accused of murder, though she says that is unjust. She has had her ear clipped for desertion, though that hardly matters. They have a very few silver pennies in their purses, and they are conscripted in an army that is already half-beaten, and is about to be completely so, but from which they have not been able to extricate themselves, and now, even if they could be gone, there is nowhere left for them to go, since they have consistently lied to the only people who were ever welcoming to them, and, more than that, it is to one of these people to whom she – Katherine – whose family name no one knows, was fraudulently married while pretending to be a woman for the death of whom he cannot help but feel partially – wholly? – responsible.

When he puts it like that, when he recounts each stroke of his chance-inspired ill fortune, instead of weeping, he finds a slow smile spreading across his cheeks and a deep, chugging laugh beginning to build in his chest and it emerges in a series of sobbing and sighs and then gradually becomes loud enough so that he has to cover his face with his blanket.

It is absurd. Absurd.

At length he stops laughing, and now he finds that he is weeping.

Oh Christ, he thinks, what in God's name am I to do?

When morning comes, slow and seeping, loud with birdsong, he still has no answer, and Katherine is sick again and can hardly move. He is reminded of a far-off time, in Wales he supposes, since that is what she has told him, when he sat over her in an inn for a week or more while she slowly knit herself back together, and he prepares to do so again, to sit there and wait, watching over her while she groans in her bed and the servant ambles about the solar collecting up the sheets and the other mattresses. He will use the time wisely, he thinks, and come up with something. Some plan.

Payne returns from the kitchen with more wine to mix with his tincture and he makes both Katherine and Jack take some, and later Thomas thinks she smells peculiar but she sleeps at least, and seems at peace, and Payne says that there is nothing more he may do for her until later, and so, when the bells ring for Mass, he goes with Payne to the church, walking twenty paces or so behind the narrow back of King Henry and his small retinue of gentlemen.

'How is the expectant father this day?' Payne asks with a smirk.

And Thomas looks at him, and he wonders if, instead of shame, he should feel pride in what he has done? Perhaps if he were Jack, say, and Jack were him, then he might feel some envy for the boy? That he might even see something to be admired in what he had done? That he alone had had a woman in the castle with him all this time, right under their noses, while the others were suffering their pangs of discomfort or, worse, visiting the whore in the village? He holds that thought, but he knows the truth of it, and it is nothing so simple.

When they return from Mass, Katherine is sitting up, feeling better, she says, but still tentative, moving as if bruised, and for a short while they are shy with one another, and their conversation is formal and stilted.

'Will you take ale?'

'A little, please. Thank you.'

Thomas asks Payne what he will do now and Payne tells them that he is bound to King Henry, and that he will go wherever he goes.

'Over the sea?' Thomas asks.

'You do not place much faith in the Duke of Somerset to defeat Lord Montagu and lead King Henry to London in triumph?'

Thomas hardly cares what happens to King Henry and the Duke of Somerset. He can only think about what he and Katherine can do now.

'And what about you?' Payne continues. 'What will the proud new mother and father do now?'

Thomas glances at Katherine. She looks interested in his answer.

'I don't know,' Thomas admits.

'Do you have any money?' Payne asks.

343

Thomas shakes his head.

'Nothing of value?'

'Only the ledger, which we no longer have anyway.'

'The stolen book? Hmm. What about this Sir John Fakenham character? Would he take you back?'

Thomas and Katherine look at one another for a moment.

'Probably not,' she says.

'So?'

'So we must find that ledger,' Thomas says. 'That is all that remains to us. Our only option.'

Among the many shocks Payne has to suffer in the telling of their tale the night before, this was the most dangerous.

'But Riven has it,' Katherine says, 'of that I am sure.'

'Then we must find him. Find where he has gone. Retrieve it, if he has not burned it, and then—'

The argument that follows comes very quickly, suddenly blowing up as if from nowhere.

'And if that happens,' Katherine asks, 'what then?'

'We find the ledger, and show it to King Henry!'

'*If* we can find it,' Katherine says. 'And *if* we can somehow get it to King Henry. Which we have not managed yet, even when we had the thing in our hands!' 'And even then, it is only of value if – *if* – King Henry's cause is still valid!'

'There is still hope,' Thomas says. 'And we may—'

'No!' Katherine shouts. 'Thomas. This – it can't last! We cannot live like this! Don't you understand? Do you not remember I know what happens in childing? I do not want to do that. I do not want to do that, to do that, on my own. To be at the mercy of a midwife who places her faith in stones and bones and pardoners' scrips.'

'I have delivered many a lamb,' he says, and for a moment she looks so wild he thinks she will try to stab him, and he takes a step back.

'That is what Eelby said about his wife,' she spits.

He holds up his hands.

'Forgive me!' he says. 'I did not mean to—'

'What else could you mean?'

'Nothing,' he says. 'Nothing.'

And the heat goes out of it just as suddenly.

'So you want to go back to Bamburgh?' he asks.

'I want to be near Master Payne,' she says.

He looks at Master Payne who is looking oddly inscrutable.

'And where will you be?' he asks.

'I am bound to King Henry,' he repeats, 'so if God forbid York beats Lancaster in the field, then it must be to Bamburgh, I suppose, since that is all that will be left to us, but if Lancaster beats York, imagine! Then he might go anywhere. To Coventry. Eltham. Windsor. Westminster.'

He smiles at the thought, as if already feeling the southern sun on his cheeks, but Thomas has the strong sense that the physician's next journey will most likely be north, to Bamburgh. At least then there is a fleetingly slim chance they might find the ledger, he supposes. They can sell it, and with the money— He stops. It is a flight of fancy, he knows that, in his heart. But what else? What else is there? Christ, if only they had some money! If only they were not reliant on the charity of others.

Payne looks to be thinking hard and then he speaks, slowly, revealing some new horror.

'But should York beat Lancaster in the field,' he says, 'he will pursue the King to Bamburgh, will he not? And should Bamburgh fall, as it must, then you'd best pray to your lucky saints that your ledger is no longer there. That it is burned, which is most likely, or written over.'

'What? Why?'

'Why? Because if it is in Bamburgh, as you suppose, then sooner or later it will fall into King Edward's hands, won't it? And if King Edward finds the book, if it is shown him, then he'll want to know how it came to be where it is, and he'll soon be rounding up anyone and everyone who knows what it is about. Including us.'

He points to everyone in the room. Jack starts coughing. Katherine is pale again, and she turns to Thomas, round-eyed.

'Remember what Sir John said,' Katherine says. 'That if it were discovered that we knew what it proved, we would have our feet burned and then be hanged and gralloched as a hunter guts a deer, and everyone we knew would have the same done to them!'

'He is right,' Payne says. 'He is right!'

'But King Edward will not know it was us who brought it?' Thomas says.

She turns to him aghast.

'Your name is in the ledger!' she tells him. 'It is there, written under the picture of the rose window you once drew. You were pleased with the picture, and wrote "*Thomas Everingham fecit*" below.'

He stares at her. Christ, he thinks, could she not have mentioned that before?

'I am sorry,' she says. Her eyes are downturned and she looks miserable with guilt.

'So,' he says. 'Whatever happens, we must return to Bamburgh? We must now find that ledger!'

'But how can I go back?' she asks, placing her hand over her tummy, which Thomas swears was not so round a moment ago. 'It is all right now, perhaps, but soon I will be a surgeon who is five or six months pregnant. I cannot do it! I cannot go back and give birth to a child in the outward postern gate! I will not!'

Thomas does not know what to do or say, but Payne is looking at her carefully, then he turns to Thomas.

'Thomas,' he says. 'Will you leave us a moment?'

And Thomas, who can feel the weight of it all pressing down on him, stopping him thinking, is pleased to do so.

He leaves them, and follows the flight of winding steps up into the dark until he sees the limned outline of a small door that will lead him out on to the tower's top. He will be alone there, he thinks, and will have space to breathe and to think. He emerges out in the spring day, where cool sunlight shines and the birds are loud. There is a guard, though, a boy, in Riven's colours, bright and new-made, with a fringe that half-covers his eyes and a prick-shaft bow that will not loose an arrow a hundred paces.

'Who are you?' the boy asks.

'Thomas Everingham.'

It means nothing to him. Why should it? Thomas does not ask the boy's name in return. He doesn't care and he doesn't want to know.

'What do you want?' the boy asks.

'Honestly? For you to be quiet.'

The boy raises his eyebrows and mutters a profanity that might in some circumstances have got him killed, but Thomas is not in the mood for that, and anyway, the boy is just a boy. He seems excited and after a while, he must speak.

'They have not been sighted yet,' he says.

'No,' Thomas agrees. He looks out across the valley. The mist has lifted and the river's water slides brown through the funnel of its green-swathed banks. Where the banks are shallow cows have been down to muddy the water, but there are none there now. He looks south, to the little church in its yard, the mounds of graves, the old yew that must have been there two or three hundred years. He wonders if King Henry is back in there, on his knees before the altar. For all his praying, Thomas thinks, this king does not seem to have much luck.

The tower top is small around, only a few paces across, its walls thick stone, its merlons high. It is a good little gatehouse, Thomas supposes. He stands there, and he feels that his socks are gritty and he wonders when he last removed his ill-fitting boots, and when he last changed his linen, and he knows that he needs a wash, too, by God, and a shave and a long sleep in a bed of hay, and he feels the need for something good to happen to him today, but he cannot for the life of him think what. Then there is something else niggling him.

'Who've not been sighted yet?' he asks, realising that what the boy's said still hangs between them like an unanswered question, and that this is what's bothering him.

'Edmund's men,' the boy says.

'Edmund's men?'

'Aye. They's expected before sundown.'

Who in God's name is Edmund? Thomas wonders. The boy is looking at him as if he may be simple.

'They'll be wearing our livery,' the boy goes on, tugging on the cloth of his own tabard. 'Where is yourn?'

'Below,' Thomas says. He looks away, across the river to the trees beyond. There is something wrong here, he can feel. Edmund. It is not a name such as Everingham, but a given name. Edmund. In Riven's livery. Christ. It can only mean one thing. Edmund Riven. Here. Or on his way.

'What do you think they will do when they get here?' he asks the boy, and again the boy looks at him as if he is stupid.

'Well, they will take King Henry – him down there – won't they?'

'And where will they take him?'

Back to Bamburgh, he supposes, but the boy scoffs.

'Not bloody likely,' he says. 'Not after all this. No. They'll take him to Newcastle, and then down to London, I daresay.'

It is as if the flagstones under his feet are shifting and switching places. He knows he will expose himself but he cannot help it. He must know for sure.

'Edmund Riven is coming here to take King Henry to Newcastle, to hand him to Montagu as prisoner?'

The boy is as proud of the scheme as if he devised it himself. He has evil teeth.

'They say Edmund Riven's wound reeks enough to make sheep barren?' the boy says. 'Though I do not believe that, mind.'

'And is that the way they'll come?' Thomas asks, coming to join him, standing at his shoulder, staring down the river.

'Aye,' he says. 'From Newcastle.'

Thomas needs to reassure the boy, but he also needs time to think. To think what this means. And then something occurs to him.

'You are Sir Giles's man, aren't you?' Thomas goes on. 'And were at Hedgeley Moor?'

The boy allows it. 'Funny, running like that, weren't it?' he says. 'All the stuff you're told about never running, about never turning your back. And all the stuff they say about Towton, I mean, and then us, off like rabbits as soon as the first shafts were loosed, and everyone coming after us. Worked though, didn't it?'

Thomas nods and joins the boy in laughing. So, he thinks, it was as Roos's men said: Riven's men broke first, and took the whole line with them. They must have been on Montagu's side from the beginning, Thomas sees, but then why did they not join Montagu's men and turn on Roos and Hungerford's men? Because they were outnumbered? Can that have been it? No, Thomas thinks, it was not because they were outnumbered, or, rather, it was not only because they were outnumbered. It was because that was merely the first part of Riven's scheme. His men did not want to turn on Roos and Hungerford's men because there was still something else yet to do, some second part of the scheme, that required them to appear to be loyal to King Henry and his cause.

And that second part is being played out right now, before his eyes: the betrayal and capture of King Henry himself.

Dear God! Thomas wonders what price Riven has extracted for this, or what advantage he will expect, and from whom? One thing is certain; it must be more than merely the retention of Cornford Castle.

The boy finally reads his expression correctly.

'Who did you say you was?' he asks, and now he knows he has made a mistake, but it is too late. Thomas should kill him, but he is not able. He turns and steps through the door and draws its locking bar across into the stone holding. He hears the boy's footsteps and then his shouting and thumping on the door's thick boards. Thomas hesitates, then slides the locking bar back and steps aside to let the door open. It flies open to crash against the jamb and the boy is suddenly tipping forward. All Thomas has to do is help him past. The boy shouts as he goes sprawling down the winding steps. He cries out in rage and he only stops on the second landing, where he lies stunned, but he is a boy, of course: they can fall down steps. Thomas hauls him up by the tabard and shoves him down the next set of steps. The boy hits his head on the underside of the descending flight with a hollow tonk and his legs fly out from under him and he falls on the next flight down like a dropped sack.

Payne opens the door and looks down at the boy, then up at Thomas coming down the steps.

'What is wrong?' he asks.

'Riven is coming,' Thomas tells him. 'Both of them. Father and son. We must go.'

'Wait,' Payne says. 'A moment.'

He will not let Thomas pass into the room.

Then he does.

Thomas pushes open the door, then stops.

Katherine stands by the cold fireplace. She is staring at him, half-anxious, half-challenging, but that is not what it is about her that stops him dead. She is in a dress. It has a blue body and blue skirts with black sleeves and she wears a red belt and laces of the same at the front. She has a long white cloth wrapped around her head and it is almost impossible to see the boy who was Kit. Thomas is suddenly robbed of words. She is beautiful. He stares for a long moment. She stares back. She tilts her chin defiantly.

'What?' she asks.

He collects himself.

'Riven is coming,' he tells them. 'Giles Riven has betrayed King Henry, and all of us, and sold him to Montagu.'

There is a moment of silence. Katherine stares at him.

'You have to tell him,' Payne says. 'You cannot let him fall into Montagu's hands. He will kill him.'

Thomas looks at Payne. He is genuinely upset.

'You tell him,' Thomas says. 'You take him. I am done with this.'

'What about Jack?' Katherine asks. 'We can't leave him. They will kill him too.'

Thomas looks over at Jack. He does not look so bad, he thinks.

'Then he must be got ready to ride,' Thomas tells her. 'Master Payne can give him some of that medicine, too, and you both can ride.'

Jack slowly rights himself and rolls to his knee and then, still keeping that leg straight, to his feet. He breathes out, swearing in one long incoherent breath. Katherine comes to his side. He is utterly still in her presence, waiting for her to go.

'It is still only me, Jack,' she tells him, and though he is thrown by the fact that she is now a proper woman, he yields and lets her help him up. When he is upright, he stands, and she steps away from him and straightens her unfamiliar dress, and Thomas cannot help but let his gaze wander over her, and he sees she now fills it where it should be filled.

'Wherever did you get that?' he asks.

'It was Cecily's,' she tells him. 'Master Payne's patient.'

Another dead girl's dress.

'Can you catch the pissing evil from – from a victim's clothes?' he asks.

Payne tilts his head.

'Not so far as we know.'

Not so far as we know. Christ.

'And so, who are you now?' Thomas asks, suddenly angry again. 'You cannot pass yourself off as another dead girl, can you?'

'No,' she says, dropping her gaze. 'I am Katherine.'

There is a long moment. Payne and Jack are silent, watching.

'Katherine who?' he asks.

'I am Katherine Everingham,' she says, looking up. 'I am your wife.'

And he stops, heart-stilled, and they look at one another, and she seems timid, and in search of his favour, as if she thinks he might not give it. And in an instant his world turns again, and he regrets every harsh word, every uncharitable thought, and he thinks he has never loved so much as now.

Then she turns a curious shade. Her cheeks puff, and she hunches and vomits thin grey gruel on to her skirts.

23

King Henry does not believe them at first. He comes from prayers with his gentlemen, looking unusually regal in a blue velvet cloak against the cool of the morning, and he asks questions in that querulous voice, and all illusion of royalty is lost. Details and minor points. He misses the thrust of what Payne is saying, and his men keep interrupting, barking across him, demanding answers of Payne and Thomas, then having to apologise to King Henry for their impropriety. Most think Payne is lying. Only one wants to attack Riven's men where they stand.

'We should kill them all now,' he says.

'Please, sirs,' Thomas tells them, 'we are outnumbered many times over. If we wish to extricate ourselves, we will need guile and speed.'

Thomas cannot help but glance at King Henry. He embodies neither.

'You have picked that one out for me?' King Henry asks, indicating the horse Thomas has found for him. 'He looks larger than – than I am used to, and I was never much of a horseman.'

'Nor has his grace ever done such a thing as take a ride before,' one of his men says. 'Why should he start now?'

'And if he is such a danger to us, why then is that man wearing Sir Giles's colours?' another asks, indicating Jack, who is wearing the tabard of the boy Thomas threw down the steps. He is clutching the reins of his own pony for support while behind him Katherine is already up on a brown mare, her hitched skirts hidden under a long travel coat, and she is hunched over a fistful of herbs that Payne has given against the horse's smell.

'My Lord Montagu is a Christian,' one of them says. 'He would not dare offend the King's person. Never in a thousand years.'

Thomas is beginning to lose his patience. He is beginning to think it might be better if Montagu were to take the King, and these men, too, and do with them all as he wished. Drown them like cats.

'And whither would we go?' another asks. 'We are not arrayed for travel. His grace the King will—'

'His grace the King will no longer be his grace the King if he is still here when Montagu's men arrive,' Thomas says, 'so if his grace the King wishes to stay his grace the King, then he had better get on this horse and ride out of here just as fast as he is able. Begging your pardon, your grace.'

There is a moment's silence. The men behave as if they should have a monopoly on rudeness to the King, but King Henry is less worried about that.

'I must fetch my other psalter,' he bleats. 'It is within.'

He indicates the small keep.

'As is the king's bycoket!' another exclaims. 'It is all we have left that is of any value.'

Thomas remembers those jewels on the king's helmet. Can they get it back? He looks around at the castle gate. Riven's men are gathering on the steps. About ten of them. One is pointing. A man is being sent to fetch someone else. They have realised something is up.

'We must leave it,' Thomas says. 'And go. Now.'

King Henry is persuaded.

'My Lord of Montagu was always very – abrupt,' he trembles. 'I should not like to fall into his hands and be forced to rely on him for Christian succour.'

It comes to Thomas that he has seen King Henry before, long ago, before all this, and he wonders where, and then he remembers and can even name the place. At Northampton. Before a tent. Thomas was bleeding, in pain. His shoulder. And there were dead men at his feet, a pile of them in bloodied plate, cracked, dented, broken, and more were dragging themselves away into the shadows to die in peace, while others raged about the place with hammers and knives and there was a tremendous din. It seems an age away, yet also, only yesterday.

'Everingham? Are you all right?'

It is Payne, frowning. Thomas shakes himself awake. They must move fast.

'May I swap cloaks, sir?' he asks. 'Yours for – his?'

He picks a man among them who is the same height and build as the King, wearing a russet cloak and a scarf.

'Oh, yes,' King Henry says. He seems to want to rid himself of the blue cloak and take up the humbler russet one. Payne steps behind him and unclasps the brooch and then removes the King's cloak. One of the men is angry because that should have been his job. The man in russet is quick to take the King's cloak. It is lined, not just edged, with soft fur. He swings it to get it to spread in a circle as he puts it over his shoulders. So much for guile.

King Henry puts his new cloak on and straightens it, and in it he looks properly ordinary, a humble dredge, a cleric perhaps, and he has the face of a man you'd never want to ask a question for fear of him answering it. Thomas helps him up into his saddle. He is frail, narrow-shouldered, brittle as a bird and just as light. He smells odd, Thomas thinks. Fungal.

'Remember, sirs, we are merely going for a ride,' Thomas reminds them as he swings himself up into the saddle.

'What should we do?' the one who'd wanted to attack Riven's men asks. 'We do not want to fall into Lord Montagu's hands any more than you or the King.'

Thomas looks down at their upturned faces, all screwed up and wan and anxious, and he tells them to be seen to be going to the chapel to pray, and then to leave through the sacristy door, and make their way upriver a little while where they will find the town of Corbridge.

'Cross the river there and then when you are on the other side, go west. Make for Hexham. It is not far. An hour's walk perhaps. The Duke of Somerset's army is camped a mile south. You will not miss it.'

It does not seem much of a plan, not to him, not to any of them, but it is no worse than his own to smuggle King Henry away by dressing him as another man, and, in fact, rather better, and he wonders for a moment if they should all do that? But Jack is unable to walk, and Katherine is like to expire, and everything is better if you have a horse. There are some grumbles, some mouths opened to voice complaint, but Riven's men are beginning to move.

'We must go,' Thomas says.

And the King, a terrible horseman, lets Thomas take a lead rein and he sits there in his saddle, nervously pretending to be someone else, and they set their horses along the track, reins not quite slack in their thumbs, away from the castle gate, expecting at any moment a shout from behind and the rumble of pursuing hooves.

'Be ready,' Thomas says.

But nothing comes. They ride out, following the track through the gate of the hazel palisade and into the rough pasture, and still nothing. Then they pass behind a thin screen of new-budding aspens, and then they reach the road and nothing has come and it seems they have done it.

'You may take off the scarf now, your grace,' Payne tells him. But King Henry wears it as a badge of humility, like the poorest pilgrim, and they ride on, and Thomas has rarely seen anyone so uncomfortable in a saddle: he sits on his horse as if at stool, as they retrace their steps of yesterday back towards the town of Corbridge, picking their way over loose cobbles as fast as they dare, looking back over their shoulders for signs of pursuit. Thomas cannot help but smile. Taking King Henry from under Riven's nose is a small victory in his campaign against him, but it is something, and he tries to imagine the scene when Montagu arrives to find him gone.

But where to take him?

'We cannot go back to Bamburgh,' he tells Katherine. 'That will be to present him to Giles Riven just as if it were his saint's day.'

'But there is nowhere else to go, save the Duke of Somerset,' she says.

A couple of townsmen have come out of their houses and are watching. So too are faces in windows and there is a piebald goat atop a red-hooped barrel standing nearby which also regards them through golden devil's eyes. King Henry does not like to be looked at by goats, and he begins a whispery prayer, and still Thomas is left to decide what to do.

'There is no one else to oppose Riven now,' Katherine murmurs. 'No one else but Somerset. He is our only hope.'

And she looks so forlorn, he could weep. But Thomas thinks, yes, there is – there is me. I can do what I set out to do all those years ago. I can kill Riven myself. I will perhaps be able to start with the son.

Then the goat on the barrel lifts its bearded chin and looks into the distance, as if sniffing the wind, and after a moment, it jumps down and with a patter of hooves it is gone, and the horses swing their heads and stop chewing and are still, and then a cloud of birds flies overhead, choughs perhaps, and a bell rings to the east, and yet what is the hour?

'It must be them,' he supposes aloud. Imagining Edmund Riven and his stinking eye riding up to Bywell, certain of victory, only to find his prey gone, and there is in that, to Thomas, a sombre note of quiet satisfaction.

'Come on,' he says, and turns his horse southwards, and kicks it on, riding down through the town towards the bridge, towing King Henry behind him. He pays pontage for them all with the last of his coins and as he rides on across the bridge, Thomas looks over his left shoulder, along the bank toward Bywell, but there is nothing to be seen, and soon they are off the bridge and on to the road south, retracing their path through the pastures of the southern bank. When they reach Somerset's makeshift encampment, they are met by a patrol. The riders are suspicious, and they need persuading that King Henry really is the King, but seeing his rings, and a curious red stone he wears as a pendant, they see he must be someone, and they agree to take them to find Horner, at least, who will vouch for them, and they find him sitting upstream, fishing.

'All day and not a bite,' he says. Then he sees the King, and he stands.

'Your grace,' he bows, and then he sees Katherine, and his focus sharpens.

'But you've had more luck,' he breathes with his mouth open, staring as she dismounts. And now King Henry turns to her, and finally sees he has been travelling with a woman.

'Oh,' he says.

Katherine stands there before them in that dress. She touches the sleeve of her left arm. She is feeling better, certainly looking less waxen, and she looks to Thomas to explain, and so does Horner, and Payne, and even King Henry in his absent way, and Thomas feels as if his head is filled with tow, almost to bursting point, and he wonders why he has not thought up something in advance, but he can think of nothing, and so he says only the very first words that come into his mouth.

'This is my wife,' he says and despite it all, despite everything, he cannot help his eyes misting over and he feels very much consoled by that thought, as if it is somehow enough, or will do for them all as well as it does for him, but Horner can only stare.

'Your *wife*?' he asks. 'But she is – she is— Where is Kit?'

And now Thomas feels he might as well tell them, have done with it, for he can still devise of nothing, but now Katherine enters with a lie that makes him stop and smile again, despite everything.

'My brother has stayed in Bywell,' she says.

'Your *brother*?'

Jack starts coughing. Katherine says nothing. Horner stares at her. She stares back until he shuts his eyes and pinches the bridge of his nose.

'By all the saints,' he says. 'You do look — similar.'

She says nothing.

'Are you as good a surgeon as he?' he asks.

'Twice as good,' she says.

Horner looks over to Payne, who shrugs.

'So she says,' he mutters.

'You did not tell us that Kit was your wife's brother?'

'No,' Thomas says. 'You did not ask.'

'But all this time?'

'What can I say?'

'You can tell us why have you brought her here now?' Horner asks.

'Montagu is coming,' Thomas says, not answering the question. 'Today. He has ridden from Newcastle.'

Katherine is forgotten. So too is the King.

'We must tell Somerset,' Horner says. 'Come with me.'

Thomas nods. They turn their back on King Henry and walk through the camp together. Thomas explains Riven's ruse. Horner seems at a loss for words. He does not believe him. Nor does the Duke of Somerset. He makes them stand at the opening of his tent while he eats some sort of fowl, roasted. Grey is within, sitting on a folding stool, and Tailboys, too, likewise seated, and behind them there are others, the Lords Hungerford and Roos. All have suffered the privations of the past months: they are poorly shaved, baggy-eyed, in dirt-smutted clothes, and the tip of one of Tailboys's piked shoes is broken and turned down. The tent smells of cold river water, and of mildew and unwashed bodies. Not even the Duke's supper smells good.

'Oh, good Christ,' Somerset says. 'How could he, you fool?
Riven's been face down for three years, enduring half hell's agonies,
not sending missives to his son or making pacts with the King's
enemies. Dear God.'

And he should know, Thomas thinks, and yet . . .

'Where is King Henry now?' Tailboys asks, looking over their
shoulders for his dread sovereign, and the way he says it, King
Henry is obviously a burden they can do without.

'He is with Master Payne,' Horner tells them. 'At prayer.'

'He must be gone,' Somerset says. 'We must get him away, tonight,
back to Bamburgh. If we lose him, then we are left with nothing.'

Sir Ralph Grey is sober this morning and beats Tailboys to the
punch.

'I will provide an escort,' he says. 'I will go myself. Take twenty
men.'

The others regard him.

'You do not relish the prospect of an encounter with Lord
Montagu?' Tailboys asks.

'I merely offer, is all,' Grey counters. 'We cannot send King
Henry alone. He is the King of England, after all, and should travel
accompanied and in some style.'

'I should take him,' Tailboys objects.

Grey snorts.

Somerset brings the discussion to an end.

'I will let you know who is to escort him,' he says. 'We can spare
only very few men, and none of any use. Cripples and so forth. And
we must accomplish it with no fuss. His presence here is a boon to
the men, and his loss will be felt. So not another word.'

Thomas is bundled out.

From then on the camp is busy. Men are at their weapons and armour
as usual, tightening, loosening, polishing and sharpening. Fires have
been lit. Pots steam, and the women are washing clothes in the river

and the trees and bushes are spread with clothe Thomas cannot imagine ever drying before they will need to be packed away. A blacksmith is shoeing a horse, and a grinder has set up his wheel and sparks are flying, but here there is a man – one of Lord Roos's – trying to sell a kestrel, and another his tent. They are hoping to reduce their baggage, so that if they have to run for it, they can. Thomas is tempted to buy the tent, not the bird, for Katherine, but then he too would be encumbered with it and just like these men, they must travel light, he thinks, if they are to get away. Already his mind is turning to flight.

So now he looks around, tries to see where they will run when it comes to it. They are camped on a flat plain, in a loop of the river, at the bottom of the valley, just south of the road and its bridge across the river they are calling the Devil's Water, which flushes over a rocky bed on its way to join the Tyne to the north. In addition to the bridge there are a couple of fords along its length where the water is about hock deep, he supposes, but elsewhere it is much deeper, and the flow, after the rains, is powerful enough to create a churning cloud of mist above the low waterfall upstream. Across the river, to the west, the road cuts up a steep, heavily wooded hill on its way back to Hexham, and to the east the road from Corbridge snakes southwards until it reaches a crossroads: the west road comes across around another hill, mostly of rough moorland, just like at Hedgeley, which the men call Swallowship Hill. If Somerset were to set himself up there, Thomas thinks, on the hill's crest, then he might have a chance, but down here? He is a duck on water.

'Your wife?'

It is John Stump. Christ! He had forgotten about John Stump. Now John nudges him with his remaining elbow, and grins a very particular grin, and despite his distractions, Thomas cannot help but smile back.

'What of her?' he asks.

'Come on,' John says. 'I've been watching those hands at work all these weeks. That isn't anyone other than Kit.'

Thomas is alarmed. He opens his mouth to say something, but what?

'You crafty devil!' John goes on. 'Having her here all the time. Right under our noses. But listen. Don't you find it a bit odd? You know. How she looks so like Kit? Must be funny, when you're face to face, like?'

Thomas does not know exactly what John Stump means, but he can guess.

'Anyway,' John says, 'Horner's looking for you.'

When they find him Horner is helping one of the others brush down the stolen horses. He seems cheerful and even optimistic.

'Somerset doesn't believe Montagu knows where we are,' he says, 'and is probably fixed on taking Hexham, and so tomorrow we will take the crest of the hill there –' he points over to Swallowship Hill – 'and catch him while he is on the move, and with God's blessing, this time we will score such a victory as to set the whole country ablaze for King Henry.'

Thomas wonders if he should ask about the last time they caught Montagu's army on the move – through Hedgeley Moor – but he does not want to upset or disappoint Horner, so he keeps his mouth shut.

'Thomas,' Horner goes on, 'you are to take the archers to the front as before.'

'We have very few arrows,' Thomas warns. 'Barely twelve apiece.'

Horner is surprised, caught out. He obviously had no idea things were that bad.

'Nevertheless,' he says after a moment of anxiety, 'loose them and then retire. It is the Duke's plan.'

Then it is a foolish plan, Thomas thinks, which does not address the realities of the situation, but that is typical of Somerset, Thomas supposes, and he is pleased, for it is as he'd hoped. He will do what he must, but he can be expected to do no more.

He goes now to find Katherine. It is curious, he thinks as he passes through the camp, that now she is dressed as a woman, he must fret about her more, or be seen to fret about her more, than when she was a boy, although in fact she is in far less danger now. He has never forgotten that the French witch Joan was burned for dressing as a man.

He finds her standing face to face with Sir Ralph Grey. Sir Ralph is absolutely sober. He has his hands on his hips and is leaning forward to peer very closely at her. He is incredulous.

'His brother, you say?'

Katherine nods. She is enduring his inspection tolerantly, which Thomas thinks she would not do if she did not already know Grey to be mostly harmless. Still, though. Perhaps that is best.

'You are that boy's sister?' he goes on.

'Yes,' she says, her face blank.

'And you are married to that archer who assists him in his – his – whatever it is he does?'

'Yes.'

Grey leans back. 'Well,' he says, as if he has heard everything now.

He senses Thomas looming up and turns to him.

'This is your wife?'

'Yes,' Thomas says.

'But how in God's name do you tell them apart in the dark?'

Just as with John Stump, Thomas is not sure what Grey means. He finds himself on shifting ground.

'The need has never arisen,' he says.

No one says anything for a moment. Grey stares at them, looking from one to the other. He knows something is wrong, and that they are waiting for him to leave before he divines it.

'Well,' he says, 'I hope you are as skilled with the knife as your brother. We will have need of a surgeon or two tomorrow, I should think.'

24

The sickness wakes her when it is still absolutely dark. Thomas is next to her, and she can smell him, and what was once pleasantly dusty has become less so, and she rolls to the other side, but here is Jack, breathing a rhythmic gale in her face, and she has noticed that when a man has not had enough to eat, as Jack has not, his breath is very bad, as Jack's is now. So she turns back and looks up at the underside of the cart and she tries to pretend that if she does not move, she will not vomit, and this works, and the nausea subsides. She lies still for a moment, her hands across her belly, letting her eyes become accustomed to the dark. Most men are scared of it, thinking it a presence, rather than an absence, but she has never felt so, and she used to scorn the sisters at the priory who turned their clogs over during the night for fear they would fill with darkness and so become evil.

The baby will come in September, she supposes, and she thinks then of Eelby's wife, and how she must have lain like this at one time, perhaps next to that snoring boar of her husband, and she wonders with a start what has happened to the son, the miraculous baby? She has not thought about him since they were sent north, since coming to Alnwick. Dear God. She feels she has somehow betrayed the boy, now, by having her own, and before she ever managed to find him in those trackless green wastes into which the eel catcher had disappeared. She wonders what the boy would be like now. Walking perhaps? Learning his first word? 'Eel', probably.

She will find him, she thinks, when this is over. Next year perhaps When her own baby is born. She will show them one another. Or is that vanity? And anyway, where will she be? She simply cannot guess. She cannot even guess where she will be next week, since anything might happen today, tomorrow, the day after.

So she must come up with something. But what? Her mind does not seem so sharp as it once was, she has noticed, and she thinks it might be the sleeping rough with so little food that has done it. It is why she was so pleased to announce that she was Kit's sister, though she thinks how odd that was: the words were out of her mouth before she thought them through.

When he'd heard, Master Payne had just shaken his head, half in sorrow, half in admiration. She thinks about him now, and she prays he will stay with Somersets' army, stay with her, but she knows he is King Henry's man, and must go where the king goes. She wishes she and Thomas could go with him to Bamburgh, perhaps, however uncertain that future might seem, and that he would be by her side when her time came.

He would not wish it, of course, and would claim ignorance of her woman's body, but how could that be so, she thinks now, when he spotted her condition before she did? In one glance? He is a very fine physician, she thinks, and perhaps there is something to his theories about the planets and their position in the sky, for after all, what does she know? She has picked things up as she has gone along, from old ladies and Mayhew, while Master Payne has been to far-off countries where Christian men gather together to pursue knowledge, to dissect corpses in order to understand how they worked when they were alive. Such depth of learning is – is something.

The camp awakens around her, coming to while it is no longer night, but not quite day, and there is a curious gentleness in the soft morning air. Voices are muted, consideration and accommodation informs every dealing as lines of men and women make their way between the damp canvases of the tents down to the river, there to conduct their ablutions with a semblance of privacy. The lull of early morning lasts only until the arrival of bread and ale, brought down the hill by carts from Hexham, and a mad scramble follows during which every man must exert himself to get what he needs.

Thomas returns with a great pitcher of ale and the upper crust of a loaf that must once have been the size of a man's body. He divides it unequally in her favour, and Jack laughs. He is looking very much better. She wonders what it was that ailed him. Some miasma from the river? He is not mobile enough to fight yet, and he and John Stump both refused to leave with King Henry and Sir Ralph Grey the evening before, and so they are to stay in the camp, to keep such a baggage train as they possess, and she is pleased. They will be with her. She has volunteered for surgery, but there is even less with which to work than there ever was at Hedgeley Moor, and she wonders what she might usefully do, except sit with her hand on a man's brow while he dies, and even that worries her.

After he has eaten Jack hobbles away and Thomas watches him go with a nod that strikes her as more calculated than heartfelt, and she wonders what Thomas is up to, but then Horner comes with others in Grey's livery trailing behind. He is in rust-spotted harness that he has had little help putting on; in one hand he clutches a pollaxe Katherine has never seen before, and with the other he holds his helmet against his chest. Others are coming past, spilling out of the camp in their companies: Hungerford and Roos's men, still not trusted after last time, have the furthest to go, since they are to take the right flank, facing north towards Corbridge, while Somerset's men are to dominate the centre.

'We are to take the left, Thomas,' Horner says, 'with Neville of Brancepeth and Tailboys's men. We are to drive Montagu's flank back into the river.'

Thomas just nods. The way Horner says it, it is as if he believes it is possible, though in the very next minute he reminds John Stump to look to the baggage and the followers.

'In case Montagu sends prickers around,' he says, 'but he won't.'

John Stump nods cheerfully enough.

'Nice to have something to do,' he says.

'Where is Jack?' Horner asks. John Stump shrugs and mutters that he is about, and not likely to go far, not with that leg.

Then, in the distance there is a bugle blown. Men stop and stare quizzically at one another.

'What is it?' she asks.

'An alarm.'

'Can they –? Can Montagu be here already?'

The alarm continues, is taken up by nearer trumpets.

'By Christ! It must be them!'

The camp erupts into a frenzy of movement. A drum starts. Then another. Then another. They are coming closer. So too are the alarms as the tidings spread. Lord Montagu and at least five thousand of his men are across the Tyne at Corbridge and are moving south and west in good order. And now every man is hurrying, some are running with others still tying their points, and there is a great confusing struggle as they rush to get up the hill before Montagu can beat them to it.

'I will see you after it,' Thomas tells John Stump as he forces his helmet on. John nods.

'We'll be here,' he says. 'Me and Jack. Couple of cripples as may be, but we'll look after her all right.'

And Thomas can only nod and then he turns to her, and for the first time he is allowed to kiss her with all these other men about, and he opens his arms to envelop her, to really say goodbye properly, but she has to force herself to allow it, because he smells of sweat and horses and rust and now her insides are rebelling and so this first kiss goodbye is perfunctory, snatched, and she knows she will regret it later, if, God forbid, anything were to happen to either of them.

'Go with God, Thomas,' she says.

She realises she is crying, and she wishes she weren't, and she wishes she did not feel so sick, and she wishes she could see him off as he deserves, and as she would wish to, but she cannot help herself. And then the boy with the drum comes out from the trees and he stands by them, his sticks thundering away, and he grins at them and she thinks he might be mad, or simple, and after a moment Horner taps Thomas on the shoulder with his pollaxe, and he mouths something and gestures uphill with its point, and Thomas takes his meaning, and he turns, and so they part, for the first time as man and wife, he going one way to fight with all the other men who are trudging past up the hill, while she and John Stump go the other way, walking against the tide, back down into the trees towards the river and the camp.

When they get there Tailboys's men are busy loading his baggage on to mules. Heavy bags that set the animals staggering. Everyone else – all the women and the children and the cripples and the old men – is pressing along the river downstream, following its turns, a thousand paces or so, hurrying to where the trees thin and the ground rises, and there is a view of the hill to the east where the men will be. When she is there, she climbs up on a tree stump, awkward in her skirts, with John readying his arm to catch her should she fall, and she shields her eyes against the rising sun and watches the figures of men hurrying up the slope to the crest. After a moment John Stump climbs up beside her. More of the women from the camp join them, craning their necks. What can she see? What can she see? There are hundreds of men struggling in a swarm like ants up a hill. There is little sign of any organisation, but there are banners and standards and there are groups of men in similar livery gathering across a front that runs away from her where she stands.

While they wait, she wonders if there is any woman to ask for advice about her sickness. Behind them, along the river a little way, is a chapel attached to a small gatehouse or castle, not unlike Bywell, she thinks, only even smaller, with one small turret, filled just then with a crowd of men and women watching, just as if they were at an entertainment.

'By God, look,' John shouts, pointing. 'He's bloody well done it!'

And there is a burble of approval and admiration. Somerset and his men have made it to the top of the hill. There are still plenty hurrying to join them, but enough have made it up and now their banners and flags are raised on its crown, and she can hear the drummers and the trumpeters are up there too, going at it, and now, at the foot of the slope, she can just see more flags coming into view, and she supposes this must be Montagu and his men, though for the moment they are hidden behind the rise.

She remembers the only other battle she has watched like this – outside Northampton, standing with all the women and that Italian bishop, by the stone cross in the rain – and she sees there is a rhythm to these things. Once the men are placed, there is a pause for prayers and then a moment for something else. Reflection? Reconsideration? Regret? What? She does not know. Then when that is over, the commander might say something to encourage the men and instil within them a certainty as to the justice of their cause and that God is on their side and that He will look over them. Then the archers will stride forward and the battle will commence.

She thinks of Thomas up there, and how he must be feeling, and she prays without praying for him. Around her all the women seem to know which flags the knights carry, and they are collected in groups themselves, so that all Tailboys's men's women stand together, and all Roos's men's women stand together, and they seem knowledgeable about almost every aspect of what is to come: dispositions and wind direction, vantage points, where the pressure will first be felt, then where it will most be felt. They have a low opinion of Roos and Hungerford's men – despite the presence of their women – and are unrestrained in voicing it.

'Cowards,' one of them says. 'They'll break today, that is for sure.'

369

'Let's hope they run the other way this time.'

And heads are turned and there is some ill feeling.

She is surprised to find they are not especially concerned for the safety of their men. Or perhaps they do not talk of it? But they are on tiptoes, faces craned, like children watching a mummers' play, and then one of them says: 'Here we go' and there is a collective drawing in of breath, and after that there is total silence as they watch the arrows fly. From this distance the shafts merely smudge the distant sky, an impression, like smoke in autumn, but the women know how crucial these moments are, and Katherine remembers Walter – was it? – telling her that any battle was decided in these first moments. If everything else was the same, he said, whoever loosed the most the fastest would win.

Today those loosing downhill with the sun behind them, and even – is it possible? – the slightest wind, might be expected to prevail, to inflict such damage on those coming at them up the slope from below that the battle will end almost before it has begun, and one of the women, an old one – stained apron, green dress, sleeves rolled up to reveal arms like legs, and a great wrap of linen tucked in tight around her face – says you always know who will win the day about now, and she snaps her fingers, and though John Stump says that is rubbish, Katherine watches the woman's expression, and sees her wrinkles deepen as she frowns at what she's seeing, and then as she comes to understand it, she shakes her head and sucks her remaining teeth.

'Run out of arrows,' she says.

And she says no more. Everybody understands. Somerset's archers have loosed all they have – too few – and they have let Montagu's men off the hook, and now it is Montagu's men who keep up their attack, and it easy to imagine what that will do to Somerset's archers. There are groans among the women. Wailing too.

'We should be ready,' the old woman says. 'There will be plenty of wounded.'

370

But there is nothing to ready. This battle was not supposed to happen today, everybody said so, and there has been little time to collect urine and make bandages and so on. John Stump is quivering and bright-eyed with excitement, fuelled with a strange sort of lust, flapping his stump as if it were a wing. He does not want to go and cut cloth for bandages. He wants to watch the battle.

And now there is a swelling roar from the hill, and another great drawing in of breath around her, and she looks back and she can see that Montagu's men are moving forward in that same way they did at Hedgeley Moor – implacable, organised, relentless – and she can see their banners and standards waving, and she wonders for a moment if she can see in there among them that white flag with the black ravens, but she is imagining it, she supposes, and anyway, she is too far away to see details such as that. She watches the Duke of Somerset's men moving down to meet Montagu. They are less even, more ragged. Many fewer. Then two lines meet and a moment later she hears a slow rippling crash that breaks in her ears like a wave collapsing along the length of shingle.

Prayers are begun by the river now, a gentle hum, and hands and rosary beads are wrung. A pale-faced boy – he might be eight, and still too young to carry arrow bags, if there were any to carry – constantly crosses himself, over and over and over again, while a girl next to him kisses the cross on a wooden beaded rosary. The paternoster is begun and joined in with.

But in the end it is not enough.

Not all Somerset's men commit to the defence of the hill, and though she cannot understand it, or make it out herself, she can detect the tone of the questions the women are asking one another. Natural incredulity turns to forced incredulity as they refuse to accept what they are seeing, and then it turns to anger.

'They are! They are! Look. Oh, the bastards! They're breaking. The cowardly bastards!'

She sees first one man come running over the back of the field.

371

He streaks away from the fight, comes running around the hill, blundering through the heather and the long grass. Then there are more. All of them come from the far end of Somerset's line, and they come racing down the hill towards the camp. She is about to ask who they are, and what they are doing, but there is sudden fidgeting among the women, and some have already turned and are hurrying back toward the camp. John mutters.

'Those bastards,' he says. 'Those bastards.'

'What is it?'

'They've broken,' he says. 'Hungerford and Roos. Same as before.'

'Where are the prickers?' a woman cries out. 'Why don't someone stop them?'

'We've not enough men for prickers,' John tells the woman, but she only looks at him as if it were his fault.

'Will the others hold?' Katherine asks.

'We'll see,' John mutters, but he sounds doubtful. They watch. Nothing is clear. Long moments pass. There is turmoil in the front and back of Somerset's lines. Hundreds of men are milling about. Most will be archers, many will be those breaking rank.

'Thomas will be away by now, won't he?' she asks.

And John nods but will not look at her.

'Aye,' he says. 'Should be. Best be, anyway. He's a big lad, but without any plate, he'll not want to be caught up in that.'

They watch more of Hungerford and Roos's men come running and a little further down the stream, their women begin hurrying back up towards the camp to meet them, and they look guilty but also relieved, and they ignore the muttered insults as best they can, but no one has time for any fighting now, and most eyes are on the field above.

'The Duke'll hold!' a woman cries out. 'He'll hold!'

'Pray to God.'

But the prayers fall on deaf ears, for the men keep detaching and coming back down the hill, and soon there are more behind the line than in it, and it becomes clear Somerset cannot hold, and the news somehow communicates along the length of the front, and within a few moments, those at the back of the divisions, from left to right flanks, are turning and streaming away while they have the chance, leaving those at the front to fight alone, and now those men on the left, Thomas's wing, start to peel away and they turn their backs on Montagu's men and they run, and soon the whole army is in retreat, turning the hill black with their numbers, stumbling back, canting west, back towards the camp and the rushing line of the Devil's Water.

'Oh, Christ,' John Stump says. She looks down. Most of the others are gone. It is just her, John Stump and a few other women. One looks up.

'Best be gone, love,' she says. 'This'll soon be no place for a pretty girl.'

And Katherine knows she is right. Around them the women have turned and are racing for the fords over the river behind. Skirts are hauled up, and fists swing, and the weaker are shunted and pushed aside in the scramble. Women are wading through the brown waters, arms and legs pumping, to scramble up the far side, just to get away, to try to melt into the countryside.

'We must be across before they come,' John says. 'Come on!'

And he grabs her hand and pulls her from the tree stump.

'What of Thomas?' she calls.

'He'll want you gone.'

'No,' she says. 'I'll not leave him again.'

'You must! Come on!'

'No! He would not leave you if you were there!'

She wrenches her arm free. But now the men are arriving, coming running past, just as at Hedgeley Moor. Katherine turns into the crowd, back up the hill, but then, unbelievably, here is Thomas, or a Thomas-shaped man, coming fast, his helmet tossed aside and his hair flowing, and she sees with a great flood of relief that it is him; he clutches his bow, still nocked, and his face is red with the exertion, shoulder to shoulder with other men from Grey's company. He does not look frightened so much as intent. He starts shouting at them as he comes, gesturing with his bow, pointing southwards towards the camp, just as if he thinks they will find their horses where they left them.

'The horses!'

He is alongside them and he hardly pauses, and he catches her hand and drags her almost off her feet.

'Come!' he shouts.

'This way!' she calls, pointing at the fords where the women are crossing.

'No!' he shouts and he pulls her south. John follows. They run, back up the path, the river frothing alongside. Men and women are coming the other way. They collide and rebound off one another as they go. She is breathless in moments, her skirts heavy, but if she doesn't put one foot before the other he will drag her over. Then they are into the thicker trees and then the camp, left deserted now, everything gone save tents and cooking pots, one cart with a broken wheel. The knife grinder's wheel is knocked over. Men come hurtling through, wild-eyed, slashing at anyone with drawn swords or knives who might try to stop them. Nor Thomas does stop. He runs on, dragging her along. He is breathing heavily now, and she can hardly catch her breath. John is labouring behind. It is hard to run with one arm.

They reach the bridge where the crowds are thickest and no one would hesitate to lash out with a blade if they thought it might help them edge ahead. Anything could happen in this panic.

'Stay with me,' Thomas tells her, and she clings on to his empty arrow bag as he pushes his way into the mob. She elbows out of the way a woman who threatens to come between them, and is punched for her troubles, but John is there, bristling, growling like a dog, menacing men and women who push from behind. They reach the bridge and start to cross, shoulder to shoulder, chest to back, knee to knee, a solid mass of human flesh. The smell is of moulding clothes and sweat and unwashed bodies and someone is bleeding.

'Hurry, for the love of God!'

There is a bellow, a scream and a splash. A man laughs. Katherine watches a woman floundering in the current for a moment before she finds purchase on a sodden trunk, and hauls herself out, her clothes half-pulled off, and she turns and shouts terrible curses and gesticulates at those pushing past on the bridge above. No one listens. And then Katherine becomes hemmed in, almost in the dark, between two large men in blue-and-yellow livery jackets, and she is almost borne along on the human current just as was the woman in the river, and she places her trust in Thomas, and she clings tight and keeps her head down, and shuffles forward. Everyone is sharp elbows and foul-mouthed threats.

And at last they are across the bridge and ahead people are beginning to spread out, to walk faster, to swing their arms, and then, finally, to run again, breathlessly up the steep hill.

But Katherine stops. She lets go of the arrow bag.

'Where is Jack?' she shouts.

Thomas turns. He can hardly hear her above the din of the shouting, of the pounding feet, the steady roar of the water on the rocks below. He gestures ahead and reaches to take her hand once more. She tries to snatch it away but now John is there, shouting something into her face and pointing with his one good hand up the hill too.

'What?' she shouts.

'He is up there already.'

And they drag and push her along up the hill, to the top, where some are striking out into the woods and others are running up the road to Hexham. At the roadside are bundles of clothes and discarded livery jackets and there are already boys from the town fist fighting to claim them for their sisters or mothers to make into something else.

Thomas hurries on. She can barely breathe now. Her shoes are loose, and she's hobbling and she suddenly feels the extra burden of her growing body.

'Just a little further,' Thomas encourages.

And there among the trees are horses, waiting. Four of them. And she thinks, my God! The day's second miracle: it is Jack. Waiting. He grins, almost broadly, and he swings up clumsily into his saddle and Thomas helps her up on to her saddle and she settles herself with her skirts hitched and has not time to care nor does she even mind the smell, and they shake their reins and dig in their heels, and they ride fast over the rough road, and men and women and children scatter before them with more foul curses and she is aware that Jack and Thomas ride either side of her, and that they all have their blades drawn and that this is not over yet.

The mobbing crowd flows mostly up the road to the gates of Hexham, but Thomas leads their horses off and down across the sheep pastures and the pig pens and the new-planted furlongs and they ride for the road the other side of the town, that cuts north across the bridge, where a thinner crowd is already condensing, but by the time they get there, the pontage collector has been knocked over and lies by the roadside, pale and possibly dead, and they ride past and across the bridge and the men and women on it shout at them as they are forced aside, and they ask to be taken with them, and if there is anything they have they might spare, but soon the crowd is behind them, and they continue along the old road north-wards, until they reach a crossroads again, and Thomas looks both ways – east and west – before riding on.

After a little while they slow their horses and walk two by two, breathing heavily. She is next to Thomas.

'So what happened?' she asks, and he sighs.

'It was the same as ever,' he says.

He does not want to talk very much. There is a smear of blood and a bruise on his cheek.

'Did you see Horner?'

He nods. 'He was at the front,' he says.

She knows what that means.

'He was a good man,' Jack says. 'He will have acquitted himself.'

But it is not about acquitting oneself, is it? Not on a day like this. It is only ever about survival.

'So are we riding for Bamburgh, too?' she asks. She thinks of Master Payne and his care. She cannot believe Thomas will agree, but he nods again.

'There is nowhere else to go, just now,' he says. 'Montagu will send his prickers screaming up this road first of all, so we will divert westwards, and then cut northwards. They will not expect that.'

He hopes. A little later he takes them off the road, along a track, heading west, and they follow it winding through the spring green trees across the soft golden cloth of last year's fallen leaves. They ride in silence, until Thomas stops his horse and dismounts. They are in a narrow defile, a fold in the land filled with tall grey-trunked ash trees, and the sun does not penetrate the valley's floor where the leaves have been kicked up recently, and a long wavering muddy trail has been cut through the valley ahead.

'Mules,' Thomas says, straightening, and looking around as if for clues.

'Could be King Henry on his way back to Bamburgh?' John Stump suggests.

'Wrong way,' Thomas mutters.

'Tailboys,' Katherine tells them. 'His men were loading some this morning, remember?'

'He was supposed to have held the left flank!' Thomas says.

'Maybe,' she says, 'but he was definitely in the camp this morning, loading four or five mules.'

377

Thomas looks down at the tracks again with a frown.

'Well, they are going our way, it seems,' he says.

'By God, I hope we don't meet them,' John says. 'The sort of men to cut you to pieces, soon as look at you.'

Thomas nods, and climbs back into the saddle. They ride on a bit, cautiously scanning ahead.

And now Thomas stops again.

The track of mule prints veers off the path, along a smaller one, deeper into a ravine.

'Can you smell them?' Jack asks, and they sniff. She can smell nothing but her own horse and her own greasy woollens, but the others claim to detect a subtle difference between the mules and their own horses.

'We can't be far behind,' Jack says.

'Come on then,' Thomas says, 'let's get ahead.'

And they carry on along the original path, its leaves largely undisturbed, and they ride until she feels the evening chill and she thinks she will faint with hunger. When she asks if they might stop, Thomas is all care and concern.

'Let's follow that track,' he says, and they dismount and lead their horses along a smaller track that takes them up the slope and through some trees where they find a small trickling stream that comes down from the hill above. They refill their bottles as she eats more bread.

'How do you feel?' Thomas asks.

'Better.'

'We will have to sleep out tonight,' he tells her, 'but tomorrow we can turn north, and there will be a day or so more before we reach the castle.'

'So we really are going back to Bamburgh?'

'Yes,' he says. 'I thought that was where you wanted to be. With Master Payne?'

And she nods again, because that is right. The thought of a few days in the saddle, though . . . Jack meanwhile has found a coal pit, disused. He drops a stone down it. It must be thirty foot deep. Beyond is a tiny hovel, dry-stone built, its roof fallen in, but better than nothing. Probably the old miners' quarters, abandoned at the same time as the mine.

'Thomas,' she says. 'I do not think I can ride any further.'

Thomas is anxious.

'What do you think, Jack? John? Are we far enough?'

They are doubtful, but they too are tired, and the hovel is filled with dried leaves and though it smells of fox, they can each imagine lying down for the night, and they agree Montagu's men will probably not be out in the woods looking for men such as them, but will be searching the road's length, or celebrating their victory and savouring the delights of Hexham.

'Come on, then,' he says and they hobble their horses behind the hovel where there is a scattering of mossy bones of God knows which animals, and the men join Jack by the coal pit throwing sticks down it until the air grows cooler still as dusk leaches away to night, and then they join Katherine in the hovel, all of them with their feet intertwined, and they finish the bread and the water, and Thomas tells them about his role in the battle they witnessed: how he loosed half his arrows, always with one eye on what was going on behind him this time, and then he felt something, some lack of resolve in the others, and then there was daylight behind him, and so he turned and ran, and it was Horner who stood aside for him, and he does not know what would have happened to him, he just knew he wanted to be gone. And so he ran.

'Do you think anyone like Somerset will have got off the field?'

'Not in full harness, I don't suppose.'

'Perhaps he yielded? Went to Montagu on bended knee, after the King's grace again?'

'I tell you,' John Stump warns, 'Montagu's not one to make friends.'

'What about all the others?'

'I expect we'll see some of them back in Bamburgh.'

'If we ever make it.'

She falls asleep first, wrapped in her travelling cloak and leaning against Thomas, his arm around her shoulder, the back of his hand in her lap.

25

It rains heavily that night, and Thomas is awake just before dawn, lying damp in a pool. Katherine still sleeps on dry leaves next to him, just a bundle of clothes, and John Stump and Jack are huddled together for warmth on the other side of the low-walled hut. They too are dry. Thomas gets up and goes to the rivulet and thanks the Lord for his deliverance the day before, and he says a prayer for the souls of John Horner in particular, and the others in Grey's company in general.

His thoughts turn again to Giles Riven. Can the man really have manoeuvred himself so cleverly? To have taken King Henry from the side of his closest supporters and placed him in a trap to be sprung by his own son, without anyone even suspecting, and all this from his sickbed? Or perhaps he was never as injured as he feigned? Perhaps he lingered there to avoid King Henry's court, or to avoid being sent on any pointless sorties during which he or his men might be injured. Perhaps that was it? And when King Edward has King Henry safe in his dungeon, what will he do to reward the man who helped put him there? Cornford Castle will be the very least of it, that much is obvious.

And meanwhile, Thomas thinks, look at me. I am squatting here by a murky stream in sodden clothes with not a penny in my purse, and a woman whom I cannot marry and who is expecting a child by me in a few months. I have no prospect of putting a roof over her head, let alone the child's, let alone mine. I am harried by men determined to kill me, and my only recourse is to return to a castle that is surely about to have to endure a siege, and in which I must serve a mad lord who drinks too much, and who in turn serves a king and a cause in which I have no interest, no stake.

Just then Katherine wakes. She comes down to the stream, and she looks pallid, green even, and she falls on her hands and knees and retches. He kneels next to her, and cups water for her and strokes her back and holds her hair, and eventually she shudders.

'It is a punishment,' she says after rinsing her mouth in the water. 'Because of what I have done. With you.'

He stands, rocking slightly.

'No,' he says. But he can't think of anything else to add and she looks at him. Now she has been sick, she is very pale, almost translucent, and she looks very fragile.

'I am married,' she says. 'In the eyes of God and Man, I am married to Richard Fakenham, and so I am to be punished for my sins.'

'No,' Thomas says. 'Margaret Cornford is dead. Dead! You understand? She died twice, once more than anyone I know, and so she can never now come back.'

She looks at him levelly.

'Well, that is nice,' she says.

He sighs.

'I only meant—' he says, and he shrugs. 'Sorry. I don't know what to say. You know I will do anything and everything for you. You just need to tell me what.'

'I should like a bed,' she says, 'in which to lie.'

And he feels worse than ever.

'We shall go to find Master Payne,' he tells her, 'and you shall have a bed, and a roof over your head even.'

He remembers Sir John mentioning that those whom the Lord loves he first tempers in the flames. Well, he thinks, the Lord must love him and Katherine abundantly, for He is testing them sorely, while He must loathe the Riven family, for He gives them everything in His power. For a brief moment, Thomas wonders if it might not be better to be loved by the Lord just a little less.

And Katherine looks at him and tears fill her eyes and he realises that she is terrified. Terrified of everything. And he steps forward and he puts his arms around her and he pulls her tight and she is stiff and unyielding and he says over and over again: 'It will be all right. It will be all right.'

And he is holding her just like this, and she is beginning to soften in his arms, to come to him, when they hear shouting on the track below.

He lets her go.

'Quick,' he says, and together they run crouching back to the hovel. Jack and John are half-asleep still. He hushes them. He pulls his sword from the sheath and Jack does likewise and they wait in silence, their eyes big and white in the gloom.

The shouting continues. Someone is urging someone else on. Shouting out to get the bloody things moving for the love of Christ. The shouts are getting closer, more distinct.

What is going on? Thomas watches over the wall.

Christ!

There are men down there, coming up the track. More than a handful. He makes a sign to John and Jack: down now. They look at one another and raise quizzical eyebrows, and then he peers back over the broken-down wall.

They are much closer and, oh, dear God! It is Tailboys! Tailboys and his men. They are coming up the track toward them, labouring with their mules. Why are they here? Where are they going? Thomas has no idea. Tailboys is still shouting.

'Come on!' he screams at his men. 'Come on!'

Thomas looks over at their own horses. They are tired, cold, thirsty probably. Could they outstrip Tailboys on his mules? Perhaps. If they ran for it now. And if Tailboys has no archers with him. But Thomas is pretty certain the track ahead leads only to another coal mine. Could they hide in there? Perhaps. But not with the horses, and anyway, no, look, it is too late. Tailboys is there, on his own horse.

'Use the stick!' he is shouting at a man slapping a mule. 'Come on!'

And the rain begins pattering among the leaves on the canopy above, then silver in the air around them, and the men behind the mules are urging their animals on, beating their hindquarters with sticks and even the flats of their swords, and others are hauling on the ropes around the animals' necks, but the mules are panicking. Men are slipping in the leaves, cursing the animals, swearing at them, but they cannot go any faster because they are laden with hugely heavy bags, and they are obviously exhausted, and yet Tailboys is still screaming at the men to keep them coming.

Jack is shaking his head in bewilderment and Thomas knows just as little.

Tailboys's men move up the path. There are four mules being manhandled by eight men, with Tailboys on his horse at the front. Lagging behind are two more men, their necks craned, staring backward as if they are being followed. They have nocked bows and a bag of arrows apiece.

Tailboys calls over the muleteers' heads.

'Any sign?'

And one of the two men at the back tells him there is none so far, and Tailboys shouts again at the muleteers and now the procession is just past the hovel, when one of the mules, the one at the back, seems to stagger, just as if it has been worked to death, and it stumbles, and its forelegs go from under it. The man with the rope tries to haul it up, but it is no good and the mule keels to one side, and then the ground seems to give way from under it, for the next moment it is slipping sideways in a tangle of hooves and the man on the rope leaps back and lets it go sliding through his hands and the mule has gone, slipping, sliding, falling with a dull fumble into the depths of the coal mine.

Tailboys turns and emits a roar of such rage that Thomas flinches. 'Get it!' he shouts. 'Get down there and fucking well get it!'

But then the man at the back hisses for all to be quiet and though Tailboys is purple with rage, and spitting, he can say nothing. He jumps from his horse and stalks through the leaves back to where the mule has slipped from sight. He peers down. He looks at the men who let the animal go, and it seems for a moment that he is going to push one or both in after the animal, but sense prevails, and he glances at the other men looming over him and they do look as murderous as John suggested, and so Tailboys has to say nothing. He turns and walks back to his horse. He climbs up into the saddle and jerks his hand forward and the little party set out after him as best they can.

A long moment later and they are gone along the track, dipping into the trees, and there is complete silence in the ravine.

'Christ,' Jack mutters.

He begins to rise, but then drops back down again.

'Christ Christ Christ,' he says.

'What is it?'

And Thomas peers over, and from the track below a party of horsemen come picking their way up through the trees. They are in red livery, in helmets and matching harness, all carrying lances, moving silently. They are Montagu's prickers, and they are tracking Tailboys and his men.

No one breathes.

Thomas watches them come into view. They are grim-faced, hard-bitten and implacable, with faces like anvils, and of course they know what they are about, but because of the rain in the night, Thomas and Katherine and Jack and John Stumps's tracks have softened and leaves have folded over their prints, so the hovel attracts hardly a glance, and with their horses hidden behind, all Thomas can do is pray they are silent for the moment, and thank God they are, and then after a momentary pause when it is almost possible to feel Montagu's men looking at the hovel, the soldiers turn and continue on their way up along the tracks left by Tailboys and his men. One of them stops and looks at the scrapings on the side of the mine shaft, but he says nothing, and can see nothing down there from the saddle of his horse, and after a long moment they are gone, disappeared among the ash trees.

'Quick,' Thomas tells the others. 'We have to go. More will come. Or they will come back.'

They run around the back for their horses. He helps Katherine up into her saddle.

'What were they doing?' she asks.

'God knows,' Thomas admits, 'but good riddence to them all. Come! Quick.'

They strike north as soon as they find a path, and it leads up over ridge after ridge of rough moorland, all the way to the wall the Romans built. They cross this, and they camp against it that first night, never agreeing which side of it is the best to sit against to avoid the wind. In the morning it rains briefly, then the sun shines, and then it rains again, and then the sun shines again. It is like this all day. The wind is constant.

That day they see men on horses moving through the unfurling bracken. They are too far away for their livery to be seen, but they are riding in a solid block, unhurriedly, and they can only be Montagu's men. They stop and watch under the cover of some trees until the riders have disappeared, blending into the distant countryside.

'I suppose they are moving up to Alnwick,' Thomas says. 'Perhaps King Edward's army has already already arrived with all its guns.'

They ride all that day and the next. They see more of Montagu's men, and to avoid them they are forced to ride in a wide loop that means they cannot use a bridge but must ford a river, becoming soaked again in the process, and they must spend an extra night in the open, but they also find some men who, after a tense moment, admit to being in the retinue of Humphrey Neville of Brancepeth. They agree to travel together.

'I think Sir Humphrey got away,' one of them says, 'but we lost him in the aftermath. It was chaos. Montagu's men were in Hexham before the morning was out, and there were parties of them riding through the country, just – all over the place.'

He is coated with shame, and can barely look Thomas in the eye, but the others are fascinated by Katherine, of course, and they come riding close in an attempt to engage her in conversation, only for Jack and John Stump, who know these sorts of men, to cut them off and send them scuttling.

On the evening of the fourth day, they see the castle at last.

'There she is,' John Stump says, pointing to Bamburgh's stark stone lines. 'Looks a bit better in the spring, doesn't she? Bit more inviting.'

They join the road to the great gatehouse just before curfew, and in the sunset, the castle is rose-coloured, and the seagulls that float above it are equally tinted, and it is good to smell the sea again, Thomas thinks, but still he pulls his horse up a little short, and the others slow too, and they stop and stare at the castle walls and they say nothing for a while.

'King Henry's standard,' Katherine says, indicating the flag among the keep's battlements.

'So he made it back then.'

'Come on,' the other men say, and they ride around them, and approach the gatehouse and call up for the gates to be opened and now men appear in the battlements above.

'Whose are they?' John Stump asks.

'They are Grey's,' she says. 'They are Sir Ralph Grey's.'

'Thank God,' Thomas says.

Katherine looks washed out, her eyes huge. These last few days have done her no good. The gates are swung open and they ride up and into the barbican and behind the portcullis. Thomas recognises one of the men who was with him at the battle by Hexham, as well as one of the others who came away with Sir Ralph Grey and King Henry the evening before it happened.

'Sir Ralph will be pleased to see you,' the first one says. 'He is feeling outnumbered.'

'What do you mean?'

'Giles Riven is up there,' the second one replies.

'Giles Riven! He is here?!'

The name comes like a thunderclap.

'Aye,' the first guard answers. 'Been here all along. Might've been useful to have him at Hexham.'

'He'd only have run at Hedgeley moor,' the second guard says. 'Or turned his coat as he did at Northampton.' The first guard grunts his agreement.

'But what is he doing here? Thomas asks. 'He is – he is supposed to be with Montagu! He is supposed to have turned his coat!'

The guards are puzzled.

'Don't see how he could've done that,' one says. 'He has been here all along, and now has King Henry as his guest in the keep.'

What can this mean? Is this some sort of other element in Riven's scheme, or some alteration after the failure at Bywell?

'When did King Henry arrive?' Thomas asks. He is flailing, he knows.

'A few days since,' the guard supposes. 'He came with Sir Ralph and a few of our men.'

'And Giles Riven was here already?'

The guard is getting impatient with him.

'As I say,' he says. 'He believed himself castellan of the castle and there were some words had, apparently, between those two. You know what they're like, them sort. Strutting around the place like two cocks in a hen house. Word is that Riven thought he was governor by right of occupation and precedence, only Sir Ralph had got King Henry to promise the position to him on the way up. Not best pleased with that, was our Giles Riven.'

Thomas looks at Katherine. For once she seems equally confused. Why is he here? Why is Sir Giles in Bamburgh?

Thomas thanks the guards and he leads Katherine and Jack and John Stump out of the gatehouse and up in the gathering dark of the deserted and empty stables, where they unsaddle their horses and feed them the very last scraps of hay in the manger.

'Where is everyone?' Jack asks. 'Do you suppose this is it?'

'Could be,' John Stump says. He needs help with his saddle. 'Least we'll have our old quarters. Was getting used to them, before we left.'

So they go on foot up through the inner bailey where there are still very few men to be seen, many fewer even than before, and there are no lamps lit, save on the first solar of the keep and in the church, nor are there fires in the watchtowers, and there is a single solitary man at the inner postern gate which is open anyway, and beyond, in the outer bailey where the sheep used to graze and there were smithies and arrow makers, and men and women under canvas, there is nothing.

'Christ,' Jack says. 'There's nobody here.'

'They must have just run home,' John Stump says. 'And who's to blame them?'

They walk in silence.

'You're awful quiet,' John Stump tells Thomas. Thomas grunts.

What is Riven's scheme? Why is he not with his son and with Montagu? What is he up to.

'He is trying to take the castle,' Katherine says suddenly. 'That is it. While his son takes the king, the father takes the castle.'

There is a moment before Thomas sees this, and once it is seen it is so obvious it becomes impossible to imagine any other thing. After all, if Giles and Edmund Riven delivered King Henry and Bamburgh Castle into the lap of King Edward, then they might reasonably expect such rewards as would make Cornford Castle seem like a kestrel mews. They would be made earls at the very least, and given the estates of men like Grey and Roos and Hungerford who would have no further need of them, surely, for being dead.

'So what to do?' He says, to himself more than Katherine, because he knows of course what he must do. It is what he has almost always wanted to do: to kill Giles Riven. He cannot help but give Katherine a tight smile. Giles Riven has delivered himself into their hands. And if they can retrieve the ledger at the same time – well, that is all the better.

'And now he is waiting,' she says. 'That is what he is doing. After Bywell, he has had to adapt his scheme, but it leads to the same end anyway.'

Thomas groans with the frustration of it.

'At every turn,' he says. 'That bloody man.'

For a long moment he imagines himself perched in a tower's top with his bow and a handful of shafts, and he can see Riven so clearly in the bailey, standing alone in his livery, and he imagines nocking the arrow and then loosing it – a difficult shot downwards into a space – but he will do it. He will do it. And there will be no mistake this time. No one says another word as they cross down to the familiar arch of the outward postern gate where there is a faint glow from the window. Thomas strides ahead, gathered now, ready for what must come. He does not look at Katherine again. He is thinking only of killing Riven. He shoves open the lower door of the Great outward Posten Gate and the four of them file in, into the dark, and they make their way up the familiar worn steps to the room above, the one with the bread oven.

As they climb the steps in the dark, Thomas cannot help but recall all the times they coupled together, in secret, with his feet pressed to the door above, and now Katherine is paying the price, he supposes, while he – well, he is weary beyond belief, and he can hardly lift his feet, but at least there is a light in the room above and he steps up and shunts open the door, then stops.

There are three men gathered in the glow of the mouth of the bread oven, playing dice. All look up. All are bearded. None he recognises. One stands. He is in a white livery tabard, and in the light spilling from the oven, Thomas can see he is wearing the badge of the crow. Of the

SOUTH, TO TYNEDALE, NORTHUMBERLAND

raven. He is one of Riven's men. They are all three Riven's men. Two are the men who promised to cut Thomas from gut to gizzard.

'Fuck me,' one of them says. 'If it isn't the mad cunt.'

The fight is very quick. The three men come at them while they are still in the doorway, but they are not armed so well as Thomas, or as Jack, and they must first reach for their knives, and two of them are in linen shirts, and as they converge on the door they crowd themselves. Thomas backs out, up the steps. Jack steps back down the steps, but he pulls his sword out and up, and his is really sharp, and it slices straight up through one of their outstretched wrists and there is a cry and suddenly the air is filled with that terrible, shaming smell of blood. Jack throws himself forward, he is cutting and slashing, One of the men throws himself against the door. Jack is knocked back. Thomas kicks the door. It hits one of the men. Thomas shoves it wider, sending the man staggering. The wounded one wheels away, gripping his arm, and Thomas surges into the room using him as a shield. The two others cannot get at Thomas, but Thomas can at them, and he slashes and catches one. He pushes the wounded man away just as one of them swings at Thomas's eyes, but he is knocked off balance by the wounded man, and after that it is simple. Thomas closes and thrusts his blade up under the man's armpit. His sword is held sideways. It slides between the man's ribs. He pushes in. A double handspan. The man chokes, stutters. He and Thomas are eyeball to eyeball, the man looking at Thomas from the tail of his. A bubble of blood grows and pops under his nostril. There is no change in his appearance, but Thomas knows the man is dead. The point of Thomas's blade is right in his throat. Thomas pulls it out and it's as if it was the only thing holding the man up.

The room feels very small now, and the wounded man is shouting loudly. He is clutching his arm in just the way Eelby clutched his when Katherine hit him with her washing beetle, and he's shouting at it to stop it bleeding, but the wound won't, and it's spraying black blood everywhere and he knows as well as anyone that he is a dead man standing.

And now the last live, fully whole man has gathered himself, and he moves his blade quickly, darting forward, always balanced, as if he is playing at this, and Thomas can see how expert he is, and he feels clumsy and leaden-limbed before him. The man darts forward and there is a quick movement and a tug on Thomas's sleeve and he feels burning pain at his wrist and before he can tell what has happened warm blood drips from his fingertips.

'Come on then, simpleton,' the man says. 'Spared you once, won't do it again.'

And then from the side Thomas sees the wounded man gathering up his own knife in his clumsy left hand, and he is about to come at Thomas, when Jack intervenes, almost lazily, as a precaution, extending his sword to hold the man back, but it becomes a backhanded slice that stops within the man's neck, maybe against his spine, and he drops on his knees with a truncated scream and a frothing mess. But the distraction is enough, and the last of them comes at Thomas again, and Thomas is too slow. His arms are heavy, his body too large, and he is not a fighter, not like this man, however lucky he has been in the past, and he feels a punch in his chest that makes him cough and step back. He looks down to see the man's pinched little face peering up at him with a savage grimace of pleasure and victory, but then the man's expression changes as he realises he has not caught Thomas below the ribs as he'd hoped, but he has slid his knife against one of the metal plates in Thomas's jack. And Thomas wraps his arms around him in an embrace that pins him tight so that he cannot pull the knife from where it is stuck in the tow, and he turns him so that he has his back to Jack, and Jack stabs him, short and sharp.

He stiffens in Thomas's arms, and Thomas finds it repellent, and he does not want to be so close to him when he dies, and so pushes him away into the corner of the room where he twists, and falls on his front and lies with his toes scuffing irregularly in the bloody puddles on the rough stone flags.

After a moment there is nothing to hear except the sigh of burning wet wood in the oven, and his own heavy breath. Then Jack laughs without opening his mouth. They say nothing for a bit. Thomas wipes his blade on the first corpse and then slides it into his scabbard. He watches Jack wipe his own blade clean, then cross it, muttering a blessing, and then slide it away for next time. His skin is pale against the blood and now he is trembling.

'Thank you, Jack,' Thomas says. Jack waves his hand: it was nothing. Katherine and John Stump are at the doorway. Katherine has her mouth covered against the smell. She takes the knife that is still stuck in his jack and she cuts a section of linen from a cleanish shirt. Then she passes him one of the ale jugs.

'Piss in it,' she says from behind her hand.

Thomas does so.

'All right, all right. That is enough!'

She gets him to pour some of it over the wound on his wrist, and then binds it tight with a wad of urine-soaked linen pressed against the cut. She slices the ends of the bindings with the blade that would have killed him and then slips it into her own scabbard.

'Don't think we'll be wanting to stop here tonight after all,' John says. There is blood on the ceiling, all over the walls, pooling on the tiles. Thomas searches the men's belongings, rummaging around in the falling dark, going through their worn clothes, their meagre possessions: mugs, bowls, eating spoons, rosary beads. Only one of them has a spare shirt. He did not expect to find the ledger, of course, nor does he, but still . . .

'Thomas,' John Stump says, nodding at Katherine. She is drooping with fatigue, and he puts his good arm around her, and she flinches, but then remembers, and she allows herself to be helped, and he must almost carry her.

'Is she quite well?' John Stump asks.

'No,' Thomas says. 'We must find Master Payne first.'

'And before we meet anyone else who takes exception to us,' Jack adds.

'He will be in the keep,' John Stump says, and Jack shoots Thomas a look and they nod at one another. They – he – must now face Giles Riven. He eases the sword in its scabbard again and wonders if this will finally be the moment. He feels his heart flutter. He knows he is in no fit state to fight Riven, and he sees that he himself will probably be cut down by Riven's men either before or after he has killed him, and he wonders where that will leave Katherine. But then – what choice does he have? He must find Payne. He must get her treatment, or at least a bed, and if that requires confronting Riven, then – he ends in a mental shrug. Christ, he thinks, I am almost dead on my feet anyway.

There are lights burning within the keep, and Thomas pictures the great hall with a fire burning and every sort of pie and other dish spread on the boards, and he can almost taste the ale that he imagines will be flowing. It is dark now and they have no idea how well they have done in getting rid of the blood, until they try to negotiate their way up the steps of the keep, past the guard, where the captain, one of the King's men, is having none of it.

'By all His saints!' he says. 'I'm not having you in there. Rightful King of England's in there, you know? And you turn up looking like butchers from the shambles? Have you come fresh from Hexham?'

'We met some of Montagu's prickers down the road,' John says. 'Which is why we are after Master Payne.'

The captain looks warily southward as if he might see Montagu's horsemen through the curtain walls.

'Christ,' he says. 'They here already?'

And he turns and begins up the steps, on his way to report the news to someone within, gesturing to two other guards that Thomas is not to be allowed in.

'But what about Master Payne?' Thomas calls. 'The physician? Is he within?'

One of the two guards shakes his head.

'Try the east gatehouse,' he mutters. 'He is with Sir Ralph Grey, beacuse neither of 'em like the company in here.'

So they turn and troop across the darkness of the inner bailey to the east gatehouse, a smaller version of the keep, built into the curtain wall, from where a track leads down towards the beach and the sea beyond. Here lights also burn, and the guard – one of Grey's men this time – recognises them and lets them through and they climb the steps toward the brightest source of light in the solar on the first floor until they are intercepted by Sir Ralph Grey himself, who comes weaving towards them along a passageway, accompanied by a man with a glass lantern. He is clutching a cup and a bottle of something.

'Ho ho!' he cries. 'Who have we here?'

He is at the capering, eloquent stage of drunkenness, and he hones in on Katherine, raising his swaying cup in her direction.

'Goodwife Everingham!' he calls. 'Goodwife Everingham! I am delighted to see you again, here in our castle. I feared for your safety after the tidings of my Lord of Somerset's latest debacle! I feared your abundant physical charms would prove too much of a temptation for my Lord of Montagu's common soldiery, and the usual indiscriminate intimacy would be forced upon your person, but no! Here you are, eh? Safe and sound in the arms of your – your – your husband here.'

It is still not clear if he believes Katherine is Thomas's wife, and now he stares at her with no restraint while taking another nip of his drink, and after Thomas asks if he knows Payne's whereabouts, it is as if Grey's lips are numb, and he cannot form the word 'physician', so after trying it a few times, he stops, and he grins at them glassily, and he bows, and gestures that they are to pass on their way up the steps to the solar beyond. As they pass him, he makes a clumsy grab for Katherine, but Thomas shelters her, and Grey misses and staggers and they leave him smiling delightedly at the wall, propped against it with one arm, just as if he might be pissing upon its footings.

They find Payne in the solar above, sitting alone at a board, in the dim light of a rush lamp.

'Who is it?' he asks, and then: 'God save us,' when they enter the lamp's radius and he sees who they are. 'What have you brought me this time?'

'She is — I don't know.'

'Make a bed,' he says. 'Carefully.'

And Thomas and Jack and one-armed John Stump set to, finding and unrolling a straw mattress from the corner and placing it by the low-burning fire in the chimney place. They watch as Payne leads Katherine to one of the mattresses and she follows and he lies her down with her boots over the far end so as to keep it clean.

'Come,' he tells Thomas, 'and take this.'

He passes him a rush. Thomas holds it up over Katherine and in its sombre glow, she looks ready to be washed for her winding sheet.

'She will be all right?'

Payne grunts. He starts touching parts of her body.

'What have you been doing with her?' Payne asks.

'We had to get away from Hexham,' he says.

'You rode? She stinks of horses. You all do. And Christ, what have you been doing? You are covered in blood. Look at you.'

'We met a man who felt we had an imbalance of humours,' Jack says, and Payne looks up at him from under his brows.

'Phlebotomy is not something to trifle with,' he says.

Jack laughs.

Payne presses an ear to Katherine's breast. When he kneels and lifts his head he sees her new knife, there in her belt, and he takes it and holds it up.

'Mine,' he says.

'We took it from the man who tried to kill us,' Jack says.

'One of Riven's?' Payne asks.

Thomas nods.

'Why is he here?' he asks. 'Why has he not come out for King Edward?'

Payne shrugs.

'Biding his time, I suppose.'

'Christ,' is all Thomas can say.

'When we reached here the King was mightily pleased to see Riven, you know? He embraced him and called him his right well-beloved subject and so on, and his men – he had but a few of them – stood staring. They were keeping the castle almost alone then, and it would have been obvious to leave Riven as castellan of this place, but Grey had extracted a promise from King Henry on the road up here that he would be made castellan, and for once King Henry kept his word, so now Grey is castellan, which I thought would be a bitter blow for Riven, but Riven just laughed, which made Grey reach for his dagger. You know what he is like. He did not actually draw it, of course. King Henry soothed him, as best as he was able, but now Grey keeps himself here, while Riven is ensconced with the king in the keep.'

'How many men has he?'

'Riven? I cannot say. Neither has enough to hold the castle on his own against the other. I think that is the only thing that keeps the peace.'

'They could kill each other,' Jack says, 'Riven and Grey, and then we could all be off.'

Payne scoffs.

John Stump asks if he has any tidings from Hexham.

'Well, the Duke of Somerset has run his final race,' Payne tells them. 'He was caught in the woods fast by the field, and this time there was no mercy. Montagu had his head from his shoulders the very next day, in Hexham marketplace.'

'Ha!' John says, proved right.

Then Payne turns to Thomas, while his fingers feel under Katherine's jaw. He sniffs her breath. He frowns.

'When did she last eat?'

Thomas shrugs.

'It has been hard,' he says.

Payne grunts.

'Hungerford and Roos were taken, too, you know?' Payne says. 'They will seek King Edward's grace, of course, and probably get it too, for all the advantage they've afforded Montagu.'

'And Tailboys?' Thomas asks.

'Tailboys? I have heard nothing of him since last I saw him at Hexham, but he was always lucky, wasn't he? Knowing him he has probably been carried south in a litter covered with cloth of gold. Now. Listen. All of you. Get out of here. I need to take Goodwife Everingham's urine and she will not thank me if I make a public show of it.'

As they move towards the door, Thomas asks once again if she will be all right.

'I cannot say, Thomas,' Payne tells him. 'But she is with child, and whereas she should be living carefully, nursing her strength for what is to come, she's been living badly these last few months. These last years even. Have you seen the scars on her back? No. Well. Anyway. She is strong in spirit, we have all seen that, but she is much depleted in body, and she needs to regain her strength. She needs ale, and bread, and meat. Things to nourish her. We will not find them here.'

'I will do what I can,' Thomas says, and Payne nods.

'Good,' he says. 'Good.'

But Thomas can see he is doubtful.

'Come back in the morning,' he says, and they look at one another, and Thomas remembers what Payne said, that everyone has something to hide, and he nods and he walks away, trusting Master Payne in all matters.

26

She recalls almost nothing of how she comes to be under a blanket in linen sheets under the smooth white plaster of a curving ceiling, and it is only when she sees Thomas standing at the tall narrow window, looking southwards, the sun on his face, dark red hair with its white patch, freshly shaved, in cleanish clothes he might have borrowed from another man, that she remembers much of anything at all.

She says nothing. She wants to lie still and watch him, to remember him like this, remember him calm, and apparently at peace. He is watching something with interest. Time passes. She can hear birds, and men chattering not too far away, and then the slow shush of the sea against the beach. There is a gentle breeze through the window, and the sun slants down across the floor to light a slice of one of Payne's coffers and on it is a mug and a spray of dried herbs bound at the stems by another stem. She wonders what they are, but only vaguely.

'What is happening without?' she asks. Her voice slips and slides. It has not been used in an age.

He turns to her with a great smile.

'You are awake,' he says, smiling at the stupidity of the comment.

'Yes,' she says. 'Fooof. How long have I slept?'

'A while,' he says.

'I am hungry,' she tells him.

'We have fed you ale only,' he says. 'Nothing solid.'

She tries to remember. She sees only vague interludes, peopled by vague shades, Payne and Thomas, perhaps, pushing her, pulling her, lifting, lowering, a low susurrus of deep voices and always, until now, warm release back into deepest slumber.

He comes and brings her some ale and there is also bread.

'No wonder then,' she says, tearing a piece off. Her fingers feel weak, and her teeth loose. She lets the ale soften the bread before swallowing. Thomas beams at her still, but there is a noise beyond the window and his eye is drawn that way.

'What is happening without?' she asks.

He stands and crosses back to the narrow window.

'The Earl of Warwick is positioning his guns, I believe.'

'The Earl of Warwick? He is here already? With his guns?'

She tries to sit up but she's too weak. How long have I been here?

'He has been bringing them up all this morning,' Thomas tells her. 'But stay. Master Payne insists. I will describe them to you. There are two very big ones, monsters, each needing three teams of oxen if they are to be moved, and there are many more besides, smaller but just as long, and like to throw a ball further, I believe. There must be twenty in total, I suppose. And there are many thousand men, and horses, too.'

'Dear God!'

'Oh, do not fret,' he says. 'They will not be fired. They are here for show. To prove Warwick means business. He will now offer terms, and Sir Ralph Grey will accept them, for he has no choice, and he will be afforded the King Edward's grace, as will we all, and then the gates will be thrown open, and we can leave this place at last. We can all go home.'

Home. Where is that? She closes her eyes again for a moment. She does not want to think about that.

'What about King Henry?' she asks. 'What will happen to him?'

'He has already left us,' Thomas says with a shrug. 'Three days since. After Dunstanburgh capitulated. Grey insisted he would be safer elsewhere, so he rode away in the night with just a handful of his gentlemen, and those two priests. No one is saying where, but there can't be many places, can there, in this country anyway, or across the Narrow Sea?'

She is silent for a while, thinking. Trying to imagine the scene.

'What did Riven say to that?'

'There was nothing he could do,' Thomas tells her. 'He was outnumbered two to one, and King Henry himself – he wanted to go. Riven lacked the strength to be seen to harm him or his interests, so he stood with clenched teeth and watched it happen. The sight of that has sustained me, I can tell you.'

She manages a sibilant chuckle. Thomas returns to looking out of the window. She holds up her arms. They are encased in linen. For a moment she does not know if she is a man or a woman.

'What day is it?' she asks.

'Yesterday was the feast of St John,' he says.

She cannot believe it has been so long.

'What have you been doing in the meantime?' she asks. He is looking well, she thinks, as if he has been eating enough for once.

'I have been hunting every day, even the Sabbath. Payne has ordered it and Grey lets me, knowing you are here, and that I won't try to ride south. It has let me avoid Riven, and his men, too.'

'But the siege? Warwick's men?'

'They have just gathered these last days. They have been at Dunstanburgh, and now it is our turn. It is – civilised.'

'That is a relief. And what of Master Payne? How is he?'

'He is well. He has been here every day. Tended to you in person.'

She sees, and feels vaguely ashamed. She lets her hand rest on her tummy. It is rounded a little bit, and she who knows her own body best, feels other subtle changes too. Either that or she has been fed March ale for a month. She had thought for a moment, on waking, that perhaps she was not pregnant after all, or that perhaps she had lost the baby, or any number of alternatives, but when

they were dismissed, one by one, and she was left with the knowledge that the baby was still there, she felt, for the first time probably,
a sense of satisfaction and even pleasure.

She tries to get up again, and Thomas comes to her side and helps
her and this time she makes it. She hobbles to the window; her body
feels soft and boneless. She rests on the stone of the window ledge
and looks out.

'Good Lord,' she says.

'Yes,' he agrees. 'There are a lot of them.'

Through the stone arch, two bowshots away, is a sea of men, a
tide of them swirling around the rocks of those great guns, and their
tents, hundreds of them, stretching almost as far as she can see. At
their fore edge are the long bodies of five or six guns, but two are
much larger than the others, and they are being canted around by
slow-plodding wheeling teams of oxen, and she wonders if she can
hear the carters' whips from here. Men are digging the guns' rears
in, lowering their hindquarters and piling the rock and earth in front,
raising their forequarters above breastwork of woven hazel. Soon
she will be staring at the guns' big black mouths.

'So you see, we are surrounded,' Thomas says. 'They even have
ships out at sea.'

'But you say I am not to fret?'

'Grey says King Edward will not want this castle harmed in any
way. He says it is too near Scotland for that, and it is necessary for
the defence of the realm, so—'

Thomas shrugs.

'It is just something they have to do, he says. He says they – the
Earl of Warwick and King Edward – will offer terms, just as they
have done at all the other castles – Alnwick and Dunstanburgh
over there, which have already opened their gates to King Edward
– and now King Henry is gone, Grey will accept them. He admits
he more or less has to, whatever they are, and then we will have
to lay down our weapons, open the gates and walk out, and

Warwick's soldiers will be there to mock us and so on, but after that we will be free.'

She nods. She notices he does not use the word 'home' again. But still the question of what happens then looms between them, and she knows instinctively that in the time since last they spoke of this Thomas has come up with no plan further than 'it will be all right'. She watches him studying the view through the window, and she sees how bright his eyes are, and she imagines what he can see, and she supposes it is the Earl of Warwick's army, and she is taken back to an earlier summer, a happy and now seemingly carefree time when they were with Sir John Fakenham's company and everything seemed so simple. She recalls the busy little Earl of Warwick with a tinge of distaste, but then she remembers the boy who has since become King Edward, and she remembers a lanky youth with a glint in his eye. Everything seemed a laugh to him, she thought, until it wasn't, and then it was in deadly earnest. He had valued Thomas, she remembers, and she wonders if Thomas is thinking about him now, and she supposes he must wish he were not stuck here, with her, when he could be out there.

'Have you any tidings of the ledger?' she asks.

'No,' he says, dropping his gaze. 'Even though King Henry has gone, the keep is still guarded, and if I go up there, the captain will recognise me. The last time I saw him I was stained with blood from the men who attacked us in the outward postern gate tower.'

She can remember virtually nothing of the fight, and he shows her the scar on his arm as proof it happened.

'And Jack is unharmed?' she asks.

'Yes,' Thomas says. 'We have been hunting together, one of us on the lookout for something to shoot, the other for any of Riven's men come looking for us.'

'Do they know you killed those three men?'

'Not yet,' he says. 'Riven has accused Grey of ordering it, which Grey has denied of course, but he has hardly tried to discover the

403

truth of it. He also saw us that night, with their blood on us, but he was drunk, and cannot recall, or has chosen not to, so all we have had to do is avoid the captain of the guard of the keep—'

'—which has meant you have not been into the keep to see if there is any sign of the ledger.'

'Exactly.'

'I know Riven has it,' she says. 'I just know it. I don't know why, but I just do.'

He tells her about the knife they took from Riven's men being the one stolen from Master Payne. She nods. It is as they suspected. Riven's men were given free access to Master Payne's goods, and took what they wanted.

'But why the ledger? It looked valueless, and there were all Master Payne's clothes hanging there. His cloaks. His shirts. Everything. All of it so much more covetable than a battered old book.'

Thomas shrugs.

'They must have taken it for fire splints,' he says again.

She shakes her head.

'There was something he said,' she says.

'But if he has it,' Thomas says, 'he cannot have grasped its significance. If he had done so, he would have already taken it to King Henry, surely? And now he's gone, so . . . ?'

He shrugs.

'What would he do now,' she begins, 'if he realised its significance? Riven.'

They are silent for a moment, thinking, and she supposes that with King Henry's power so diminished there is no one to make use of the ledger's secret.

'He should destroy it,' Thomas says. 'If he has not already done so. He will not want King Edward to find that he knows such a secret as that.'

She nods, remembering the threats of tongue-tearing and foot-burning, and she sees this makes sense, but – but now that his other schemes have come to nothing and Riven has neither the King nor Bamburgh in his hands — might he not cling to this last weapon? Might he not secrete it somewhere, storing it against the uncertainty of the future? After all, there is no telling where King Henry has gone. It might be across the sea to find allies in France or Burgundy, it might be to Scotland. And there is no guarantee that Horner's much longed-for rising across the country will not come to pass, especially if it can be proved that King Edward is not his father's son, and should not occupy the throne. And if it were widely known, how then would the Earl of Warwick feel about supporting a king with no right to his crown? If the ledger's secret were to surface, might that not drive a wedge between King Edward and his mighty subject?

'So he is sitting in the keep,' Thomas says, 'just keeping out of trouble until Grey capitulates to the Earl of Warwick, and then he will march out with us, only he will be greeted by his son, and he will be honoured and rewarded for at least trying to hand King Henry over, and at least trying to take Bamburgh for them.'

'And his reward will be Cornford Castle.'

'It is not so great a reward as he was hoping, perhaps, but it is enough.'

'Yes,' she says. 'I suppose it is, but where does it leave us?'

Thomas shrugs.

'I don't know,' he says, 'but it will be all right. I know it.'

She looks at him, then out at the guns and all the many thousands of men and their banners that snap in the breeze of the sea. Christ, she thinks. Christ. I hope you are right.

'I think I shall have to lie down now,' she says, and he leads her back to her mattress and he pulls up the blanket.

'And you are really certain the guns will not be fired?' she asks and he smiles down at her in a manner she knows is intended to be reassuring, and then he bends and kisses her forehead and he tells her he is absolutely certain the guns will not be fired, and she smiles, for she trusts him in this at least, and she places her hand on her belly, closes her eyes and goes to sleep.

The first stone is fired just before midday on the following day. The noise of the explosion in the gun rolls over them like thunder that seems to come and go, lasting unnaturally long, setting the seagulls wheeling and screaming above the heads of the men who are clutching their ears. It falls just short of its target, but it is not a complete waste, for the stone – black and round and large enough that only a tall man might get both his arms around it – skips across the ground between the meres and hits the footings of the southward curtain wall with a sharp crack and enough force to send a shower of dust and stones higher than the battlements above. The shock of its impact ripples through the castle with a clink of loosened masonry and a falling cloud of dust. The first smell is of hot, chipped stone but that is replaced by a sulphurous stink that makes them all think of hell itself.

'Haha!' Grey roars. 'Haha! They've not the elevation!'

'That is one head gone,' a man beside him mutters.

Grey turns on him. 'Shut up!' Grey shouts. 'Damn you! Shut up!'

The next shot, from the second of the two big guns, is louder than the first, and this time the charge is perfected, or the angle is made right, and the ball thrums as it comes. It hits the southern curtain wall halfway up, a hundred paces to their right, and there is an instant burst of dust and the air is filled with fizzing missiles – chunks of fractured stone and cement – and the castle walls tremble, and then there is a slide of clinking stones from the spot where the stone collided, and the larger blocks fall to land with a thud Thomas can feel through his boot soles.

'Two heads,' another mutters.

'God damn you!' Grey roars. 'I will have the next man's head myself!'

Thomas and Jack are already wondering if they want to remain on the tower's top when a third gun is fired. This is smaller, and it throws a lighter stone which they hear throbbing through the air, passing over their heads, and they spin around to see it hit an inner wall with another boiling swirl of dust and stone. No one is injured, for there is no one nearby, but when the dust clears, the crater in the wall is as round as a man is tall, of very pale stone, and after a moment the line of masonry above it slumps, and its dressed blocks slide forward and the wall collapses along its length.

'God's holy wounds,' someone murmurs. They look at one another. Then at Grey, who is still there, waving his gloved fist at the guns, bellowing some incoherent defiance. None of the other men join him, and after a moment, one by one, they begin stepping through the door to the steps that will take them down from the tower's top and to the safety of below. Thomas and Jack join them.

'Could pray for rain, I suppose,' a man mutters.

'Or for a lucky shot to carry Sir Ralph away,' another says.

'By Christ,' yet another adds, 'it should never have come to this.'

And he is right.

When Warwick's herald rode across from camp to castle, the day before, Thomas had been behind the battlements of the main gatehouse, with Sir Ralph Grey and the man he'd made his deputy in Riven's place: Sir Humphrey Neville of Brancepeth, who had come to the castle late and was blamed for the early botched ambush of Montagu before the battle on Hedgeley Moor. They were both drinking Grey's distillation and they were already quite drunk as they watched the heralds coming up the track, led by a man with the Earl of Warwick's coat of arms on his tabard, and another carrying his lord's banner.

Grey would not let the men into the castle, lest they see how poorly provisioned they were in both men and material, and so Warwick's herald pulled his horse up below the main gatehouse, and craned his neck up to the battlements. His coat was blazingly ornate, a composition of past coats of arms that served as a testament to his lord's ancestry, and he was finely harnessed, though he carried no weapons, and he was escorted by ten other men in Warwick's simple red livery, equally well arrayed in plate, equally unarmed, but on good roan horses. The matching horses was a typical Warwick touch, Thomas thought, until Grey arrived with a few of his gentlemen, and he was shunted aside to make way for better men to have better views. He went to sit with Katherine, and so listened to the negotiations unfold sitting on her mattress, his hand on her ankle.

Grey and the herald were previously known to one another, and so they began with a strained exchange of formal pleasantries that stuck in both their craws. Then Warwick's herald asked for the keys of the castle in the name of his dread sovereign Edward, rightful King of these Isles and this Commonwealth, and Grey, not quite yet eloquent with drink, had called down to him that he could not understand a word he was saying for he had a turd in his teeth. Warwick's herald then asked if Henry of Lancaster, late king of the realm, was within. Again Grey claimed to be unable to make sense of what the man was saying.

Warwick's herald retained his patience. He'd pointed to the line of Warwick's men and the guns that were being sighted and he'd reminded Grey of their power. Grey had laughed and asked what such a power might do to walls this thick, and then he'd boasted that he had many thousands of men and provisions enough to endure a siege indefinitely.

'I am not sent to argue with you,' the herald had called up. 'I am here to relay the King's offer.'

'Very well,' Grey had called down, feigning boredom. 'Which is what?'

'That in return for the keys to the gatehouse, his most gracious sovereign Edward will grant life and liberty to all men who lay down their arms and seek his merciful grace.'

There was a pause during which Sir Humphrey Neville said 'Ha!' and he and Grey both breathed a stifled gasp of relief.

But Warwick's herald was not finished.

'Save,' he'd gone on with sombre relish, 'save the persons of Sir Ralph Grey and Sir Humphrey Neville of Brancepeth, who will remain out of King Edward's favour and without redemption.'

Both Grey and Neville had looked at one another. They were both very pale, but small florid patches enlivened Grey's sunken cheeks, and then both men went for the jug at the same time, and each yielded to the other, as if a show of kindness now might somehow redeem them. Once Grey had drunk, he steeled himself, and he gripped the window's frame, and extended his head to shout all the more loudly at the herald.

'Damn your Earl of Warwick! Curse him! A thousand bloody damnations on his bloody head!' he bellowed at the herald. 'Do you hear me? I wish him dead. I wish him every hell! I will see him rot! I will see him strangled in the goddamned marketplace! I will see his corpse mauled by dogs in four corners of the kingdom! Let him come! Let him try to get us! By Christ! By Christ! By Christ!'

'You will not yield then?'

'No!' Gray shouted back. 'You do your worst, you dog! You jumped-up little bastard son of a whore! You treacherous coward! You do your worst. My men are loyal and my walls stronger yet. So, no! I do not yield.'

'Very well,' the herald called, and he rode a few paces from the castle walls and then turned his horse back, as if to address everyone within.

'Then hear this!' he'd shouted. 'All of you. Every man. Listen to this, for it applies to you all. Because we stand so near our ancient enemy Scotland, our most dread sovereign lord King Edward especially desires to have this jewel of a castle kept whole and unbroken.'

He'd gestured behind him at the guns.

'If you are cause of our guns being fired against these walls, then for every strike, one of you will have your head struck from his shoulders. None exempted. From castellan to spit boy!'

There was a bleak silence. Even the birds were quiet. And every man there watched Warwick's herald turn, finished, and ride back to his camp with his escort, and there was not one of them who did not wish he were among them.

So now the fourth stone comes. This one flubbers across the meres. It does not even hit the slope but sends a great slough of water up and once again the birds take wing and wheel about, screaming in the sky.

'That doesn't count,' Jack says.

But the fifth cracks into the south-eastern wall again, and this time Thomas feels it in his teeth.

'Christ,' he says, and then there is a cascade of stonework, and a gap appears in the wall through which they can see the beach. Across the meres there is a billow of black smoke drifting slowly above the troops.

'Katherine!' Thomas says.

And he and Jack set off down the winding steps.

'We can move her up to the keep,' Jack says.

Thomas thinks of Riven, lurking there like a spider.

But when they get there, Katherine is in her blue dress, and has her head dressed in linen, and she is unsteady on her feet after so long in bed, and she is plainly scared. Payne is with her, his arms filled with his things. Around them Grey's servants are bustling about collecting books and ewers and a plate of pewter, and tossing them in wicker chests.

'We're moving to the northward gate,' she says.

There is another great crack from across the fields and the servants duck. The stone hits the wall below and a candleholder jumps on a coffer.

'By all the saints,' one of them says. 'That is another head!'

410

'Why is he doing it?' Katherine says. 'Warwick is mad. All he had to do was tell Grey he would be spared. He could have lied. He could have avoided all this.'

He takes her hand just as another stone clips the battlements of the southern wall with a spray of rubble, and thick dust drifts in the air like a heavy rain. Someone starts screaming.

'Should we help?' Katherine asks.

'There is nothing to be done,' Payne tells her.

Grey comes up the steps. He is red-faced with drink, back to his furious best, railing against Riven who will not let them move to the keep.

'Dear God!' he says. 'He was much more tolerable when he was sweating with pain in his stinking little chamber. Now he is strong enough to practise his swordplay, have you seen him? Out in the bailey with a hand-and-a-half, or that bloody pollaxe of his, making all these grotesque moves as if he were a German dance master.'

'Is he out there now?'

'Not if you did not see him. The bastard. He is probably ear deep in a suckling pig. I have to say – he is the only reason I am hanging on here now. If every one of these bloody stones means one of his men gets the chop, so be it! Eventually we will get to him!'

He stops a servant and rummages in one of the wicker trunks and pulls out a large costrel.

'Blow me! I am almost to my last bottle.'

He unstoppers it and they smell his distillation.

Another boulder crumps against the walls. Dust drifts from the ceiling.

'Close,' Grey says. 'I think that was one of the big chaps – "Newcastle", perhaps, or "London". Next one'll be "Dijon", I'd wager.'

There is sand in Thomas's mouth.

'We can't just stand here,' Payne says. He is deathly pale, shaking.

Grey takes a long swig, almost emptying the bottle. He gasps afterwards and shudders. His eyes are instantly bright and his outlook, too.

Another stone.

'*Jesu!*' Payne cries. He is weeping now.

'Pull yourself together, man,' Grey says. 'Have some of this.'

He passes the bottle to Payne, who holds it to his pursed lips and takes a sip that makes him cough and his eyes water. He passes the costrel to Thomas.

'We should arm ourselves,' Grey declares. 'Put on harness and sally out. We could do battle with them in a place of our own choosing. Not be stuck here like voles in a bucket.'

Thomas drinks and is forced to gasp.

'Good, isn't it?' Grey says. 'D'you know, if I get out of this alive, I might go into trade. Set a son up, perhaps, or a daughter, and sell this stuff for proper coin. A groat a go. As was drunk by St Christopher himself. Why not?'

Another crash makes them all jump. Grey shakes the costrel. It is empty.

'You bugger!' he says to Thomas. 'Finishing my supplies! Lucky I've another. Ahah.'

And he turns just as two more servants pass with another hinged coffer, and he stops them and opens it and fishes out a bag. It is a long-strapped bag, shiny with wear, with a mended hole in its side. Katherine gasps, and Thomas finds too late that he has taken a stride forward and has snatched the bag from Grey's hands.

'What the——? You!' And Grey is reaching for his knife, but Thomas ignores him. His heart is thundering but as he unties the points he already knows it is not the ledger within, from the weight and shape of the thing, and sure enough, it is a leather bottle, a costrel of Grey's distillation. Grey makes no move, but stands clutching the knife and glaring at Thomas with his nostrils flared and the blade shaking in his hand.

Thomas hands the bag and bottle back. 'Sorry,' he says, 'I thought—'

'What did you think, you little weasel? Snatching it from me like that. I was going to offer you some, as a Christian gentleman, but I do not think I will now.'

'Do you mind telling us where you acquired the bag?' Katherine asks.

Grey is calmed by her politeness.

'This? Why?'

Another stone hits the castle, close enough to make the table jump, and Thomas thinks he can hear the stones of the wall and ceiling grind against one another like loose teeth. Grit falls from the rafters. Payne begins a prayer.

'It contained something that we lost,' Katherine tells Grey, straightening up from where she had ducked. 'Something we held dear.'

'Something *you* held dear?'

'It was ours,' Thomas says, too quickly.

Grey looks at him through compressed eyes.

'I got it from Giles Riven,' he says.

'He stole it from us.'

'Did he? Did he now?'

He stares at them. He is trying to make up his mind about something.

'It is just a book,' Thomas says.

Grey scoffs.

'Is it?' he says. 'Just a book? Where did you come by it?'

Thomas and Katherine look to one another. Can it be that Grey knows its value?

'We were given it,' Katherine tells him.

'Given it! Given it! By? A man? A man you met? In an inn?'

Neither says a word.

'But do you know what it is? What it shows?'

Again, neither answers.

413

'Dear God,' he says. 'You know! You brought it here, and you – dear God. So it is true. It took me a while to see what it is, d'you know? But I knew what to look for, didn't I? The moment I saw it, I thought, ahhhh! Sir Ralph, this is it. This is it. Now you can check, see if that fucking Frenchman was telling the truth.'

He lets the bag drop by his feet and as he unstoppers the bottle he watches them with glassy eyes, his Adam's apple bobbing twice, three times. Christ, Thomas thinks, how can he stand it? When he finishes he wipes his mouth with the back of his hand.

'You know what he told me?' he says. 'That Frenchman? Billbourne? Blayburgh? Name like that. He told me something I'll never forget. Thought he was lying at the time. Nearly killed him for it, though by Christ he was a big fellow. I thought, no. He is a liar. Not Proud Cis. He means some other lord's lady. She would not lie with an animal such as this. Not a French animal such as him. Blaybourne?'

He looks at the bottle again. He smiles at it. Then up at them.

'Do you think the Earl of Warwick will let me live? I was thinking. If I gave him this book. I've got it here somewhere.'

He looks around. There are fewer and fewer places it could be. Another stone. A sprinkling of dust from shifting rafters.

'Where is it?' Thomas asks.

Grey's head seems to wobble. He grins. He is wholly drunk again. He waves his arm to indicate the room. A servant returns, crouched over. He is about to take a coffer.

'Don't take that!' Grey says. 'I need it. I need it to just . . .'

And he sits on it with a gusty sigh and looks up at them, pleased with himself.

Thomas and Katherine stare at one another. She nods. He starts to walk toward Grey, and he means to help him to his feet, so that she can retrieve the ledger from the coffer beneath, when there is a huge din and suddenly the room makes no sense. The floor seems to have been whipped from under him. It yaws and he finds himself staggering as the planks fall away. There is a tremendous noise and the wall comes billowing in toward him. It is almost as if liquid. Until he smacks against it and his cry for Katherine is not even half-formed before it is cut off. He is thrown back and out and down and out into the darkness. He can feel booming pain in his arms and his legs and his chest and his face and he cannot breathe and then – nothing.

27

Thomas wakes in total darkness. He cannot move. Not even his eyelids. He does not know if they are open or closed. He is being pressed from all directions, lain upon, flattened, pushed, pulled. Pain throbs and flares in every part of his body. With each beat of his heart it seems to course up and down his limbs. Boom boom. Boom boom. But he is alive, at least, he thinks, though for how long and to what purpose, he cannot say. He is conscious though. He can feel grit between his teeth. He spits. The spit does not come back on him. He is lying face down. Well, that is something. He moves the fingers of his right hand. It is by his right hip. Dust and dirt. The same with the left hand, though they are flung out behind him on the left. They feel as if they are moving. Then he moves his hands. They flap as they should. He draws his left hand towards himself. It is blocked by something hard and angular. A block of dressed stone, a rafter, something like that. He tries to roll on to one side. He can. He is not trapped. It is only that – by Christ it hurts. Now he can see daylight. It is grey, swirling, and it stings his eyes. It settles on him like grit. It is grit. He spits again. And again. He is on his right side now. He lifts his head. He can hear voices. They are very vague. Not distant. Just muffled. Then there are hands. A man in hose and short boots, russet doublet under a russet jack. Thomas feels himself explored, felt for handholds. Strong hands under his arm, and then another one cradling his head. He is being pulled out. Dragged out. He feels plucked from something, though not so cleanly.

'You lucky bastard!' the man is saying. 'Look at that!'

Thomas is held up. More hands. Someone slapping his chest.

'Give him some water.'

'Sit him down. Careful!'

He has to cough. It is burning and hacking.

'That's right, get it out. By the Mass, you've eaten a bloody brick.'

Thomas feels the water turning all the dust into mud in his mouth.

'Steady!'

He opens his eyes fully. Looks up. Closes them again. Opens one. It is less gritty than the other. He aches all over.

'Katherine,' he says.

'What? What's he saying?'

'Katherine?'

He stands.

'Whoa! Sit down, boy. You're bleeding from every bit of your body!'

'Katherine!'

He is standing outside, behind where the eastward gatehouse used to be. Its wreckage is all around him, a slew of masonry and stone and spars and rafters. There are tiles. Broad sheets of slate. Tiles. Plaster dust. Lengths of splintered wood. The gatehouse has lost its top storey and is a stump, a gap in the already pocked wall. He can see a booted leg. He clambers toward it and then stops. He does not want to tread on anyone. The three men with him look uncertain.

'How many of you were there?' one asks.

Thomas tries to think.

'Five,' he says. 'No. Six. No. Five.'

He looks around. For a few moments the world is swimming, floating; up is down and down is up. It slips and spins. He is dizzy.

'Katherine!'

There is nothing. Thomas picks his way to the booted leg. He knows it is Payne.

'Help me,' he says and after a moment they do. They come

awkwardly over the blocks and rubble and they help him with a long beam that they shift away to expose Payne below. He is dead, bleeding from his nose and his ears. Even his eyes.

Thomas feels grief welling within him like an illness. It is not for Payne, though. It is for himself and for what he knows he will find when he lifts the next stone, or the one after that.

'Katherine! Katherine!'

He starts pulling at stones, hurling them behind him. He hefts a rafter and levers it away. The three men are impressed.

'Must be an archer,' one mutters.

'Handy for this sort of thing,' the other says.

'Let's give him a hand. Who're we looking for?'

'Stupid question.'

They begin, all four of them, to work from one edge toward the gatehouse. Some pieces are too big to move.

'Least there's no one under that one.'

They leave Payne undisturbed.

He calls her name constantly. His hands and shoes are torn and they were right: he is bleeding from every inch. He leaves smears of blood, and dust turns to thick mud.

'Katherine!'

He finds the stone Warwick's gunners used. It is a rough ball, chipped by many hammers, and it is cracked, and has fallen apart into two almost perfect half-spheres. But Katherine is not there.

He stops and looks up. The men are puzzled.

'You sure, mate? Five of you?'

Could they be on the first floor? Still in the solar? He scrambles up the pile of broken building and on to the first floor. He sees Grey straight away. On his back. Half in, half out of the blocks, a rafter across his belly, mouth open, dust so thick on his face – even on his tongue – that he might be an unpolished statue. He is still clutching the costrel of spirit. Thomas feels a moment of savagery. You brought this on yourself, he wants to shout. You brought this on yourself. He clenches his eyes but cannot stop the tears squeezing out. If only you had died sooner, he thinks.

He stands. He takes the costrel from Grey's not quite limp grasp, wipes the top, takes a long pull. Christ, it is strong. It burns all the way to his stomach. One of the other men has climbed up to join him. Thomas offers him the drink and the man doesn't mind if he does. But before he drinks, he stops, and gestures with his hand. Pointing. There. Thomas looks. And oh, Christ. There she is. Her feet, in her grey woollen socks. Her shoes have gone. She is face down, under a pile of slates and beams. Thomas scrambles over. He starts tearing at the slates, sending them slipping away. They slide down the staircase to the floor below.

There is a shout.

'For the love of God! Thomas!'

It is Jack, alive, knocked down the steps.

'Help!' Thomas shouts at him. 'Help me. She's trapped.'

And Jack comes slowly scrambling up the steps on all fours. He is bleeding from a cut on his forehead, and his eyes are bloodshot, and his left hand does not seem to be working so he is like a limping dog as he comes. When he is there, he helps as best he can, dragging stones away one-handed, splintered beams and a piece of broken rafter.

'Careful,' Thomas says. 'Careful.'

After a moment she is clear. There is nothing across her, unlike the other two. He stands and he does not know what to do. Dust crumbles from her dress.

Oh, thank God. She is breathing. She is alive.

'Katherine?'

He bends so that he is by her face.

'Katherine?'

Her eyes flicker. She is definitely alive. He can hear the soft whistle of her breath. Her spit darkens the dust on her skin.

'Help me,' he tells Jack, but the other man steps in.

'Let me,' he says. 'You look – like you've seen better days, mate, that arm of yours?'

They both look to see a long splinter sticking from the meat of Jack's arm. It goes right the way through and out the other side.

'Don't take it out,' Thomas says. He has learned something, he thinks.

One of the others is on the first floor now, picking his way through the debris toward them.

'A woman?' he asks.

'His wife,' Jack says.

'Oh.'

'We need a plank,' Thomas tells them. He has seen this done before. They find a bench, the seat of which will do, and the legs are already broken off. They place it next to her and lift her up and on to it as gently as the four of them are able. It is not easy work. The rubble is thigh high, and it slips and falls away down the steps and over the side of the wall. When they have her on the bench they carry that.

'Which way?'

They go down the outside of the gatehouse, stepping on the slew of the broken building, passing her down. She slips and they should have tied her to the bench but they save her from falling again, and they carry her away from all the rubble and they lay her on the worn grass of the inner bailey.

'Where's Master Payne?' Jack asks.

Thomas shakes his head.

'Pity,' Jack says.

You could say that, Thomas thinks.

'So what d'you want to do with her?' one of the men asks. 'Can't leave her out here.'

As he says that, there is another crack and then the distant rippling boom of a gun.

'Newcastle,' the man says. 'Third time today, that is.'

'We should lay her on her side,' Thomas says, 'so she can breathe.'

'All right.'

They roll her over.

'Use this,' the man says, and he pulls out a fat book from a shattered coffer. The ledger. He brushes the dirt and dust from it, and he slides it under her head. A gift from the Pardoner.

'Made for the job,' he says.

Katherine is very pale. Very still. But she is breathing. Shallow little gasps. As if to breathe in deeply is too painful.

'What d'you reckon?' one of them asks. 'She going to pull through?'

No one has an answer.

Thomas cannot stop himself weeping so he stands and moves away from them, walking around in a circle, tears dripping, mouth loose and square, snot in his beard. He can't help but gesticulate his hopelessness and he starts talking, beginning one word before finishing another, a series of questions. Self-sorrow, despair, grief, but at least he feels no physical pain. He can sense the others watching him. He knows he could go mad now, and fall to beating the ground and wailing. He could tear his clothes, such as they are, or the skin of his cheeks. He could beat his chest until that bled. And all these things seem sensible. But after a while spent tripping around crying out, nothing has changed and he begins to slide the other way.

'D'you have a surgeon?' he asks the men staring at him.

They shake their heads.

'Ralph Grey's got two,' one says. 'A physician and a surgeon. Though maybe the surgeon went away.'

Jack is looking at Katherine closely.

'If we could find one,' he says, very carefully, 'that would be good.'

'But where? Where? Has Riven got one?'

Thomas knows he hasn't. That is why he used Payne and Katherine.

421

'Old Warwick'll have one,' one of them says. 'Probably have hundreds.'

Jack turns on him.

'What the fuck use is that?'

But he's right, Thomas thinks. Of course the Earl of Warwick will have a surgeon. They must get her to the Earl of Warwick.

'Shouldn't be impossible,' Jack says, 'now Grey's dead.'

But then, suddenly, Grey isn't dead. Suddenly there is a commotion on the floor above. A sneezing and then a truncated cry.

'Christ!'

Thomas thinks he might climb up there now and kill him. But he does not. He lets the others scramble up and they stand around Grey's prone body for a while without doing much, while Thomas just sits in the mud and holds Katherine's hand.

'He's alive, all right,' one of them calls down. 'But he isn't none too clever.'

They shift the beam across him and let it slide down the rubble. Grey is groaning. He sits up and rubs his head. He looks utterly lost and stares around him terrified. He says nothing. They help him to his feet. He needs support. He grimaces and clutches his head, then slips into blankness.

'He's out of his wits.'

'Let's get him down,' one of them says, and they help him negotiate the ramp of shattered masonry and they sit him down next to Katherine and after a moment he lies down and looks up at the seagulls and there is not a scratch on him.

They stand in silence for a moment.

'We need a horse. Two horses.'

Jack says he will get them.

'Be in the stables,' he says. 'I'll bring them up.'

Thomas sits and watches Katherine sipping the air. He listens to the ringing in his ears and there is an occasional crump of a distant gun, but perhaps the big ones are too hot now, and cannot be safely used, for there have been no big stones for a long while, only the little ones, and though he hears them land, he never sees them, so supposes Warwick is using them to pick holes in the curtain walls. He uses Payne's knife to cut some of Grey's linen into long strips and while Grey sits there in silence, alternately grimacing and blank as a pebble, Thomas shuffles over and ties his wrists together. Thomas ties him tight, wrist to wrist. Grey does not move, but he blinks, and a frown appears.

A little while later Jack brings two horses, both saddled, clopping up the track from the stables below. You can see their ribs, and they look half-dead, except their eyes roll and their ears are flattened and they snap their teeth and wave their heads on spindly necks.

'What are you going to do?' Jack asks.

'I am going to trade Grey for a doctor,' Thomas tells him.

Now Jack is looking at him oddly.

'It is all I can do,' Thomas says. 'I will not let her die.'

But Jack's gaze is not on Thomas. It slides past him and over his shoulder. Thomas turns.

It is Riven, of course.

He stands there, and he is in a broad-shouldered velvet gown of very deep red, and he wears hose of deepest blue, and his riding boots are turned down at the knee. Strapped to his belt are a sheathed dagger and a heavy purse. On his head is a broad black cap, sewn with tiny pearls, and on his breast, a white circle in the centre of which flies a delicately stitched raven. He is carrying a pair of gloves. Behind him are three of his men in their usual livery, and one of them is carrying a long sword in a leather scabbard, while the other is carrying the pollaxe.

Seeing it again chills Thomas. It is so lethal, so purposeful and so bent on just one object: the death of a man. It seems to have a personality and presence of its own, and it draws the eye.

Riven stops at the steps and he looks down at Thomas for a long time.

423

Thomas can think of nothing to say. He is unmoving under the gaze.

'Well, well,' Riven says, with a smile forming. 'Well, well. How you've changed, Brother Monk. How you've changed. That's why it took me so long to work it out, to remember where I saw you last.'

'And have you now?'

'Shall I tell you what annoys me most, Brother Monk? Shall I? It is that I won't hear the story – from you – of how you came to be here after all these years. I won't find out your real name, nor where you went after—'

And now he stops.

'What in God's name are you doing with Grey there?'

He looks at the bindings and the horse and he concludes correctly.

'Well, well,' he says, with a regretful admiration. 'You have got there before me, and for once, you have done me a favour. I was just on my way to collar the fool, but what is—'

And he cranes his neck to see who is lying with her back to him on the plank.

'A woman? Here? Who is she?'

'Said it was his wife,' one of the men answers.

'His wife?'

Riven steps around Thomas with a humourless smile. He walks over to Katherine. He walks beyond her, and bends and stares at her. Then he is startled, unable to believe what he is seeing, and he crouches before her and tilts his head to see her properly. After a moment, he rights himself. He is wild and wide-eyed. He looks at Thomas. Then back at her. Then back at Thomas.

'By Christ,' he breathes. 'By Christ. What has gone on here?'

And Thomas says nothing and now Katherine wakes, with the gentlest, most puzzled mewing sound.

'Is this? Is this? Is this who I think it is? Is this Sister Nun? Is that it? Is that what this is?'

And Katherine, hardly moving her head, looks up at him and

424

they look at one another and she tries to say no, perhaps, but it doesn't matter, because he knows the truth of it, if not the why and the how of it, and he says:

'Do you know I promised my son I would do this if I ever saw you again?'

And he kicks her, once, very hard, in her guts.

Thomas has killed the man even before the pain in Katherine's belly subsides. She does not see it, not exactly how it happens, but it isn't difficult to imagine. He moves very fast. He snatches the pollaxe from the startled liveryman's hands, and he is on Sir Giles Riven before Riven can even move. He is just stepping back, and later she will wonder if he was going to take another kick at her, when Thomas comes. She cannot say which part of the pollaxe he uses to hit him first, but she supposes that any part of it, swung with that ferocity, would have killed him.

Riven is thrown to the ground by her feet. His head is absolutely caved in. It is like a rotten apple left to the wasps, except more so. The pollaxe is driven through his head and into the top of his throat. It almost passes through him and comes out above his hip. It bursts his head and rips a great piece off him. It cores him, guts him, brains him, all at once and all in an instant, and it turns him from a human being into just a pile of meat, and if a man found this on the side of the road, or washed up on a beach, a man might think it had been shovelled there, and was part of something else, an offcut of something.

The pollaxe is embedded beyond its langets and it stays that way, sticking up, while blood spreads sluggishly on the ground around the twitching pile of flesh.

No one moves.

Thomas is standing with legs spread wide and there is a great spray of fresh blood across his face, chest and arms.

Riven's men are staring open-mouthed.

'By God,' one of them says. 'You fucking killed him.'

425

And then the one who lost the pollaxe starts an incredulous laugh. 'Wish someone'd done that five years ago.'

Thomas comes and bends over Katherine. His eyes are very white against the blood that marks his face.

'Are you all right?' he asks.

She feels as if something inside has been torn, and that if she moves she will only tear it further. And she feels such a depth of sadness that she can hardly look at him. So she nods her head and closes her eyes, and she hopes no tears will come, and she wonders why she is on a plank.

Then she hears another man come. She hears him shouting from a distance, asking questions in one of those voices, and then she hears him bark with incredulity and then he's silent. He swears once, and then stops. He talks to Grey, asks him questions, slaps him, and seems to get the answer he wants. Thomas tells him something. Then the man goes away and they stand there a moment longer and Thomas drapes a cloak over her, and he says something about it being all right and that it is over now, and that they will take her to a physician and she knows Payne must be dead or else where is he?

Then she hears the axe being removed from Riven and she opens her eyes to see his body slump further, and then she watches two men she does not know helping Sir Ralph Grey on to one of the horses, and he seems very confused, she thinks, and he is looking around as if he is not sure he was ever supposed to be here. And then they lead the horse away and Thomas comes back with some ale for her and she is thirsty and hungry too, so she drinks and she spills some and she says she is sorry and he tells her of course it does not matter and she realises she is resting her head on the ledger, and she also realises he has done it: he has found the ledger and he has killed Riven, and she says: 'Well done, Thomas,' but she cannot have said it very loudly for he has to bend in close to hear.

Then she tries to say goodbye, and to tell him that she loves him, because suddenly, she is certain she is dying.

28

'Sirs!' Thomas shouts. 'Sirs! For the love of God! Please be out of the way!'

He and Jack and John Stump are carrying Katherine on the same bench seat they used to lower her from the wreckage of the great eastward gatehouse, and they are trying to push past men in various liveries who are flooding out of the main gate of the castle, men who have been permitted to leave her walls for the first time in three months, on condition that they lay down their arms and make a solemn oath never to take them up, or make fences against the King's majesty, ever again. This they have gladly done, and now they must endure a lengthy and humiliating walk through the ranks of Warwick's men, who mob the roadside, and jeer at them as they pass.

'Please, sirs!' Thomas calls. 'Make way.'

He has no idea where he must go first, but he knows there will be a physician or a surgeon somewhere in the camp ahead. So he makes his way with the flow, but men are reluctant to let him and Jack past them for fear it will slow them up and mean they have to endure more mockery from the Earl of Warwick's troops for longer. When they reach the camp, when they pass under the snouts of the great guns that are raised up above them, and where the air smells contaminated by the smell of burned powder, the press becomes even worse since now they must go against its flow, and they have no hands with which to bat men away, but must endure collision and subsequent derision. Men laugh and shout, and it feels very

427

dangerous, as if anything could go wrong at any moment for any number of reasons, and the result would be fatal.

'Please, sirs,' Thomas keeps saying. At one point he has to stop. He nearly turns and runs. Ahead are five men in the pale livery of Edmund Riven. They have their heads craned, looking for someone. He ducks his head and he can only pray it is not him they seek, but others in their livery, and that they do not yet know what has happened to Giles Riven. When they are past the five men, Jack calls out.

'See them, Thomas?' he says. 'They'll soon be looking for you, won't they? Edmund Riven won't be happy when he finds out what you've just done to his father.'

The pollaxe, roughly cleaned now, wiped on a dry bit of Riven's cloak, is lying by Katherine's side, its business end by her feet. She is asleep, deathly pale. He is too frightened to check if she is still alive.

'Only take him a day or two to find out who you are,' Jack goes on. 'A couple of questions in the right place. He could even ask Grey, couldn't he? If Warwick lets him live long enough, that is. And Grey's no reason to thank you, has he? Not after you tied him up and turned him over to that Neville of wherever it is to exchange with Warwick for his life and liberty.'

Thomas feels the truth of this settle on him like rainwater.

'Jack,' he says over his shoulder, 'Jack, please, just stop. Please. For the love of God.'

'All right,' Jack says, 'but if I were you, I'd be thinking of – well – elsewhere.'

'I am bloody thinking of elsewhere!' Thomas says. 'It is all that's bloody left to me now.'

Eventually the crowd thins. Then, ahead, are the canvas avenues of tents belonging to the nobility of the Earl of Warwick's army with their banners and flags. If he is to find a physician, this is where they will be. He meets two men who will not let him pass until they have had their moment of fun with him. One of them is horribly scarred down one cheek; a great pock of flesh is missing, with a tail of hardened skin that slides into the collar of his jack. An old arrow wound.

'What you got there?' he asks, as if suspicious they may be looting something before he has first rejected it himself.

'My wife,' Thomas tells them and he turns his head to indicate Katherine on the makeshift stretcher. 'She needs help. A surgeon.'

'A surgeon, is it?'

'Yes. It is urgent.'

'Got any money? No point asking if you haven't.'

Christ, Thomas thinks, Christ! Of course he doesn't have any bloody money.

'No?' the soldier says with a shake of his head. 'Well, then you had better take her to the friars over yon. They might do for her. And if not, then you'll not have far to carry her when it is all over, will you?'

Thomas sees they have a black bull's-head badge on their jacks, and each carries an unnocked bow.

'You are William Hastings's archers?' he asks. He almost doesn't know why, or how he knows the badge, but the two men are proud of it and straighten themselves.

'Lord Hastings, it is now, since three years ago,' the older of two says. 'Who wants to know?'

'I am Thomas Everingham.'

The name means nothing to the younger one, and why should it? But the older one narrows his eyes and looks at Thomas carefully.

'Christ on His cross,' he says. 'Thomas Something. I remember you.'

Thomas feels the air go out of him. Is this good or bad?

'We found you in the woods outside Mortimer's Cross, didn't we?' the archer says. 'Pulled your fat from the fire then, and no

429

mistake. You were with some fancy lady, weren't you? A surgeon herself, I recall.'

Thomas nods mutely. The archer peers around at Katherine. He pulls a face.

'Well, it's her you need now, then, not old Mayhew,' the archer says. 'He can only stitch cuts and grazes, not bring folk back to life.

'If I did not get the chance to thank you,' Thomas says, 'I do so now, and will again, only please, sirs, if you would show me to your surgeon. This Mayhew.'

The archer nods.

'I will,' he says, 'for that woman you were with – she showed kindness to me. This would be a deal worse had she not stitched it up right tight.'

He points to the silvery whorl of his cheek.

'Oh, Christ,' he goes on. 'And I recall you then were favoured by Lord Hastings, yes! And King Edward! You were at the front when the three suns come out weren't you? What a day that was, eh? He rubs his wound as if it aches to be spoken of. Thomas can only nod.

'Please,' he says.'

'But look at us,' the archer says, 'We're dawdling like old soldiers already. Come the fuck on.'

He relieves Thomas of half his burden, joining him at his end of the plank, while Thomas joins Jack at Katherine's feet. She lies eyes-closed, bone-white and she looks halfway to death already. They set off through the jostling crowd again, the archers shouting and bullying their way through the throng.

'Stand aside! Mind your backs! A Hastings! A Hastings there!'

Thomas feels the weight of sorrow shift in his guts. Mayhew, he thinks. Mayhew. He is taking her to see Mayhew, and Sir John Fakenham, and then , of course, inevitably Richard Fakenham. The man who believes himself to be her husband. Oh Christ. What is he doing? What will they say when they recognise her? They will see she is this Lady Margaret Cornford whom they believed dead. They will recognise that she is not as dead as was thought? They will want her back! They will want her back! They will take her back! She will no longer be his. He almost stops then. He raises his face to the sky and he almost cries out in his grief and anguish at what he is giving up.

'It will be all right, Thomas,' Jack says. 'She'll live for another day.'

'You're right, Jack' he says. 'You are right. That is all that matters now,' and his voice catches. 'All that matters is that she lives. She must live. Otherwise . . .'

Otherwise what? Christ. She is slack on her board. Her head is lolling.

'Katherine! Katherine! We are to see a surgeon! Stay awake, my love, stay awake!'

There is a flutter of resistance to the plank's rolling as they hurry, and it is as if she is not yet gone.

'Mind your backs! Coming through! An injured man! Coming through!'

They are between two rows of grand tents now, all striped linen and pennants, and there is straw underfoot and servants and women and men standing aside as they come through, their pale faces staring down at Katherine, and Thomas will kill the first who makes a sign of the cross to mark the passing of the dead.

And then here they are: the surgeon's tent, smaller, shabbier, more worn than those around. Thomas is given no time to hesitate, no time to gather himself or decide if this is indeed what he wants to do. A servant lingers by the door, mouth agape, arms filled with a sack of something. He is barrelled past, left watching, and they carry Katherine into the centre of the tent and stand there a moment looking around in the cool gloom. A man with eyeglasses looks up from where he lies on a pile of sheepskin-covered mattresses. He is in dark hose and very dark doublet, his shirtsleeves rolled to his elbows. He has been studying a sheaf of parchment filled with shaded pictures of the moon. He looks familiar.

'Who are you?' he asks.

The first archer tells him that Thomas is a friend of William Hastings and of King Edward, and as soon as he mentions Thomas's name the eyes behind their glasses sharpen, and the man's features concentrate. He tosses aside the chart and rolls to his feet. His hands are gangly.

'Thomas Everingham,' he says. 'Thomas Everingham, by God. But you are dead. You were killed at Towton, or are you some other Thomas Everingham?"

'Difficult question, that one,' the archer answers for Thomas, but Thomas nods. The surgeon stares at him. His eyes are very wet.

'We can talk of this later,' Thomas says. 'Sir. I have — my wife. She is . . .'

He can hardly say the words. Tears sting the corners of his eyes. They are still standing with Katherine held on her plank between them.

'Your wife?' the surgeon says. 'Dear God! Is this her? Yes. Put her down. What is wrong with her? Is she wounded?'

While they set her down Thomas remains crouching, and tells Mayhew about the gun's stone, and about the collapsed building, and about Riven's kick, but he does not mention that she is pregnant. He talks quickly, in a rush, but before he has finished he realises that Mayhew has stopped, frozen, and is staring wide-eyed down at Katherine's face. He is speechless with confusion.

'But she — she is—'

'Please,' Thomas says. 'Please. Just save her. We can — discuss whatever needs discussing later.'

Mayhew is struck silent for a long moment. He blinks behind his eyeglasses.

'How — how did she come to be here? She is known to be dead already and yet—'

'I know,' Thomas says. 'But she. Please. Just – save her.'

Mayhew asks him to repeat what has happened to her and while he listens he runs his hands over Katherine's body just as Master Payne did in the eastward gatehouse. He presses here and there. Opens an eyelid. Smells her breath. Then he works down the body. He frowns. Presses again. Then he looks up.

'You two,' he says, to the lingering archers, 'leave us.'

The archers turn to troop out.

The old one squeezes Thomas's shoulder as he passes. Good luck. Thomas thanks him. Jack looks to Thomas, and Thomas nods. Jack goes too, taking John Stump with him.

'We'll be outside,' he says.

When they are gone Mayhew turns to Thomas.

'She is with child,' he states.

Thomas can only nod. There is a silence. Thomas can hear Mayhew breathing quickly while he thinks.

'This is out of my experience,' Mayhew says. 'We should find a wise woman, or a midwife, or someone who knows the bodies of women. I can stitch and cut. I can remove an arrowhead, but that is all.'

'Please,' Thomas says. 'Please. She would have wanted you to treat her. She did not want any midwives with their magic stones and incantations. She said so. She spoke often of you. Of how much you taught her. How much you showed her. She would want you to treat her.'

Mayhew stares at Thomas a long time.

'Please?' Thomas says. 'At least look at her. And then we can decide.'

Mayhew nods.

'May I?' he asks, indicating her skirts. Thomas nods. Mayhew rolls them up. He places his hands on Katherine's body, feeling under the weight of her gown. He looks up into the roof of the tent and he nibbles his lips. He stops. Looks down. Then he removes his hand from under her skirts. He holds it out flat and his palm is dark with blood.

'No!' Thomas cries. 'No.'

Jack comes back in. Mayhew is on his feet. He eases past Jack and shouts to the servant waiting beyond the tent flap.

'Bring linen,' he says. 'Hot water. Rose oil. Fresh urine. Bring salve. Quick, man!'

Thomas is stricken. He cannot move. He looks down at Katherine with her skirts and underskirts pulled up around her blood-fingered thighs and her hose bunched around her knees and he lets out a wracking sob.

'You will have to wait elsewhere,' Mayhew says.

Thomas shakes his head.

'Come on, Thomas,' Jack says. 'Come now. Let the surgeon do his work.'

But Thomas will not go. He will not leave Katherine there on the soiled floor of a stranger's tent, especially a stranger who thinks she is someone she is not.

'Very well,' Mayhew says. 'But you cannot abide there.'

'I will sit here,' Thomas says. He scrabbles to place himself by her head. Jack too. Her linen cap is loose, her hair spilled. Something makes him tuck it back in, and hide her quartered ear. He strokes the pale hair at her temples, and smooths the dirt from her forehead.

'It is all right,' he says. 'It is all right.'

Her eyelids flutter. She is still alive.

'I will wait outside, Thomas,' Jack says quietly. 'Within earshot, so if I can help . . .'

Thomas nods. Jack places his hand on his shoulder.

'I will pray,' he says. Thomas nods again. Jack meets the returning servant at the entrance, and holds the flap open to admit him and one other, and together they bring steaming jugs of water and urine, a fat fold of virgin linen, a clutch of earthenware bottles, some good candles and a brass crucifix. They gather around Mayhew who snaps quick orders. Cloth is ripped. The candles lit. Bottles are unstopped. A coffer is dragged up and on it, the crucifix.

Mayhew washes his hands in the urine. Then he dries them very thoroughly on a piece of linen and then he begins his examination. He lifts the skirts and begins dabbing and discarding bloodied cloth. Thomas sits and watches Katherine for signs of enduring life. It takes a long cycle of prayer while Mayhew crouches over her spread legs, his servant holding up a candle, his eyes averted, murmuring the prayers, until finally the surgeon lets out a long sigh and throws down his cloth. He removes his misted eyeglasses. Sweat beads his forehead, has dampened his shirt. He pulls the skirts down and looks at Thomas.

He shrugs.

'It is in God's hands.'

Thomas says nothing.

'Should I call the priest?' the second servant asks.

Mayhew frowns in thought. Thomas can hear his own heart booming in his ears.

'Not yet,' Mayhew says. 'Let us see how she goes through the night.'

The four of them lift her and carry her to Mayhew's bed. She seems much lighter than before. She lets out a murmur and moves her thin arm to cover her tummy.

'A good sign,' the first servant says, though Thomas cannot believe him.

They place the pollaxe and ledger next to the bed, and prop the board against the side of the tent.

'Find wood for a fire,' Mayhew tells the servant. 'Both of you. Ask Lord Hastings himself for some if you cannot find any. He will want to provide what he can for the wife of Thomas Everingham.'

Thomas cannot interpret the tone of his last remark, but both servants disappear. There is a long silence. He watches Katherine, consumed by the thought that if he looks away, she will die. Mayhew offers him a drink of something. Thomas takes it and wets Katherine's lips with the wine.

'Thank you,' he says.

'Don't thank me,' Mayhew says, 'for I will not be able to save the child. I cannot perform miracles.'

'No,' Thomas says, because he cannot mourn for the unborn child yet. Perhaps there will be time enough in the future for that.

The silence is awkward for a long moment, broken eventually by Mayhew.

'I do not expect you to tell me,' he says. 'But others will wish to know.'

Thomas allows himself a glance at Mayhew. When he looks back, she is still alive.

'It is not an easy story to tell,' he admits.

'No,' Mayhew supposes.

And Thomas leans against the bed, with a hand on Katherine's arm, and he intends to start to try and tell her story, in the manner of a confession, to expiate his sin, to make a downpayment on the sum he would willingly pay to have her live, but fatigue overtakes him. His eyes close, and a moment later his chin is against his chest, and he is asleep.

He wakes at Matins when it is still dark and he touches her hand.

It is still warm.

He wakes again at Prime, and her arm is yet warm.

He is woken some time in the morning by Mayhew's servant. She is still alive.

Mayhew is there. He is looking serious.

'She is still bleeding,' he says.

Thomas holds her hand, and he is certain she knows it is him, and that she squeezes his fingers.

'You must keep up your own strength,' Mayhew says. He offers him ale. It is very good.

'There is someone waiting to see you,' Mayhew tells him.

And Thomas knows that this is it. This is where he must explain to Richard Fakenham why he has brought the woman who was once his wife, whom he thought dead, back to him, half-alive, and with child. He takes another series of swallows of the ale. Mayhew is right. He must have some strength for this.

He hears voices without. Long and grumbling. Then the flap opens and Mayhew brings in Thomas's visitor. Old, almost as round as tall, a swag of white hair under a dark cloth cap he has bent to one side, he is in very sombre clothes, as if in mourning, and unsteady on his feet.

'Thomas!' he cries. 'By all that is holy! Is that you?'

It is Sir John Fakenham. He is peering at him through his eyeglasses.

Thomas cannot speak for a long moment. Something is blocking his throat.

'Sir John,' he manages. 'Sir John.'

'Let me have a look at you, Thomas,' Sir John says. 'Let me rest my eyes on you again, though for the love of God I can hardly see a thing these days. And these bloody things only seem to make things worse.'

Thomas stands before him while Sir John peers long and hard at him. His eyes are very vague, milky even, and his eyeglasses so scratched and chipped it is a wonder anyone can see a thing through them. He has aged sharply this last year.

'Ha!' he says. 'Still got that red hair!'

'As if he should not?' Mayhew chides.

'Hush, Mayhew,' Sir John says. He takes a drink from him with clumsy, grasping fingers and then Mayhew guides him to a chair and helps him sit. He does so with a heavy sigh and then looks over at the pile that bears Katherine, pale and still as a marble effigy.

'And Christ, this is her, is it?'

Neither Thomas nor Mayhew says a word. Thomas holds his breath.

'I am sorry for your pains, my boy,' Sir John says. 'And hers. She looks like a pretty girl. Only you could have plucked such a jewel from out of so miserable a place as this, Thomas. My congratulations, boy!'

He raises his cup and drinks again. Thomas does too. He sees that Sir John has reached that age when nothing now bothers him much, and it is as if he is meeting someone he knows he will never come to know very well, so why become involved? Thomas feels the warmth of relief at having an obstacle removed, but it is tempered by the thought that none of these obstacles matters if Katherine is dead.

'But tell me,' Sir John goes on. 'Tell me, my boy, what you have been up to? What news of Kit? Where is he?'

Thomas is struck silent for a moment. Kit! Dear God.

'Kit returned home,' he mumbles. Sir John raises an eyebrow.

'Home, eh?' he says, and once again Thomas is left wondering what that means. How much does Sir John know? He cannot tell.

'I have the ledger,' he says, to change the subject.

Sir John is instantly still, his face a passive mask.

'The ledger, my boy? The ledger? What is this ledger?'

'There,' he says, pointing to it where it sits behind Katherine's head on the board.

Sir John does not even bother to look. He could have his fingers in his ears. It is an act.

'No,' he says, shaking his head. 'I know of no ledger.'

Thomas sees what he is saying, and he might almost laugh. The trouble it has caused, the dangers it has led them to, the price it has cost; and now it lies there, something to be ignored. He might throw it on the fire, were there one alight.

'And Giles Riven is dead,' he says. 'By my own hand.'

And now Sir John looks truly alarmed. He holds out his hands and hisses at Thomas.

'Shush! Shush! Christ! Keep your voice down. Dear God! If any should hear you saying something like that it will be straight back to that bastard Edmund Riven, and he will send his murderers and assassins and what-have-you and that will be that. I will be in mourning for another six months.'

Thomas says nothing. Mourning? For whom?

'But great God in heaven, boy, I am glad to hear that. It is bad enough that that little shit Edmund Riven is alive, even with us in the camp, can you believe it, though the Earl of Warwick will not tolerate him at council for the fearful stink of his eye – but he is still here! Still alive, and as far as I know – well, he has Cornford still, and had been aiming for greater things yet, with all his schemes. I am glad to hear his father is dead and gone to hell as he deserves. Was it a painful one? God's bones, I have imagined it so often over the years.'

Thomas tells him how it happened.

'But it was not before he kicked Katherine,' he says.

Sir John nods sadly.

'The trouble that man has caused. Makes you wonder why God allows it, sometimes, doesn't it? My wife Isabella says these troubles are God-sent to harden us, to prove us, as a swordsmith might a blade, but she is increasingly devout thanks to that infernal canon you left with us, and I think I don't know what to think.'

So he is not mourning for Isabella, Thomas thinks.

And now Mayhew glances over at Katherine and he frowns and comes quickly to her side. He presses a point on her neck and then shouts for his servant.

'She is bleeding again, from within,' he says. 'We have applied a coagulant. There is only so much we can do.'

'Just your best, Mayhew,' Sir John says. 'No man can ask for more.'

Thomas crouches next to her. She is very pale now, very drawn, the bones of her cheeks sharp, the skin drawn tight, her lips bloodless.

The servant comes. Sir John is moved. He sits next to Thomas
while Katherine's skirts are raised. There is more linen, spools of
it, more urine. The faint smell of rose oil and something else that
is pungent and bitter and catches at your throat. The servant mumbles
prayers. He raises the crucifix in one hand and the candle in the
other. Mayhew is quick, working frantically. Katherine twitches as
if she were dreaming and her breath is very shallow and fast. Mayhew
curses. Then he does something and he is still, applying some
pressure. He looks at them both significantly, and Thomas knows
this is it, the last chance. If this does not work, nothing will. A priest
will need to be summoned.

Time ekes past. The light fades. The tent linen closes in on them.
The servant lights another candle from the stub of the first. Mayhew
is still there, pressing. Sir John slips in and out of sleep. His snoring
is a light buzz. Katherine's breathing has slowed. He can see the dark
trace of her blood vessels through her pale skin. One is jumping
rhythmically. A tiny beat. Then it is too dark to see that. No one says
anything. A little later the other servant brings bread and soup and
ale, sent by Lord Hastings. Mayhew does not move, or even look up.

Sir John wakes and mumbles something. The servant pours him
ale.

'Still with us, is she?' Sir John asks. 'Good. I have been praying
for her. And Mayhew, he knows his stuff.'

Thomas can stand it no longer.

'Sir,' he asks. 'Whom is it that you mourn?'

Sir John looks at him over the rim of his mug, and the candlelight
glints in his rheumy eye, but for the first time Thomas thinks the
old man has really focused on him, is really seeing him.

'Tcha,' he says, putting aside the mug, and looking suddenly very
powdery and older yet. 'You have been away for almost a year,
haven't you? You will not have heard. Richard. My boy. My only
boy, you know. He died. Late last year. Just before Christmas. I
used to love Christmas, you know? But no more shall I. It was – oh,

it was always going to happen, that I knew. Once his Margaret died he was bound to follow. Still though. It was a blow. A great blow.'

Thomas returns to Katherine, and he presses her hand in his own, and relief, hope, guilt and regret plait together and coil through him. Richard Fakenham is dead. Dear God. Suddenly a vast obstacle is removed, like an old man's stone, he thinks, and he begins to think that there is hope for them – until he remembers that nothing matters if Katherine is not there with him.

And then Mayhew makes a subtle move, a slight relaxing of his shoulders, and afterward, he is stopped still for a long moment, head bent, crouched, staring at something, and then he looks up and allows Thomas to catch his eye, and his expression, bone weary, is just about readable and he nods his head very slightly, and behind him the servant begins the Te Deum, a prayer of thanksgiving, and Thomas feels tears welling in his eyes again, and he turns to look at her, and he thinks for a moment that she has her eyes open.

'Katherine,' he says. 'All is well. All is well.'

At that moment there is a booming ruffle of the heavy linen walls of the tent as the east wind off the North Sea picks up, and the candle flame wavers on its wick, and Sir John wakes with a start, and all the men look up fearfully as if something is passing overhead, and the servant crosses himself twice.

A Note from the Author

The great castles at Alnwick, Dunstanborough and Bamburgh are perhaps the mightiest of the castles in Northumberland, but they are just three of the many that stud what was in the fifteenth century known as the East March, each constructed during the early Middle Ages to protect England from the marauding Scots, and – to be fair – to serve as bases for marauding Englishmen heading the other way.

Many of them still stand – rebuilt, buffed-up, Victorianised in the case of Alnwick and Bamburgh, preserved as an austere ruin in the case of Dunstanborough – and today they, and many of the others, can be visited following a well-signposted castle route running from Warkworth in the south to Norham in the north. In the twenty-first century they are almost serene; cool and mossy and damp, often hard by meandering rivers below, romantic monuments to a distant past, but it does not take too great an imaginative leap to see them as they might have been 500 years ago, absolutely dominating the landscape as cathedrals did further south, each one a complex, whirring hub at the centre of an extensive eco-system sucking in men and materiel, food and fodder, animals and wood to burn, from miles around, and they would have been busy, loud and smelly places.

It was to these castles that, after their power was very nearly destroyed at the battle of Towton in 1461 (the subject of the first in the Kingmaker Trilogy, *Winter Pilgrims*), such Lancastrian forces as survived the rout withdrew, and it was among them that the next phase of the conflict we have come to know as the Wars of the Roses played itself out.

As with the longer span of the wars, the history of these next few years – from 1461 to 1464 – is often confusing, occasionally nonsensical, sometimes comical. Everybody changes sides at least once, usually twice, there are two kings, and everybody else is called Richard or John.

Before Thomas and Katherine arrive in the autumn of 1463, each of the three castles had been besieged by the Yorkists and taken from the Lancastrians at least once already, only for the wrong man – from the Yorkist point of view – to be given the keys afterwards. Each newly

443

appointed castellan almost instantly reverted to the Lancastrian cause and it was from the chilly confines of these borrowed castles that the adherents of Henry VI holed up, in some discomfort and almost powerless to influence events while they waited for help from France or Burgundy or Scotland or, in fact, from more or less anyone with 'un peu d'argent'. Meanwhile in London the Yorkists under Edward IV scrambled to secure their grip on the throne, and to cut off any chance of outside aid coming to those men in the castles.

Life must have been very bleak.

Options began running out very quickly, and Henry VI – not the leader his father had been, nor in fact the leader his wife, Margaret of Anjou, was – was not the man to bring the Lancastrians out of their bind, so one can imagine the excitement the beleaguered garrisons must have felt when the Duke of Somerset reverted to Henry's cause and turned up on the drawbridge, under-equipped for the weather at that time of year having had to leap out through the window of an inn to escape Lord Montagu's men.

Although not a markedly successful general – he led the Lancastrian army unsuccessfully at Northampton and Towton – he was full of vim, a very fine jouster, and it must have been wonderful for Henry's men to be away from the castles for a while as he led them in search of Lord Montagu's men, though I do not suppose many would have appreciated the rugged beauty of the Northumbrian countryside as we do today. I have looked for any mention being made of Hadrian's Wall, incidentally, but have found none, and so I still wonder what they would have made of it. To many Englishmen of the time, any foreigner was a 'Frenchy' so what they would have thought of it, built by the despised Frenchies so long ago, is anyone's guess.

The two battles described in this book – Hedgeley Moor and Hexham – were small-scale affairs, and somewhat frustrating after the incredible rigours of Towton, but they are intriguing in many ways. Very little is known of them, and such accounts as exist are, again, and as is usual, contradictory, and do not fit with the topography or military probability. Legend has grown up around Percy's Leap at Hedgeley Moor, but did it really happen? At Hexham I have placed Somerset's men atop Swallowship Hill facing north, which seems to me to make the most sense, but others

444

may disagree, and be proved right, and if that is the case, then I can only admit that my guess will have turned out to be incorrect.

In both cases I have tried to understand why the men belonging to Lord Hungerford and Lord Roos capitulated apparently so speedily, and have advanced a theory that, since it is predicated on the existence of a fictional character, cannot possibly be the real one, but there may have been some other similar forces at work on those days. Whatever the cause of their running, it saved lives in the end, and perhaps that was reason enough? The men in both camps would have been very similar types, from adjacent neighbourhoods, and perhaps their hearts weren't really in it? Perhaps they remembered the trauma of Towton too clearly, and this was an outbreak of genuinely civil civil war?

As for William Tailboys and his mules carrying what remained of King Henry's war chest, that is true. He was captured after the battle hiding in a coal mine with an unknown but large sum of money, quickly distributed among Lord Montagu's men, and was executed in Newcastle in July that year, two months after the battle. Quite what he had been doing in the meantime is one of the gaps in our knowledge wherein fiction writers thrive.

Meanwhile, though, poor old Henry VI continued to evade capture until 1465, when he was finally caught and taken to the Tower of London. In some ways he was probably better suited to captivity than kingship, since he was a simple soul, given to prayer, and he was to spend the next five years there until he was winkled out to play one last, fateful role in the continuing story of Katherine and Thomas . . .

Acknowledgements

While I was trying to finish this novel, I was convinced my slog was solitary, but since looking up from it I have seen that it would have been much less fun, and much harder work, without the support and friendship of a hundred different people, some of whom I'd like to thank by name.

First, I'd like to thank those of you who were so encouraging about my first novel, *Winter Pilgrims*. Without Ben Kane and Manda Scott's kind words, and Hilary Mantel's unexpected endorsement, this second one might have been a trial of endurance, but your very generous encouragement really gave me wings, as did that of Robin Carter and Kate Atherton, who were so kind about me in their excellent blogs: Parmenion Books and For Winter Nights. I can't tell you how cheering your comments have been, so thanks very much, guys.

Second, thanks are due to my lovely agent Charlotte Robertson, who has been wonderfully positive and calm in all things, as well as my editors Selina Walker and Francesca Pathak, who have tolerated my endless deadline dodges. I'd very much like to thank the amazingly patient Mary Chamberlain for applying her eagle eye on matters of plot and plausibility, as well as Tim Byard-Jones for his terrifically astute nit-picking on matters concerning the fifteenth century. Thank you too, David Allison, for all your brilliant suggestions. Without your help, this book would not be half the book it is, while at the same time being double its length.

Next, my thanks are owed to Johnny Villeneau and Leslie Bookless for putting me up and putting up with me, and to Jacko for being such an easy and enthusiastic audience. Thank you, also, Kate Summerscale and Sinclair McKay, for your continued support – you know what I mean – as well as, all too familiarly, Anna and John Clements, for, again, you know what. I'd also like to thank Nick and Lilian Philips, who have been models of generous support and very tolerant friendship. I could not have finished this without you.

Most of all, though, I'd especially like to thank Kazza and Martha and Tom and Max, too, for continuing to make it all the subject of high comedy.

'Magnificent. An historical tour de force, revealing Clements to be a novelist every bit as good as Cornwell, Gregory or Iggulden.'
Ben Kane

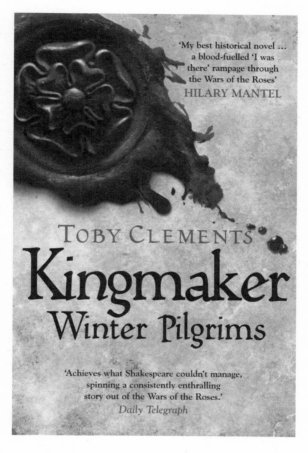

'My best historical novel ... a blood-fuelled 'I was there' rampage through the Wars of the Roses'
HILARY MANTEL

TOBY CLEMENTS
Kingmaker
Winter Pilgrims

'Achieves what Shakespeare couldn't manage, spinning a consistently enthralling story out of the Wars of the Roses.'
Daily Telegraph

Book one of the
Kingmaker series

OUT NOW